LEDGE

THE **DOMINO EFFECT** BOOK ONE

GREY HUFFINGTON

TRIGGER WARNING

PLEASE READ THIS SECTION!

Seeing this note means the book that you are about to read could contain triggering situations or actions. This book is subject to one or more of the triggers listed below. **Please note that this a universal trigger warning page that is included in Grey Huffington books and is not specified for any paticular set of characters, book, couple, etc. This book does not contain all the warnings listed. It is simply a way to warn you that this particular book contains things/a thing that may be triggering for some.** This is simply my way of recognizing the reality and life experiences of my tribe and making sure that I properly prepare you for what is to unfold within the pages of this book.

violence

sexual assualt
drug addiction
suicide
homicide
miscarriage/child loss
child abuse
emotional abuse

PAPERBACKS
HARDCOVERS
SHORT STORIES
AUDIOBOOKS
MERCH
AND MORE...

instagram.com/greyhuffington

STAY IN CONTACT

want live updates?
text **greyhuffington** to 1 (833) 315 2372

instagram.com/greyhuffington

LEDGE

THE **DOMINO EFFECT** BOOK ONE

GREYHUFFINGTON

PROLOGUE

HALO

DRIP. DROP.
    Drip. Drop.
    Drip. Drop.
    The sound of the slowly leaking water landing in the bucket that sat in the middle of my bathroom floor was most prominent in the silence. And, as much as I hated a soundless moment because it gave my thoughts the opportunity to grow louder, the simple thought of television or music overstimulated me. With a heavy sigh, I

closed my eyes and welcomed the abundance of emotions that were behind my conjoined lids.

*Urrrrrrrrrn. The front door closed, slowly, signaling my mother's departure. Though it occurred every night at the same time, it never got easier. In fact, it was the most difficult part of my day. **Please don't go**. I wanted to scream but the words wouldn't come out. **She's gone**. My six-year-old brain quickly processed as my eyes began to sting in the darkness of my bedroom.*

*Across my nose and onto the side of my face, my tears drained. The others hit the bed, making the loudest, most silent scream one would ever hear. I wished, desperately, that I had the gumption to rise from my bed and call after her, but I didn't. I couldn't. **There's no use**, I summed.*

Not only would she ignore my pleas and continue with business as usual, but the consequences were far too horrid. Fear confined me to my room. Sometimes, it was safest here. At least until the sound of the door slamming against the threshold rocked my core. At that moment, each and every night, there was no place safe enough to run or hide.

"It's going to be okay Mr. Stuffy," I whispered, tearfully.

More than anything else, I was remorseful for the things that my incredibly soft, brown teddy had witnessed. Just like me, he didn't deserve the experiences he'd been forced to endure. Every day, I wished we could take each other's pain away, but I'd learned that it was impossible.

"It's going to be okay," I said, again, patting his round belly to prepare him for the inevitable.

Or, maybe, I was preparing myself. Maybe it was me who I was comforting. Maybe it was me who I was coaxing. Maybe it was me who I was reminding that everything would be okay. Maybe that was it.

Discomfort and anxiousness quickly followed my words. A deep, weighted sigh pushed through my lips. It was the first of many that I knew was to come while sleep dodged me. I closed my eyes anyway and began counting upward.

"One. Two. Three. Four."

Seventy-six. That's how far I counted before the familiar thudding halted all movement and thought. The method I used to cope to silence the craziness in my head no longer sufficed. The altering, very dominating sound of large feet stomping in my direction canceled all else.

My thin frame began to shiver as if I was jacketless in negative twelve-degree weather. But, I wasn't. In fact, I was in my bedroom, tucked underneath my cover which was believed to be the safest place for a child. However, it wasn't.

Run. Hide. Scream. My thoughts sounded off in my head. Had any of those ever supported my case in the past, then I would've. But, because I knew they wouldn't, I remained still, unmoving other than my quivering frame that rattled against my sheets, involuntarily.

Urrrrrrrrn. The door that desperately needed fixing crept open.

It's going to be okay. It's going to be okay. It's

going to be okay. *Over and over, at an insanely rapid pace, I repeated in my head.* **It's going to be okay. It's going to be okay.**

But it wasn't. My delusion stemmed from my optimism and pure innocence as an six-year-old who only saw the good in humans, even those who were evil. My little heart couldn't help but believe that things would be okay. Telling myself that there was greater on the opposite side of this all gave me something to hope for and I didn't hope for much. Not often at least. Probably not at all.

Though my eyes were already closed, I squeezed my lids tighter as the halted stomping started up again. This time, they were so close that I could hear the creaking of the floorboards underneath the pressure they caused. The pungent and very familiar smell of filth and disgust seemed to be the chosen fragrance, topped with notes of brown liquid that burned your throat, chest, and tummy. Hadn't I been forced to drink it on one too many occasions then I wouldn't have known what it felt like sliding down your internals.

Oh no. Oh no. Oh no. *I began to panic.*

Vomit rose from my belly, threatening to spill from my mouth. Knowing that it would result in a much harsher punishment if it surfaced, I swallowed it back. Thick and chunky, it went down my throat with resistance. My eyes popped open in the dark as I tried to fight the anxiety that swelled in my throat.

The heat from the burial of my body underneath the cover was revoked. The pink comforter was flung backward, down to my ankles. Simultaneously, my mattress shifted to accommodate the body weight that was added.

And, now, instead of the one person that belonged in my twin-sized bed, there were two.

The covers were brought up and over my body, again, but at this point, they didn't matter. I still shivered from the sheer and raw reality of what was next to come. Then I felt a large, uninvited hand snake up my stomach, starting at the tail end of my Princess-covered pajama shirt. It was my favorite out of all the sets my mother had bought.

Because I believed that in some far, far away place that I was in, I was waiting to become a queen, and was being treated so well. I closed my eyes and imagined so much more than my reality could contribute. However, there was a place that could. And, to that place is where I drifted as I felt the same fingers brush across my tiny, very young, and barely even visible nipples.

MY EYES POPPED open as I gasped for the little oxygen that seemed to be left in my lungs. With each deep and sharp breath I took, my chest rose and sank. On each rise, it collided with the side of Mr. Stuffy's face. I squeezed him tighter as I tried to rid myself of the memories that plagued my existence and altered my future.

Those founding moments that finalized my identity were ones that I desperately needed to forget but I couldn't. The stress and trauma that my mind, body, and heart were put under for the duration of my elementary years were paramount to my presence. There wasn't such a thing as forgetting any of it. I lived with the results each and every day. And, as unfortunate as it was for me, it was life.

"I can't do this anymore," I said aloud, wiping the fresh, hot tears from my cheeks.

A new, very unfamiliar emotion diluted every other one in my body. Rage centered my line of sight and consumed my thoughts. Before I was able to stop myself, Mr. Stuffy was flung across the room.

It's not going to be okay... not unless I make it that way. Exhaustion from the constant state of fear, paranoia, and vigilance that I was in was daunting. Just once, I wanted to feel something else. Normal. I wanted to feel normal for once. Because, since the day that my innocence was stolen from me, I felt like a zombie that served as a walking billboard that displayed the hurt and pain that my trauma caused.

Though I didn't encounter many people, the ones that I did ever so often, I had a deep, unsettling feeling that they knew. Everybody knew. They had to. At least that's how it seemed—according to the constant stares to the sudden private chatter with friends and family standing closest to them.

So, to spare myself the embarrassment, I made my home my safe haven. It's where I spend the majority of my time. All of it, truthfully. It's my place of refuge and I'd never even consider trading it for the discomfort of being around or accessible to others. *Home.* It's exactly where I want to be.

Home. The loud, thunderous footsteps had long ago disappeared, and clutching Mr. Stuffy happened to dissolve my desires for companionship rather than uninvited company. The sound of my mother's car starting in the driveway didn't cause saltiness to seep from my eyes anymore. The smell of brown liquor and tobacco didn't haunt me nightly. *Home*. Not here.

Everything in my world, now, was dictated and created by me. Almost nothing was out of my control, anymore. This kept my anxiety at bay, my paranoia at tolerable levels, and my head above water. Everything... I controlled everything.

Drip. Drop.

Drip. Drop.

Drip. Drop.

Except that. It was a persistent problem that required assistance beyond my capabilities. The maintenance team had fixed it twice already. But, with the issue stemming from an elderly's apartment upstairs who often forgot that she was running bath water, it felt like a neverending cycle. One that required an unwanted presence in my space, forcing me to surrender control of the safe haven I'd created for myself.

It was a grueling few hours each time they showed up at my door. And, for the length of their visit, I was confined to my bedroom with my back and door stopper against the door. *Surely, they can't get in*, I always thought with trembling hands and legs.

"I can't let this hinder me forever. I can't let *him* hinder me forever. Then, *he wins*... again," I whispered through deep, heavy breathing.

As I stood to my feet, revelations stormed my

thoughts. *Maybe I'll just go outside. Maybe I could go get a drink. Maybe I could visit a bar. Find a handsome man to go home with. Gain control of my body and vagina and my life again. Yes.* I nodded, considering all the possibilities. This one sounded the scariest but I was ready to face my fears. It was the only way to begin to fix what had been broken.

That's it. I just know that if I willingly give my body to someone and it be my choice, I'll feel so much better. Okay. That's what I'll do. I have to so that I can at least start healing. This is for the best. I can do this. I've been working toward this. I can leave the apartment. I've got this. I have no other choice. I owe this to myself... to the child and adult in me. I convinced myself. Suddenly, the labored drag disappeared from my breathing and I was able to take much lighter, easier breaths.

But, wait. What will I wear?
Kamber!

Anxiously, I skipped out of my bedroom. My feet tapped against the carpeted floor as I rushed through my apartment, down the long hallway, and into the living room. My shoes were neatly stuffed into small cubbies beside the couch for easy access. I despised shoes inside my home.

I slid my feet into a pair of sandals. Ahhhh. I sighed, inwardly. It felt like I was walking on clouds. The fluffiness of the shoe's sole was carefully thought out and skillfully executed. Each time I stepped into them, I was reminded why I paid seventy-five dollars for them. They were worth every tearful penny I stressed over before hitting the complete payment button.

With my shoes on my feet, I was prepared to make my exit. My adrenaline, hypothesis for what could happen, and curiosity of what could transpire over the next few hours pushed me forward. My hand stretched, ready to make contact with the silver knob until reality kicked in.

DOOR. My movements came to a screeching halt.

With an outstretched hand, I stood still, unmoving. Sweat beads formed on my forehead. Dryness lumped in my throat. And, the pressure, it consumed me. Finally, I rested my eyelids on top of one another and took a deep breath.

You've got this. You can do it. You've been preparing for this moment. There's no one who will hurt you on the other side of the door. There's, in fact, no one at all. I coached, determined not to.

Before opening my eyes and losing a battle that I'd lost for the last fourteen years of my life, I reached forward and grabbed the handle. Agoraphobia has plagued me since the young, immature age of fourteen. Life had already worn me down mentally, physically, and emotionally by the time I reached high school. And, it wasn't until then that I was freed from the hell I was living in. Unfortunately, the damage was already done.

Door. It's just a door. I twisted the knob and the lock above it, one right after the other. One foot in front of the other, I stepped forward. The night breeze swept across my skin with perfect timing. It was the gentle hug from nature that I needed to assure me that things were okay. *But are they?* I wondered.

WHAM! My apartment door slammed behind me, pulling me from my thoughts and back into the moment. *I'm outside!* I screamed, internally. *I'm outside!*

As the realization socked me square in the eyes, swelling them, the sound of a door unlocking and detaching from its threshold captured my attention.

WHAM! I ran into my apartment door trying to get back inside.

"Damn girl, at least open it first. Shaky-ass," Kamber cackled, causing my eyes to roll one way and then the other.

"What are you doing out here?" I asked, sighing deeply while holding onto the handle of my door. I had just made it outside and I was already ready to get back inside.

"Nah. The question is, what are you doing out here?" She countered, placing a hand on her hip.

With a shrug, I revealed my truth. I hardly knew myself—not for real, anyway.

"I was sitting on the couch in silence, minding my before-work-ass business, and heard your door slam. I had to make sure that I wasn't hearing things. Now, I have to make sure I'm not seeing things. Halo... outside?"

"Stop it," I sighed, "I'm trying here, Kamber."

"And, I see. I'm just trying to grasp it all. I see the desperation in those brown eyes of yours. What is it? What are you thinking?"

"I was thinking that I was headed to your place to knock on the door."

"And borrow some sugar or nah?"

"Noooo. Some clothes, maybe?" I tossed out with a knitted right brow.

"Some clothes?" Kamber shrieked, "Girl *for who? For where? For what?*"

"Shhhh," I hushed her, "Can you keep it down?"

"Forgive me if I am in total fucking shock right now, but my homie from the other side of the door is actually out of the door... asking for clothes which could only insinuate she's going somewhere. Not to mention she's not on the other side of the door right now. She's in my fucking face. Do you understand my excitement right now? Hmmm?"

She bounced from one side to the other like a cheer-leader in the middle of a chant.

Embarrassment burned the peaks of my cheeks. I was almost positive my dark skin had turned a shade of crimson as if I'd blushed my jaws. With a shake of my head, I turned toward my door and pushed it open, again. *I can't do this*, I quickly summed.

"Nevermind."

Kamber was swift on her toes, catching the defeat on my face and in my posture as I took one step forward. I felt her body rush past mine as she threw herself against my door. Her back landed with a thud that I was sure ached.

"Nooooo. Not nevermind, Halo. This is good, really good. I apologize but I was just a little shocked. Well, very. Come on. Let's not ruin this very important moment, huh? I'll go back into my place and mind my business so that you can finish the task that you set out to complete."

"I was coming to your door," I reminded her.

"I know… so come to the door. I'm stepping back inside, okay?"

"Okay."

She was sure to close my apartment door before tiptoeing down the two steps that led to the sidewalk and then up another two that led to her apartment. Once she was inside, I debated whether or not turning around and going into my own apartment would feel better than walking the very short distance to Kamber's place.

I can't do this. Finalizing, I twisted on the tips of my toes and reached for the handle of my door, again.

Knock.

Knock.

Knock.

"No. Come on. You've got this!" Kamber yelled through the window that she was knocking on. "Let's go Halo, let's go! Let's go Halo, let's go!"

Her impromptu cheer coated my uncertainty with assurance. Instead of opening the door and locking myself into my apartment again, I took one step in her direction.

Then another.

Then another.

Then another.

Then another.

The sound of loud, roaring clapping was the boost of confidence I needed to continue.

Another one.

Another one.

Another one.

Another one.

My right foot hit the door in front of me, signaling my arrival. Panic-stricken, I stilled my body and looked from one side to the other. *Run!* My voice screamed in my head. It took every ounce of strength not to pick up my feet and dash back into my apartment. *My apartment. It's not locked. What if someone... Oh no. Oh no. Oh no.*

"Where are you going?" Kamber snatched her door open and ran onto the small porch that we both had alike after seeing me make a run for it.

"It's unlocked," I told her.

"What?"

"My door. It's unlocked."

"If you go back inside, you won't come back out. I know this, Halo. Don't go inside."

Her words stopped me in my tracks. She was right. If I went inside to retrieve my keys, I wouldn't return.

"I'll go get your keys. You, on the other hand, come inside of my house."

My hesitation was a result of the screeching in my head. So many thoughts. So little space.

"And, get out of your head, Halo. Everything is fine, friend. You're okay."

I am. I admitted. Because I was. The anxiety that

contributed to the stress of even the thought of leaving my apartment was tolerant. Mild, even. I turned my palms upward to find them free of sweat, but I wiped them on my pant legs, anyway, out of habit.

"I want to go have a drink," I exclaimed, feeling the weight of the world lifting from my shoulders. I felt that if I spoke it into the universe, then maybe it could actually happen. And, if I revealed my plans to Kamber, she'd make sure they happened.

"And, maybe meet a guy. You know, take control of my life, again."

"Aka, knock the cobwebs out of that pussy."

"Kamber," I pled.

"Okay. Okay. Sorry. A little too much, huh?"

"Yes. But, also, yes to your question. I'm so tired of breathing but not living. I feel cursed. I just want to feel normal for once. You know, in control of a situation involving my body and my vagina but not alone. With someone."

"Tonight?"

"Yes. It's either now or never."

"Not Halo wanting a one-night stand. If you'd told me this was in my deck of cards, I would've sworn you were lying to me!" She howled.

"Do you have to be so dramatic?" I whined.

"Yes. In fact, yes the fuck I do. This is big shit, friend. Now, come inside and let's get you all the way together. Don't worry about your door. I'll lock it up. What size are you?"

"An eight."

"Perfect. I figured as much, anyway," she mumbled as she grabbed my hand and pulled me into her apartment.

It was so contrasting to mine. The vibrance and palette of bright colors brought a smile to my face. I hardly noticed when she snuck out to go lock my door. It wasn't until she was gone that I remembered to tell her where my keys were.

"My keys are–," I started, but cut the statement short when I realized I was the only one standing inside of the apartment.

Preoccupied with the large, artful pieces displayed on the wall, I quickly lost track of time. Instead of leading with my head, for once, I led with my eyes and my heart. My thoughts were silenced, but my eyes slowly danced from one section of Kamber's living quarters to the other. And, my heart galloped with glee, crashing into my chest cavity with each beat.

Something other than a novel held me captive. The revelation wasn't lost upon me as my lips stretched from one side of my face to the other. I could feel the thin lines underneath my eyes as a result of the happiness the colors brought me, especially cream. The fuzziness I felt inside each time I laid eyes on it was revealing.

My favorite color? I asked. *My favorite color!* I followed up immediately. After twenty-eight years, I finally found it.

"Ha," I chuckled, thrilled with my new discovery. "Cream."

"What the hell are you smiling so hard about," Kamber asked.

She'd reentered her apartment, undetected. Her sudden presence startled me, but I tried my hardest to suppress the feelings that accompanied the disappointment I felt for not being vigilant enough. Too consumed with the beauty of her space, I gave anyone the opportunity they were possibly waiting for.

No one is coming to harm you, I reminded myself.

"I just learned that cream is my favorite color," I shared, slightly embarrassed. My cheeks blushed red as they burned.

"Well, lucky you. I still haven't found my favorite color. I feel like it's something new every month. Yellow. Black. Orange. Blue. Gray. Cream. Girl, I have no idea. I like them all. I guess that's why I've incorporated them into my decor. I just can't choose."

"I love your apartment," I confessed.

"Well, unfortunately, you can't hide out in here."

We both shared a soft, hearty chuckle.

"It wouldn't be tonight, at least," sighing, I joked.

It added a cool point to my book. It wasn't often that I did, but the moment felt right.

"Sure not. I'm about to call in so that I can take you to this new bar I've been hearing about for the last few months. I still haven't had the chance to visit because I work at night. Tonight though, they can kiss my ass."

"I don't want you missing work on my account."

"Girl, this is big shit. Okay. I've been dreaming of the day you come over and say fuck everything, let's hit brunch or go grab dinner. Something. Anything. A bitch don't have friends. They've all misused my kindness, betrayed my trust, or fucked my ex."

"Your ex?" With crinkled brows, I questioned.

"Another story for another day. Let's first get you loosened up a bit."

"How?" I wondered... *aloud*.

"We're starting with a shot. Which do you prefer, clear or brown?"

"Clear or brown what?" Confused, I asked for clarification.

"Liquor!" Kamber scoffed, "Stop playing."

"I'm not. I don't drink."

"As in don't drink or never had a drink?"

"Never had a drink."

"By choice?"

No. The word echoed in my head.

"Yes."

"You're a strong human being. There's no way I wouldn't be popping wine bottle after wine bottle in the house all day. Choose one, though."

"Brown," I stated, confidently, though I was everything but.

After being educated on the subject at hand and what Kamber was referring to, I chose the opposite of what I'd often seen growing up as a kid. Our kitchen counter was full of clear bottles filled with clear liquids.

"My girl!" Kamber chanted before rushing off toward the kitchen.

I looked around, nervously, wondering what was I to do next. The discomfort began to intrude my thoughts as my unfamiliar surroundings threatened to drive me to the point of no return. It felt as if the room was spinning and there was nothing around to support my weight as dizziness overcame me.

"Halo!" I heard Kamber scream, commanding my attention.

"Hmm?" I asked, feeling woozy.

"You're okay, friend. I promise. Here, take this."

Kamber handed me a small clear glass that was half full. When I accepted it, willingly, silence followed. I brought the cup near my nose and regretted it instantly.

Sweaty, musty, and clammy skin brushed against mine. The smell of fruit that had soured permeated the air and seeped through his pores. It was as bold as it was disgusting. I'd grown to hate it over the years. Grown-up juice. That's what my mother called it, daring me to ever touch it. She didn't have to worry. I never would. I hated the smell of it and I hated that it was the only juice that he wanted.

"Halo," a familiar voice called out to me.

"Huh? Uh. Sorry," I whispered, pushing a heavy sigh through my nose and mouth.

Before I could stop myself, I tilted the glass until it was bottom-side-up and my neck was stretched backward, as far as it would go.

"Shit na. We didn't even get to toast."

"Pour me another one," I breathed. "We can toast with that one."

"Oh, I see what type of night you're trying to have. Let me put my boss on notice and make sure my little friend on standby. You're not the only one trying to control some shit in the bedroom tonight. I'm going to work these pussy muscles and milk this nigga for all his cum. I have one more Plan B in the drawer in there. I'm trying to use it!"

"You can do that?"

"Do what?"

"Use your vaginal muscles to make a man... you know."

"I don't. Say it."

"Cu— Ejacul—," I stuttered, unable to bring myself to say any of it.

"Say it. Gone ahead. You got it," Kamber joked.

"Seriously, can you?"

"Yes, ma'am. And, he'll love you for a lifetime for doing it, too."

As I allowed her words to sink in, she poured another glass of brown liquor.

"Here," she said as she handed it to me.

"What if I can't do it right?" I asked.

"If it's something you really want to do, then it will come naturally. Is it something you really want to do?"

"Yes." Immediately, I knew the answer to that question. Though spontaneity wasn't my style, I was tired of my norm. Because, truthfully, it wasn't normal at all.

"Then, I think you'll be fine."

"I don't even know what to say to a guy. 'Hey, I'm a really weird adult who was sexually assaulted from the age of six to the age of fourteen and has never freely given my body to anyone. But, tonight, I want to give it to you?

So, please take it and also take the awkwardness that comes with me and my socially inexperienced self? Please?' Is that what I'm supposed to say?"

"No. We're just going to make sure this milky skin is popping and those big, brown eyes are on full display. You won't have to say anything. They'll be waiting to get a word in with you."

"How do I choose which one is my best option?"

"Follow your gut, it'll never steer you in the wrong direction. Plus, I'll be there with you."

Ping. Just as soon as she finished her statement, her cell pinged.

"Oooooor not," she sighed. "My boss says we're already short two people and she really needs me."

My heart sank into my ankles. Initially, I was prepared to explore a night out in Channing alone, but once she added herself into the picture, it got clearer. Now, the thought of her not joining me was causing my chest to ache and my eyes to blur.

"But, if we head out in the next... thirty minutes or so... I can make it happen. I have another hour before my shift begins. She won't mind me being a few minutes late. If your luck is low and you don't encounter anyone worth your time, then you can text me. I'll sneak off to bring you back home. Deal?"

"Deal!" I agreed.

"Now, a toast to a night of good laughter, good music, good drinks, and a good dick down."

"Kamber!"

"Just drink!"

I swallowed all the liquor in the glass at once. The first portion of my consumption was already beginning to take effect. I could feel a difference within me, though I couldn't quite describe it.

"I know that's right," Kamber squealed. "Now, let's go get dressed."

LEDGE + HALO

EVERYTHING HAD LOOSENED. Anxiety wasn't knotted in my throat and there was a permanent smile on my face. I felt as if I was floating on clouds. Nothing made sense, but that was okay. I was okay and that was most important.

"IDs, please," the big, tall guy standing by the door requested.

"It's already in your hand," Kamber said, reminding me that I was already prepared. She made sure of it before we left her apartment so that I didn't feel indifferent about anything for the night.

I lifted my hand, slowly and waited as he examined it. Kamber did the same. My locked knees and elbows were signs of discomfort that Kamber immediately picked up on. The close vicinity of the large male figure to my frame was alarming.

"Straight ahead and through those doors. Enjoy your night," he insisted.

One foot in front of the other, I rushed past him and

through the doors of the bar that Kamber suggested. The second I was on the other side of them, I sighed in sheer relief. Still, slightly loosened, I chuckled as I clung to the wall with my right palm.

"I'm outside," I tittered. "Like, outside."

"Not at this very moment. You're actually inside and broke your neck trying to get here."

"I feel like... like I've got this."

"That's because you do."

"For so long, my past has controlled my world. I'm tired, Kamber. I just want to feel normal... even if just for one night."

I bowed my head, the shame of my expectations for the night falling at my feet. Tonight was all about me and breaking the chains that have held me captive since six. It wasn't until I turned fourteen that I was rescued from the shitty life my mother subjected me to.

I lived with my paternal grandmother throughout high school, up until I was nineteen when she died of a heart attack. It happened to be the night that I finally revealed my truth and finally admitted that I had been victimized far longer than she'd imagined and much more had transpired than Child Protective Services led her to believe.

She was my safe space for five years and then she died of heartache. No one could convince me otherwise. She loved me with everything within her, though she didn't know that I even existed until she received a call from CPS. My visit to the emergency room from severe bleeding, cramping, and a high fever led to the discovery of an ectopic pregnancy. Questions were asked for the first time and without anyone near that had caused me harm, I answered them all truthfully.

"Those batteries worn out, huh?"

"Hmm?" I lifted my head to ask.

"The batteries on your vibrator. They're worn out?"

"Are you ever serious?"

"I try to be but it's just too serious."

"Really, Kamber?"

"Really!" She exclaimed as we continued down the hallway. "But, are they?"

"I'd never used one until about six months ago," I whispered, my 5'4 frame lifting slightly to reach her ear. Kamber was a bit taller than me, but not so much.

"I knew you weren't always in that apartment just staring at the walls. How'd you like it?"

"I can't say that I did for the first four months. I tried it once and never touched it again for that long. I've never felt good about anything sexual so it was very hard to focus. I was too in my head. But last month, I tried it again. Then, again this month and—" I sighed.

"Now you want to experience the real thing," she finished.

"Yeah. It's like, I thought I'd be taking control of my body so that I could feel better about myself but I just feel dirty after using it."

"Oh, you're not the only one that feels dirty after they get what's theirs. I be tossing my shit across the room like, why are you even by me?"

"Get theirs?"

"After they nut."

"That's the thing, Kamber, I never get to that point. I'm too stuck in my head. But, I want to. I feel like if it's not the real thing, then it doesn't count. Not my orgasm, but the control aspect of it. Like, if a man isn't involved then I'm not really owning my sexuality and my body. I'm just... having an orgasm."

"Never gotten to that point? Oh yeah. We're getting you some dick, tonight."

We were so close to the loud music that I could feel it on my cheeks. Kamber pushed forward but I stepped backward and pressed my back against the wall behind me.

In and out.

In and out.

Deep breaths, Halo.

In and out.

In and out.

"Hal—" Kamber called out after noticing I had stopped mid-stride. She backtracked until she was in front of me.

"Listen, I got you. Okay? You don't have to worry about anything. If you're uncomfortable, we can leave."

"No. I'm fine. I'm okay. I'm just taking it all in," I lied.

I wasn't exactly okay, but I wasn't overwhelmed either. I simply had a plethora of emotions that were swarming me, simultaneously. In order to move forward, I had to confront them.

"I'm serious. If you want me to hold your hand

through the entire time we're here, I will. And, when I leave so will you. I don't want you here alone and suddenly get overstimulated."

"No. No. I'm okay. Please don't babysit me tonight. I really, really need this. In fact, when we go in, can you just stay a little distance from me so that I can take this moment to stand on my own two feet? You don't understand what that would mean for me. I want to be proud of myself when I'm home alone, again. I want to have something to look forward to whenever I decide to come out again."

"Alright. Alright. I understand. But, the second I think you're in way over your head, I'm stepping in. Deal?"

"Deal."

"You need to loosen up a bit more so make sure your first stop is the bar. I'll be there, but with distance, of course."

"Of course." I smiled with a nod.

Kamber led the way. Slowly, I followed her lead while still maintaining a small distance between us. She was the most confident woman I knew. And, though I didn't know many, I wasn't a stranger to society as a whole. I'd gone through twelve years of school and encountered girls, boys, women, and everything in between. Kamber, however, stood out amongst them all.

I wish I had that, I admitted. As I watched intently at her form and every movement of her body, I began to adjust mine. I squared my shoulders and exaggerated my height by stretching my neck and holding my head high.

Just like Kamber, I gave head tilts to the people we passed along our journey to the bar.

I feel silly. My thoughts were loud but my desperation was louder. *But, you look normal.* There was a war going on in my head as I walked what felt like the longest distance to the bar. Thankfully, the lounge wasn't crawling with patrons. There were a handful of people every few feet. There was plenty of sitting room and a small dance floor. Approximately sixty percent of the tables were taken and there were a few people hanging around the bar. It wasn't completely empty, but it wasn't at full capacity, either. I'd take that over an overcrowded spot any day.

"What you having, pretty lady?" I heard beside me, jerking me from my thoughts and observation of the bar.

I could feel my heart try to escape through my breast as I whipped my head in the direction of the deep, lacy tenor. It felt like forever before I located the source and the moment I managed to, it required every ounce of strength that my body possessed for me not to call out to Kamber.

Our eyes locked. His brown ones and my brown ones, different shades and gazing in different directions. The unfamiliarity of the moment and emotions that accompanied him left me gasping for oxygen that I knew was all around me; otherwise, I would have curled over and suffocated a long time ago.

My heart drummed.
Mouth dried.
Throat swelled.

Eyeballs blossomed.
Palms clammed.
Stomach knotted.
Head swam.
And, my vagina... it secreted.

What is happening? I panicked. I was on the brink of wooziness and it had absolutely nothing to do with the two drinks I'd had at Kamber's or my agoraphobia. It was him. Whoever "*him*" was.

Say something, Halo.
Say something.
Anything.
Just say something.

A thick lump of nothingness formed in my throat, stopping words from exiting. It wasn't my fault. Not really, at least. My body was betraying me. With each second that passed, our eyes stayed locked. Though I desperately wanted to break eye contact, his magnetic presence wouldn't allow it. I was immobile. My systems were disabled and decided not to contribute to the moment.

Say something, Halo.
Say something.

Nothing. Nothing would escape me.

"I'll give you time to think about it, but whatever it is, it's on me."

He started in the other direction and I could feel my heart tearing as he turned his back toward me. The thought of him leaving me so soon was far too much to bear, forcing me to swallow back the lump in my throat and trash the thoughts in my head that forbade my actions.

"Grown-up juice. I'll have grown-up juice. Brown."

His brows folded as he turned in my direction again.

"Grown-up juice?" He asked, confused as I was as to why I'd said that.

Dammit, Halo. Did you just say that? I chastised myself.

"Enlighten me," he smiled, crumbling my heart into pieces.

A man so perfect it's painful to watch. I concluded.

"Alcohol," I said, lowly, clearing my throat right after.

Embarrassment stained my cheeks. The peaks burned as my mouth overcompensated itself with constant saliva pools that needed to be swallowed every other second.

"We're at a bar, pretty lady. I wouldn't assume you were talking about anything else."

Without even seeing them, it was obvious he stood back on his legs. I didn't miss the moment they locked and his arms folded in front of him. His bright jewelry was very contrasting to his dark skin, but they both glistened in the dark, taking control of my body.

No. No. Wake up! I demanded of myself. *You're the one in control here.*

I straightened and squared my sagging shoulders, just like Kamber. Then, I hiked my chin up just a bit to lift my head and stretch my neck. When my posture was appropriate, I found the words to follow.

"I'd like something brown and sweet, please," I replied.

"Something brown and sweet. Sounds like somebody I just met," he chuckled.

Oh God. I shuddered.

Something was released from my center. My eyes bucked and my hand immediately cupped my lady parts. Through the fabric of the black pants that Kamber had allowed me to borrow, I could feel moisture and warmth. Both exaggerated beyond familiarity, causing me to wonder exactly what was going on down there.

"You good?" he asked, concern etched across his face.

The study of human behavior, expressions, and logic in my downtime that once seemed pointless because I had no plans of ever leaving my apartment had finally come in handy. The hours and hours of studying felt silly until this very moment. I didn't feel as lost as I thought I would though uncertainty and discomfort still lingered.

"Uhhhhh, yes. I'm okay," I assured us both.

The assurance was more for me than him, but I'd never tell. It was an oath that I'd repeat several times throughout my life and the night as a point of validation for self. It was necessary and always needed to get to the next second and the one after that. Affirming myself, constantly, coaxed my nervous system and kept my thoughts from overcoming me.

"I'm Ledge," he shared, moving about the bar and mixing things up in a glass.

Each time he was required to move further down toward the other end, the crack in my chest grew a little longer. Finally, he'd finished whatever the concoction was and sat it in front of me. I was stupefied. His closeness was as invigorating as it was daunting.

"When someone gives you their name, you're supposed to give them yours in return, pretty lady," he leaned forward and whispered as if it was a secret that was meant to be kept between us two.

I hated secrets. I'd kept one for years and it destroyed me. I didn't want to keep another one, especially one from a stranger. Shorter, quicker breaths followed the ideation.

Calm down. It's okay. My eyes searched the length of the bar until I found a smiling Kamber. They shifted from Kamber to *him* and then back to Kamber. She lifted a hand, slowly, and raised her thumb. Her head nodded up and down.

"That's your people?"

His voice was so close and so alarming. I felt my entire body jerk from its impact.

"Uhhhh, Halo," I replied, deflecting. I didn't want to talk about Kamber or her reason for being so close.

"Huh?" He asked, tilting his head in confusion.

"My name... my name is Halo."

"Figures. Some shit like that fits you."

"What does that mean?" I wondered aloud, furrowing my brows in the process. That hadn't been in the studies of behavior, expressions, and logic.

"Shit, really. Your mother was spot on when she named you. It fits you," he clarified.

"How so?" Surprisingly, I challenged, still not understanding.

"Alecic. Soft-natured. Gentle. Fragile. Mild-mannered. I'd use those words to describe what's in front of me. Their relation to an actual halo isn't coincidental. The name suits you."

"You just met me."

Though appreciative of the words used to describe me, I didn't understand how he'd managed to conjure them for a person he'd only encountered a minute or two ago.

"I've met enough people in this lifetime to be a good enough judge of character. A nigga doesn't need too long to figure someone out. That includes you."

"I highly doubt you've figured me out so soon," I admitted.

"Then stick around until I do," he suggested.

I said nothing. Instead of responding, I dropped my gaze and stared into the clear glass full of colors and a large cup of ice. Just like I'd seen on my computer screen during my Youtube searches on human behavior, I gripped the black straw between my index finger and thumb before swirling it around.

"Drink up." He patted the bar as he stepped away.

My heart sank into the size seven shoes that I'd borrowed from Kamber as well. I was usually a six and a half, but the seven fit perfectly. *Please don't go*, I wanted to scream but the words stayed lodged in my thoughts as I watched him move on to the next customer.

Drink up. I obliged. The dependency I instantly felt for someone I didn't know was disheartening. I shook my head from one side to the other as I placed the small straw to my lips and pulled against it. The sweet, flavorful liquid tap danced on my tastebuds, causing me to close my eyes for a brief second.

"It's our anniversary," the singer belted over the track that was blasting in the background.

It is. The track was symbolic of the moment, my moment. On this very day, I'd been violated for the very first time by a man that I loved and cherished. This anniversary was the reason I decided to stop feeling sorry for myself and get ahold of my life. There was no doubt about it, I was wasting away behind the door of my apartment. The depression was heavy and the burden of my brutal assaults was even heavier.

"Anniversarrrry," he sang.

For 62 days, I'd prepared myself for this. One foot on the small porch in front of my apartment. A cracked window to let in the fresh air that I never got the chance to enjoy. The opening of my blinds. Grabbing the handle of my door. Locking and unlocking the locks. Standing in the mirror repeating the twenty-six affirmations I'd written to replace the simple phrases that I found myself clinging to daily. *I'm okay. It's okay. It's going to be okay.*

I watched, intently, as the man I'd discovered was named Ledge, serviced any and everyone who stepped up to the bar to order a drink. His unchanging expression left me baffled because it wasn't the same one he wore the few minutes he was in my presence. Hoping I'd shrunk a few inches and was possibly invisible to everyone in the room, I remained focused on him and the drink he'd poured, only to find myself shying away when his eyes landed on me.

His eyes. They were cold and mysterious and wondrous, forcing mine straight ahead to avoid getting lost in them. After so long and so many sips, it was inevitable, facing him.

"Another?" He asked, holding my empty glass in the air.

He smelled like nature wrapped in a bow. The subtle yet intrusive scent that he wore reeked of wood, pines, grass, florals, citrus, and musk. Then there was pineapple, oakmoss, apple, and berries. Together, they made the most sophisticated fragrance.

Maybe being a homebody isn't so bad, I concluded. The online perfumery course that I'd taken helped me identify the notes of his cologne without much thought or too many whiffs. It came with a kit that contained fifty popular notes and half of them seemed to be plastered on his skin at once. I wasn't complaining, however.

"Yes, please."

And another.

And another.

LEDGE + HALO

I watched as Kamber tossed her head backward in laughter as the guy standing in front of her entertained her. *So carefree. So effortless. So endearing.* The simple act was agonizingly beautiful to me, bringing saltiness to my eyes. My emotions were spilling over and there was nothing I could do to stop them. *I want that for me. I think I deserve it.*

"Is it that bad," he asked, handing me the fourth drink.

"It's worse," I sighed, completely loosened and unable to hold onto my thoughts any longer. They exited my lips as soon as they came to mind.

The first man that I'd grown fond of stood behind the bar pondering with a hand across his chest and another under his chin. I felt myself unraveling as he moved in my direction. My body shifted forward instead of backward this time when he leaned on the bar and eliminated a great amount of distance between us.

"How can I help?"

"Make me forget about everything in my heart," I challenged, unsure of who was speaking.

Halo SaraBella? Is that you, baby girl? My heart voiced as my head prepared its response. *Yes.*

"If the liquor didn't do it, I have something that will," he responded with a smirk on his nice, fluffy lips.

"Yeah?" I questioned with squinted eyes, curious to hear what he had in mind.

He leaned in even more and brought a hand to the side of my neck. Slightly shaken, I flinched at the feel of someone, anyone's, but especially a man's hand on my skin. My hesitancy didn't deter him. Instead, he brought me closer to his mouth as the sound of his voice began tickling me between the legs. I could feel my nipples harden through the thin fabric of the shirt that I would've never considered hadn't Kamber forced me into it.

"It involves me taking you to my house, eating your pretty pussy until you beg for me to have mercy on you, then you putting my dick down your wet, slippery throat right before I slide into the mess we both create between your legs," he articulated.

I swallowed back the overwhelming amount of saliva I'd collected in such a small amount of time. As he pulled away slowly and released me from his grasp, I gazed at the bulge of his throat that signified his manhood.

"Is that what you had in mind, pretty lady?"

"Ummm. I—uh."

"You're a big girl, sound it out," he encouraged as he hovered.

Say it. Say yes. This is what you want. This is what you need. Say it.

"Yes."

The words rushed from my frame, relieving me at once.

"Good. My bartender called in sick so I'm holding it down tonight. Can you hang out with a nigga for about another hour and a half?"

"Drinks on you?" I breathed out.

"Drinks on me," he confirmed with a wink.

My head whipped around as he walked off toward the other end of the bar. Kamber was still there being entertained, but her eyes were on me. I nodded and this time, it was my thumb that went into the air. She lifted her arm and tapped the watch on her wrist.

"Work," she mouthed with sad eyes.

In response, I nodded. I understood. It was alright. Her leaving me didn't feel like the end of the world anymore. Not the world where Ledge existed, at least. Though I'd just met him, I felt like he'd take good care of me for the night.

Kamber stood and headed in my direction. When she approached me, her arms lifted.

"Can I?" She asked without getting too close.

"Yes."

Slowly, she hugged my frame. I shrunk within her embrace. It was the first time since I was nineteen that anyone had wrapped me in their arms. My grandmother was the last person on earth I'd felt comfortable enough to share moments of intimacy with. Noticing the slight discomfort, Kamber quickly retracted.

"I have to go. Do you want me to drop you off at home before I head to work?"

"No. I think I'll be fine."

"Yeah? Is that what your gut is telling you?"

"Yes and my panties," I whispered. "I think I need new ones."

"Someone is on her level, I see. Had a lot of that grown-up juice. I counted. You sure you're fine?"

"Yes. I'm sure."

"If you feel a way at any point, please call me. Also, remember that there is no timeframe or limit on consent. Even if you're already in the act and decide it is not what you want to do, you have the right to say no. You're in control here. Remember?"

She transformed into a mother bear before my eyes. Having someone to look after me and genuinely care about my well-being again after so many years was a blessing that I didn't take for granted. Kamber had been my neighbor for years and though we didn't see each other much, she made sure to check on me often. She was aware of my condition and had made it her business to make sure that I was well every chance she got.

"Yes. I remember."

"Good. Text or call me every hour you're awake or I will come searching for you. I already turned your location on."

"Okay."

"I'm serious, Halo."

"I knoooooow."

"And, I'm happy for you. You did it, friend."

"Please go. You're already late."

"I am. I am. See you in the morning," she said, finally stepping off.

"Scc you."

LEDGE + HALO

"YOU GOING to come in or stay out here?" Ledge asked as we sat.

I was hardly sure of when we'd arrived or how we'd

gotten here. To cope with the motion sickness that I felt after starting the engine of his truck, I sealed my lids. I opened my eyes to find us in the driveway of a beautiful dwelling.

"Oh God," I breathed, holding my chest as I attempted to stop my heart from falling flat onto the floor rug.

"You good?" He asked for the fifth time tonight. The welfare checks were confirmation that I hadn't made a foolish mistake by leaving the bar with him. For that, I was thankful.

"Yes. Yes. I'm fine."

"More water?"

He'd been suggesting a few sips every few minutes since my fourth and last drink. According to him, I needed to sober up a bit. However, he didn't understand that the sober version of me wasn't the one that would've ended up in his car or at his house. In fact, she'd be curled up in bed snoring. I needed to keep my blood alcohol level up as long as I could because once it came down, I wasn't sure what to expect.

"No. I'm okay."

I am. I nodded. *I'm okay.*

"Aight, then. Let me get you inside."

Ledge was out of the truck and on the ground in seconds. His long legs cut the journey's time in half. I imagined he was easily over six feet, towering over my five-foot-four frame. Strangely, though, the difference in height and the thickness of his frame was far from frightening. I found myself wanting to be wrapped in his arms and cuddled through the night, but that was wishful thinking.

Although I'd watched him round the truck, I was still caught by surprise when he opened the door. I wasn't quite ready to face the cold so soon. Or maybe the realization of what would be happening once I exited had begun to settle in my bones.

"Hey," he started, softening his voice as he reached up and grabbed the handle hanging from the roof. "You sure you're good?"

I nodded, slowly, keeping my eyes forward.

"Then, what's the matter? What's with the sad face?"

"Just a lot on my mind and my heart. But, that's what we're here for," I reminded him with a half smile.

"It doesn't have to be."

The tips of his fingers brushed my skin as he cupped my chin and pulled my face in his direction. *My God, he's beautiful.* The sight of him made me ache all over. His hand rested on my cheek, sliding from the top to the bottom. I leaned into his gentle caress. Firsts. There were many of them tonight that he was unaware of and I hoped I wasn't giving him a clue about them, either. *You're okay*, I repeated as I familiarized myself with his palm and fingers and hand.

"But, it is. I want it to be. I need it to be," I admitted.

"Whatever you want, pretty lady. It's your world."

You're in control. I quickly translated his words. He was suggesting that I was in complete control, not understanding just how much those words meant to me. What this moment meant for me.

"Let's roll."

I slid out of the truck as he stood back to give me room. But, just when he started toward the house, he laced his fingers with mine and slowed his pace. Smaller, less swift steps allowed me to keep up. With my eyes on the ground, I followed his lead. *Only this once*, I soothed the part of me that demanded control of the night.

On quivering legs and a slightly trembling frame, I entered Ledge's place. The two-story home was breathtaking. It was obvious that time and attention were plentiful when completing the masterpiece. It was far from the bachelor pad I'd read most men had with barely a decent amount of towels in pool the linen closet or sitting room for guests.

"Anything to drink?" He asked me, securing the locks on his door and causing the breath in my throat to hike. "Water? Apple juice? Lemonade?"

"No thanks."

"This way," he responded, tilting his head toward the stairs.

Taking me by the hand, he led the journey through the foyer and up the stairs. I felt as if I was in a stop-motion film as we traveled up and toward what I assumed was his bedroom. One second we were at the bottom of the modern set of wooden planks with black guardrails and the next, we were in the middle.

Finally, we reached the top, leaving me baffled and trying to adjust to what felt like a timelapse. It wasn't though. We'd successfully tapped each step with the soles of our shoes.

Click.
Clack.
Click.
Clack.

My heels collided with the solid, light-washed wood beneath me. The silence of the home was a worship ground for my conscience. I could hear my voice as it began to scream from within. I buried the sound with words that surfaced, praying the others stayed at bay.

"This is a lovely place," lowly, I spoke.

"Appreciate that."

That was it. That was all. That was his response. I wasn't sure why I was expecting him to say more or needing him to say more, but there I was longing for his sultry voice and choice words.

"Right here," he said, catering to my desires.

He stepped forward, into the room that our stride halted in front of. Again, his head nodded in the direction of our path, signaling his urge for us to move forward. With my eyes on his extended arm, I stepped into the room first.

My heart drummed against my chest as I entered. What I found was what was to be expected. There was more beauty to behold. The black, cream, gold, and hints of brown throughout the space were well coordinated. Everything came together so well.

The large bed that was stationed in the center of the room and pushed up against the wall was the statement piece. It was velvety and black with gold trimming and metal to stabilize the frame. Large pillars made up the thick headboard that looked soft to the touch. Sheets lined the bed to match, black in color and thick as well.

"The bathroom?" I cleared my throat to ask.

"Straight through here."

Ledge trekked through the enormous bedroom, his long legs reaching his destination much sooner than I ever could've without running at full speed. The darkness of the bathroom was immediately illuminated at the flip of a switch. As I approached, he slipped past me and back into the bedroom.

Mindful of just how unnerving the sound of slamming doors was for me, I carefully closed the bathroom door behind me. Once securely inside, I placed my back up against it and dropped my face into the palm of my hands. My shoulder-length hair fell forward, serving as a blanket that wrapped me snugly in its threads.

One thousand and eighty-two emotions ripped through my core, but there was one far more prominent than the others. *Thirst*. It burned my throat and heated my center like an old, wooden furnace.

Thirst for *more*. Thirst for *better*. Thirst for *normalcy*. Thirst for *intimacy*. Thirst for *sexual healing*. Thirst for the *best version of myself*. It all dictated what was next for me, shoving me to the edge of the sink's counter with one hand deep into the small clutch I'd borrowed from Kamber.

Wet wipes. The sound of the pouch they were in rumbling upon physical contact was music to my ears. I hurriedly removed them from the purse and pulled back the clear plastic that protected their moisture. The wetness seeped through my skin as I hunched over the sink, slid down my pants, and then my undies.

From front to back, I wiped my flesh carefully. In the seat of my black, seamless panties was a mound of white, sliminess that could only be a result of everything I felt for the man on the other side of the door. A perfect pair of panties had been ruined, but I didn't think complaining was on my agenda.

Satisfied with my level of cleanliness, I tossed the wipes I'd used and then quickly removed the pants and shoes I was wearing. The underwear was next to go and into my purse they went. I pumped soap from the stone dispenser and scrubbed my hands. The effects of the alcohol I'd consumed were still slowing my movements and delaying my speech, but I felt the best I had in so many years.

When I reentered the bedroom, Ledge disappeared into the bathroom. I used the moment alone to pull out my phone and shoot Kamber a quick text to let her know that I was fine. Barely a second later, she responded.

Ledge is his name. I'm safe and at his home.

He owns the place! The bar. Jilted.

Really? That was news to me.

Are you naked, yet? She asked, with an eggplant emoji that confused me.

Wait. I should be naked? I wondered. Instead of wasting time texting Kamber back, I began getting rid of the threads that my body was wrapped in. As much as I wanted to take a second and slow down, I knew that it wasn't best. Backing out wasn't an option for me, so I was willing to go to great lengths to make the night a success.

Just as I picked up my phone to assure Kamber that I was indeed naked, seated on Ledge's bed, shaking awfully, and waiting for him to return, he appeared. I didn't bother with the reply, choosing to lay my phone beside me and train my eyes straight ahead. With my shoulders squared and my chin high, I mocked the behavior of what I believed to be normal, confident women, one of those women being Kamber.

"That's how you feel?" He tittered, rubbing the hair on his chin.

"Ummm hmmm."

Surprisingly, I maintained eye contact, though I was on the brink of disengagement. Head up. Eyes straight ahead. You've got this. I watched, intently, as Ledge placed one foot in front of the other to obliterate the space that divided us. As he did so, I shifted positions on the bed, feeling the effects of the alcohol as they led my movements.

By the time he reached me, my legs were wide, show-casing the very part of me that had been brutalized from the age of six until I was fourteen years old. For the first time, it was my decision and it was my world. I was in control. That made parting my legs much easier, espe-cially for a practically perfect man.

One minute he was standing tall and the next he was on his knees in front of me, pulling my body toward the edge of the bed. Feeling his fingers against my skin, in places that hadn't been touched since I was fourteen, resulted in sharp, short breaths that were heard in the silence of the room. While they were once forceful and unwelcomed, Ledge's were contrasting.

"Come 'er," he grunted as he placed me exactly where he wanted.

With care, he caressed me. Gentle and carefully, he slid his fingers up my legs, gripped my thighs, and somehow widened the gap between them in the process. I could feel my center creaming and soiling his comforter.

First, it was his thumb that I felt against the hooded nub. Instantly, it swelled, peeking from underneath its cover. Simultaneously, his middle and index fingers circled my entryway, getting a fix of my personal lubrication. And, when I least expected, they both entered me at once, causing me to gasp. My chest inflated as I waited for the pain that I was accustomed to, but there was none. There was only pleasure.

"Relax," Ledge whispered.

Naturally, my body submitted, although I wanted to remain in control of everything and anything I got myself involved in. He made it so easy to succumb to his authority. And, that gut feeling that I'd been told to follow, made it clear that I wasn't making a mistake.

My cheeks scooted back and forth on the black comforter, grinding against his fingers and thumb as he painted masterpieces inside of me. Waves crashing against the coast was the only way to describe the feeling that consumed me.

There was no pain.

There weren't any tears.

And, the silence wasn't ringing in my ears. Just the sound of comfort, pleasure, and appreciation as I opened my mouth and allowed a moan to escape.

Oh my God, this feels so good.

Just as the thought crossed my mind, his thumb exposed my clitoris to the open air. My sealed eyes opened, staring down in an attempt to figure out what was happening. It wasn't until I saw him lower his head and extend his tongue that I understood the assignment. This was oral sex, the one thing I'd never experienced.

"Ummmmmmm," I groaned, leaning back further on his bed as I grabbed the sheets to relieve the mounting pleasure in my lower belly.

Up and down. Around and around.

His tongue drew a road map on my vulva that only he could understand. As he created each landmark, my chest rose and once he moved on to the next, it fell again.

Euphoria.

Heaven.

Jubilation.

Ecstasy.

Bliss.

Pure rhapsody.

Those were just a few words to describe my state. With eyes trying to find their way to the back of my head, I clenched my core. Something was on the horizon. Something big and something consuming. To brace myself for impact, I squeezed my legs together, locking Ledge in place, and grabbed a fist full of fabric. This time, I balled it until it fluffed between my knuckles and separated my fingers.

"Please," I begged. "Please."

Release me. I wanted to scream.

"Please."

It was the only word that would surface. But, apparently, it wasn't enough to appease the serpent with his head between my legs. Instead of giving me the air that I needed to breathe, he latched onto me and flickered his tongue rapidly. Over and over, sending me off the deep end and closer to wherever it was that he was taking me.

"Please stop!" The words ripped through my core and exited my lips.

Just as they did, everything came to a halt. Ledge's dark, handsome face rose, slowly, his beard leaking of my juices. It reminded me of the images and videos of lions with blood trickling from their mane after a fresh kill and a decent meal.

"Why... why'd... why'd you..." I stuttered, lifting the top half of my body from the mattress.

"Because you asked me to."

"I didn't mean it."

"Then don't say it. Don't say shit," he advised, sternly but with concern etched across his forehead.

I nodded my head, swiftly, up and down to confirm my understanding.

"I'm sorry," I apologized.

"Show me. Open that pussy back up and show me."

Obliging, I rested my body back on the bed and spread my legs as far as they would go. When I closed my eyes, I felt his lips on me, again. This time, they remained fixated on my flesh until I saw stars. My body shook violently as I released years of build-up.

"Ahhhhhh. Ummm. Oh God. Oh God. Pleaeeeeeeese."

Every nerve in my body shattered. Every limb in my body weakened. Every bit of oxygen in my body was depleted, leaving me gasping for more.

"FUCK," I cried out, producing profanity for the first time in my adult life.

As if the levees had been broken, every ounce of fluid rushed from my vagina. There wasn't anything I could do to stop the overflow. I tried and tried and tried.

"What is... what is going ooooonnnnnn?"

"Your pussy is thanking me. That's what the fuck is going on," Ledge snarled as he tapped my center with his hand, bringing more of the waterworks.

"Oooooohhhhhh my God!"

As I began my descent, I felt the weight of Ledge's body sinking into the mattress on both sides of me. Then there were his lips. With ease, they found mine as if they belonged. His wet beard brushed against my skin. The smell of my flesh startled me just as he lowered his lips onto mine.

Is this how I taste? The bittersweetness was profound and tasty, nonetheless, keeping me engaged in the very first kiss I'd ever shared with a man of my choosing. Hungrily, I devoured him, never wanting to release him. When I did, it wasn't on my terms. It was his. Heavily, he breathed as he backed away.

"Shit," he said to me. "I got something for you to eat, but it ain't my face, pretty lady."

Astonished by my lack of shame, I pushed out the stream of air that I'd been holding while I tried to have his facial features for a late-night snack. My appetite for him hadn't been satisfied, not just yet. But when Ledge stood his full-length and shoved his boxers downward, toward his feet, I was met with the next portion of my full-course meal.

At the sight of the entree, I knew that it would fill me to the brim. Fear etched its way into my thoughts with my eyes fixed on the veiny, round-headed, master tool between his legs. *What am I supposed to do with all of this?*

"Put 'em in your mouth," Ledge groaned as if it was painful to project. He'd heard my thoughts and answered my question. But, although he had given instructions, I was still unsure of how to carry them out.

Instead of his rod being as straight as an arrow like all the ones I'd seen in training, it featured a curve. A sickening one that I'd only had the pleasure of reading about but never actually seen on a video and certainly not in person. Yet, here he was standing in front of me with what was considered a gem in the bedroom, according to the women who'd experienced them.

Besides the training videos I'd paid good money for, I didn't have any real experience with handling a man with girth and length. At the sight of Ledge's massiveness, one thing was made very clear to me. Decency wasn't the only area that my rapist lacked.

I felt silly as I widened my jaws and pushed my head forward to accommodate him. He was as thick as he was long, making it hard for me to adjust. But, it didn't stop me from trying. Complete satisfaction was the only thing on my agenda and I'd studied for months to make sure that it was checked off my list.

Discomfort struck me like a bolt of lightning the second his dark skin touched my taste buds. It had absolutely nothing to do with him, but everything to do with me. I tried my hardest to remember what was next, but my mind went blank. Ledge sensed my hesitancy and lack of skill. The smile on his face when I looked up at him revealed that he didn't mind the inexperience a bit.

"Practice makes perfect, pretty lady. Open a little wider so I can teach you how to suck this dick properly."

He fisted my hair, gently pulling my head back until our eyes locked. My mouth was wide open as he'd requested. He'd sent me to heights I never knew were reachable and I wanted to do the same for him. But, he was right. Practice does make perfect and I hadn't practiced at all.

"That's right, baby girl, open up so I can fuck that throat nice and slow."

As the words fell from his lips, my center creamed and my mouth watered. True to his word, he moved slowly, deeper into my mouth until he couldn't anymore and then he retracted. Saliva pooled in my jaws, my thirst for his satisfaction driving me to the point of no return.

When I felt confident enough that I could handle the task on my own, I slapped his hand away from my head, used the muscles of my jaws to suck him deeper into my mouth, and then slid backward to watch his shiny pole as it drew back.

"Shit," he gritted. "That's it, pretty lady."

My head and neck were in sync as I tried my hardest to drain him of everything inside of his sack. Slob dripped from my mouth, onto his lengthiness, and onto my chest each time I pulled him out to catch my breath. My level of focus was unmatched as I licked and sucked and continued to spit on the yummy, chocolate skin until I felt resistance. Confusion plagued me.

"You gone make this mauh'fucker cum," Ledge alerted me, simultaneously stepping back and pulling his... *Say dick, Halo. Just say it*. My thoughts rang out.

"Stand up."

Instantly, I was off the bed and standing in front of him. Without warning, he lifted me up and into his arms. My legs wrapped around his waist, instinctively, as my lips lowered onto his. Feeling a bit of control in my favor, I stuck my tongue down his throat. I could still taste myself on his personals.

Just when I thought things couldn't get any better, I felt the head of his ***dick*** poking around my hole, trying to find the entry path. Very swiftly, he discovered it and before I was able to brace myself for intrusion, he'd hit rock bottom, sending me into a world far beyond my imagination.

"Whaaaaaaaaaaat is haaaaapening?" I exclaimed, tightening my grip on his shoulders and burying my head underneath his left ear.

"Dick, pretty lady, that's what's happening."

Ledge was as quiet as he was cocky and he had every right to be. He'd been blessed in every department. God spared no material when creating him, especially not when it came to the third leg he was toting around as if it was normal. *Wait. Is it?*

With ease, he lifted me up and down his shaft. I waited and waited and waited for the pain to surface. It never did. And, once I realized I was giving the past way too much opportunity to ruin the present, I shut down my thoughts and allowed my feelings to lead the way.

"Ledge," I cried out, feeling the pressure mounting.

"This shit gripping," he grunted. "Fuck."

My vagina was as wet as my mouth while he was inside of it. It was slippery beyond my control. My cream soiled my thighs and trickled down my butt crack. Finding it extremely hard to hold onto my sanity, I closed my eyes and allowed the crashing waves to overcome me. Just before the stars aligned behind my lids, it all ended.

"Ledge, please."

"Please what?" He asked, making strides toward the other side of the bed.

"Please," I repeated, feeling helpless and hopeless as I chased the same ending I'd had with his head between my legs.

"Say it," he encouraged while laying me down on the clean, dry portion of the bed.

"Put it back in. Please," lowly, I rephrased.

"I can't hear you. What do you want me to do?" He asked, frustrating me.

"Ledge, please."

"Open your fucking mouth and say what you want me to do!" He fussed, hovering over me with his lips so close to mine that I could feel the air that he pushed out with them.

"Fuck me!" I shouted. "Fuck me!"

Without uttering a single word, Ledge reentered me with so much passion that it rattled my heart and my head, simultaneously. I wasn't sure what love felt like but I was almost sure that it was exactly what had struck me as my eyes blossomed and gazed into his. There was so much adoration and admiration within them. The contortion of his features as a result of our divine connection wasn't even enough to conceal the depth his orbs possessed.

I gushed from below as I pulled his body closer to mine. Letting go wasn't an option, not now, anyway. I clung to him as if he was the last human left on earth and could vanish at any moment. He dug my insides out with little mercy on me. I thoroughly enjoyed each and every thrust of his performance.

He touched my soul, serenaded my body, and sewed the fragments of my heart together. *Halo*. I cried. Hot tears burned my eyes. *This is your moment*. It was and the man that had made it possible seemed to understand it, too.

"Let that shit go," he breathed into my ear.

His permission to dissolve the trauma of my past and take full control of my future couldn't have come at a better time. The double entendre, as it related to the orgasm that was on the rise and my history, was taken to heart.

"It's haaaapennnnning."

"Let it go," he growled. "Fuck. I'm cumming."

Everything around me blackened.

LEDGE + HALO

DARKNESS WAS ALL AROUND ME. It covered every inch and every corner, blinding me. But, even with obstructed vision, the unfamiliarity of the space around me was apparent. *Where am I?* My breath hiked in my chest as my throat swelled. *Where am I?* The question arose again.

Light snores in my left ear assured me that I wasn't alone and was in fact laying beside someone. *What is going on?* I pondered as my head began to throb. Afraid to shift and relieve myself of the discomfort of my position, I remained still and tried my best to relax my limbs. Being that I was unsure of where I was, what was going on, or what was next, relaxing any parts of my body was almost impossible.

Brown. The first memory of the night flooded me.

Jilted. The second came soon after.

Ledge! His face appeared in my head.

We... we had sex. A lot of sex.

Suddenly, the muscles of my vagina contracted. I could feel him between my walls, again. *Oh my God.* It felt celestial. However, it was nothing in comparison to the anxiety that grabbed my neck and squeezed it tightly.

I couldn't breathe.

The fear of suffocating forced me to my feet and toward the bathroom that I'd been shown hours earlier. It wasn't until I was inside with my back against the door that a bit of relief found me.

I'm at his home? The question quickly shoved the pinch of relief down my throat, choking me. I attempted to balance myself on weakened knees, barely managing the short distance to the sink. I twisted the right handle and water fell from the hole immediately. Parched, I lowered the top half of my body and placed my mouth underneath it.

My hair, my sweaty but still gorgeous hair, was instantly drenched in some spots but remained dry in others. Gulp after gulp, I didn't stop drinking until my belly felt full and my temperature lowered. However, when I turned the handle toward the back and the stream of water ended, my neck began to close again.

Hurriedly, I rushed toward the end of the bathroom and scooted my frame between the toilet bowl and wall, then began focusing on my breathing. It felt as if I was drying, rotting, and dying all at once.

Breathe. I told myself.

Breathe, Halo.

Breath...

The lack of silence interrupted my thoughts. *Footsteps.*

The sound was so familiar. Fear nearly swallowed me

whole as I looked from one side to the other with big, cowering eyes.

In a tight knot, I curled, as the sound of large feet echoed on the floor. He's coming. It registered in my head as my eyes closed and I began counting.

"One. Two. Three. Four," I whispered.

Eight. That's how far I was about to get before the familiar sound of footsteps halted. Shivering as I sat on the cold, lonely floor, I stared at the door with my head tucked between my hands. Run. Hide. Scream. The commands appeared at once, but I was unable to follow either of them. Instead, I remained on the floor, body quivering and throat clogged.

Urrrrrrrrn. The door crept open.

It's going to be okay. It's going to be okay. It's going to be okay. I repeated in my head, over and over nonstop until...

"Halo?" Ledge's voice sounded, reeling me in and bringing me back to my reality. Our reality.

I said nothing. My eyes were fixated on the floor as my body burned all over. Suddenly, I wasn't cold anymore. I was embarrassed and ashamed. The coolness of the floor didn't register. I felt like I was on fire.

"You good?" He asked, rushing to my side. "You okay?"

I'll never be okay, I cried inside. Never.

"What's the matter?"

Say something, Halo.

Anything.

This doesn't look so good.

Explain.

"Can you take me home?" I asked instead.

"Right now? It's like four in the morning. You want to come back to bed and I take you when the sun rises?" He squatted down, establishing a less scary height difference. With us leveled, I felt much better about his presence.

"I... I uh," I stuttered as the tears broke through the air.

Why is this happening to me? My heart broke as I came to terms with the fact that maybe I was as weird as others thought I was and maybe a normal life just wasn't in my deck of cards.

"Hey. Hey. I can take you home. Just tell me what's with the tears?"

The back of his calloused hands graced my cheek. Ever so gentle, he was as he swiped my tears away. To his dismay, more fell and wouldn't stop.

He was winsome inside and out. That fact, I didn't deny. To be honest, I didn't even think I was worthy of being in his space. Instead of freaking out as I melted away on his bathroom floor, concern plagued him.

I wish I could tell you. But... you're a stranger. I concluded before conjuring a few words. I at least owed him that much, I believed.

"I'm having a really hard time, right now," I admitted and it was the honest to God's truth. But, unfortunately, the hardships didn't stop. Like, ever.

"Let me get you home. You putting your shit back on or do you want to borrow something of mine?"

"Can I have a shirt?"

"You want some sweats and a hoodie, too? It's cold outside, pretty lady."

How could he still think that? I swallowed back the words and nodded.

"Come on, let me get you dressed and home safely."

Ledge stood up straight and started toward the door. When he realized I wasn't following him, he retraced his steps until he reached me and then extended his hand. Hesitantly, I took it. He pulled me from the floor with ease and we both exited the bathroom together.

Once back in the comfort of his room, I wished I could stick around longer. However, I understood that things from this point on, for me, would only get worse. Home was my best option and that's where Ledge prepared to take me.

LEDGE + HALO

DRESSED IN HIS BIG HOODIE, t-shirt, and sweats, I clung to the passenger door, putting as much distance between us as possible. It wasn't intentional, but it felt so much better, so much safer this way.

"Right here," I said to him, finally finding my voice after an entire thirty-minute ride to my place.

My address, I'd punched into the navigation of the enormous Cadillac truck as soon as I was settled in the passenger seat. It had led us all the way to my building. I pushed the door open, forcefully, and bolted. But, just before I stuck my key into the lock, I felt familiar hands on my waist, pulling me backward and spinning me around. Once my body stopped, I was face to face with an angel on earth.

"Come 'er," he said, his deep voice warming my heart. "You just going to leave without saying goodbye?"

"Goodbye, Ledge," I responded.

I could hear the sadness in my tone. The sag of my shoulders supported my case. I wished I was strong enough, normal enough, to spend the rest of my night with him and wake up to his handsome face. But, it was just too much.

"You got a phone so I know you got a number a nigga can hold on to reach you later."

As he spoke, he pulled me into a hug, wrapping his arms around me and holding me tightly. *Please don't let go.* I wanted to beg, but I knew that I didn't have the bandwidth to withstand what would happen if I did. In the little time I'd known Ledge, I'd learned a lot about the person he was and if I didn't want him to let go, he wouldn't.

When he let go, my heart ached. He patted his pockets, only to realize he'd left his phone behind. Though he was peeved, I was a bit rejoiceful. Silently, I was already preparing to tell one of the few lies I'd ever tell in my life. His phone not being in attendance only saved me a guilty conscience later.

"I'll remember it. Just give it to me."

"Or, I could just have yours," I suggested without the

intention of using it. My phone was already in my hand. It unlocked when my face was close enough.

"That's a bet. 555-702-1220."

I tapped each number he called out and saved his contact under his name. Once that was settled, I stuck my key in my door, finally. When I turned, Ledge's tilted head and sad eyes almost made me invite him in. Unfortunately, I just couldn't.

"Goodbye, Ledge," I said, again, stepping into my apartment.

"See you later, Halo. It's never goodbye."

But, it is. For me. I'm different. I'm not like the others. You'll never, ever see me again. I know because I'll never come out of my home again. I wanted to scream, but kept my thoughts to myself.

He stepped off the small porch and back onto the pavement. I watched closely as he rounded his truck and took one final look in my direction. Satisfied, I closed the door behind me and locked both locks. A large, heavy breath escaped me as I slammed my back against the door and my face began to contort to my emotions.

Pain.

Relief.

Frustration.

Worry.

Defeat.

Victory.

It all hit me at one, like a blow to the chest.

I did it. I did it.

My eyes burned as my cheeks rose. I'd conquered one

fear, slaying one of the demons riding my back day and night. But, there appeared to be a hundred more that needed to be tamed and I wasn't up for the task. While my body belonged to me for the first time in my life, complete ownership of my person simply wasn't enough to cure me of all the mental and emotional illnesses that haunted me.

I'm doomed. I cringed. With blurred vision, I stomped through my apartment until I reached my bedroom. Though I knew that I needed a shower, I wasn't ready to wash the evidence of such a glorious night off my skin. And neither was I ready to shed the clothing he'd shared with me.

I climbed into my bed and pulled the covers on top of me. Ledge's hood went over my damp hair and the neckline rose to my nose. Deeply, I inhaled until my lungs were filled to capacity. Before exhaling, I savored the remnants of his fragrance that were sprinkled on the hoodie. As I released the long, slow trail of oxygen, I closed my eyes and allowed the pain of my existence to fall from my eyes.

I'm never leaving again.

DEDICATION

To me.

*Did I think I could write a series of full novels?
No. I'm a short type of girl. Did I think I'd
write a series of 100,000 words+ novels? Heck
no. Did I think I'd start a new series with
novels over 100,000 words immediately after
the first series?
Okay, someone has to be lying. I did that? Me?
No fucking way. Shoutout to me!*

LEDGE

THE **DOMINO EFFECT** BOOK ONE

GREY HUFFINGTON

1

LEDGE

EIGHT MONTHS LATER...

"CAN you shut the fuck up for one second and listen, my nigga?" Vexxed, I growled.

There was only one motherfucker on earth that was able to raise my blood pressure and get me going for real. He happened to have the same face and DNA as me. We'd shared the same womb at the same time and were born only minutes apart. I kissed the air first, four full minutes before he did and it was most obvious during conversations like the one we were having.

"Listen to you for what? Fuck that nigga. Fuck his kids. Fuck his bitch. Fuck his family. And, fuck you for wanting to be a part of it after thirty-something years. Nigga, we're not kids no more. We're grown-ass men. The fuck I need a daddy for now? I ain't been had one.

"This nigga been in the same fucking city and was never there when moms needed nothing. This nigga is the man in the city, Ledge. Not even thirty minutes away, his kids are eating grilled cheese sandwiches for dinner just so that our stomachs aren't touching our backs when we try to get a good night's rest. Him and them fucking privileged kids of his can suck my dick," Lawe fussed, his anger overcoming him as he banged on the bar in front of us.

"He had no idea. If there's anyone you should be upset with, it's our mother for keeping us a secret and keeping us from him."

"Our mother just died, Ledge. The fuck I'm going to be mad at her for?"

"You telling me this shit like I don't know it already. I read the letter to you, bro. As much as you hate to see it, none of this is that man's fault."

"It is! Him living a perfect fucking life that she didn't want to intrude on... that is his fault."

"No it's not. It's her kind ass heart that forced us to live the life we lived man, not his. If he's anything like the man and father that she described in this letter, then

68

it should tell you everything you need to know. Had he known we existed, we would've been well taken care of."

"Fuck that nigga!" Lawe exclaimed, taking a sip from his drink.

His anger was valid but it was aimed in the wrong direction. The misery we lived through was no one's fault but our mother. And, though her death was still fresh in our hearts, I wasn't too blind to see her faults.

The letter I'd found in her nightstand after finally having the courage to clear out her home explained that our conception was a mistake and the result of a night of spontaneity that was orchestrated by Laura Eisenberg, the wife of the infamous Liam Eisenberg. Hearing we were his seeds was as stunning as it was unbelievable. The odds just weren't leaning toward the Eisenbergs at all. I'd seen them a few times in passing.

Everyone in the city knew exactly who they were and what they did, but it was rare to encounter one and even more rare to converse or do business with either of them. Their shit was sealed tight and you had to have your money in order to play on their turf. Before I turned in my hustler's card, I was on the verge of breaking bread with their crew, thanks to my first cousin who was already in business with them and had been for years. Til' this day, they kept his pockets laced.

"So you're not going with me?"

Shifting backward until my legs locked, I folded my arms over my chest and tilted my head, waiting for a response from my knotty-head ass brother.

"Nigga, is you deaf? I told you that shit when this conversation first started."

Unlike Lawe, a father was something I'd always wanted. I never got used to being the man of the house, because I felt as if it wasn't my job to have. Lawe and I both deserved to experience the love of a father. Had we, then I doubted he'd be so angry and resentful. It was the only way to mask his true feelings of hurt and confusion.

It went from him asking why we weren't good enough for our father to stick around when we were young boys to him lashing out as a pre-teen. By the time he was sixteen, he'd transformed and become someone I barely recognized and had to acclimate myself with over the years. Now, I knew him inside out. Even though he didn't know it, he was still lost and still holding onto that pain of not feeling good enough or important enough for our father to stick around.

Liam Eisenberg being unaware of our existence made his feelings invalid, but he refused to let go of them. He'd clung to them for far too long and they were part of his identity. If he released them, then he wouldn't know who he was anymore. The barriers he'd built would come crashing down and he wasn't ready to expose himself in that way. He wasn't equipped for vulnerability, especially not at the hands of a stranger.

"Aight. Suit yourself. I'm headed that way. If you change your mind, I've given you the address."

Lawe and I stood to our feet, simultaneously, and stretched our arms out to wrap around one another. It was out of sheer habit. Though we had Malachi, Milo,

Makai, and Mercer on speed dial, all we really had were each other. The undying love we shared for one another was all we'd ever needed. Everything and anything else was a bonus.

Our chests collided. My hand went around Lawe's neck as his did mine. Toe to toe, we embraced, neither of us in a rush to let go.

"You really don't have to do this shit," Lawe gritted in my ear.

"But, I do."

The gaping hole in my chest that had been there since I learned that our father wasn't around and was never coming around was still there. Unlike Lawe, I hadn't filled it with artificial beliefs or packed it with far too many emotions than my frame could handle. I dealt with the consequences of my parents' actions head on and they made me a much better man. Lawe's choice to cover up his wounds made him stronger and tougher, but the poorly packed wound had infected his blood in the process.

I released him from my grasp and patted his shoulder while putting distance between us. As I exited Jilted, the bar that I owned and Lawe was part-owner in, uncertainty bubbled at the bottom of my stomach. Down the long hallway, I scanned the wall of founding faces. After ten months in business, I was still appreciative of the people who'd supported the vision since day one. Every chance I got, I stamped the wall with one of their faces.

Jilted was on the brink of something major. I could feel it in my bones and in my tired eyes after my thoughts about it kept me up at night. I'd cashed in nearly all my life's savings and given up the only hustle I'd ever known to see my vision come to life. Ten months later and it was just beginning to pull its own weight and turning a reasonable profit. Most businesses didn't survive their first year, so I was grateful just to see an ROI before our first year up and running.

When I stepped outside, sunlight violated every inch of my face. The El Camino SS that I'd finally finished remodeling was only a few feet from the exit, but it felt like a mile-long walk with the sun kicked into high gear. The late September and early October days were always unpredictable in Channing. It was the November weather that required your coat and sometimes your gloves. Shit switched up in a matter of days when Channing winters began rolling in. Until then, it was a coin toss each day.

I hopped into my whip and started the engine. The loud roar brought a smile to my face. It never got old. The subwoofers in the back began beating, rattling the seats and windows. Jay-Z's *Heart of the City* continued exactly where it'd ended when I turned the ignition to disable the engine an hour earlier.

This nigga. I scoffed. An hour and I was still no closer to convincing him to join me than I was walking into the bar. With a shake of the head, I threw the car into gear and wrapped my arm around the passenger seat to get a good look at what was behind me. Seeing that the coast was clear, I began exiting the parking lot.

Carefully, I cruised through the streets of Edgewood,

admiring the perfectly paved streets and visions of the successful Black population. It was where the middle and upper-class met, thrived, and lived out the rest of their lives. Just a few miles north was Huffington Hills, where the rich who didn't mind the hefty price tag got richer, got divorced, or went broke. Either way, it was always a joy sliding through and seeing faces that resembled mine.

"Turn right and your destination is on the left in eight hundred feet," the GPS warned me.

I followed the directions given to me, realizing upon my arrival that Jilted was only a hop and a skip away. My crib was a mere twelve minutes away. All this time, the man my mother claimed to be my father was a short car ride away.

As I pulled alongside the curb, I noticed a group of three men standing near a sweet-ass King Ranch. I shut off my engine and opened my door, only to be smacked in the face with the smell of fresh, unrefined buds that reeked of richness and potency. A nod of approval was my only response to the poignant fragrance.

Though I would've loved to taste the burning buds on my tongue, the fellas seemed to be deep in conversation, and interrupting them wasn't exactly on my agenda. Keeping my eyes straight ahead and my sight set on the fat ass crib in front of me, I lifted my chin and planted my feet with each step. My mission was nearly complete.

"Does this nigga not see us or what?" I heard from the group.

"I know the motherfucker not blind because he can

obviously see the house he's headed up to," another added, puffing from the blunt in his hand.

"My nigga, take another step and you'll have a minimum of three bullets in your body. Neither of us will miss. I'm hitting your kneecap," the bigger of the trio stated.

"Are we killing 'em or?" Someone asked.

"Na." Disappointingly, the larger one answered.

"Then, I'm hitting the stomach. A shit bag will teach 'em a lesson."

"I want to see the nigga dance. I'm hitting that big toe. Knock a nigga balance off," the darker one claimed, puffing on the blunt in his hand.

"Not that any of that will be necessary," I finally spoke, cutting through the grass and backtracking my steps.

As comical as all these niggas were, they were right. As I neared the group, I was able to identify them all at a closer glance. Luca was the larger of the three with Laike being the tallest and whoever the black ass nigga was coming right behind him. I was somewhere in the middle when it came down to my weight, between both Luca and Laike. But, as far as my height, I could see that I was toe to toe with the rowdy one of the brothers. As I stared at their features a little more closely, I could see the resemblances we all shared. It was as if I was staring at a less-melanated reflection of myself.

This nigga's genes are strong.

"Oh, it's very necessary," Laike stated as a matter of fact.

I grew up with a nigga that's hell just like you, pipe the fuck down. I wanted to reveal but decided against it. I wasn't here on bullshit and I needed that to be known out of the gate. But, I also needed them to know that there wasn't any hoe in my blood. Shit, we shared the same nigga's DNA.

"You look like smart men. I'm sure you know they didn't stop making guns when they made yours," I said with a smile and tilted my head.

"State your business, nigga, or you won't make it to yours," Laike assured me, but he was wrong. It was on my hip and I was certain they all knew it.

"I didn't come for any trouble." With raised hands, I shook my head. *But, I'm with whatever y'all niggas with.*

"Then what you come for?" Luca asked.

"'Cause, that's what we're all trying to figure out," with a shrug, the darker one stated.

"I... uh. I'm looking for Liam Eisenberg." I shrugged, lowering my hands.

"For what?" Laike spoke, again.

"My mother died three months ago. I just mustered the courage to go through her shit at the house. I came across a letter in her nightstand drawer that explains a mystery that's haunted me my entire life."

"And, what's that?" Luca questioned.

"The identity of my father. According to her letter, Liam Eisenberg is the father of my brother and me."

Without hesitation, Laike bolted for the door of the home I was headed up to. He disappeared after a few seconds, leaving me with Luca and whoever his friend was.

"You and your brother?"

"Yeah. So, is he here?"

"He's here," he admitted, nonchalantly, before turning toward his friend, "What you think?"

"Nigga do kind of look like a black ass version of an Eisenberg. This how you niggas wish you looked... the way y'all be acting and carrying on nobody would ever guess y'all light-skinned."

"Fuck you."

"Nah, I'm good," their friend said, shaking his head from left to right.

"This Ken, what's your name homie?"

"Brother, call him brother," Ken joked, forcing Luca to whip his neck in his direction.

"I'm Ledge," I responded, extending my hand.

Stunned by the name I'd just given, Luca remained silent and allowed my hand to fall, again. He was trying his hardest to keep his composure, but on the inside, I knew that he was coming undone. His father was a legend around the city and not just for the keys he sold, but for the man that he was. Luca was a very smart and calculated man. He knew that my presence meant it all could very well become the furthest from Liam's reality. Children outside of his marriage didn't exactly describe a standup guy.

"And this nigga's name starts with an L? Oh, he's an Eisenberg for sure."

"Ledge," he began after composing himself. "I'm

Luca. The nigga that just went inside, that's Laike. We also have a sister, Lyric. What's your brother's name?"

"Lawe."

"Aw. Liam got some explaining to do, dog," Ken cackled. "Laura about to be on this nigga's ass. I mean, imagine Lyric finding out—" he started.

"I'm not imagining shit 'cause the day she does will be your last day on this earth, my nigga. Know that," Luca warned Ken.

"How quick are you niggas to forget that you are trust fund babies that learned to be tough. Nigga, I was born a motherfucking rider. My guns blast too, and when they run out of ammunition, my fists bang."

"Liam?" I asked, not caring much about their banter.

"Right this way."

Luca led the way up to the front door of the address listed on the letter in my possession. One of them, at least. There were two, one for us and another for the Eisenbergs. My mother had given much thought to this shit long before she died of an aneurysm. She'd suffered a stroke just a month shy and survived to tell the story.

It was the stroke in the brain that she didn't recover from. *Blood clots.* They were the culprits and the cause of both. After being on life support for two days without brain activity, Lawe and I made the decision to remove the machines and allow nature to take its course. Hooked up with no signs of life left was no way to carry on and we both knew it. That was the one thing we'd quickly agreed on our entire lives.

Because the letters were fresh and the paper was still

in perfect condition, it was obvious that she had recently written the letters. My guess was that the first stroke led her to act on the thought that had been brewing for a long time. She knew that her time on earth was coming to an end and wanted to make sure that she didn't leave us wondering who our father was for the rest of our lives.

"Pops!" I heard as we entered the home.

It was as sweet on the inside as it was on the outside. The Eisenbergs were, in fact, living a good fucking life. Any further up the road and they'd be part of Huffington Hills. They lived on one of the bordering streets, which was just as expensive as a few of the houses but a bit more modest.

"Make that the first and last time you raise your voice at me," the old man chastised. Though I hadn't seen his face yet, I could hear the maturity of his voice.

"This nigga out here saying he's your son and all you're worried about is me raising my voice? My nigga, you've got some explaining to do!"

There was a moment of silence as we approached the hallway where a few were gathered. Immediately, I recognized Laike. The man in front of him, I knew as Liam Eisenberg. Not because I'd ever met him, but because he was a Channing City legend that was known far and wide. Today though, he was simply my father, and seeing his face brought joy to my heart.

Unbalanced and unsteady, he visibly weakened before me. I wasn't sure if it was my presence or his age.

He looked like he was in pristine condition to me, so I had a feeling that it had nothing to do with his health. For a moment, his eyes and mine locked and moved not one bit.

Thirty-five years. I'd waited thirty-five years for this moment. And, though I was older and gave a fuck a lot less, it was exactly as I thought it would be. My heart pushed against my chest, beating at a rapid pace. Dramatically, it sounded in my ears as I stepped a bit closer and closed the gap between us. We'd been separated long enough.

"I'm Ledge," I said, sticking my arm out.

My mother didn't take any shit from us. Though Lawe was a fucking menace now, he hadn't always been. Our mother had raised us to be polite, respectable men and she'd done a damn good job too. Even in death, my desire to make her proud didn't waver.

"Liam," he responded, pulling me in for a hug instead.

"Really?" Laike hissed.

"Shut up, nigga," Luca gritted. "This ain't bout you right now."

"Na. It's not. It's about this cheating ass nigga here," Laike growled before pushing past us all.

"What?" The woman I'd quickly discovered was Lyric shouted.

Damn, she's gorgeous, I thought as I pulled back and watched her heart break in front of me. Already, I was a sucker for those angelic eyes and perfect face. I felt like shit when she placed a hand on her chest. This was partially my fault. I figured I could've picked a better time. It seemed as if they were here to celebrate something and I'd fucked that up for everyone.

"This nigga got another kid, Lyric," Laike informed her.

"What?" She yelled, again, still confused.

Fuck. I cringed, feeling like a villain. In an attempt to rectify the situation, I began explaining the situation to everyone.

"My mother died six... I mean three months ago of a blood clot. It was sudden and unexpected. I finally went to her crib to clean it out... ya' know. Finally able to deal with it all. I stumbled across this letter in a lock box she'd left for us that was full of memories from our childhood on up. I never even knew it existed until yesterday.

"Sorry to impose the way that I have, but I've wanted a father all my life. Knowing that he was in the same city and a few miles away, I couldn't just sit on that information. I had to come to see for myself after I read the note. I tried to get my brother, Lawe, to join me but he never cared who our father was. His anger suggests otherwise, though. I think it stems from not having you around."

"Brother?" Laike bellowed.

"Meaning like an entire side family right up under our noses?" Lyric followed. "Okay, wow. This is far too much for me right now. Where's my husband? I can't with this right now. Keanu!"

Ken? It made sense now. He wasn't only a family friend. He was married to the family, too. They made the perfect match.

"Right behind you, sis," Laike hissed.

Luca, on the other hand, stayed put. I could see already that he and I were much alike and would probably get along just fine. Laike, on the other hand, would need some work. The thought of him and Lawe bumping into one another was a headache that I wasn't ready to deal with.

When the door finally slammed behind Laike and Lyric, I sighed with relief.

"Brother?" Liam questioned.

"We're twins," I explained.

There was silence, again. Then, the door cracked open and Laike's head popped in.

"Baisleigh, come on baby. We're leaving!" He shouted, but with much less bass in his voice and with softer, kinder eyes.

I wasn't surprised to see a beautiful woman appear from the shadows of the hallway. In her hand, she held a baby that was attached to her breast. Over her shoulder was a blanket that gave them both privacy.

"Is everything okay?" She asked.

"Nah. I'll explain in the car," Laike assured her. "We can leave his shit. We have enough of it at home, already."

Everyone watched as Laike ushered her out of the door. When it slammed again, there was silence once more. Because no one else said anything, I felt the need to continue.

"According to the letter, we're..."

"Are you hungry, honey? We have plenty of food here. We're celebrating today, so you're in luck."

"Thanks, but I've had a little something to eat."

"Well, I'd be offended if you didn't at least try this cake that Ever made. I'm Laura by the way."

Laura. My mother mentioned her several times in the letter. She was the reason for our conception. It was her bright idea to celebrate her husband's birthday by plotting a threesome. Together they indulged in a night to remember, resulting in the birth of twins that neither Laura or Liam ever knew about. *This some wild ass shit.*

"Me too," Luca chimed in.

"Your wife?" I asked, quickly catching on to how the Eisenbergs rolled. Everyone was mated and seemingly starting their flock. Even Lyric had a kid in her hand and one at her side when she stormed out.

"Yeah. She owns a bakery and she's sensitive about her shit, so make room, nigga," he said lowly, leaning closer so that only I could hear him.

"Whatever he just told you about me is probably a lie," a soft voice opposed.

When she was finally in clear view, so was her extended hand.

"I'm Ever. Ledge, right?" She'd obviously heard the whole, crazy ass story.

Her belly protruded, revealing what was to come in a few months. A twinge of jealousy flowed through me as I realized each and every one of the Eisenbergs had something that I wanted. They had families complete with children and a loving set of parents.

"Yeah."

"Enjoy."

She handed me the plate that was in her other hand. It was loaded with cake and ice cream.

"What are we celebrating?" I asked, heading to the long table that was massive in size and looked like it cost a grip.

"Moms just beat cancer, again."

"Again?"

"Second time around. A blessing," Laura exclaimed.

Everyone piled into the kitchen to have their slice of cake before joining me at the table. Liam was at the head, still quiet and processing things. Luca was a chair or two away with Ever at his side, and Laura was next to Liam. The reassuring hand on his wrist and gentle sliding up and down his arm every few seconds told me everything I needed to know about her. *She's a rider*. The conclusion was easily made.

"Daddy, Lucas is fighting us, again."

"Him hit me!"

"Please, please get your son dad."

What sounded like a million little footsteps ended in chaos, everyone speaking at once. All girls. Whoever the kid was they were upset with was obviously a boy but he hadn't shown his face, yet.

"Lucas!" Luca yelled.

"He's faking sleep."

"Go tell him that if he hits anyone again then he's coming in here with us and not having any ice cream and cake."

"Can we have ice cream and cake?" The one next to the oldest asked.

"Pweeeeeaaaaaassssse." The youngest exaggerated.

"Yes, baby. In a minute, we're going to call you guys into the mini dining hall so that you can eat there," Ever told them.

"Yeessss!" The oldest whispered.

Then, they were off and down the hallway.

I'd counted four, but I wasn't sure if there were more of them.

"How many you got?" I found myself asking aloud.

"We're on number six."

"One didn't survive the pregnancy," Ever said with pain visible in her smile.

"What are you expecting this time?"

"Another girl."

"I can't get away from them. Lucas is looking like my only boy."

"Maybe not. I'm willing to try until we luck up on another one."

"I don't have intentions of stopping until we do," Luca chuckled. "Unless we should," he quickly added.

"I'll let you know when that day comes."

"Bet." With a nod, he turned in my direction and asked, "Got any? A wife?"

"Nah. It's just me, man. I hate it, but it's really just me. I'm trying to be on the same sh—stuff y'all on. The kids and the wives... I love to see it, fam."

"It'll come and when you least expect it. It isn't easy, so enjoy your time alone. I can't even shit in peace now. And food, it never really belongs to me. It belongs to everyone," he explained.

"So, I hear."

"What about Lawe?"

"We're not getting any babies out of that nigga. I can bet he's going to his grave a lonely, angry old man."

"Sounds like Laike," Laura scoffed. "But, there's always one to tame them. He just hasn't come across her yet."

"Yeah. Laike reminds me of Lawe, a lot."

"Figures. You're the oldest?" Liam finally spoke, again.

"By a few minutes."

"That's why you remind us of Luca. I can see him all in you. Identical twins?" Laura wanted to know.

"Yes ma'am."

"Don't do that. I'm not even all that old, really. Call me Laura or mom like the others."

"You sure you're cool with that?"

"I offered, didn't I?"

"You did."

"Then alright," she sassed.

I stuffed the cake in my mouth, figuring it was time for me to shut the hell up. My heart was full and my brain was overstimulated. The hatred and the animosity I expected to find here was lost on smiling faces, kind hearts, and pure curiosity. There was no malice to be managed and no love that was lost.

"Let me holler at you," Luca demanded the second my cake was finished.

He stood from the table and I quickly followed his lead. When we made it outside, he dug into his pocket and removed an already rolled blunt. He placed it between his lips before lighting it with a lighter from his other pocket.

"You look like you've had enough for the day, so consider this your lifeline."

"Appreciate that."

He passed me the blunt in his hand. I took it without hesitation.

"Everybody you saw today, I'd die for. I have no issues welcoming you and your brother into our circle. But, our circle, is one hell of a circle my nigga. And, blood alone won't keep you in it. I've got a good feeling about you and I take it as our brother might need a little time. I get it. But, I need you niggas to know that we solid over here and we don't take any stragglers. We hold ourselves to a certain standard but we don't mind getting down and dirty. This isn't a threat so don't take it as one. It's a promise. We're not expecting you niggas to come begging to be part of the family if that's what either of you are thinking. And, we could never hate you for our father's actions. That's on him, not us. We ain't got shit to do with that. It's just been us all this time. It's going to take some getting used to but we're all up for the challenge."

"Even Laike and Lyric?"

"They'll come around. Both of them motherfuckers spoiled, though Laike would never admit the shit. What about your people?"

"Lawe? Accept my apologies on his behalf in advance. He's built differently."

"It's all good. Welcome to the family."

With that, he walked away, leaving me outside alone. His dismissal was my chance to flee and get my shit together. My head was all over the place and I desperately needed to center my thoughts. Still pulling from the blunt I'd been gifted, I headed to my car.

A family. Finally. Though I'd always had my mother's people, I wanted to know what my dad's side was like. There was always so many miles between us, but we'd always been close to our cousins in Berkeley.

Malachi, Milo, Makai, and Mercer sometimes came up for the summer, but most of our summers were spent down in Berkeley with them and our grandfather. He was their father's father, which only made me wish my father was around even more. Just like him, my uncle Mitch was a good man who'd been killed unexpectedly. My grandfather gathered the boys and took them all in after tragedy struck and hadn't batted an eye while doing so. He loved us all as if we'd come from his nutsack.

By the time I got to the stop sign at the end of the street, my phone chimed. A text from an unknown number popped up on my screen. Because I was at a standstill, I took the opportunity to unlock it and open the message to read it.

Luca. Lock me in.

How'd this nigga get my... I shook the thought after realizing it was Luca I was talking about. The second I gave my name, he'd already started digging into my resume.

2

HALO

"I can't," I sighed. "I'm busy."

"Doing what? Counting the little prickly shit on the walls?" Kamber joked with plenty of attitude.

"No. For your information, I'm doing exactly what you want to do, but online."

"Why when the store is not far from our place? You have no idea what you're buying, how it really looks, how soft it is, how small or big it is, how comfortable it is, or none of that. You're shopping blindly. Please... I am begging you. Please come to Target with me."

"I thought I made it clear that I wasn't coming outside, no matter how much you begged."

"I thought I made it clear that I didn't give a damn and I'll create a disturbance outside of your door if you don't."

"That's childish, Kamber."

"Maybe it is but it is not beneath me, please understand that!"

"I don't wannnnnna," I whined, hoping she'd take it easier on me.

"But, you have to. You know it and I know it. There's no sense in continuing to prolong the inevitable. Be ready in five minutes or I'm causing a scene. We know how much you hate that shit, so don't make me do it. I know that window is open and I know you don't want me coming through it but I will."

"I don't feel good," I admitted.

"A runny nose that you've been having for the last few weeks is nothing, Halo. Five minutes and I'll come in peace. Play with me and I promise you won't be able to shut me up."

With a shake of my brown twists, I exhaled. "Alright. See you in five."

After a full two months of convincing myself, I was ready to take Kamber up on her offer. Everything that I'd been ordering online was admittedly mediocre and didn't give me the joy that shopping in-store would bring. However, I sufficed. The last thing I wanted was to spike my anxiety and overwhelm myself by stepping out of my home. I hadn't in so many months that I'd stopped counting.

"Good. It only took two months to get your ass to agree!"

I couldn't respond fast enough. She'd already ended the call. A slow, widening smile spread across my face as a spark of joy hit me. I wasn't at all excited about going outside, but I was happy to finally get my hands on some things I'd been needing to grab. My last shopping adventure was so many years ago that I hardly remembered it.

I was already dressed and my hair was intertwined with an extension method that I perfected over time. It was my third attempt at the bohemian-themed twists that fell right at the tip of my butt. They were small and lightweight with curly hair poking out, making them fuller and prettier. I was extremely impressed with the outcome and prayed they lasted me at least six weeks. That was about the same amount of time I'd kept the ones in before. These were smaller, so an additional week was possible.

In an oversized shirt and joggers that coincidently coordinated well, I stepped toward the row of comfortable slides that covered my entire foot. It was October and Channing loved playing with the weather around this time of year, every year. It never failed. To be safe, I slid into full coverage slides and grabbed my favorite hoodie. If there happened to be a chill or sudden downpour of rain, I wanted to be prepared.

A few sprays of my favorite perfume and I was off to

the kitchen to grab an apple and start my journey out of the door. It was never easy. I needed at least two of the five minutes that Kamber had given me. When I took a look at my phone, I realized that was all I had, honestly.

Apple in hand, I stood face to face with one of my worst enemies. My front door hadn't done a thing to me but it felt like it was only there to remind me of how miserable my life really was. I just couldn't get past it. But, Kamber, she didn't want to hear it. I'd been giving her the same excuse for the last two months.

Strangely, I was happy she hadn't given up. I wasn't quite ready to give up on myself either. There was so much I had to look forward to if I could just get from behind the door. That was the challenge. As simple as it sounded, it wasn't.

The two locks were twisted with ease. I'd done so countless times with the intention of exiting, but didn't quite make it through. This time would be different though. The confidence I lacked every other occasion was thick in my throat as I narrowed my line of vision and focused on the silver nemesis of mine. *The handle.* I stretched my arm and reached for it. In one swift motion, it was in my grasp. Contentment filled me as I twisted it downward and the door cracked.

Sunlight beamed through the small hole, nearly blinding me on contact. I raised a hand to block its rays and buy myself a bit of time to gather my bearings. Short, hard breaths rushed out one after the other as I inhaled the fresh, evening air.

My God, this is glorious. Suddenly, my apartment felt

like the muggiest place on earth. The air quality was nothing in comparison to the crispness of nature's oxygen. I smiled up at the sun and thanked it for its grand appearance on such a glorious day for me. Its magnetic rays pulled me further into the open and further from my door. A shadow quickly covered its brightness, shading everything around me.

"Boo!" Kamber jumped at me, forcing me backward and onto my door.

"Gosh, you scared me!"

My right hand landed on my chest as I leaned forward, attempting to catch my breath. Kamber's appearance had rattled my core. Although I was expecting her, I was far too focused on the task at hand to see her round the corner.

"Didn't take much," she cackled. "Are you ready?"

"Yes. I think I am, actually. I just need to lock my door and maybe take a second to collect myself before we get into the car. Is that okay with you?"

"As long as you don't try to flee into the house, then take the time you need, honey. I can wait a few minutes to spend my money."

"Kamber, I can really just get everything online. What's the big deal with that?"

"Or, you can save 50 percent on everything you need by switching to Kamber's method of shopping... *U-scan*."

She tried her hardest to sound like one of those insurance commercials, causing me to hunch over in laughter.

"Okay. Okay."

She'd secured the sale with that bit of information. Though I tried my hardest to live an honest life, I wasn't opposed to saving money if she insisted. I'd just keep myself busy while she handled her business.

It was enough already that I was pinching pennies and my bank account was dwindling with each purchase. I'd saved a hundred dollars from each paycheck for the last few months. But, that fourteen hundred was probably not enough to last very long.

"So, lock up and take your time. My car is right in front of your unit. I'll be inside when you're ready, okay?"

"Yes. Be there in a second."

With her head in the clouds, Kamber walked off into the sun. She was cute and comfortable in her matching jogger fit with her hair pulled into a high ponytail that showcased her natural beauty. I could feel the smile that stretched my lips as I watched her disappear.

Okay, Halo. You've got this. It's not going to be long. It's just one store. You're okay.

I bolted down the stairs as fast as my body would allow. When I made it to the car, Kamber opened the door for me. I stuffed myself into the passenger seat and rested my head on the cushion behind me. My emotions were in turmoil. Lava flowed through my body, kicking my temperature up a few notches.

"I can't do it," I breathed out. "I'm sorry. I can't do it."

"Get out of your head, Halo. You can do it. Stop saying that, because you'll begin to believe it. You've already gotten through the hard part. Now that you're out of the house and in the car, what's stopping you?"

"Nothing," I confessed.

"Exactly. Shut the door and let's go. I know the perfect place to calm your nerves. That's what you need right now."

I leaned over and slammed the door. Back in the upright position, I closed my eyes and rested my head. The tips of my fingernails clawed at my sweats. Anxiousness seeped through my bones, rotting them without mercy. My nerves rallied against me, leaving me feeling muggy and sweaty. The motion of the car was the only thing that lulled me though I had fully expected it to make me ill.

I wasn't sure how long we'd been driving before the quiet of the car was interrupted by slow, calming sounds that reminded me of water and the waves it created. To my surprise, I opened my eyes to find us inside a machine that produced loads of it along with soap, bubbles, and brushes. Instantly, my body and mind settled.

"It's a car wash," Kamber informed me.

"Figured."

Now that my surroundings were no longer a mystery, I closed my eyes again and listened to the sounds of the drive-thru wash. They were as relaxing as they were fierce. They were everything I needed in the moment to quiet my head and my heart.

LEDGE + HALO

"WOULD you like to use my headphones before we go inside? There will be a lot going on in here and I don't want you getting too riled up."

"I'm fine, Kamber, but thanks. This isn't my first time, you know. I used to love shopping with my grandmother. It's just been *a while*. I can handle it."

"Just offering. You go ahead. I'm going to grab one of these baskets out here just in case there aren't any inside. It looks like they're all in the damn parking lot."

"I'll wait by the door."

"Alright. Coming right behind you."

I slid out of Kamber's Camry and shut the door once I'd cleared all clothing. By the sharp winds that were beginning to pick up, I knew that I'd made an excellent call by bringing the hoodie along. With it draped over my hands, I made slow strides toward the big red sign. It was so nostalgic. The magic of the moment leading me straight into the store, past the door that I'd promised to wait by, and down the aisles. I didn't notice how far I'd ventured off or how long I'd been gone or how much I'd acquired until I heard Kamber's voice behind me.

"There you are," she sighed. "You had me scared. I've been around this entire store looking for you. Where's your phone?"

"Uh. It's in my bag."

"This bag?" She asked, holding up the purse that I'd obviously left in her car.

"Yes. That one," I chuckled, walking toward her and dumping my things into the cart she was pushing.

"Please stay over here. I have to use the restroom and I'll be right back. I don't want to have to chase you down, again."

"I'll stay over here. I promise. Go ahead."

"At least answer your phone if you leave this area," she told me before stomping off.

It was clear that she was concerned. The look on her face was priceless.

I turned around, ready to grab the pretty yellow blanket that I'd laid my eyes on before Kamber found me, and ran right into another customer. Quickly, I stepped back, giving them the personal space that was rightly reserved for everyone. My cheeks flushed with embarrassment, contradicting the smile on my face.

"I'm sorry," I apologized.

"It's all good," a very familiar voice rang out from the man who was kneeling, picking up the things that I'd made tumble from his hands.

My brows creased and raced to the center of my face. My body stilled as I watched him stand to his feet, again. His presence was paralyzing. *Run. Hide.* Thoughts rushed through my head, but I was too rooted in astonishment and diseased with an inexplicable gravitational pull that didn't allow me to move a muscle.

"Halo?" He squinted his brown eyes and asked.

"Le... Ledge," I choked out.

"Long time no see," he tittered.

His eyes left my face briefly, landing on my protruding belly before they raced back up to meet mine. Nervously, I shifted my weight from one foot to the other. Suddenly, I wished I'd followed Kamber to the restroom because my bladder was about to burst.

"Looks like you're about to pop. How far along?"

"Eight months," I blurted, immediately chastising myself.

Why, Halo? My nerves splintered, leaving me to vomit words in an attempt to mask my undoing. Having Ledge standing in front of me was not in my plans for the day. I should've followed my first mind and stayed home.

He was as handsome as I remembered. Since I'd last seen him, he'd done nothing but get more attractive. His very dark, smooth brown skin glistened under the light. Those perfectly aligned teeth that he showed each time he uttered a word or smiled made my heart throb. Memories of the night we shared consumed me, forcing me to close my eyes briefly. I was convinced that I'd never experience anything as monumental.

"Yeah. It's about that time." He nodded.

"About seven weeks to go, give or take a week."

You can't shut up, huh? The words flowed like a faucet with broken knobs. They just kept going and going without an end in sight.

"What are you having?"

"I'm unsure. Figured I'd wait until birth."

"That'll be a pleasant surprise."

"I guess." I shrugged.

"Well, congratulations to you and the lucky guy," he exclaimed, his eyes dropping to my stomach, again.

"And congratulations to you and the lucky girl."

My follow-up was in reference to the items from the baby section that he was holding in his hand. The salt the vision poured onto my reopened wounds burned every inch of my beating heart. *A baby?* Being that I'd spent a few hours getting to know Ledge, I was certain that if he had a child on the way, then there was a happy woman somewhere, too. *It could've all been very simple.* I reminded myself. Once again, I'd cheated myself out of something decent due to the scars from my past.

"This, ah nah. Not yet, at least. After thirty-five years, I met my father today. I met him and my three siblings. Apparently, them motherfuckers love having kids. I can't go back empty-handed. My oldest brother has a daughter on the way," he clarified.

My raging heart slowed as I caught my breath. I wasn't exactly sure why gratitude surfaced at the sound of him denouncing the child I thought he had on the way with someone else, but it did. My smile returned as I nodded to assure him that I understood.

"Well, still, congratulations on meeting your father. I bet that was unnerving."

"I thought it would be, but it was the opposite, actually. It was as if they'd been waiting for me all my life. Not for real, but in a sense, ya' know? Like, they felt as if some pieces to their puzzle were missing. My brother and I can now fill that void they didn't even know they had."

"Your brother?"

"I thought I mentioned that to you?".

"It's possible you did. I don't remember much from that night."

"I remember every single detail."

Please don't ever forget them... don't ever forget me.

"It's been nice seeing you again, Ledge."

"Same, Halo. This all you're getting for the baby?" He pointed at the cart with the pile of items I'd dumped into the basket.

"No, I'm just getting started. I haven't gotten much over the last few months, so this will be a long trip for me."

"I feel you," he admitted, digging into his pocket. "Congratulations on the baby, again. If that nigga ever fuck up, I'm ready and willing to be stepdaddy."

The sound of the word always brought vomit up my throat, but coming from Ledge it didn't sound so bad. I watched as he stuffed his hand in the slightly opened bucket bag that was in the cart, leaving the hundred dollar bills that he'd removed from his pocket.

"You got the number, use that motherfucker. Aight?"

"Okay, Ledge," I chuckled, feeling my face tingle all over.

"You look good in my shit, by the way."

My head dropped as he walked away, leaving me weak in the knees. Dizzy from the spell he'd put on me, unintentionally, I tried to make out the words on the shirt that I'd worn a thousand times over. They were all a blur.

"Either I'm seeing shit or that was..." Kamber whispered as she approached.

I hadn't noticed her until she was too close for comfort.

"It was him," I agreed, stepping back and placing a hand on my chest.

At any second, I was sure my heart would jump out of it and run in Ledge's direction. Though I hardly knew the man, with him is where it felt like it belonged. The gravitational pull was so potent that I had to secure my body by holding onto the edge of the basket, otherwise, I'd be running through the store with my eight-month pregnant belly to flag him down.

"Did– Did you–" she stuttered.

"No," I exhaled, finally gaining control of my emotions.

"Why not? That was your chance."

"To what? Let another man into my life, grow to trust him, and then tragedy strikes?"

"That's not everyone's story, Halo."

"But, it's mine. What if I have a daughter?"

"What if y'all have a daughter? Then that'll just be what it is!"

"Can we not talk about this right now?"

"The man was literally right here. I don't understand."

"And, you never will, Kamber."

"Enlighten me, please. Are you planning to keep this poor man's child away from him because of your past?"

"What was I supposed to do? Hm? 'Oh, hey Ledge,

by the way... the night that we had sex and you woke up to me being a weird, scared, mentally unstable turd was the night I got pregnant. It was the only night I'd been out since I was nineteen. You were also the first person I've had sex with... only person I've had sex with, consensually.'"

"But, I wasn't a virgin, not by far. That's because my stepfather has been fucking me since I was six years old. I even got pregnant by him at fourteen and it wasn't until then that the madness ended."

"Did I mention my mother found out when I was eight and didn't do shit about it. As long as he was fucking me then it meant she didn't have to lay down with his drunk, abusive ass? To top it all, her guilt led her to drugs as a coping mechanism. The day that I went to the hospital and discovered I was pregnant was the day she overdosed. But, I'm normal, I swear... Sometimes, at least. *Hmmm?* Right in the middle of Target, is that what you wanted me to say?"

Silence followed. Gritting my teeth, I begged my tears not to fall. Just as one escaped my eye, I turned the basket in the opposite direction and decided to look elsewhere for more baby essentials.

"Halo, I'm sorry."

"It's fine," I lied. "I know you mean well, Kamber, but this isn't a front for me. It's my life. It's my world. We live in two different hemispheres. Your confidence, your resilience, your ambition, your fearlessness, those are all things I wish I had. But, I don't and probably never will, which makes me a target for predators. To protect my body and my heart, I have to keep them locked away. I'm damaged and people like that can spot it from afar. They prey on people like me, people that have already been broken just so they can break us some more. I'm not giving anyone that privilege."

"I get it. I promise. It just breaks my heart to see you missing out on everything you deserve. You're such a good person."

"That will get me nowhere, Kamber. Trust me. I'm not cut out for any of this. I'm not the average woman, I'm just a shell of one. That's my truth. That's my story."

"Okay, so what your story isn't like anyone else's. It's awful, the things that you went through. You couldn't control or dictate what happened to you back then. But, from here on out, you can. You have the right to. For what it's worth, secure a happy, healthy future for your-self. You can do that! You're not a kid anymore."

"But, I feel like one. I'm scared and lonely and just scared. Life is cruel, Kamber. It's been nothing but cruel to me. Why should I expect anything different? It's mean and ugly and just... *cruel*."

"Is he?"

"What?"

"Ledge. Is he mean and ugly and cruel?"

"He's none of those things."

"So, why are you punishing him as if he is?"

I didn't have the words she was searching for. Instead of responding, I allowed her question to sit with me. I pushed the cart along the aisles, deep in thought, tossing in everything that I thought the baby would need. With the extra money that Ledge had given me, I knew that I'd have more than enough to get us through the first two or three months. As a minimalist, only the necessities were on my list. Kamber, on the other hand, was grabbing everything in sight.

LEDGE + HALO

"ARE YOU OKAY?"

"I'll be fine."

"I'd believe you if you'd talk to me. You haven't said anything in the last hour. Are you sure you're going to be okay?"

"Thanks for saving me hundreds on baby essentials by switching to Kamber's U-scan."

That brought a smile to her face and then mine.

"That's not what I said, but it's close enough."

"Seriously though, thanks."

"Of course. Since you won't let that man be, I've got to be the baby's daddy and I take my job seriously."

She sat down the last bags from the car and propped a hand on her hip.

"I gave some thought to what you said."

"Annnnnnnnd?" She dragged, waiting for a response.

"It won't be forever. I'm just not ready right now. While in conversation, he told me that he'd just met his father today, after thirty-five years. He seemed so happy. He even said to me that if whoever my child's father is messes up to call him. I wanted to scream, it's you! But, I didn't. I couldn't."

"Just don't keep that man waiting too long."

"I'll try my hardest not to. I just want some time alone with my child. Maybe the first few years of their life."

"Halo," she warned.

"I'm serious."

"I know you are and that's what's scary."

"I just want to protect them from so much."

"But, from a man who hasn't given you a reason to believe that your kid needs to be protected from him? I've said it before and I'll say it again. Your gut knows. Trust it. What is it telling you?"

"That Ledge is everything."

"Because maybe he is."

"But, what if he isn't?"

"It doesn't mean he's a rapist, drunk, or an abuser."

Kamber was right, again. I tossed my hands in the air with a shake of my head.

"I'll tell him, Kamber. I promise. I just need a little time. A lot of time. Maybe a year or two. I don't know."

"The longer you wait, the harder it'll be to tell him. You're an adult and I can't force you to see my reasoning, but I can make suggestions. I suggest you use that number you've been sitting on for months and call that man up. He didn't hurt you, Halo. Stop treating him like he did."

Kamber turned on her heels as she ended her statement. I watched as she twisted the handle and stepped out of my front door with ease. Before closing it behind her, she turned and smiled.

"If you need me, give me a ring. I know you need a moment, so I'll let you have that. When you're ready to put the baby's things up, I can help if you want."

"Thanks," I shouted.

"Of course."

Alone with my thoughts wasn't exactly where I wanted to be at the moment. And, excited as I was to do so, putting away everything I'd just purchased was the last thing on my mind. A shower sounded like a much better idea.

With my belly leading the way, I journeyed to my bedroom. One by one, I collected the things I'd be needing post-shower and tossed them on the bed. Three of the products were strictly for the stretched skin on my stomach. There was an oil, a butter, and some lotion. I'd made them all myself and they'd gotten me through the entire pregnancy without a mark in sight.

After closing the bathroom door behind me, I secured the lock. I was unable to take a step in the opposite direction. My conscience kept me grounded. *No one is coming Halo.* The sound of the younger, fear-stricken version of me surfaced. Turning without haste, I glared at the knob, waiting for it to rattle.

No one is coming Halo. She repeated. *You're okay, now.*

My nostrils flared as small, fine bumps covered my skin. My core contracted and released once, then twice. By the third time, my eyes were still fixed on the knob and my shallow breathing had transformed into long, jagged breaths.

In one swift motion, I twisted the center of the knob to unlock the door. Still staring at the silver knob, I waited for the rattling, banging, and knocking. There was none. *No one is coming Halo. You're safe.* Comforted by the constant reassurance, I took small, calculated steps away from the door. My eyes never shifted, staying locked on their target.

"Shi—" I yelled, nearly letting a bad one slip.

The rattling of the shower curtain behind me had nearly ripped my soul from my body.

"My God."

Leaning over, I rested my hands on my knees and lowered my head. I couldn't resist the smile that lifted my features. A ridiculous, horribly-timed chuckle followed. Someday, I'd be the death of myself. That was for sure. Today, luckily, wasn't that day.

To be sure that there weren't any more unprovoked scares, I turned my body around and began preparing my shower. Twisting knobs helped me get the perfect temperature and water pressure. Once everything was suitable, I dropped one piece of clothing at a time. Everything except the shirt I was wearing hit the floor.

Instead of it joining my pants, underwear, and bra, I folded it neatly and placed it on the counter. I'd be wearing it again soon. Most likely, I'd be pulling it over my head once my body was dry. It was one of the few pieces of Ledge's that I'd kept and the one that made me feel closest to him. It felt as if his arms were wrapped around my body, around my stomach.

In a sense, I felt as if he'd been with me through the entire pregnancy. The hoodie was an added bonus. It was a gentle hug from the gentle giant. It had caught way too many of my tears on frightful nights and during times of uncertainty.

I grabbed two hair ties from the jar next to his shirt and tied my hair up as best as I could to keep it from getting drenched in water. The sight of my reflection in the mirror halted all movement. My incredibly large belly was still the most striking thing I'd ever seen. The only thing that had ever come close was *him*. And, it was *him* who'd made it possible.

For that, I'd forever be in his debt. He'd given me something that I never knew I needed or wanted. He'd given me a reason to keep trying and keep pushing. He'd given me purpose. He'd given me love like I never knew it. I hadn't met my tiny human yet, but I loved them with every fiber of my being. He'd given me that. He'd given me joy.

From one position to another, I changed in the mirror. My brown skin had stretched far beyond my imagination to accommodate the life that was growing inside. A life that had been created the first night I willingly submitted to a man that I'd just met. And, I didn't have a single regret about it or what came of it or who I spent that night with. It was, undoubtedly, the best night of my life.

When I climbed into the shower, the warm water

massaged my pain away. The stress of the day was easily forgotten as I scrubbed my skin with the strawberry kiwi-scented wash. My neck. My back. My arms. My legs. My toes. And, my stomach. With a body full of thick, white suds, I closed my eyes and allowed myself to feel everything the moment had to offer.

God, please fix me. Heal me. Restore everything within me that has been broken.

The simple prayer rose from the depths of me. I wasn't sure why or how, but the alleviation that trailed it was everything I needed. My anxiety diminished as the water rinsed the soap from my skin.

Amen.

Led to end my shower, I turned the water off and stepped out carefully. I'd nearly fallen one too many times with the extra weight throwing my balance off. I couldn't afford a fall of any kind at this stage in my pregnancy, so I took my precious time. The towel on the rack slid off with ease when I pulled it. For support and a little grip on the tiled floor, I bent over, held onto the counter, wiped my feet, and slid into my slippers one by one.

On carpeted flooring, I felt much safer. Reaching my bedroom was always a milestone that I didn't take lightly after a shower. Seated on the bed with my towel wrapped around me, I began the methodical process of moisturizing my skin.

It was the most sacred part of my cleansing process. It was more of a ritual than a routine. Hydrating my skin was one of my favorite tasks. It kept it soft and shiny, and the elasticity intact. The butter was always first. A light, thin layer did the trick every time. The oil and lotion made a perfect mixture that I slathered on top.

My belly was always last. It was where I spent the bulk of my time. It was also the part that needed the moisture most.

"Hey, baby."

Touching everywhere there was movement, I tried keeping up with the little being inside of me.

"Hey there."

It never got old, feeling the kicks and twists and turns.

"Are you having fun in there? Mommy can't wait to meet you soon. I ran into daddy today. He knows all about you," I choked out, becoming increasingly emotional as the words continued.

"I'm going to tell him that you're all his very soon, baby. I promise. Mommy just has to get used to the idea of letting someone into her world. It's not as easy as I'd like it to be. It's actually hard, extremely hard. Almost too hard, but it's not impossible."

Tears tapped against the skin of my belly and fell to the side.

"It's not impossible. And, one day, I'm going to do it. You hear me?"

It wasn't the baby I was trying to convince, it was myself. I needed convincing.

"I promise."

3

LEDGE

Shit. I cringed as I moved the towel from behind my ear. Staring at it, I searched for signs of blood, but there were none. I'd damn near scrubbed my skin off as the words that I'd heard a week ago replayed in my head for the millionth time. No matter what, every moment I spent alone and it was quiet enough to hear my thoughts, they resurfaced.

Eight months. Halo's voice echoed in my head.

"Eight months," I said aloud, trying to calculate the numbers in my head. "Eight months?"

February? Or was it March? I tried remembering our time spent together and when it was.

Seven weeks or so. I remembered her mentioning that was how long she had before her child would be born.

With my body still covered in suds, I hopped out of the shower and nearly busted my ass. But, reaching my phone and unlocking it as water dripped onto my screen made that near tragedy worth it. I immediately typed google into the search bar.

How many weeks does a woman carry a baby? I spelled out and then hit the button next to the words.

Forty weeks, I read. Although, *38–40 weeks is considered full-term. Thirty-six week deliveries are considered low-risk and generally produce healthy babies with little to no complications.*

The math began. *She's thirty-two weeks. She was thirty-two weeks. She's thirty-three weeks, now.* I corrected, noting that a week had passed since I ran into her.

Fuck! The revelation sat on my wet chest like a sack of bricks. I couldn't shake the unnerving feeling that the lucky man I'd congratulated was more than likely me. *But, she was dealing with some shit that night. Maybe she was already pregnant or getting back at her nigga.* I reasoned. *Nah.* I quickly put those thoughts aside. She didn't come off as that type. Nothing felt like a logical explanation other than my DNA matching the child growing in her belly.

I exited the safari browser and accessed my contacts.

Scrolling through and down to the names that began with the letter H, I searched for her name amongst the three that were listed. Hers was nowhere to be found. With knitted brows, I tried to remember if I'd saved her number under another name. Instead of some pet name I'd probably given her coming to the forefront, the memory of me leaving my cell inside the truck popped up.

Gritting my teeth, I recalled the two or three times that I searched the same contact list because I wanted to spend more time with her, inside of her, and getting to know her. I'd come up empty-handed then, too. She'd taken my number instead and never got around to using it. Visiting her crib seemed like a little too much then, but now that the ante had been upped, I couldn't get to her shit quick enough.

I laid my phone on the counter and hopped back in the shower. My thoughts were all over the place, but my heart's location was obvious. Its thunderous pounding made sure that it was known. *A father?*

I cleansed my body a second and then a third time before ending my shower. Just as I stepped out, my phone chimed. I leaned over as I dried my skin, peeping to see who it was trying to reach me.

Big Bro. Luca's contact popped up on the screen. According to my mother, he was three years older than Lawe and I. Laike was only a year older than us and Lyric was a year younger. We were all very close in age, but luckily there weren't any ages that overlapped.

Knowing exactly what he wanted, I didn't rush to

respond to whatever it was he was saying. It wasn't until I'd made it to my bedroom with my phone in my hand and a fully dried frame that I unlocked the screen and read his message.

See you in forty-five.

He texted, confirming his attendance for the meetup that him, Liam, and I were scheduled for.

A week later and neither Lawe nor Laike were interested in a sit-down. The few of us that were on board didn't want to lose any more time together, so we were actively attempting to get to know one another. Admittedly, the effort that Luca and Liam were putting forth was both surprising and appreciated.

Bet.

I responded and tossed the phone onto the bed. I had twenty-five minutes or so to get dressed and out of the door.

Eight months. I couldn't shake it and I wasn't sure if I wanted to. I'd heard the piece of information in my head so many times that I doubted it would ever leave. While pulling my briefs on, images of her swollen belly and pretty face flashed before me.

She'd done something new with her hair. I wasn't sure what it was called but it made her features stand out. That cute ass nose and those high ass cheekbones. She was just too fucking good to be true.

My pants slid on with ease. They matched my shirt, which was black in color. It was next. I lowered it on my head and when it hit the waist of my jeans, another thought came to me. *She was wearing my shit. Still. After all this time and while pregnant.* The facts were adding up and leaning in my favor.

That can't be another nigga's kid, not unless she's mad disrespectful. I added. *Nah. She ain't that type.* I kept returning to that observation. *But, if it was mine, she would've told me. Called me. Texted me. Even visited the bar. Something. Anything. So, it can't be mine. Or, maybe there's just a possibility. Maybe she doesn't know.*

"Get out your head, nigga," I scolded. "Get out your fucking head and go see 'bout it."

Fully dressed, I stood in the mirror and sprayed the Creed cologne onto my chest, arms, legs, and back. I took the stairs two by two until I made it to the first level where I grabbed my coat and headed out of the door. The choice was easily made as I opted for the Cadillac versus taking the old school for the day. Though I barely drove it since getting the El Camino in tip-top shape, it held something valuable and necessary to complete my tasks for the day.

After starting the engine, I pecked away at the navigation system. It brought up my most recent locations as well as the few addresses that had been manually entered in the system. The first one, I remembered right away. It was the one that Halo had entered. It led us straight to her apartment. With any luck, I'd be able to pull up on her right after my meeting with Luca and our father.

Jilted was my first destination. I didn't need the navigation system to find it. I could almost find the bar with my eyes closed. That's how familiar I was with the route and how many times I'd driven. I hiked the volume on the stereo and bobbed along to the beat of Yo Gotti's *Pure Cocaine* track. It was still rocking all these years later.

About eight songs later and I was pulling into the parking lot. Pride swelled my eyes and my heart each time I shifted the gear to park in the spot that was reserved for the owner. I'd nearly cleared my account to make Jilted come alive and I was still waiting to regret it. Even with the hardships, I was still enjoying the process.

As expected, there were only a few stragglers hanging around the bar enjoying a bite to eat on their lunch break, more than likely. It was only noon and the bar wouldn't be in full swing until around the five o'clock hour. That's when everyone was ending their work day and needed a place to decompress. Jilted was the perfect place and we made sure to treat them well enough to tell their co-workers. Word of mouth had been our number one source of marketing and we wanted to keep it that way.

"You have two really, really fine-ass men in the conference room waiting for you. Mind telling me who they are?" Jade asked.

She'd been down since our grand opening and wouldn't be going anywhere anytime soon. The customers loved her and she loved their money even more. Her tips were astronomical at the end of each night. I'd watched her count them enough times to know that her pockets weren't hurting at all.

"Married and married. That's their name."

"Married men have a little fun, too. Marriage doesn't mean the world has to end."

"Having fun in their marriage is how I got here. I doubt if my father wants any more of that shit. And as for my brother, I doubt he's trying to get down like that. I've seen the material he's working with."

"Are you saying she looks better than me?" She scoffed, whipping her neck from side to side.

"I'm saying it's just not worth it," I admitted with a shrug. "Did you get them something to drink?"

"Yes. They ordered damn near everything off the menu, too. I hope this isn't on the house."

"It is."

"Well, my tip better be worth it!"

"I'm sure it will be. Just make sure their shit is hot and fresh."

"Got you, boss."

I entered the conference room to find Luca and Liam seated near the projector screen with drinks in their hands. The conversation they were having amongst each other stopped immediately, and they both stood to their feet. It had only been a week since I met them both but it felt like a lifetime since I'd seen them.

"Ledge," Luca greeted with a nod.

"Son," my father called out, acknowledging my presence.

"Y'all good in here?" I inquired, making my way to

the end of the room where they stood to greet them properly.

I reached the eldest of the two first. He pulled me in for a quick hug that ended with a few pats on the back. Luca and I embraced just as quickly, but as we pulled away, our hands locked while his features contorted as if he was pondering.

"This your spot?"

"Yeah. For the most part. Lawe owns a percentage of the company, too."

"Plenty potential," he declared with a nod of approval.

"Yeah? You see it too, huh?"

"The vision is very clear. What's holding it up?"

"We'll talk about it," I assured him.

"Fa' show."

"For you."

I turned my attention toward my father and handed him the second letter that my mother had left in the box I'd found the other. It was addressed to him and Laura. Whatever was on those pages wasn't any of my business, so I didn't bother opening it or reading it.

"What's this?"

"The second letter I found in the box. It's for you and Laura."

He stuffed it in his back pocket without giving much thought to it. A smile covered his face as he looked back up at me and had a seat.

"This... this is nice," he claimed, referring to Jilted.

"Thanks."

"How long have you been in business?"

"Ten months and counting," happily, I revealed.

Eight months. Her voice appeared, shifting my focus.

"I... uh. Give me one second. I'll be right back. Can I get either of you anything else? I won't be long."

"Nah, we're good. Handle your business."

"Bet. I'll be right back," hurriedly, I responded to Luca.

On my heels, I twisted my entire body and headed out of the conference room. Down the hallway, into the bar area, and then toward the main entrance's lengthy hallway, I kept going until I'd made it to my destination. The founder's wall. It was littered with pictures of our founding customers with the dates they visited scribbled beneath them.

One by one, I searched the wall until I stumbled upon the caramel complexion that was true to its nature and sweet to the taste. *Bingo.* Vividly, I remembered the black top and pants she wore, making sure to highlight her curviness. *It was February.* I realized.

February 22. The date read at the bottom of the frame we'd both posed in. It was Jade who'd snapped the shot of us at the bar. For the first three months in business, you had to pry the camera from her hands.

Swiftly, I unlocked my cell phone. Google was the first stop. *What's my due date if I conceived on February 22?* I typed in completion and tapped the search icon next to the inquiry.

November 15, the results displayed.

"My birthday... *almost, at least.* My shit on the 18th, but still."

"You talking to yourself, now?" Jade chuckled, walking past.

"Nah. Just trying to figure some shit out."

"Maybe I can help," she offered.

"I'm good. Their food ready?"

"Not yet, old man. But, it's about to come up."

"Aight."

I didn't want to keep them waiting much longer so I shoved my phone into my pocket and made my way back to the conference room.

"Sorry about that. Now, what's up?"

"Shit. Just wanted to touch base." Our father was the first to speak.

"And give you the rundown on our squad. Hopefully get to know yours a little better, too."

"Yeah. Yeah. Of course." I nodded and took a seat.

"Luca is the oldest of the bunch. His wife is Ever, whom you've already had the pleasure of meeting. They have Essence, Emoree, Elle, Lucas, and Emilia on the way. Then there's Laike who is married to Baisleigh. They have a son, Laiken."

"Baisleigh as in Baisleigh's House?"

"Yes, as in Baisleigh's House."

"That's what's up. Love that spot."

"You, me, and the entire Channing City."

"True. True."

"And, there's Lyric. She's married to Ken or Keanu.

Their daughter's name is KJ, short for Keanu Jade. Laura, that's my wife and their mother. It's not too many of us, but we're a close-knit bunch."

"I see. I'm fucking with that, though. Speaking of children, I grabbed a few things for the babies the day I left. Remind me to hand it over the next time we meet. It's in the other whip."

"Or how about you bring it by yourself. I'll send you my address. You could also bring it by our parents' place. You're family now. You don't have to wait for meet-ups. Come through."

"Bet. Bet."

"Here's that food you guys ordered," Jade announced as she walked in with our large black serving tray in one hand and the mount in the other. She sat it down first and then the tray on top. The large tray was full of dishes. She hadn't exaggerated. They'd ordered quite a bit from the menu. I wanted their honest opinions, so I couldn't wait for them to dig in.

There were buffalo wings, tacos, mini burgers, philly cheesesteak fries, supreme queso, tenders, and some other shit in the mix. They'd chosen wisely from the menu. Looking at their plates had my stomach growling.

"Jade, bring me some BBQ wings and seasoned fries when you come back."

"Who said I was coming back," she joked.

"I did."

"Alright, boss man," she sniggered, leaving the gentlemen with their food.

"That's you?" Luca asked once we were alone again.

"Nah."

"You really out here single? Pops, we should've brought the swabs. This nigga can't be an Eisenberg." Luca was the culprit behind our sinister laughing.

"I'm trying. I'm trying. Just been busy. When the time is right, I have someone in mind."

"The time is always right when the person is," our father interjected. "Get her before someone else does, whoever she may be."

"Noted," I responded with a nod.

As his advice sunk its claws into me, I allowed the silence we'd entered to have its way. Their mouths were full and their bellies would be soon. Having my father and brother enjoying the fruits of my labor was a sprinkle of contentment that I never knew I needed. The pride on both of their faces swelled my heart and head. Unfortunately, my victory lap didn't last very long and neither did the silence we were all basking in.

"Ayo, Ledge," Lawe called out in search of me.

Quickly, my contentment transformed. I straightened my relaxed posture in the conference chair and waited for my twin to enter the room. There weren't many places for him to look, so I knew that it would only be a few seconds before he found me.

"Ledge," he commented once he noticed me. "You—."

He stopped mid-sentence. I watched as his brown eyes darkened. They panned the room as his face scrunched in ways I'd never seen before. I could almost feel the steam radiating from his frame. It was damn near painful to watch him storm into the conference room and slam the door behind him.

WHAM! It collided with the frame.

Both Liam and Luca placed their utensils on their plates and gave Lawe the floor. It wasn't as if he was asking for it. He'd consume it whether it was given or not. It was just the type of nigga he was. And, as knotty-headed as he was, I'd back him each and every time. Only this time, he wasn't up against the enemy. This was family, whether he liked it or not.

"Ledge, tell me one motherfucking thing, bro," he paused, "Why the fuck these light-skinned ass niggas in my bar."

"This isn't your bar, Lawe. Not yours alone, at least."

"Answer the fucking question," he barked. "Why these niggas got seats at my table, eating from my table."

"I'm not answering shit until you calm your ass down and have a seat."

"I'm not sitting at the same table with these niggas," he rebuked.

Standing to his feet, Liam extended a hand, "I'm Liam, your father."

"Nigga fuck you!" Lawe's words were like knives to my chest.

Slowly, Luca stood from his seat. In no hurry, he stepped forward and in Lawe's direction.

"What we're not going to do is be disrespectful. I suggest you lower your fucking voice and show us the same respect we're prepared to show you."

"Lower my voice? Nigga, my mother died months

ago. You ain't got that type of ranking over here. This ain't the streets."

"It's not. You're right. Because if it was, I would've put a bullet right down your throat the second I even felt like you were raising your voice at me. Because we share the same blood, I can't and won't do that. So, like I said, calm your ass down. You're not scaring nobody in this bitch. Everyone is relaxed except you. Do you need a drink in your bar? Would that help?" Luca finished by asking.

"Like I said, nigga fuck him and fuck you!"

"You're a disrespectful ass nigga," Luca chuckled, sarcastically.

"They say I get that shit from my pussy ass daddy, but I wouldn't know. I've never knew the nigga."

"They were right about one thing... the disrespect. What they didn't tell you is that he doesn't tolerate it. Niggas like you were my favorite to end...with my bare hands. You're not as tough as you think you are, son. I've seen it all and you ain't shit. Pipe down, have a seat and get to know the nigga you never met. He's trying to get to know you," Liam warned.

"I'm thirty-five. The fuck I need to get to know you for? I ain't been had a daddy and I don't need one of them motherfuckers now."

"But you do," Liam stated calmly, taking his seat again.

Before I could catch him, Lawe was already at Liam's side with his piece in his hand and aimed at Liam's chest. To my surprise, Liam wasn't moved, not even a little.

"I'm okay with my shit ending here. I've lived a good life, young nigga. Have you? Because, before you can clutch the rigidness of your gun tight enough to let that bitch blast, your brains will be splattered all over *your* establishment. Choose wisely, because your brother won't give a damn about ending your life and then making sure that you're buried like a fucking king right next to me. Ain't that right Luca?"

"Already," Luca responded, his gun was against Lawe's temple.

"Come on now, fellas," I sighed. "Are you fucking serious, Lawe?"

"You're a baby. I can smell the milk on your fucking tongue. But, if you're ready like I'm ready then let that shit bust," Liam taunted. "If not then get that fucking gun out of my fucking way."

He slapped Lawe's piece away from his chest and reclined slightly in his chair. At that moment, any and everything I'd ever heard of Liam Eisenberg was proven to be true. He was as fearless as he was feared. He was as haunting as he was haunted.

"If your father was present, he would've taught you to never pull your piece if you aren't planning to use it. Luckily, I'm here now and willing to teach you all that shit I didn't get to."

"Lawe," sternly, I called his name.

"What?"

"Sit down. Ain't nobody in here done hurt you, bro. Let that shit go. Whatever you're holding onto, let it go."

"For what it's worth, I didn't know. Had I, then

things would've been a lot different and we wouldn't be meeting for the first time. The pain you feel in your heart right now, son, I feel it too."

"We haven't even taken DNA tests. We don't even know if we're yours."

"With a temper like that, I don't need a DNA test. Your brother is your twin flame. His name is Laike. You'll meet him soon enough."

"I'm good," Lawe responded, tucking his gun away. "Call me when these niggas out of the way."

Without another word, he exited the space that seemed to get smaller with his presence. The second he left, it expanded, again. Instantly, I began expressing my sincerest apologies.

"My bad. He's jus—"

"No need to explain. He's not the first or last nigga I've encountered like that. I can handle him," our father replied. "Tell that little waitress to bring me a stiff one. I'm going to need it."

"Mom is expecting you in a few, old man. Did you forget?"

"Oh shit, yeah. I guess I won't be needing that drink, son. Save it for next time because I will be back. Me and my golfing buddies might make this our spot. The food is good and the drinks are right on time."

"Sounds like a plan. The more the merrier. Bring them on by."

"Luca, I'm going to get out of here. We're going to grab the girls for our movie date this evening. If you need us, don't. We're taking the rest of the day to ourselves."

"But, my kids will be with you. If I need you, I'm calling."

"Suit yourself. You won't get an answer. I'm warning you now."

"Then I'm pulling up."

"I've told your mother to change the fucking locks. She still won't listen," he grunted.

"She ain't gone listen, so stop asking."

It was comical, their banter. Our father's love was apparent in the way he spoke to Luca. Once he left, it was only Luca and I sitting at the table. The urge to spill my latest news came over me. My instincts led me to believe that I'd get the sound advice I needed from him.

"So, I got something I want to run by you really quick. You got time?"

"I can make time. What's up?" He continued snacking on his food.

"Last week, the day that I came to the house, I ended up at Target buying a bunch of baby shit for the kids."

"Appreciate it."

"While I was there, in the baby section, grabbing a few things, I bumped into someone I'd been involved with...once." I paused, remembering just how big and pregnant Halo was.

"Nigga that's all or is there more?"

"There's more."

"I'm listening."

"She's pregnant. Like, big and pregnant. About to pop pregnant. Eight months pregnant."

"And what does that have to do with you?"

"We were involved eight months ago."

"Word?"

I'd truly captured his attention, then. He dropped the wing he'd just finished and began cleaning his hands with the napkins Jade had provided. His eyes enlarged as his head tilted, reminding me of myself so much that it was scary.

"Yes. When I ran out for a second, it was to go check the date on the picture she and I took the night she visited the bar. According to the date, she'd be eight months pregnant today. And, shit, she's eight months pregnant today."

"Damn. What you thinking? How are you feeling?"

"Like I have a kid on the way," I admitted.

"Then, you most likely do."

"I know. I'm just trying to figure out why she wouldn't hit me up if there's even a possibility."

"Were you involved, involved or just fucked?"

"We fucked, but I wanted it to be more. I left her with my number instead of taking hers."

"Bad decision. You left the ball in her court and she did not shoot that motherfucker."

"Exactly, that's why I'm wondering if the baby is mine or if I'm just tripping and want it to be mine."

"Do you?"

"Yeah. I guess. Kind of. I really liked her. She was a vibe. Then, meeting our pops and seeing y'all with your kids and shit. I'm just feeling a whole lot right now. I can't really explain it. Like, what are the odds of bumping into her the day that I meet Liam? I feel like shit was just aligning in my favor that day."

"What's next?" Luca asked.

"That's what I'm trying to figure out."

"If it was me," he started, "I'd hunt her ass down and try to get some answers. She would've never gotten away from me. When I want something, I don't stop until it's mine. Ask my wife. She knows what's up. She was on her independent, fresh out of a relationship and not looking for love bullshit when I met her. It was my first day out. She's Lyric's best friend. They pulled up on me to pick me up from doing a bid for offing Lyric's ex.

"That day, I knew she'd be my wife and I stopped at nothing to make her just that. The first chance I got, I put her pussy ass ex in the mud. Niggas like him don't deserve to walk the same earth as me – as her either. So, yeah, nigga. Go figure that shit out and if it ain't yours, then make it yours. If she ain't involved with nobody, snatch her ass up. Ain't a motherfucker on this planet can tell me that Essence and Em don't belong to me. I swear if you test them today, they might have the Eisenbergs blood running through their veins."

"She had them before you met?"

"Yeah. But that doesn't leave this room."

"Fa' show. Fa' show."

"So you need some info on her or what? I have people. Within five minutes, I can get everything you need to know about her. I just need a name to start."

"Nah. I drove the truck today for that exact reason. Her address is still in the navigation."

"Smart man."

"I'm 'bout to pull up on her ass and see what's up."

"Handle your business then. I'm staying my ass right here until I finish my food."

4

LEDGE

"YOUR DESTINATION IS ON THE RIGHT," THE GPS announced.

Seeing the first-floor apartment brought everything back to me. I remembered her pointing toward the right just a little further up than the GPS had taken us. Fortunately, there was a parking spot right in front of the door she'd gone into the morning I dropped her off. I parallel-parked and hopped out of the truck, locking it up as I stepped onto the sidewalk.

As I neared the door, I could hear the ruffling of the blinds. I marched up the few steps that led to her door and pounded my fist against it. To give her space, I stepped back a bit and waited for her to open up. The seconds turned into a full minute and then another without a response, prompting me to knock again.

"Knock, knock," I voiced as my hands hit the door, again.

Afterwards, there was complete silence. *The fuck is she doing?* I wondered, stepping up and knocking again. When I stepped back, I noticed the blinds were parted and a set of eyes were staring straight at me. With a tilted head and crinkled brows, I twisted my body to confirm the identity of the person on the other side of the window.

"Halo?" I said.

Simultaneously, I noticed a small crack in the window. Her eyes followed the trail of mine. Before I was able to utilize the space, she slammed it down and closed the space she'd left in her blinds.

"Fuck is you doing?" I asked, heading for the door, again.

"Halo, I saw your nosey ass peeking out the window. Open the door."

This time, I knocked a lot harder and with a little more speed. When she didn't answer, I knocked again. Then, again. And, then again. Until finally, I felt a pair of hands on my arm, forcing it down by my side.

My opposite hand brushed the barrel of my gun. But, when I heard the feminine voice in my ear, I knew that there wasn't a threat near. I'd more than likely caused a disturbance.

"Uh... hi."

"What's up?" I turned and faced whoever the fuck was next to me.

"She's not going to answer," she told me with more confidence than I thought she should have.

"How do you figure?" I challenged.

"Because she's not. She doesn't come outside."

"What you mean she doesn't come outside?" I couldn't remember asking so many questions in my life, but they were steadily coming.

"She suffers from a condition that forces her inside. She doesn't come out, seriously. You're wasting your time."

"What condition?"

"Agoraphobia."

"Agora— what?"

"Agoraphobia," she revealed.

"The fuck is that?"

The words were out of my mouth before I could stop them.

"A condition that leads to the fear of people, places, and things that are beyond your control. In there, she can control her reality... Out here, she's like a fish without water. She's not coming out. I'm telling you now."

"Then she can let me inside," I suggested.

"Well, that's probably not going to happen either, but I'll let her tell you about that."

"She really not coming out?"

"No. She literally never does."

"I just saw her at Target like a week ago."

"I know. I took her. Do you want to know how long it took me to convince her to go to Target?"

I didn't respond, because of course I wanted to know.

"About two months. She had to mentally and emotionally prepare herself to leave and to be around people."

"She was at my crib eight months before that, and she was nothing like the woman you're describing now."

"You're right. She was at your place eight months ago. I know. I took her to Jilted."

I knew she looked familiar. She was the girl that Halo kept eyeing from the other side of the bar.

"Before then, she'd never been outside. Not since she moved in six years ago. She had been in her place before that since she was nineteen and her grandmother passed."

"Damn, so... that means it is," I stammered.

Without words, she nodded. "She's going to kill me but you do the math."

"I've done that shit in my head over and over and over. That's why I'm here."

"Yeah, I figured when I heard you banging on her door."

"Why didn't she tell me?"

"She's afraid of losing control." With a shrug, she stated.

"Agoraphobia?"

"Yes. She has a severe case of it. Now, though she

upsets me quite often, I can't front. That's my girl in there. Her fear is looking like a freak to the public because of her condition. It's debilitating. I love her and all of her craziness and it's my job to protect her at all costs. If you can't exercise patience, then you might as well leave now. This isn't going to be easy, I'll tell you that right now. It's hard, even for me. But, Halo is an angel. She's worth every headache she's ever given me."

"I like her," I blurted, unsure of where it had come from but it was my truth. "Like, really like her ass. Shit hit me where it hurt when I saw her poked out and shit in Target. The whole time, that's a little me she's carrying around."

"It is. I've tried to get her to tell you since I noticed her growing belly. The girl had no idea she was pregnant until I brought home a few tests. We discovered your little one growing in her stomach at around four months. She's been in love ever since. So much has happened in her world that she's just trying to protect her child for as long as she can."

"There's no need to protect our child from me. I mean them no harm."

"It's not that simple for a woman who has experienced the ugliness of the world since she was just a little girl. It's not."

It was apparent that she knew much more about Halo than she was willing to share at the moment. I wasn't tripping. Her loyalty wasn't to me. She was doing exactly what she was supposed to be doing and protecting her friend.

"Do you know what we're having?" Shifting the conversation, I tried acquiring as many details as possible.

"We don't. She hasn't been to the doctor."

I couldn't say I was pleased with any of the information I was being given, but there wasn't much I could do about all that had transpired so far. My job was to change the narrative moving forward.

"How is she surviving? Making money? Does she need anything?"

"She works remotely in marketing. Money pays the bills but I doubt that it will give the kid the life she wants them to have."

Hearing that she wasn't struggling was relieving. That would've crushed me knowing that I wasn't hurting for a thing. Immediately, I considered my mother's audacity during hard times while my father was just a few minutes across town without a financial flaw.

"The life they deserve," I added, the thought of my father not being around leading me.

"Right."

"I can handle that. She doesn't have to worry about any of our child's expenses. I got that. I just want to make sure they're both healthy and everything is good."

Health was the priority. Birthing a healthy baby and having a healthy mother to care for them mattered more than anything else.

"I know. Me, too. I just haven't been convincing enough to get her to a doctor. I wonder if anyone can come to her."

"Probably so," I added.

"They have these big ass machines and shit. I don't know. It's something worth looking into but I'm sure it'll cost a fortune."

"Good thing I have one saved, then, huh?"

"I guess so," she scoffed. "I'm Kamber, by the way."

"Ledge."

"If it's a girl, she wants to name her Lailah. If it's a boy, she wants to name him Ledger."

My heartstrings were tugged.

"Lailah. Ledger," I repeated, loving the sound of them both. "She got this shit all figured out without me, huh?"

"That's what she thinks, but I think she knows she'll need you at some point."

"She needs me now."

"I'd say she does. She's in way over her head. I'm already worried about her. When the baby comes, I'm going to lose every strand of hair on my head."

"Nah. You ain't got to do that. I'm going to make sure they're good."

Now that I was in the picture, they were no longer Kamber's responsibility.

"If you can get her to let you in." Her brows rose and fell just as quickly.

"I will. Just got to have patience and help her understand that I'm not here to fuck her over. I'm here to help."

"Yeah."

"Anything she likes, be craving, need for the baby?"

I felt useless in a sense. There had to be something I could do for the time being.

"For the most part, we took care of the necessities when we were at the store last week. Your donation helped a lot."

"It wasn't a donation," clarifying, I stressed to Kamber.

"Whatever the fuck it was, it helped. She got everything she'd put off for later."

"Did she have anything left?"

"Yeah. I think like two hundred dollars."

"Does she let you in?"

"Yes. By now, she knows she has no other choice or I'll cause a scene. She hates those."

"Is that what I need to do cause I will?"

Whatever it took, I was willing to do. If causing a ruckus would get Halo out of the door and in front of me, then I had no issue disturbing the peace.

"No. Please don't. It's a little different for me."

"Aight. Well, get this to her and tell her to call me. I just want to talk about the baby. Until she does, I'll be out here every day. She'll get tired of my ass eventually and let me in."

I shoved a hand in my pocket and pulled out every dollar that was there. The entire wad, I handed to Kamber. With a nod, she looked up at me and smiled. Obviously, she approved of a nigga. I just needed her friend to do the same.

"I think so, too. If you ask me, she wants to let you in now. She just can't bring herself to do it."

"Yeah?"

"Yes. You said you like her. She likes you, too. The first full month after meeting you, you were all she talked about. I'd never seen that smile on her face that you put there."

"I waited for her to come back to the bar, to call, to text, or anything. I got nothing. Thought she hated a nigga or something."

Heavily, I sighed, remembering just how long I'd waited for her call or text. For months, I thought about her each and every day. With Jilted just being open, it was hard to focus on anything but its success. After a while, I tucked thoughts of her away.

"The furthest thing from hate, I promise. She's just different and needs someone who understands that, understands her."

"I don't, not yet. But, I will."

"That's all that matters."

"I got some work to do so I'm going to jet. Make sure you give her that paper. Tell her whether she believes it or not, I'm already in love with the little baby growing in her big belly. She has nothing to fear. Everything will be everything," I shouted as I rounded the truck, thrilled beyond explanation.

Kamber shook her head, but the smile on her face wasn't to be mistaken for anything else. That gave me a little hope. She knew like I knew that shit between Halo and I was just beginning. We had a long road ahead of us.

Before I could get my door closed good enough, I'd dialed the most sacred number known to me. It wasn't until I got the automated recording that advised me of the number no longer being in service did my heart break all over again.

She's really fucking gone. My mother was no longer a call away. I'd never hear that voice of hers again or feel her arms wrapped around me. As I pulled off and into traffic, the thought stuck with me. My main lady had left Lawe and me in the world without her. *Fuck*. I squeezed the steering wheel in an attempt to keep the tears that threatened to fall at bay.

There wasn't a day that she slipped my mind but it was moments like these that really rubbed salt in my wounds. Hearing the news that she would be having a grandchild would've made her entire year. She'd been trying to get one out of Lawe and me for the last five years. Neither of us was budging. Until *her*. Until *Halo*.

I tossed all caution to the wind and let my minions roam her womb all night. We'd gone a round as soon as we hit the bedroom. Another not long after. And, then a final one around the three o'clock hour. If she hadn't gone home after four, then I had every intention of sliding in that shit again. Her pussy was a fucking mess. The sloppiest I'd ever slid into.

My tires stopped spinning when I hit the end of Lawe's driveway. The plan wasn't to end up here, but just like my mother, he was another safe space for me. I hopped out of my whip and made my way to the door. Using the key that I'd been given, I entered his home in search of two things, something to put on my stomach and something to take the edge off. I was certain he could help me with both.

"Bro?" I called out as I stepped through the door and toward the living room.

However, my line of vision blurred at the realization that I'd walked into some shit that I had no business witnessing. Butt ass naked, Bianca, Lawe's on-again off-again girlfriend, was bent over the back of his couch as he drilled her from behind.

"Fuck. Yes. Please don't stop."

I covered my eyes and turned around to head in the direction I'd just come from.

"That's right. Take that dick. Nah, don't run. Where you going?" He boasted, caring nothing about my presence or my disgust.

"Please. Please. Oh my God."

I sped up, leaving the two to finish handling their business.

"I'm outside, nigga," I yelled over my shoulder.

"You been asking for the dick for a fucking month. Back that shit up you been talking." Lawe was so caught up in the moment that he didn't respond. Instead, he continued his assault on Bianca's insides.

Finding the couple as comical as Tyrese and Taraji in *Baby Boy*, I couldn't help but shake my head as I exited the house. On the front steps, I parked it and removed my phone from my pocket. As I stared at the blank screen, I couldn't help but wonder if and when Halo would decide to hit my line.

The thought to grab her digits from Kamber hadn't

crossed my mind and I was kicking my ass for it too. I was so wrapped up in the new details of her life and mine that the only questions being asked pertained to her sickness and health. Those were my top priorities. As long as I knew where she was and how to get to her, having her number was the least of my worries. In due time, she'd call. And when she did, I'd answer.

The rattling of Lawe's door notified me of his presence. When he stepped onto the porch with me, he reeked of balls and freshly beat pussy. I was regretting sticking around already. But, the news I'd just gotten had to be shared. Keeping the shit to myself wasn't an option.

"What's up?"

"Nigga, I could've waited until you showered."

"No you couldn't have. I'm hitting that shit when we get in there, too. What's up? Something on your mind for you to stick around with Bianca here."

He was right. She wasn't good for him and we both knew it. Their toxicity was hard to watch over the years. I kept my distance from their relationship and their drama.

"I thought y'all were done."

"Yeah, a nigga just be talking sometimes. When I'm done for real, you'll know. I won't have to say it, either."

"Nigga, she was just on the passenger side of Damon's whip."

"She was on the passenger side of mine today. What's your fucking point? We still fucking but that ain't my bitch. She's just mine when I'm fucking her."

"Whatever you say, my nigga. I hope you know what

you're doing. She's bad for you. That's been proven time and time again."

"We're not here to talk about me. What's up with you and them niggas that were in the spot today?"

"Listen, Lawe, I get it. I do. I understand your frustration and pain. It's valid. You deserve to let that shit ride, but you're aiming it at the wrong people. Tell me, honestly, what have they done to you? What have any of them done to you?"

His silence was everything that I needed to know.

"You see what I'm saying?"

"Nah, I don't."

"Yes, the fuck you do. You're just too hard headed and stubborn to admit it."

"Where the fuck that nigga been all our lives? When the water was off? When the lights were off? When we were boiling water to bathe? When we survived off noodles for weeks. When toasts were the only breakfast we had? When our shoes needed a serious upgrade? When our shirts wouldn't even reach our wrists? When mom cut the long sleeves to make short sleeves in the summer? Where the fuck was this nigga?"

"In the dark. He was in the fucking dark. Let me be the one to do it since she didn't have the chance to. Let me apologize to you for her shortcomings. For shielding us. For protecting a man's marriage who would've welcomed us with open arms. For making our lives a little harder than it needed to be.

"For keeping us a secret that didn't need to be kept. She apologizes. She meant us some good. I know she did.

But, it's not their fault. They're only trying to be for us what we've always wanted and always needed. What the fuck is wrong with that?"

"Nothing. I just don't need them now."

"We lost our mother, Lawe. Who the fuck else do we have here? Hmm? Grandpa, Malachi, Milo, Makai, Mercer, and the rest of our people are down south in Berkeley. We're all we got here."

"And we're enough, my nigga."

"No the fuck we're not, dog. It's always just been us and we've never felt anything remotely close to being fulfilled."

Again, he grew silent.

"What about when I'm unable to watch your back? What about when you're unable to watch mine? Family, nigga, that's what we've always wanted."

"What you always wanted," he rebuked.

"Because you were too fucking bullheaded to see it. That water and them noodles and them little ass clothes that had us feeling naked out here," I chuckled, "That's how I've felt since mom died."

"Me, too."

"I don't want to feel like that for the rest of my life, man."

"Me either."

"Then just try to put that pride aside for me. Put on your big boy drawers. You're going to need them mother-fuckers, anyway. In about six weeks, you're going to be an uncle."

"Who? I'm not claiming none of them spoiled-ass Eisenberg kids as my nieces or nephews."

"Yes you will once you get your head on straight. But, I'm not talking about them nigga. I'm talking about the one from my nutsack."

"Nigga, you don't even have a parking ticket. You think I'm going to believe you nutting in bitches?"

"You're right. I'm not. But, I did let my shit loose in a fine ass woman that stopped by the bar late February. And, remember I'm the same nigga that put your first sack in your hand. I'm just careful enough. You should take my lead."

"The one in the black you showed me on the wall?" He asked, ignoring everything else I'd said.

"Yeah. Her."

I'd forgotten I'd shown him Halo's picture earlier in the year, bragging about her sloppy ass twat along with the sweetness of it. I'd never tasted anything as divine.

"Aw shit. That's going to be one black ass, pretty ass baby." Lawe whistled.

"Just like their mother." Agreeing, I nodded.

"And your black ass."

"Nigga, you're blacker than me."

"We're twins, bro." His face knotted as his neck whipped in my direction.

"Right. I forgot." Shrugging, I sucked the skin of my teeth.

"What y'all having and why the fuck you just telling me?"

"I just found out like a week ago. Today it was

confirmed. I'm geeked about the shit, but there's one issue."

Visions of the night I met Halo surfaced as I stared off into the distance.

"What? She got a nigga? We can end that shit today. That's no issue at all. I can put Bianca's ass out and we can go handle this shit."

As much as I hated it, he was as serious as a heart attack.

"Nah. She's single. But, her single ass won't open the door. Had me out there beating and shit."

"Pick the lock. I don't see an issue. This ain't your first rodeo. She got windows in the motherfucker, I know."

Sharing that bit of information with him should've never crossed my mind, but it had. His ignorance was the reason.

"Yeah."

"Then, there is no issue. You should be talking to me from inside the house *right now*," he emphasized.

"According to you, I don't even have a parking ticket."

"Nigga, that might be true, but I ain't forgot who I'm talking to."

"Act like it then. But, I can't just break into her shit. She has this condition her neighbor was explaining to me. Some phobia of people and shit. I still need to do my research."

"She wasn't scared of that dick," he laughed.

"Nah, she took that motherfucker like a champ."

"And walked away with the grand prize.".

"I ain't mad at her, not one bit. I just got to convince her ass that she can trust me. Kamber swears she doesn't trust a soul."

"Kamber fine?" He tooted his nose in the air and shifted his eyes downward in my direction.

"Are you serious right now? You literally got somebody in the house ass naked waiting for you."

"I told you she ain't mine unless she's sliding down this fucking pole."

"I got to hit the bookstore. I just wanted to come by and make sure you were straight and share the news with you."

"Soon as I slid into that pussy, I forgot all about them niggas. Shit is a miracle worker, for real."

"I'm out, man. I'm not trying to hear all that."

LEDGE + HALO

WITH TWO BAGS full of books on various topics as they related to or spoke directly about anxiety, introverts, agoraphobia, co-parenting, home births, and relationships, I entered my home from the garage. I'd never done this shit for real before, not like I wanted to do it with Halo. So, the more help I could get, the better off I'd be.

There had been women, several of them. There had been flings, several of them. But, a relationship, I couldn't say that I'd truly dedicated myself to one because I'd yet to find a woman ready to dedicate herself to me. My ideal love centered around devotion, protection, romance, patience, kindness, respect, and a bunch of filthy ass sex.

I hadn't come across a woman that could give me that or that I felt compelled to offer every single one of those to. Whenever shit between someone and me began getting serious, I quickly learned that it wasn't the right time or the person. The red flags were always bright and obvious, disguised as other men, spending habits, addictions, immaturity, or lack of compatibility.

Either way, the first flag I recognized in any given situation with a woman was my sign to dead the situation. Run far, far away. And, I had, over and over again. This time, though, shit wasn't like that. I hadn't gotten to know Halo, but instead of running from her, I wanted to run toward her. There were a few red flags, but I didn't feel as if they weren't anything I couldn't handle or didn't want to handle.

The chiming of my cell urged me to empty my hands a bit swifter. With high hopes, I swooped my phone from my pocket and glared at the screen. The unsaved contact I'd expected to see didn't appear. Instead, it was Luca. Upon unlocking the phone, I saw that he'd sent over his home address. A simple nod was my response before locking the screen and placing the phone on the counter.

"Let's see what we've got in here to eat."

I combed through the fridge and the cabinets in search of ingredients to whip up something quick that would settle my rumbling stomach and get me through a few chapters in one of the books I'd picked up from the store. With the ingredients of a turkey burger in front of me, I decided it would be the route I was taking.

To be sure that it didn't lay my ass out on the couch in a few minutes, I opted for a small one. I also decided against a shower before finishing my reading session for the night. Otherwise, I wouldn't make it through the first page without nodding off.

The ground turkey had been in the fridge for three days, so it was still nice and soft. Before removing it from the tube, I unlocked my cell phone, made sure that my Bluetooth was connected to the surround sound, and tapped the Pandora icon.

I scrolled through the list of stations until I came across the R&B station that I preferred over the others. It was a mix of late nineties and early two thousand hits. Maxwell was the first voice to croon through the speakers.

After a series of ahs and oohs, he began the masterpiece with, "Pray to God you can cope."

This Woman's Work was and always would be a classic. And, for the moment, it was fitting. The warm water started flowing as I turned the knobs, preparing to wash my hands and rinse the vegetables. I wasn't sure what Halo had suffered through in life, but it had left its marks on her heart. As I recalled the night that I found her curled up in my bathroom and the ride to her house, my chest tightened.

Her fragility contributes to her beauty. The thought occurred as I chopped onions and stuffed them into the folds of the ground turkey meat. After the incident, I thought no differently about her. In fact, I was drawn to her a little more. I didn't ask questions because the answers didn't matter.

Whatever pain she was feeling, all I wanted to do was stop it. She robbed me of the chance when she didn't use the number I'd given her. But, now that we were back at square one, I'd make it my business to help her heal from whatever it was she'd suffered through. With me around, the suffering ended. For our child, I needed Halo to be her happiest and healthiest self. Another option wasn't available.

The sizzle from the skillet that I'd dropped the burger into reminded me of the sounds emitting from the kitchen on the days that we had enough groceries to make a full meal. My mother loved getting in the kitchen. It was the place she felt most comfortable and most confident. She'd even taken a job as a chef, but the pay was barely enough to cover our monthly expenses and afford us the latest of anything.

That drove both Lawe and me to the streets by the tenth grade. High school was a much more complex time. Showing up with cut-off sleeves in the spring and small ass shirts in the fall and winter wasn't something we could get away with. To get the respect we deserved, we had to dress and act the part.

It didn't take me long to realize illegal money wasn't my cup of tea. After ten years of the same hustle and bustle, I was ready to put that life behind me. The only issue was that I'd been spending my money as fast as I was making it. When the idea of Jilted struck me, I had a mere six figures in my account. To make it happen, I needed at least seven.

I spent the next eight years securing a solid seven figures in profits while scaling back altogether. I wasn't ripping and running the streets, hanging out like I used to, or blowing my bread. I sat my ass down, bought a crib, began business courses at the community college down in The Heights for a couple of thousand, and ended up with a bachelor's degree by the end of it all.

I toasted the buns for the burger once it was cooked to perfection and sitting on a napkin to cool. Once the bun was good and crispy, I added ketchup, mustard, and a little mayo. The pickles were plentiful. Combined with the meat and cheese, I'd made the perfect sandwich. On a glass plate, I carried the quick bite to the couch along with a book and bottle of water.

I stretched out on the couch and opened the first page of the text that described Halo's condition in detail. Everything about the moment reminded me of the long nights of studying for exams, quizzes, and the random tests that some professors loved giving. Instead of business, this time I was studying Halo and I refused to fail the course.

A father. The revelation was still fresh on my mind and heavy on my heart. Since my exit from the illegal trade of drugs, it was a role I wanted to have. I'd gone my entire life without one, which made me want more than anything to become one. And, a great one. I'd grown up believing that my father was a worthless piece of shit that didn't care enough about us to stick around and see to it that we were alright. That was the furthest thing from the truth.

Because I didn't know it back then, I was determined to be a better father, a better person, than he was. But, even with me meeting Liam and learning the truth behind his absence, I still wanted to be the dad I never had. Strangely, Liam was the exact father that I aspired to be, just not to me or to Lawe. It wasn't his fault but I'd be damned if it hurt any less.

A son. I thought. *I want a son.*

Though I'd be satisfied with whoever God decided to give me, a son was my preference. The desire to pour into him all the love of a father that I'd been robbed of was the reason. He'd be my redemption. There wouldn't be a day that would pass that he didn't feel the love that I held for him.

Or a daughter would be cool. I flipped, unable to settle on either.

So that her mother could have the chance to see how much beauty the world has to offer. So that her mother has the chance to experience a better life through her eyes. So that her mother could begin to heal through her.

We've both got scars, I discovered. *Wounds that still need healing.*

5

HALO

Ugh.

It had been nearly twenty-four hours since Ledge's visit and I was still obsessing over every detail. *You could've easily just opened the door*, I kept telling myself although I knew that there was nothing easy or simple about opening the door. It was never simple, nothing about my life was.

Ping. My phone sounded on the other end of the couch.

As I stared at the muted computer screen with over twenty employees participating in the virtual team meeting, I began counting down the seconds until it ended. If there was nothing else I appreciated about my employer, it was their commitment to quick and efficient team meetings so that we could end the work day on time and not ride their clock. We were seconds away from the five o'clock hour, which meant that the screen would blacken very soon. I was holding my breath until it did.

"Thank God!" I whispered when everyone disappeared. One by one, they all began logging off. I followed suit, shutting down my computer entirely by lowering the top half and stacking it on top of the bottom.

When I grabbed my phone, I wasn't surprised to see that Kamber had sent another text. It was the third one of the day and they'd all gone unanswered. I'd heard every word of the conversation between her and Ledge. Though I knew she meant well, I wasn't too fond of her methods or her commitment to fixing something that would be forever broken. I wasn't a project and I, especially, wasn't her project.

> Open the door and get your money or I'm going to start spending it myself.

Without hesitation, I was up from the couch and at the door. Whatever she was holding onto of mine that Ledge had given her, I wanted. Kamber was many things but she wasn't a liar. If she said that she'd spend the money, then it was far from a threat. She'd spend it.

I twisted the lock and clinched the door handle. The

excessive amount of saliva that pooled in my mouth upon contact with the cold surface, I swallowed down and exhaled deeply. When I finally cracked the door, Kamber was standing behind it.

"Seriously?" She taunted.

Without responding, I stuck my upright palm out and waited for her to fill it.

"I'm not handing it over until you let me in."

"I'm not letting you in, Kamber. I'm not up for company. Besides, I'm mad at you."

"You're not. You just need someone to be mad at so that you're not beating yourself up and I'm cool with being the fall guy."

She was right and we both knew it. However, I was upset with myself, too. There was no escaping it.

"I feel like a freak as it is. What you did yesterday didn't help one bit."

"I did exactly what I was supposed to do. Being your friend doesn't end with me keeping your secrets. It includes stepping in when I feel like you're in a tight situation. It includes tossing you a lifeline when you're sinking. It means pulling you out when you're in too deep. My friendship doesn't have stipulations, Halo. I'm a friend, through and through. I gave you months to come clean to this man. I didn't go searching for him. He showed up at your door because he figured the shit out himself. All I did was confirm his suspicions. He'd already put two and two together."

"It doesn't matter."

"Yes, it does. And, another thing, you're not above

chastisement. I will let you know when you're wrong and leaving that man in the dark like that was wrong. I understand your circumstances, but you opened your legs for him. You used him to help with your healing. Then, tossed him to the side although he seems to actually like you and care to some extent. Now, you're expecting his child, and literally expecting to carry out a delivery without his presence. It's not right, Halo."

"I never said it was."

"Then, what are you doing?"

"It's not right, Kamber, but it's my life. Okay? If I could have it any other way, don't you think I would? Ledge isn't the only one with feelings. I like him too, a lot. But, we could never be anything. I'm too messed up and he's too freaking perfect. He deserves someone that can reciprocate the love he has to offer. I can't."

"Then at least give his child a chance to," she begged.

"I will."

She stared at me through the small crack, questioning my response without even saying a word.

"I will. I promise."

"Good. Now, can I come inside?" She tried again, handing me the money.

"No. I'm still mad at you and I'm about to take my after-work nap. Bye!"

I slammed the door in her face and locked it before she had the bright idea to push it open. The large wad of money she'd handed me was much more than I'd expected. In disbelief, I carried it over to the counter and sat it down. One by one, I separated the bills, piling them according to their value. After they were all in their respective places, I began counting.

Five thousand forty-three dollars. Woah. I whistled as I counted the last dollar. I couldn't remember ever holding so much money at once. *He carries around this kind of cash all the time?* I wondered, recalling his generous contribution to our baby's fund when we bumped into each other in Target.

I converged the money and headed toward my bedroom where I kept my savings. In the box underneath the bed, I stuffed the money inside and lowered the lid. It wasn't until it was time to stand again did I realize how much of a bad idea it was to get on the floor. Though it took some time, I managed to make it to my feet again.

Ah-chu! A sneeze rocked my core, shaking my entire body.

Ah-ah-chu. A second one came right after, dramatically ending with shooting pain up my spine.

The moistness felt below my nose caused me to cringe and flip on the bathroom light. During my entire pregnancy, I'd suffered from a slight cold that I couldn't shake. Some days I was perfectly fine, but most of them were filled with sneezes that made me wet my panties, a stuffy and runny nose, congestion, and a sore throat. My little one was giving me hell, but it was the most amazing part of hell I'd ever visited.

I placed a piece of tissue on my face, right underneath my nose, and blew gently. The insides of my nostrils were sore from the consistency of the mild cold. It was important that I didn't blow too hard or wipe too hard. Otherwise, I'd be sorry for the rest of the day.

The moment I reentered my living room, I lifted the window that always produced fresh, much-needed air. A slight crack was all I ever needed. I placed my computer on the table in front of me and grabbed the blanket from the basket full that was next to the couch. My back pillows never left my work area. They were my saving grace. I grabbed three and stuffed one between my legs. The other two, I propped underneath my head.

"Just an hour," I told myself as the sounds of nature began blasting through the speaker on my counter.

It was the same routine every day for the last six months or so. After work, I took a power nap so that I could recharge for a few more hours and be back in bed between nine-thirty and ten. Sleep wasn't always on the agenda at that hour, but bed was. Most nights ended with my head lodged between a book until I fell asleep.

Alexa was scheduled to play nature sounds every day at five-thirty. That was always my sign to lay down. Today, I didn't have to wait for the signal, I was prepared. As the sounds began to serenade the room, I closed my eyes and tried my hardest to shut off my thoughts.

I wonder what he's doing. One escaped me.

Does he think I'm weird? Another got away.

We're having a baby. A third one fled.

Oh my God. Shut up! I screamed, internally. *And, go to sleep.*

It was easier said than done, but I managed. And, in a

few minutes, the sheep that I'd started counting were counting me.

LEDGE + HALO

BOOM. Boom.
Boom. Boom.
Boom. Boom.

The deafening silence of the evening made the knocks at my door sound much louder than they were. I wasn't expecting anyone, so I wasn't sure who it could be. I checked my phone but didn't find any missed calls or texts from Kamber. Confusion tugged at my contorted features as I swept my body upward and sat up on the couch. I leaned over as far as I could and used a finger to part the blinds.

Ledge? His frame was unforgettable. The way he stood back on his legs had to be the sexiest thing ever. *Or, maybe it's his smile. Or that laugh. Or the curve in his... Oh God.* I could never forget either. I spiked with adrenaline, hopping to my feet a little too quickly and nearly pulling a muscle.

"Ouch," I whispered.

"Halo," he called out to me. "You wanna open up the door, pretty lady?"

Silence tailed his question, rattling my bones. The words were at the tip of my tongue but wouldn't come out. I put a bit of space between myself and the window, afraid that he'd realize it was open if I didn't.

"Or at least come to the door and talk to me. I just want to hear it from you that you're okay. I brought some shit with me, some stuff I think we could use for the baby. And, some food. According to the shit I've been reading, y'all always hungry."

At the sound of food, my stomach howled. I silently prayed that he hadn't heard it. *Shhhh*. I warned.

Like a moth to a flame, I was drawn to him. Without intending to, I ended up with my ear against the door, listening for more. I clung to his last words for support, but I wanted more. *Speak*, I demanded, *though I had no right. Speak to me. Speak to my heart. Speak.* I begged.

"Halo," he paused, "Just tell me you're okay."

"I'm okay," I choked out, trying to weed out the sadness in my tone.

"Good. Good."

Talk to me. Convince me. Force me to open up for you.

"I know the number one thing in this situation is patience. I won't force you to let me in or come out."

I closed my eyes as defeat crept in my soul. *Please.*

"That shit will come when you're ready. Just don't keep me waiting too long. It's seven pretty lady. You can expect to see me here around this time everyday. Use my number if you need me. I'm leaving all this shit out here for you. Don't let your food get cold."

The sound of the mail slot opening startled me. An envelope fell to the floor. For a few seconds, I could only stare at the unruly handwriting on the outside of it. I sucked my cheeks to keep from freeing the face-splitting smile that was pending.

"I'm out, pretty lady."

Stay. Stay a while. My eyes darted toward the door. Fear dampened the desire within, causing me to suppress the urge to open the door and invite him into my world. *Please, just convince me.*

The sound of his door slamming was proof that he wouldn't be sticking around. I stood there unmoving, until I heard his engine roar and his tires screech. Once I was sure that he'd gone on his way, I gripped the handle and twisted the locks.

At a snail's pace, the door crept open. My eyes clung to the brown bag with Manuel's written across it. I wasn't sure what was inside, but I was certain it was delicious. Twice, I'd ordered and had their food delivered to my door. Both times, I was pleasantly satisfied with my choices. From the size of the bag, Ledge had made sure I had plenty of them.

Once my food was secure and on the counter, I returned to the door and scooted the bags inside the house one by one. Ledge spared no expense for the baby. Inside the large bags were neutral color clothing that was fitting for a boy or a girl, a brand new breast pump, loads of wipes, diapers, a baby monitor, a sock that kept their vitals on record, expensive bottles, several packs of socks, onesies, and nursing bras.

His requests for a breastfed baby didn't go unnoticed. He didn't have to worry. It had been the plan to begin with. With milk being another huge expense, I eliminated it the day I discovered my little one growing inside my belly.

As I gobbled down the shrimp pasta and side of garlic bread from Manuel's, I took a look at the large pile of bags and boxes that Ledge had delivered. Behind it were boxes stacked against the wall with bags on top from the haul last week. I still hadn't gotten around to unloading any of it.

"I'm going to need more space."

My one-bedroom apartment seemed a lot smaller when considering adding another human to the equation. When it was just the baby and me with my minimalist approach, it felt possible. With Ledge and his new obsession, I doubted it would happen. I had every right to believe that this wasn't the last haul of his. There would be more. I could feel it. And, before I knew it, there would be far too many unnecessary pieces taking up unnecessary space and driving me crazy, *unnecessarily*.

"This is really, really good," I moaned, stuffing my face. "Really good."

God, this is way too much stuff. Will we really need it all? My ability to focus was not lost on me. There was far too much going on at once. On one hand, I wanted to begin unpacking the baby's thing. On the other hand, I wanted to finish my food. More than anything, I wanted to read the handwritten letter that sat on the table in front of me.

Just open it. I finalized, knowing that I wouldn't be able to restrain myself too much longer. With the lid, I covered my pasta to trap the heat inside and keep it as warm as possible. Beside it was the letter that I pressed between my index finger and thumb.

To Halo, the envelope read. As I slid back onto the couch, I looped my finger between the fold of the paper inside and pulled it out. There was even more of the awful, hardly legible writing that I quickly fell head over heels for.

> To the mother of my child,
>
> Somewhere in one of the many books I've started in the last twenty-four hours, I read that agoraphobia is the fear of being in situations where you feel helpless, trapped, embarrassed, or stressed. The types of situations that aren't easy to escape and cause panic, stress, or depression.
>
> Can I admit that before opening a book or showing up at your door or speaking with Kamber, I had no idea what the fuck agoraphobia was? But, I've been obsessing over the shit since I learned about it yesterday. The truth is, I hate being in the dark of the unknown. I take pride in being well-versed on almost everything necessary to survive this thing called life. But this, this is new to me. You're new to me.
>
> And, I'm in the dark. About the pregnancy,

the baby, your health, the baby's health, your world, everything. I'm lost. I'm on the outside hoping to be let in so that I can start this journey of being something that I've always wanted to be. A father.

The day I bumped into you at the store was the day that I met my father. I don't think it's coincidental that I ran into you the same day. He lost thirty-five years of life with me. I've lost a few months with our child and it sickens me to my stomach to think about losing another.

My intentions aren't to make this about me. The ball is in your court. But, agoraphobia has no place in our world. You have nothing to fear. I'll protect you and our little one you're carrying until my dying day. I'll never purposely put you in a situation that will leave you feeling hopeless, trapped, or helpless. I'll devote my time and my energy to making sure that you're at your best and our child has the best of every single thing.

I'm not a bad guy, Halo. I just want the chance to prove that to you. Will you let me?

Anything you need, no matter the hour, call me and I'm here.

Ledge

P.S. Belly pictures. Let me see.

TEARFULLY, I cackled at the last two sentences. I had a camera roll full of belly pictures starting from the day that the pregnancy tests came back positive. Somehow, I felt compelled to produce new content, especially for his exclusive collection since I'd been keeping the rest of them to myself. I made a mental note to snap a few once I got myself together. For the most part, I looked a mess. Now wasn't the time for photos.

My face was stained with tears and the box of Kleenex that sat on the table was empty. I'd used them all as I fought through the sniffles and sneezes the lingering cold caused. I stood to my feet, stretching my limbs one by one, and headed to the bathroom. Paying little attention to my path, I stumbled forward to avoid knocking over the stacked boxes I'd brought inside.

Oh God. I cringed as I felt my body lowering. Luckily, my extended arms and living room table stopped me from hitting the ground. My clumsiness would be the source of my ending. I'd said it a million times before and I would say it a million times more.

I maneuvered until I was on my hands and knees, crawling toward the bathroom. Standing wasn't an option, it seemed. As I made my way toward the bathroom, through my peripheral, I noticed a fuzzy figure that had found its way out of one of the bags that Ledge had brought over. Shifting my body, I headed in the opposite direction.

"A stuffy?" I whispered as my emotions crashed into me like a tsunami.

"Oh, God, Charles. You got her a gift, baby?" My mother beamed, watching as my stepdad kneeled before me.

"What do you think, Halo?" He asked, rocking the stuffed teddy from one side to the other. The ears lifted and fell with each movement made.

"You like it?"

"Well, of course, she does, honey."

With a nod, I answered the question with a smile.

"Yeah?" His brows lifted in satisfaction.

My cheeks rose a little more as my head bobbed up and down a little faster. And, when he handed the teddy over, finally, I squealed.

"Thank you!"

"Anything for you, Halo. Now, what are you going to name him?"

"Mr. Stuffy," I blurted, the name coming to me at once.

"Mr. Stuffy. Keep him at your side. Whenever you're afraid, feeling sick, or just need a friend, remember Mr. Stuffy is right there. Okay?"

"Okay."

. . .

MY THREE-YEAR-OLD BRAIN had no idea that it was him Mr. Stuffy would be comforting me because of in the next three years. I had a friend now –a soft, cuddly friend. That was all that mattered to me. The memory was repulsive.

Getting on my feet wasn't as difficult as I'd imagined, because within seconds, my toes were tapping the floor as I made my way into the kitchen. I lifted the lid of the empty trash can and tossed the brown bunny with the biggest, prettiest ears inside. When the top slammed shut, I rejoiced.

But the guilt cut me rib-deep as I stood next to the trash can, watching its stillness. *He's nothing like him.* I tried convincing myself. The internal struggle to surrender clawed at my organs and scraped my skin. It was like nails on a chalkboard, sitting and waiting for the madness to end. Until finally, I lifted the lid, stuck my hand into the trash can, and retrieved the brown bunny.

Everything halted. Aside from rugged, untimely breaths, all there was left to hear was silence. *He's nothing like him.* With the bunny in my hand and a soaking wet chest, I picked up my feet and carried the weight of my world into the bathroom with me to wipe away its evidence. *He's nothing like him.*

Twenty-five minutes and a warm shower later, I stood face-to-face with the newest addition to the family. *Bunny.* With his long ears and brown eyes, he was the most adorable thing ever. He was even softer than he looked. His presence left me conflicted. With folded arms and fixated orbs, I stared at the ball of fur that I'd sat in front of my pillow.

Inch by inch, I lowered my body until my knees touched the carpeted floor of my bedroom. I placed both hands in front of me and joined them near my chin. Naturally, my eyes closed as I gave way to my vulnerability. My chest cracked wide open, exposing parts that I'd patched over the years, wounds that were still infected without any signs of healing, and scars that were left from the few that did manage to heal with time.

Dear God, I'm at the end of my road. There's nothing more that I can do to fix my brokenness. Without you, this road is impossible to travel. I've met a man, a fairly decent man from what I've learned so far. Together, we're having a child and as selfish as I want to be, I can't be. He deserves to love on, care for, and be with our child as much as I do. And, I want that for him, for me, and our unborn. But, I have no idea of how to let him in.

The only man I've ever trusted destroyed me, ravished my soul, tainted my heart, abused my body, and turned me into someone I don't even recognize. That's not who I want to be anymore. That's not who my child needs. That's not who Ledge deserves. I want to be better, feel better, think better, love better, trust more, and open my world to let someone in. I'm just scared. I'm terrified. Life hasn't been kind to me. But, I know that it can be.

I'm begging for your love, peace, and protection. I'm ready to loosen the shackles and be freed. I'm ready to be whole. I'm ready to be happy. I'm ready to be healthy, mentally, physically, and emotionally. Make me well, Lord.

Amen.

Moving toward the other side of the bed, I searched for the teddy that I'd been given as a child. Under my bed, it had hidden, out of plain view, and drifted into the darkness of the underworld. Certainty rested on my shoulders as I stood to my feet and journeyed to the kitchen where I lifted the lid of my trash can and dropped Mr. Stuffy inside.

LEDGE + HALO

SEVEN O'CLOCK ROLLED AROUND TOO QUICKLY the next day. For the first time in ages, my work day flew by. The several times I'd looked at the clock, I wanted to stop it from ticking. But, I knew that stopping time was impossible. *One more time*, I urged myself to read the letter I'd written to Ledge. It was simple and a little too long for my liking, but I felt that every word on the page was necessary. I'd tried, twice, to shorten it but only ended up adding everything again because it felt like something was missing.

Ledge,
This wasn't ideal, I'm sure. And to be

honest, I'm sorry that I'm the one you're stuck with as the mother of your child. Some things were beyond my control and developing this condition was one of them. Because we know almost nothing about each other, I figured I'd share a few details about myself so that we don't feel like total strangers for much longer.

I'm Halo. Halo SaraBella, an only child. My mother died when I was fourteen and I never knew who my father was either. I'm twenty-eight, but I'll be twenty-nine on February 1st. I'd just had a birthday a few weeks before I met you.

I'm eight months pregnant with a November 15th due date. I've had my suspicions but according to all the myths, I think that we're having a baby boy. Either would bring me joy.

I'm a very antisocial person, but it's not by choice. Life chose for me. The night that I met you at the bar, I'd faced some of my biggest fears. Without knowing it, you helped me conquer everything I'd set out to overcome that night. And, well, even gave me something to look forward to.

I haven't visited a doctor and I never plan to. I'm in several pregnancy groups and I pay

$89.99/month for a virtual midwife. Everything is going well with the pregnancy according to her. We meet for twenty minutes, once monthly.

If ever there is a problem, I've been instructed to contact her. A home birth is the plan, along with breastfeeding and cloth diapers. I'm not too sure about the diapers, but I want to contribute as little waste to the planet as possible. I'm still deciding. I imagine I could use your help, huh?

I've been inside since I was nineteen years old. That's when my grandmother died in her sleep of a heart attack. She was my person, my strength, my heart, my world. Since she's been gone, I've felt so alone—until I met you. For the first time in almost a decade, I felt like someone saw me, heard me, and felt me. And quite honestly, it scared me.

I thought that our time together had come to an end as swiftly as it had begun, but I was wrong. We made magic that night. And now, I'm hoping that this baby becomes my person, my strength, my heart, my world. It has to be. I need that feeling again.

That's part of the reason I couldn't bring myself to reach out. Part of the reason I've been so selfish. Part of the reason I wanted this baby to myself. But, I was wrong. I'm wrong. I can admit that it wasn't fair. Still isn't fair. But, I hear you and I see you and I feel you and I know that you deserve this moment, too. I promise to give it to you... in due time.

Halo.
P.S. Manuel's was amazing. The baby kicked the entire time I indulged and then slept the night away.

"KNOCK. KNOCK," Ledge whispered near the crack of the window.

"Sheesh! He scared me," I mouthed, but my voice was nowhere to be found.

The paper I held crumbled in my hands with ease. Suddenly, everything I'd written sounded ridiculous and useless. Nothing made sense anymore.

Hurriedly, I pushed a single blind down with my finger, creating a space small enough for me to see outside. Ledge had made his way to the door. Again, he wasn't empty-handed. I could smell the food he sat by my door.

"Your food has been delivered, pretty lady. I'm sure y'all hungry."

Just as I neared the door, the mail slot opened. In slid another letter, making me cringe at the fact that I'd tossed mine in the trash on the way over. I bent over to pick it up, admiring the words on the front of the envelope.

Pretty Lady.

An idea struck me, halting any further movement toward the door and trading it for a swift stride toward the kitchen. Though I couldn't provide him with a letter, I could give him something that I was certain he'd appreciate. Something he'd already asked for and that I would gladly give, now that I'd tossed my letter in the trash.

Month 4.

Month 5.

Month 6.

Month 7.

Month 8.

I swiped the last five instant pictures from the fridge. When I reached the front door again, the sound of Ledge's footsteps retreating silenced me. I leaned down, slightly, lifted the mail drop, and stared as his Nike's fled the scene.

But, wait. Silently, I pleaded.

As the words surfaced with promises to fall from my lips, Ledge's movements stopped. I waited, watching from the small slit in the door, for his next move. And, when he turned back and headed in my direction, I stole every ounce of fresh air my lungs would allow.

Thank you. My inner voice screamed.

It was as if our hearts and heads were in sync. Just as I

found the strength to stand up straight, I heard that familiar baritone. It was close, very close. A little too close, but it was so magnetic that it immobilized me.

"Hi," he greeted me.

Kneeling so that we were eye level, he peeked through the same hole I was looking through.

"Hi," I responded.

His brown eyes never left mine. I blinked back the tears that my heart produced for my eyes. With every bit of strength in me, I raised the picture in my hand and slid it through the slot. With a smile that was charming enough to heal any heart, he accepted it.

I wish I had just any heart. I scoffed as I stood from the door and allowed the mail drop flap to fall. My feet were like anchors, keeping me in place as I waited for something, anything from the man on the other side of the door.

The letter he'd left was partially under my left foot. I scooted it over slightly, my lack of strength barely giving me the ability to do that. When I bent over to grab it, the faint laughter from the other side of the door soothed every bit of my soul that ached. Letter in hand and ear to the door, I listened for more.

"You look staggering, pretty lady."

I pressed my back against the door and rested my head just above it. My lips rose, trying their hardest to reach my ears as my left hand laid against my chest. *Still, my heart.* I warned. *Still.*

"See you tomorrow. Same time."

6

LEDGE

"ALL I KNOW IS THAT'S SOME WEIRD ASS SHIT. But, you're a weird ass nigga and that suits you."

"It's not weird."

"Nigga, you're at her crib every day at seven like this the old days and her parents won't let her come outside. So, you camp out by her window and shit. Throwing rocks to get her attention, letting her know you're out there."

"It's nothing like that."

"Rocks, flowers, same shit."

"Nah. She loves the flowers I've been getting her. They're nothing like rocks, nigga. And, it's only been a week."

"You one patient ass nigga and that must be some good ass pussy cause ain't no way."

"Top fucking tier, my nigga."

"Say no more."

We both sat with our thoughts for a second. When the silence became a little too much, I continued the conversation.

"You ready for this shit?" I asked, referring to our meet-up with our people that we were headed to.

"Doesn't look like I have much of a choice."

"You don't. Not for real, anyway. Just be on your best behavior. You flipped the fuck out the other day."

"Yeah. Yeah. Whatever, nigga." He brushed me off.

"I'm serious, Lawe. Mom taught you better than that. She'd be so disappointed in you for that shit you pulled."

"And, I'm disappointed in her for the shit she pulled."

"Me, too," I confessed. "But, I'm ready to make the most of it. Sulking won't get me anywhere."

His only response was a head nod.

"I'm trying to cut Tank out the equation, anyway."

"Awwwwww. That's why you finally agreed. You want a direct connect. Nigga, you ain't slick."

"Aye, We family, right? Why not?"

"What happened to leaving that shit alone and going full force into investing?"

"You need paper to invest, right? I'm almost done. I just need another twelve months and I'm out."

"You said that twelve months ago."

"Well, I'm saying it again, nigga. Twelve months ago, I didn't know the fucking plug was my father and his minions."

"True. True."

"Exactly."

"Well, we're almost here, so get yourself together. Leave your gun in the car!"

"I never took you for the foolish kind, but you're sounding like a fucking fool thinking I'm leaving my shit in the car."

"I'll have mine."

"And, what the fuck that got to do with me?"

"Lawe."

"I'm not doing it. Anywhere I go, so does my Glock. If he can't come with me, then you can let me out right here. I'll find a way back to the crib."

"You're the most fucked up individual I've ever met in my life."

"Yeah, whatever."

I hiked the volume up on the music as our trip neared its destination. Per usual, Baisleigh's House was swamped. We managed to find a parking spot at the edge of the parking lot. One would've thought they'd just entered a car show. The whips in the lot looked like they were fresh off the showroom floor or on their way to it.

"You see that shit?" Lawe whistled.

"Did you see that?" I asked. "And that? And that one?"

"The owner gots to be slanging out the back door or something," he sniggered.

"I wouldn't be surprised," I added, remembering that Liam had mentioned the owner being connected to the family through marriage.

The second we walked through the door, we were greeted by the hostess with chubby cheeks and pretty white teeth. As Lawe and I approached, her smile widened.

"Welcome to Baisleigh's House. There's a bit of a wait right now. How many are we talking?"

"Uh... Five," I told her, counting the three we were waiting on.

"Oh, there's more where you came from?" She smirked.

"Yeah," Lawe chimed in, stepping forward to return the energy that the hostess was giving.

"Well, in that case, let me see what I can do to cut this thirty-minute wait down a bit."

"You do that, baby girl, and I'll have a nice, big reward for you," Lawe promised, cuffing his dick in his hands as he planted his feet and locked his legs.

"Sounds like a great idea. Uh. Just... Just one se—," she stuttered.

"I've got this one, love." We heard from our left.

The woman I'd seen briefly back at our father's place

appeared behind the stand we were near and grabbed a few menus.

"Right this way," she instructed, waving us over with a hand.

"You don't have to tell me twice. I swear you don't," Lawe responded, taking the lead and leaving me behind. From one side to the other, I shook my head. It was all I could do. He was a very special nigga and I'd learned that trying to tame him only added fuel to the flame.

"She's married," I stated but doubted he heard a word I was saying. He was far too focused on Baisleigh's backside.

Her legs didn't stop moving until we were at the rear of the restaurant at a table with a reserved sign.

"Here we are, fellas. Someone will be right with you."

"How about you, though?" Lawe asked before she was able to walk away.

"What about me?" She chuckled, obviously amused by his antics.

"You can't wait on us? I'm ready to order right now. I know exactly what I want."

"You haven't had a chance to go over the menu, yet," she reminded him.

"I'm looking at a full-course meal right now. What the fuck I need a menu for?"

As the words came from his lips, I noticed the party of three that would complete our party of five approaching. I cringed as I witnessed Laike's skin redden as his brown eyes blackened.

"Lawe," I called out.

"Don't you see me talking to this pretty woman, my nigga? Give me a second."

"I'm a married woman. Lawe, is it?"

"Yeah. Remember that shit. Who's worried about your husband? If you were mine, you wouldn't be in this bitch slaving. You'd be at home with your feet kicked up."

"Lawe!" I gritted, needing him to shut up and sit the fuck down.

"I own the place for your information. I hate being at home with my feet kicked up. Have a seat and someone will be right with you."

"Nah, I want you to take my order."

"I said that someon—."

"If you know what's best for you, you'd fall the fuck back and let the lady get back to work. I'm sure she's informed you that she's married to a nigga that doesn't have every screw."

"Luckily, she's talking to a nigga with all of his missing and couldn't give a fuck less about her nigga. I'm trying to be her friend."

"Nigga back the fuck up out my wife's face," Laike barked.

His tone immediately shifted.

"Make me," Lawe challenged, stepping closer to Baisleigh.

"Baby," she called out to Laike, turning and heading in his direction. "Please. This is not the time or the place."

"That's right. Talk some sense into that nigga before he bark up the wrong tree."

"Any time, any place, my nigga. I couldn't give two fucks."

"LAIKE!"

"That makes two of us," Lawe voiced with a shrug.

Knowing that shit could get extremely ugly if I didn't put a little more distance between them, I stepped forward. I felt a hand on my chest as I did so. Liam shook his head, instructing me to fall back. Luca was within reach but remained as calm as Liam as he watched the two butt heads.

"I'm not one for conversation. What's up?"

Within a flash, Laike's jacket was in Baisleigh's hand and he'd stepped closer to Lawe. He didn't stop until he reached his personal space where he lingered, waiting for Lawe to make a move, any move. Nose to nose. Eye to eye. Face to face, they stood, grilling one another.

"Y'all nigga gone squabble or shut up? I've got shit to do, so decide quickly.

"Pops, just say the word. I'm ready to lay this nigga on his back."

"You could try," Lawe scoffed, "After you get your dear daddy's permission, of course."

"When I put you down, you won't get back up. Believe that, my nigga. So, I'm making sure he's ready to care for a disabled son, not asking for his permission."

"Stand down, Laike."

"Nah. I think a lesson needs to be taught here."

"Teach me," Lawe taunted.

Just as Laike stepped back and prepared to draw back with his right hand, Luca stepped in. Quick on his toes, he pulled Laike in the opposite direction. Using this as my opportunity to have a word with Lawe, I pushed him toward the bar that happened to wrap around the entire spot. It was massive and very fitting.

"I told you to be on your best behavior."

"I am. My Glock still on my side, ain't it?"

"Yeah."

"Aight, then. You ain't say nothing about not using my fists."

"I told you she was married."

"You ain't say to one of the light-skinned niggas."

"Would it have fucking mattered?"

"No, but still."

"Exactly. Chill out. If you can't get your shit together, then we can bounce. I can continue meeting with our people on my own. You've been trouble the last two meetups. Get your shit together, bro. It's looking really fucking tacky."

"Fuck how I look to them niggas. I'm not looking for their approval."

"I never said you were. I'm talking about me. The shit beginning to look like a fucking circus. Tighten up, Lawe. I mean that."

"Yes sir."

"Really fucking funny. Ugly ass nigga."

"If I'm ugly then what that make you?"

"Fuck you!" I spat, leaving him where he stood and heading back to the table where everyone was seated.

When I heard his footsteps behind me, I silently prayed that he'd gotten his shit together. The minute his ass hit the chair, he made it clear that he didn't have anything together.

"Aye, just to set the record straight, I would've beat your ass. You don't even look like you can fight, my nigga."

"Lawe," hissing, I scolded him.

"What? I just needed him to know that he ain't seeing me. Suburban ass hands. Don't look like they've ever seen hard times."

"You finished?" Laike asked, calmly sitting back in his seat. "Cause, whenever you're ready, you can get these motherfuckers and find out what they're really about."

"I might take you up on that offer."

"You niggas serious?" Luca wondered out loud.

"Laike, this is Lawe. Lawe, this is Laike," Liam interjected, finally introducing the two of them.

"I've gathered that," Lawe replied, sarcasm dripping from his tone.

"Yo, why this nigga even here?" Laike shrugged.

"Same reason you're here. Now, both of you need to put your big boy drawers on and play nice." Luca grabbed the menu and tuned them both out as he decided on what he'd be eating.

"Too much alike," I voiced, doing the same.

There was so much shit to choose from. I'd been to the spot a few times, but each time I had the urge to try something new. Soundlessly, we all busied ourselves with the words on the menus and trying to figure out what we'd be eating.

"What's good on here?" Lawe broke the silence.

"Everything," Laike answered.

Simultaneously, they both lowered their menus and stared at one another.

"I can't stand this nigga, already," Lawe admitted.

"The feelings are mutual," Laike responded, unable to hold back the laughter that we all joined in on.

"Y'all going to get along just fine," Luca stated the indisputable.

"Hi, I'm Chasity," the spunky waitress hopped over and introduced herself. "Can I get you guys something to drink?"

"Water."

"Water."

"Water."

"Hennessy," Luca grunted, "I'm going to need it."

"Yeah, give me that water, but add a Hen on the rocks," Lawe recanted.

"Same," Laike added.

"Water," I finalized.

"Are you guys ready to order or do you need more time?"

"Tell my wife to get us together. You niggas can hand in your menus. B got it," Laike assured us.

"Sure thing, Mr. Eisenberg. I'll be right back with those drinks." Chasity grabbed our menus and was off to find Baisleigh.

"Aye, B got a sister?"

Laike remained silent as he stared holes into Lawe's face.

"What? Nigga it's a yes or no question."

"She has a brother," he shared, causing a fit of laughter from everyone at the table except him and the one that had asked the question.

"And her name is Baisleigh. Don't ever call her B."

"Somebody please confirm this nigga has a pussy down there because ain't no way he's this fucking sensitive all the time."

"Have you met you?" Luca spoke directly to Lawe.

"He did the second Laike walked through the door." I gnawed the inside of my lip as I stated God's honest truth. Laike and Lawe were reflections of one another. That's why they were still bumping heads fifteen minutes into our late brunch.

"For the sake of my brother, I'm going to chill out. I know he's sick of my shit. But, let's all be clear, I'm not kissing no ass to be included in your family. I've gone thirty-five years without y'all. I can go another thirty-five."

"Do it look like either of us like having our asses kissed? By niggas, anyway?"

"I'on know. This nigga did eight strong. Two more years and he would've probably considered it. Then, all y'all light-skinned. I heard they be into some weird shit or whatever."

No one at the table was able to keep a straight face as Lawe explained his logic.

"Man, where the drinks? This is about to be a long brunch." I could see that already and we'd just sat down.

"Tell her she can really just bring the bottle," Lawe suggested.

"Sounds ideal," Liam agreed.

LEDGE + HALO

WITH A TABLE full of different dishes, we all dug in. There were cheese eggs, french toast, extra-stuffed omlets, pancakes, fresh fruit, chicken and waffles, breakfast potatoes, hash browns, turkey meats of all kinds, and a bottle of Hennessy.

"Luca told me y'all own Jilted."

"Yeah," I confirmed for Laike.

"That's a cool little spot. I went around the time it first opened. How's that going now?"

"Ahh," I winced at the thought. "It could be going a whole lot better. It's not doing bad at all, but trying to turn a reasonable profit after putting so much money into the startup is like pulling teeth. We're finally starting to see some bread, though. Trying to set aside as much as I can to put back into the business. The grand opening was supposed to put the money we spent back into our pockets. I expected to see the return within six months. That shit didn't happen. We have the perfect location, menu, vibe, and all that good shit. Just need to get the word out there. Maybe get some famous faces in the spot once or twice a month to get it going."

"Shit taking a minute to get off the ground, but it's going to happen," Lawe added.

He wasn't into the logistics of the business, but finances were his thing.

"Yeah. When I was there, I could see the potential," Laike claimed.

"Me, too. It's really dope. I ain't seen nothing like it in Channing. The whole black scheme is legit."

"Yeah. The idea was like ten years in the making, almost. I put damn near all my life savings into making it happen and I'm more than satisfied with the outcome. I've wanted to own a bar for some time now."

"What gave you the idea?" Laike asked.

"Niggas like us. You see how we opted for the entire bottle instead of a few glasses?"

Nods circled the table.

"I realized one day, just how much money we spend on heightening the moment. Enjoying our time just a little more with a little influence. Liquor is associated with a good time for the most part, which makes us consume it at an alarming rate. I wanted to capitalize off that. Create a place for everyone to enjoy themselves on another level. Something that's a real vibe. Something luxurious. Something classic. Something legendary."

"How much?" Liam blurted, causing Lawe and I to look in his direction.

"How much what?"

"To make Jilted the success that you dreamed of," Luca clarified.

"To get the famous faces in once or twice a month? Have an official grand opening? Do shit on another level? Turn it up a notch," Laike explained.

"How much?" Liam repeated himself.

Before what they were asking could fully register, Lawe was already responding.

"See, this the shit I'm talking about, bro," he scolded.

"I don't follow." Liam was the first to respond.

"We're not for sale. If that's what you niggas thinking, then you're wrong. We're not up for sale."

"Was that ever insinuated?" Liam tittered, looking around the table and waiting for a response.

"We don't want shit from you, my nigga. We already got some shit in motion. Ledge is securing some funds with the bank soon. Whatever they don't give him, I'll make sure that he gets. We're good. We don't need you dangling nothing over our heads."

"I'm not some weak ass bitch with a weak ass motive." Calmly, Liam let Lawe know.

"And, if you would shut up for just a second to think with your head and not your broken heart that neither of us had anything to do with, you'd realize borrowing money from the bank is what you don't need. That shit will be hanging over your head for what, ten, fifteen years? We're the fucking banks, my nigga. You got Big bank," Luca said, pointing to Laike, "big bank," he referred to himself, "and, the biggest bank." He pointed in Liam's direction. "Our money spend just like theirs, probably better. So, what's the issue."

"Shit, $1.2 million."

The math had already been done. Lawe and I had crunched the numbers several times and always came up with the same amount. To get Jilted exactly where I wanted it, a million dollars was necessary.

"Consider it done." Liam tapped the table as the words left his mouth.

"Just like that," I chuckled in disbelief.

Lawe was stunned into silence, unable to think of anything shitty to say.

"Call your sister and tell her to move some money around. Get this boy what he needs to make whatever he's trying to make happen," he instructed Luca.

"Tell her to put three hundred in from my account," Laike spoke.

"I got four."

"The rest comes from mine," Liam finalized. He watched Lawe from across the room. He was exercising his right to remain silent which was new to me.

"Don't give it too much thought. As much as you might hate it, I'm a father. Whether I found out about you thirty-five years ago or a day ago, the same principles apply to you as Luca, Laike, and Lyric. Being a part of this family will teach you that it's always the best of everything for my flock... y'all included."

"Appreciate that."

"Your sister will need your account numbers and a visit before she moves any funds. She's pretty fucking upset that we barred her away from brunch today. I just wanted to spend some time with the guys."

"What's her address?" Lawe beat me to the punch, shocking everyone at the table.

"What?" After realizing all eyes were on him, he belted.

"Nothing, nigga. I just swear momma should've gotten a check for your ass. Bipolar!"

"Whatever. I kind of always wanted a little sister."

"Since when? I've never heard this. Enlighten me."

"Nigga, I don't have to tell you everything."

"Cause you sure didn't tell me that."

"I hate to be the one to break up the party, but I'm about to head to B's office. I've had enough of you fellas for the day. I think my blood pressure is up and I need my medicine," Laike coughed out.

"Yeah, aight," Luca called his bluff.

"I guess I should tell your mother to start preparing for that second kid she swears she ain't getting out of you." Liam shook his head.

"I don't blame you," Lawe taunted.

"These hands are readily available. Any time. Any place," Laike reminded him.

"I'm just saying. I get it. I really get it."

"Just shut up," Laike advised.

"Hey. It's a compliment." Lawe threw his hands up. "And she can cook?"

Laike continued to stare at Lawe, waiting for him to seal his lips.

"Alright. Alright. I'm shutting up. I thought you niggas liked sharing."

"I'm not that generous," Laike told him before stepping away from the table.

"Well, in that case, I'm about to go see what's up with that hostess. I got some luck with her."

"That'll be your best bet," Luca encouraged his foolishness.

"I guess that's it for me, boys. I'm headed to the holes. I enjoyed our time together. See you cats later. Ledge, you and Lawe stop by the house this week. He needs to meet Laura."

"Don't forget to give me Lyric's address. We're going to get by there this week as well."

"Your brother got you."

"I'll text it to you."

"Bet."

Liam stood and so did Luca. I followed suit. The two embraced quickly and then Liam headed in my direction. To make things easier for us both, I moved the chairs and met him halfway. He wrapped his arms around me just as he had Luca, but they lingered a while longer.

"I'm so happy to have you. I love you and I love your brother. I just hope you feel it right here." He released me and tapped my chest.

Nodding, I confirmed the mutual feelings. I'd just met the man, but I was quickly growing to love him and the way he operated. He reminded me a lot of myself, so did Luca.

"Alright. I'm out of here. The guys are waiting for me."

Again, Luca and I were left alone while everyone went about their business.

"I see how this is going to end every time," I chuckled, taking my seat.

I wasn't finished with my food and neither was he. I dug into the stack of cheese eggs on my plate, enjoying each bite of them.

"Whatever happened with that situation?"

"Situation?"

"The baby. You mentioned it last time."

"Ooooh. Shit. I did mention that to you."

"Yeah."

"I pulled up on her last week when I left the bar. I'll admit that I wasn't expecting the shit I ran into, but it's all good."

"Elaborate," he prompted.

"She's sure as hell pregnant, eight months, and I'm 100% certain it's mine."

"There's a but, huh? I can see the shit all over your face."

"Yeah. A few. She's not... She's a little different. When I went over, she wouldn't open the door for me and I'm thinking maybe she's involved and her nigga at the crib or something."

"So." He shrugged.

"Same. Same." I nodded. "But, that wasn't the case. I'm banging and I know she's in there. Finally, her neighbor comes out and lets me know that she ain't opening the door for me. I'm confused, like what you mean? She goes on to tell me that she doesn't come outside. I explain that I just saw her the week prior at Target and she confirms that she took her—after two months of convincing. Then, I go on to explain that eight months ago she was busting that shit open at my crib. She confirmed that as well, but also let me know that it was her first time coming outside since she moved into their complex years ago."

"Agoraphobia," he called out.

"You know about this shit?"

"Yeah. Lots of inmates end up with it after they do long bids. In their case, it comes from institutionalization. In other's cases, it comes from fear coupled with anxiety. She's scared of something or someone or both. The question is, who? Or what?"

"Still trying to get to the bottom of all of it. But, I've been going over around the same time every day for the last week. I'm hoping that I can get her outside or get into her crib before the baby gets here. The other day, she gave me this."

I reached into my pocket and removed my wallet where I kept the picture that Halo had handed me through her mail slot. I'd stared at it at least a hundred times over the last three days. Luca grabbed ahold of the picture and gazed until a smile curved his lips upward.

"You're going to have a beautiful kid, bro," he praised. "She's gorgeous."

"Prettiest thing I've ever seen."

"Ah. She got your ass wrapped around her finger and won't even let your ass in the house."

"Got me feeling like a fuck nigga."

"Nah, a real nigga. I'd be on the same shit. Outside with a full band, dinner table, and some more shit. I'd go to the ends of the earth for Ever and she knows it. After our last one, Lucas, baby girl was down and out for about two months. Postpartum depression was kicking her ass. I didn't even recognize her. I wanted to cry like a fucking baby, but I had to put on my game face and see us all through it. She's happier now than she was before Lucas and neither of us even thought that was possible."

"See, that's what I'm trying to be on. I've had every kind of woman I could ever want, but I've never wanted them like I want this one. I knew that night I met her at my bar that she was something special. I'm a nigga of patience. I'm not rushing anything. I'm willing to keep at the pace she sets, but my mind is made up. I want a family and why not make that happen with her."

"Do you know her any?"

"Nah, but my heart does. When I'm at her crib, I can hardly keep it in my fucking chest," I tittered, "It's like I'm not in control when I'm over there. Whatever my heart says at that point goes. And though I'm not actually spending time with her, I'm always so happy for seven to come every day. She doesn't say much, but I can feel her energy. She likes when I'm there. She's just... I don't know."

"Scared. Take your time. I know that feeling. I went through the same thing with my wife."

"*My wife.* I know that feels good rolling off your tongue."

"Feels wonderful."

"I'm trying to get like you, big bro. Wife. House full of kids. Overflow in finances. Man, that's my definition of living. Fuck all that other shit."

"That's all that matters, really. There's nothing in this world that makes me happier than my wife. Coming home to a house full of brats, showering me with love, and then a wife willing to bend over backward for me," he whistled, "Nothing like it. Paradise."

"I'm already knowing. Speaking of the wife, does she know anything about home births? I have a feeling that's what Halo is on. She ain't going to a hospital. She ain't been to the doctor since finding out she's pregnant."

"That's all Ever will consent to. She had both of our children at home. She has a doula, midwife, and birth team. I'll text you her number right now and let her know to expect your call."

"How long does it take to get things set up? I want her to get checked out and make sure everything is good before the baby comes."

"Call her today. She'll get you set up by morning. They can visit whenever you're ready. They love us. We pay their asses enough. They'll jump at the sound of baby coming from Ever's mouth."

"Appreciate that."

"You got that? I just sent her contact and Lyric's. Lyric's address is coming through now."

My phone buzzed in my pocket. I put the picture

back into my wallet and replaced it with my phone in hand.

"Got it. You mind if I shoot her a text right quick just so I can get a headstart on all of this?"

"Yeah. Go ahead."

"I'm going to hit Lyric up, too. Man, she's... She's like something off a runway. I don't understand how you niggas stayed free with her roaming the Channing streets."

"We didn't."

"Oh, shit. That's right."

"Smoked her ex. He put his hands on her."

"I'm just glad I wasn't around. We'd be cellmates. Can't let Lawe find out. That nigga will be digging the motherfucker up to shoot him again."

"Some days I want to," Luca divulged. "But, that shit behind me."

> It's Ledge, sis. Luca gave me your contact. I have a baby on the way and my child's mother is anticipating a home birth. I'm almost certain. She hasn't visited a doctor since finding out about the baby. She's eight months along and we need assistance ASAP. Forwarding her address. Her name is Halo.

I bit the lining of my jaw as I sent the necessary information. The fact that I didn't even have Halo's number to share in case Ever needed to contact her was nerve-wracking. But as quickly as the frustration rose, I deaded it. Three gray dots popped up instantly.

> Oh good! Congratulations. Can you give me the date of conception if you remember it? I'll get right on it.
> Answer your phone tomorrow. I'll call with the next steps.

> Thanks.

I replied.

> Congratulations, again. We love little Eisenbergs. Make sure to let Laura know. She owns a daycare and will get you squared away with childcare.

"Your mom own a daycare?"

"Our mom?" Luca corrected. "We don't do step shit over here."

"Yeah. She owns a daycare?"

"Yup. Your kid is already signed up and she has no clue they exist, yet. She won't take no for an answer, so don't try to convince her she should or y'all will be beefing. You don't want to beef with her. Trust me!" He forewarned me.

"Noted."

"Go get your boy," Luca advised, peeking in Lawe's direction.

"Way ahead of ya'. See you around, man."

"Always," he responded with a head nod and a fist in the air.

I pressed a closed fist against his and made my way toward the door where Lawe was holding up the line to talk to the hostess.

"Boy, bring your ass on. She doesn't want shit to do with you," I fussed, pulling him out of the door by the collar of his shirt.

"I was just about to get her to agree to suck my dick tonight. Nigga, what are you doing?"

"Call Bianca. She'll do it without hesitation."

"She was going to join us. I was getting the whole thing set up."

"Too bad."

HALO

REWETTING MY LIPS FOR THE HUNDREDTH TIME, I watched through the blinds as the cars flew by at alarming speeds. Once again, seven o'clock had come around briskly, leaving me with shattering nerves and a million thoughts at once.

Not him. Not him. I observed the passing cars, waiting for a familiar one to approach. *Get out of the window before he sees you.* As the words came to mind, I lowered my body on the couch and rested my sweaty palms on my knees. When lifting my right hand to place it on top of my pounding heart, I noticed the spot its wetness had left behind.

"Now, I need to change," I fussed. *Or do I? He's not going to see me.*

The battle within began as I stood on my feet and began pacing the floor.

"I really should've forced myself to sleep," I continued. "I just couldn't."

Sleeping after my five o'clock shift ended was getting harder and harder with each day. My deprivation and change in scheduled daily activities left me in shambles. Anxiety swelled in my throat as my feet tapped the floor beneath me. I closed my eyes and halted my stride, hoping to gain control of my elevating temperature and crushed nerves.

You're okay. Everything is okay.

I hated everything about the way that the hour made me feel. Just a week ago, my evenings were just another part of the strict schedule I'd maintained for as long as I could remember. Now, my evening naps are getting shorter and shorter. Today, it was impossible, leaving me with too much time on my hands and nothing to do with myself.

A quick glance at the clock forced movement again. It read 7:01 p.m. *Where is he? Is he coming?* Expectations of others, I despised them and myself for having them. I'd learned a long time ago to never expect anything from anyone. It was the quickest way to get let down and I'd been let down enough times already.

The dessert that expanded in my throat left it dry and

unbearable, prompting me to unscrew the cap on the water on the table beside my computer. *Ahhhh*. I quenched my thirst before screwing the cap on carefully. Instead of putting the bottle back in its rightful place, I held onto it, tapping it against my left palm.

A dreadful, thunderous rumble sounded in the still-ness of my apartment. The emptiness of my stomach registered as I realized I hadn't been able to eat much of my salad for lunch. It was a first, but I was certain that it had everything to do with the mental and emotional consumption the anticipation for my daily visit managed to burden me with. From the moment I woke up this morning, it proved to have lasting effects that still hadn't ended.

My eyes glossed over, simultaneously widening, as I silenced my thoughts and welcomed the sound of the roaring engine that could be heard down the street—possibly around the corner. When I closed them, my senses heightened as contentment covered my face. With a far more relaxed posture, I placed a hand on my chest to feel the excitement of my heart. At a rapid pace, it beat against my hand.

Shut it off. The engine quieted.

Get out. The car door slammed against the frame.

Come here. Footsteps began, the cracked window making it easy to locate him without a visual.

Pretty lady. Say it.

"Pretty lady," he called out.

My God, you're impossible. Spellbinding.

"I got Manuel's today. I hope you're fucking with

this jerk chicken I got you. In case you can't stomach it, I went ahead and grabbed some pasta, too," he explained, close enough to the front door that he didn't have to yell.

I heard every word as I listened through the window, not missing a thing. Not even the unusual sadness in his voice as he spoke to me. I could smell the defeat. The food that he'd mentioned didn't stand a chance as the familiar scent of exhaustion permeated the air.

My eyes popped open as I rushed to the door and placed my ear against the cool surface. *What's the matter?*

"I– uh," he stammered, getting caught up on his words. This was unusual.

What is it, Ledge? What's wrong?

"Don't even worry about it."

I heard the mail slot open. The letter that he'd dropped in landed on my right foot. Without a second thought, I bent over and picked it up. This time, there wasn't an envelope and neither was there scraggly writing on top to obsess over it.

What's the matter, baby? I wondered, paying close attention to detail. The urge to open the door, pull him into a hug and tell him the one thing that always made sense to me was strong, so strong that it forced me to take a step back and away from the door.

I lowered my head and focused on the letter in my hand. It was much shorter than the others. A pain in my heart surfaced at the sight of the single paragraph he'd shared. *He's running out of words?* I asked myself.

Everything about this visit was different. I hated it all. It was nothing like the others. As I read the first line, the cause for his defeat and exhaustion became obvious, blurring my vision and causing my eyes to sting from the tears that fell onto the page.

It's me. I'm wearing him down.

Please, Halo. I'm trying. I would love to see your face. Hear your voice. Rub your belly. And, kiss the baby to sleep. Please don't keep running away from me. I'm not here to harm you. I'm here to hold you, love you, and help you. I'm ready when you are. We can start by you telling me one thing... Who hurt you?

"See you tomorrow, Halo."

I reread the final question twice as the gloom of the evening rested on my shoulders. My intentions were never to cause Ledge any hurt or harm, but those were the results of my inactivity and silence. By saying nothing, I'd said far too much. By doing nothing, I'd done far too much. My aching heart left me with no choice but to fix it.

Suddenly, the urge to open the door transformed into a burning desire that could only be settled with action. Before I changed my mind or ran in the opposite direction, I twisted the locks and pulled until the setting sun exposed my face.

Stopping in his tracks, Ledge turned around slowly. Disbelief was written all over his handsome face. It forced him against his car as he bent forward with a hand on his head. Bewilderment was in every move he made.

I stepped up to the door's threshold. It was the closest I'd get to the outside world for the moment, but it was enough for me. Our eyes locked and we held one another's gaze until my vision blurred to the point that I couldn't see him. I couldn't see anything.

"My stepfather," I breathed out. The words were like blades to the throat.

"Huh?" He called out, pushing off the car and slowly walking toward me.

"My stepfather. That's– that's who hurt me."

Unable to maintain the lie that my high head and chin told of my confidence, I finally dropped them both. My shoulders sagged and my heart hurt, really hurt.

"May I?" He asked, referring to his closeness.

I nodded. It was impossible to respond verbally.

He etched away at the distance a little at a time.

"I'm not him, Halo."

"I know."

"Then, please... Please stop treating me like I am."

"I'm trying."

"Try harder for me, for the baby, for you."

"I will."

"Wipe those tears away, love. They have no use here. I'd do it myself if I didn't think you'd run back inside and lock the door on my ass," he chuckled.

"I'm sorry," I apologized, wiping my tears with the

back of my hands. "I know you think I'm some crazy girl and you're probably tired of me already."

"I'm the furthest from being tired of you, Halo. I haven't had enough of you, yet. I'm tired of not having more of you. That's all. That's it. And, I don't think you're crazy. I think you're fucking awesome, okay? I think you're special and somehow was made especially for me. Look at you," he gasped.

My skin tingled under his gaze. I wasn't sure what to do with myself.

"Can I touch you?"

Though he didn't quite understand, the question he'd posed meant more to me than he'd ever know. Besides when with him the night we conceived, there wasn't a time in my life that a man had asked for consent to touch my body. Whether it was an innocent hug or forced penetration, I never got the chance to accept or decline.

"A little."

Getting to say how much, how long, how often, or how not to, gave me the power that I'd always wanted and always needed.

"A little is enough for me," Ledge responded with a smile.

The dress that I wore was cut in the center, exposing most of my belly. His access was automatically granted. My dark, round belly was all his—*a little*.

His long, slim hands rested against my skin, causing me to experience every emotion imaginable in 1.5 seconds. But it was the overflow of love from a man I considered a stranger weeks ago that was most prominent. Through his consistency and determination, I'd grown closer to him, ultimately finding myself experiencing premature feelings that were as scary as they were intriguing.

Overstimulated and overwhelmed, I stepped back into my apartment. His hands fell to his waist as he nodded in understanding. My heart broke as I watched his smile drift away.

"I'm sorry."

"Stop apologizing," he demanded. "It's all good. Thank you for that. You've made my fucking day, pretty lady."

"I look forward to your visits," I admitted, cringing soon after.

Shut up. Say nothing else. I fussed.

"I look forward to the day that you let me inside. The day that I can share dinner with you, rub your belly, feel the baby's movement, shit like that."

"I know," I added with a pained expression. "It hurts to be such a disappointment."

"You're not a disappointment, Halo. Don't say that shit."

"Tomorrow."

"Tomorrow, what?"

"Tomorrow, I'll be ready."

"Ready for what?"

"For dinner."

"Yeah? Like, out here or in your crib?"

"Inside," I sniggered, finding his reaction hilarious. The look on his face was priceless.

"Fuck, I want to hug you right now."

"Please don't," I begged, my chest tightening at the thought. I'd had enough human contact for the day. Any more would send me spiraling.

"I won't. I won't. But, damn. Thank you. Thank you. I'll see you tomorrow at seven?"

"Seven."

"Any special requests? I can get anything you got on your mind. What does the baby like most?"

"Ice cream," shyly, I admitted.

"I can do ice cream after some real food."

"Okay."

"Okay."

"Okay," I repeated with a shrug, feeling the smile as it appeared on my face.

"Okay," he responded, all thirty-two of his teeth showing.

"Okay." *Stop saying that.* I forced myself to oblige.

"Aight. I'm leaving now."

"Okay," I voiced, again. *Halo, cut it out.*

"See you tomorrow."

Instead of saying anything at all, I shut the door. Once I'd locked it, I placed my back against it and my hands on my head. I wanted to scream, but nothing would come out.

Knock.

Knock.

The rattling of my door and the light knocking

scared a tiny bit of pee from me. I knew that I'd need to change my panties without even checking. A shower and some fresh threads were next on my agenda.

"Pretty lady," his voice rang out.

Why is he still here? I thought.

"Your food," he commented, answering my question.

I could hear the fading of his vocals, meaning he was already on his way to his car again. I waited until I heard the door shut and his engine roar before unlocking the door. It wasn't until he'd pulled off that I opened it and snatched my food off the porch. Before I could get back inside, Kamber's sassiness stopped me.

"Ummm hmmmm. Y'all real fucking cute. Maybe I need to take a page from your book so that my Knight dripped in gold jewelry can come save me from my first-floor apartment," she joked.

"Whatever, Kamber."

"Don't worry. I'll be over there as soon as you get off the clock. I heard y'all. I'm going to make sure you don't talk yourself out of this tomorrow. And, I'm going to get that baby's shit out of the front room. I know you haven't touched it, yet."

"How do you know that?" I challenged.

"Open the blinds and let me see."

"No."

"I thought so. I'll be over there tomorrow to transfer it to your bedroom. Don't try to do it yourself. I've seen every delivery that man has made and I know it's a lot by now."

"It is. I think I'm going to need a bigger apartment," I sighed.

"We both know you're not moving so we'll figure it out. Some of it can come over here until you need it if necessary."

"Thanks, Kamber."

"Girl, bye."

LEDGE + HALO

THE SHOWER and hot meal were everything I needed to prepare for a good night's rest. With me missing my evening nap, an early night was inevitable. Curled up in bed with a book from one of the many I'd purchased since finding out I was pregnant, I used the small flashlight to read the words on the page.

"But, mom, there's no more." I read aloud. "Have you taken a really good look, Ally?"

I lowered the light from the book to my belly. There was an incredible amount of movement, shifting my focus from the pages to my pregnant stomach. I wasn't sure what was going on in there, but it felt like a party.

"What are we doing in there, honey?"

Feet, hands, elbows, and knees pushed and stretched my skin.

"Are you trying to escape, little guy? We still have a few weeks to go. Don't you want to hang out with momma a little longer?"

Most days, I still couldn't believe that I'd be a mother soon. My growing belly was hardly enough to convince me. It was the highly active child that wiggled, flipped, and flopped in the late evening that made me a believer. There was no denying my new, endearing title while watching summersaults happen internally.

"Or are you ready to meet daddy, already? Mommy saw him today. He's so patient and so kind and so amazing. One day, we're going to be a big, happy family. Maybe give you a sibling. You'd like that?"

Though it was highly likely that this would be my only child, I couldn't help but dream. Ledge did that for me. He made me do something that I never did. Dream. I dreamed of the days when my illness wouldn't have me bound and I was free to live my life, with him and our child if it was possible. Somehow, someway, I knew that it was.

I'd enjoyed every bit of my pregnancy. It was something I wanted to experience more than once and with the same person. If fate would have it, it would happen. If not, then I was more than happy with the one I was carrying being my only child. A year ago, no one could convince me that I'd even have the chance to be a mother.

"Yeah, I'd like that as well. When mommy gets better, maybe we can tell dad all about it. What do you think? I think he'd like that idea. Mommy just has to get better first."

The book that I'd been reading to the baby was no longer of importance. I placed it on the bed beside me and focused on the performance inside my womb. The smile plastered on my face pained my muscles but refused to fade.

"Seriously, kid, what are you doing in there? Are you having fun at your solo celebration?"

Remembering that babies were sensitive to direct light, I quickly shut off the flashlight. Darkness coated the room as I scooted deeper into the bed and pulled the covers up to my chin. My right hand rested on my belly while my left lay flat against the sheets.

What are you doing? I wondered, Ledge crossing my mind.

The bed felt so much bigger and so much lonelier at once. A breath that I didn't realize I'd been holding was released as the hairs on my arms and the nape of my neck stood straight up. Small, fine bumps littered my skin. My body shivered though covered in a warmth that wasn't exactly provided by the comforter I was underneath. It was a rare and very peculiar warmth that could only be explained by the presence of one person. *Ledge*.

The smell of his cologne tickled my nostrils. Those perfect teeth and round, brown eyes made my heart flutter. *I miss him.* There was no doubt in my mind about it, but I hardly understood how. He'd come to my doorstep every day for the last week and all I'd given him was my silence until a few hours ago. Now, I wanted more. More of him. More of his time. More of his words. More of his hands. More of his heart.

He makes me feel so good inside. I swallowed back the glob of saliva that sat near my throat as I admitted to myself. Fear twiddled with my nerves but my sudden yearning for the father of my child had the upper hand.

Pretty lady. The name he'd given me caused low, belly-quaking sniggers to pierce the silence. *He thinks I'm pretty.* From the night I met him, it was easily concluded. But, upon seeing the look on his face as he openly admired me a few hours ago, it was made perfectly clear. Though it felt absolutely childish for loving that simple fact, it didn't make me love it any less.

Unable to settle in bed, I stretched and bent my legs again and again trying to determine which was more comfortable. *Ugh*, I scoffed, realizing I wouldn't find the comfort I was in search of. I flipped from one side to the other, closing my eyes and trying to envision the moment we spent together. It was swift, but it felt like an eternity that we stood face to face, eye to eye.

"I should just call him... or text him," I whispered, "What's the worst that could happen?"

I patted the bed beside me until my fingertips grazed my cell phone. When it unlocked, I pulled up my text threads. There were only two of them. One was from my midwife and the other was from Kamber. My phone was as dry as they came. It was pathetic, but it was life. With any luck, I was hoping to add another thread tonight.

> Hey. It's Halo.

I typed but quickly erased it.
"Too bland."

It's me.

"Me who?" I whispered, erasing the second message I'd typed.

It's Halo. Are you busy?

"He'll think I'm being nosey."

I miss you.

"You're really pushing it, Halo. That's not even like you."

Come over.

I erased it as soon as I finished typing it.

"So you can make him stand outside and talk to you, again?" I hissed.

Nevermind. I tossed the phone to the other side of the bed. Strangely, the comfort I'd been searching for had found me. I fluffed the pillow underneath my head and released the hot air that was building inside of me. *Baby steps,* I reminded myself before closing my eyes and trying my hardest to allow sleep into my life.

8

LEDGE

4:06 A.M.

The digital clock on my wall displayed the time as the blurriness of my sight subsided. My buzzing phone was the reason they were open to begin with. I grabbed it from the nightstand beside my bed and tapped the big green circle. Though I could hardly see, my fingers were programmed to work my phone's screen even in the darkest of spaces.

"Yeah?" I answered.

Silence.

"Hello?"

Silence.

Immediately, I was up with my back against the headboard of my bed. I could hear my beating heart as it galloped, forcing me to say something more. It was far too loud in the silence. I pushed the wetness around in my mouth as I prepared to speak again.

"Halo," I called out to her. "Is everything okay? Is the baby okay?"

I could feel her. She was becoming as familiar to me as I was to myself. Even twenty minutes in the opposite direction couldn't disturb the connection that we were developing. She didn't have to mumble a word and her contact didn't have to be saved for me to know that it was her. *I can feel you, pretty lady.*

"Talk to me," I commanded as gently as I possibly could. "Are you guys okay?"

"Yes."

I released a stream of air. The weary spell that the call casted upon me was lifted and replaced with joy. It didn't matter that it was 4:06 a.m., she'd called. She'd finally used my number after eight and a half months.

"Then, what's the matter?"

"I'm hungry."

My cheeks lifted and I could feel the air touching nearly all of my teeth. Since my discovery of the baby, I'd been waiting for a moment like this.

"Yeah?"

"Yes."

She was the most angelic, fragile being I'd ever encountered. I loved that about her. Her name suited her.

"What do you want to eat, pretty lady?"

"Is it too early for that ice cream?" She asked.

My smile widened as I shook my head, "Nah. It's not too early. What kind do you have in mind?"

"You're going to bring me some ice cream?" I could hear the excitement in her voice. It was also apparent that she hadn't just woken up. There wasn't a trace of sleep in her voice.

"Halo, have you been to sleep?"

"I can't."

"Why not?"

"I don't know."

"Does this happen all the time?"

"Just since yesterday."

"Will ice cream help?"

"I think so."

"Aight. I'm about to be on my way. You want to come home with me? Maybe that'll help you sleep? I have a few rooms. You can choose any one of them."

"I can't... I can't come outside," she reminded me.

"What kind of ice cream, love?"

"Cookies and cream."

"Aight. I'll be there in about thirty minutes. Wait up for me."

She ended the call without saying goodbye. I hadn't recalled getting dressed and out of the door so fast in my entire life. Yet, I was starting the engine and backing out of the driveway with the lights of my truck leading the way.

At four in the morning, my options were limited. Everything I passed once I hit the main roadways was closed. If she'd called a few hours later, then I would've had endless choices, but that wasn't the case. And, for now, I'd work with what I had.

Bingo, 24/7. Without a doubt, I knew they wouldn't let me down. The shitty ice cream section in most gas stations wasn't worth the visit. But *24/7* was unlike any of the others. Because they'd started in the heart of Dooley and gradually acquired locations in The Heights and Edgewood, they were accustomed to the pleasures of the hood. That's why they were thriving in the areas that rarely saw the selection they had in-store. They were always stocked on the hood's favorites no matter the location.

I shut off my engine and pushed the driver's door open. When I stepped down on the pavement, I realized I hadn't traded my Gucci slides for a pair of real shoes. Shaking my head, I couldn't help but laugh at my desperation. Halo could ask me to do a backward flip and I'd cut one. I'd never managed to complete one a day in my life but at this point, if she asked, I knew I'd make that shit happen.

Ding Dong. The loud, obnoxious bell sounded over my head when I entered the gas station. Bright lights reminded me that it was indeed four in the morning and I was supposed to be at home in bed somewhere. *Shit.* Their intensity caused squinting to minimize the effect.

I headed straight for the freezer that stretched along the right side of the store. Before I approached, I knew they had exactly what I was looking for. The freezer was enormous, much like one you'd find at a grocery store. One after the other, I combed the shelves with my eyes in search of a particular brand.

There we go. Cream of Berkeley stood out amongst the rest of the products. It was nostalgia at its finest. Summers were full of fat bellies that were stuffed with Cream of Berkeley when I was down that way with my grandfather while school wasn't in session. Me, Lawe, and our cousins would spend all our hard earned money on pints of our favorite flavors. Pralines and cream was mine. The caramel and pecan mashup was still unmatched 'til this day.

It was the first flavor my eyes landed on. I opened the freezer and grabbed a half gallon tub. Cookies and cream was right beside it. I grabbed two of those. I wanted my child to get accustomed to the caramel and its richness before they were even out of the womb. Homemade vanilla was always a hit and as classic as they came. I grabbed one of those just because. You could never go wrong with it.

On my way back to the front, I passed up all the good snacks. I had a sweet tooth as a kid but overcame it after coming to the conclusion that I hated dentist visits. Not because they were painful, but because it was embarrassing to open my mouth and listen to them count the number of cavities inside. Lawe and I both sported silver caps until our baby teeth fell out and we were given a fresh start. Since then, I've kept my cravings for sweets at a minimum.

"Will that be all for you?" The cashier asked.

"Yeah. That's it."

"How far along?" She chuckled.

"It's that obvious, huh?"

"Kind of. At this hour, especially."

"Eight months."

"Oh. Almost there. Are you excited?"

"You know what," humbly, I simpered, "I've never been happier or more excited about anything else in my life."

I just wish I had my mother to share this happiness with. My heart ached knowing that she'd never experience moments with my child. She wanted this so badly for me and for herself. Now that it was happening, she wasn't here. Crazily, my child had been conceived when she was alive and well. *Time a motherfucker.*

"This will be one lucky kid. I can see it in your eyes. What a blessing."

"For real."

I handed over a fifty from my sweats.

"Keep the change," I instructed, grabbing the bags she'd put the ice cream in and headed out the door.

My arms swung back and forward as thoughts of seeing Halo's pretty face and that big belly of hers. The soft melody of Usher's *Superstar* escaped my lips in the form of whistling.

"I'll be your groupie, baby," I sang, opening the door to the truck.

The whistling continued with frequent appearances from my horrible vocals.

"As your number one fan, I'll do all that I can to show you how super you are."

I didn't need music from the stereo or my phone. I was having my own little concert, completely acapella. One song after another, I whistled and sang my heart out until I reached my destination. The slightly illuminated apartment on the first-floor that I'd only seen the outside of let me know that Halo was up waiting for me.

Swiftly, I shut off the truck and hopped out. With both bags in my hand, I made my way to the door, still whistling. This time it was "Suffocate", a song I hadn't heard in some time.

"I can't breathe when you touch meeeee," lowly, I hummed.

Before I was able to lift my hand to knock on the door, I heard the locks turning. Barely a second later and it was being pulled open to reveal the most precious gem ever placed on earth. Shyly, she wrapped her arms around her body, a self-soothing method that I was all too familiar with. My mother had done the same almost too often.

"I got you a few extras too, including my favorite, pralines and cream."

"Thank you," she sighed, dropping one arm and extending the other.

It was apparent that my intentions to stay were completely out of the question.

"Can I come in?" Biting the bullet, I asked.

"It's dark out."

I nodded. This wasn't new information to me. "I know."

"Tomorrow? Seven? Dinner?"

"Halo, it's four something in the morning," I petitioned. "I'm sleepy. I can park it on the couch and not bother you. Before you know it, the sun will be up and I'll be on my way."

"I'm sorry," she whispered, stepping further into the house with the ice cream.

Prior to any words surfacing on my end, the door slammed in my face. Though I was sure it wasn't with ill intent, it didn't stop me from gritting my teeth from pure frustration and exhaustion. *Patience*. I redirected myself. Releasing a harsh breath, I made my way back to the truck.

The twenty-minute drive was too much to even comprehend at the moment. The excitement I once felt had dissolved and exhaustion was now at the forefront. I'd never driven while tired and I wouldn't start. If I couldn't sleep it off in Halo's, then my truck would suffice.

I lifted a leg to climb into the truck and then the other before locking myself inside. The Glock on my hip was pressing up against my skin, exposing me to instant discomfort. I pulled it from my waistline and sat it on my lap as I reclined my seat. For a brief second, I debated on starting the vehicle or not. But, once I rationalized, I knew that there was no way around it.

It was mid-October and the nights were nothing like

the afternoons and evenings. They required sleeves and sometimes the heat. That's exactly what I reached for when the lights came on, signifying the start of my truck's engine. I twisted the knobs to reach my desired temperature. Everything about the decision proved to be perfect. The warmth paired with the coziness was completely unexpected but utterly appreciated.

I leaned my head against the headrest behind me and scooted slightly down the seat, hoping that my slouched position would bring me comfort. Out of sheer habit, I shoved my hands down into my sweats. I wasn't sure what the hell it was about it, but it was extremely soothing when my hands rested at the top of my thighs while I slept in the upright position. It was as close to stretching out as my long limbs would accomplish and that was fine with me.

When my eyes finally closed, images of Halo appeared behind my lids. Her cocoa-colored skin was flawless. The new style that she wore and kept pulled off her face, highlighted her big, fluffy lips, round eyes, and perfect nose. With our genes combined, our child was bound for beauty. If they looked anything like their mother and happened to be a girl, I'd have to keep my pistols locked and loaded.

The world had a way of either giving her type everything it had to offer on a silver, diamond-encrusted platter or dragging them through its streets while dangling them in front of predators who only cared to use, abuse, abandon, or imprison their prey. From the trauma written all over Halo's poor posture, face, fears, and lack of livelihood, it was very easily determined that shit hadn't been handed to her on the platter. She'd been hunted down and wounded like the prey she was.

I could still feel her presence. Her closeness was soothing. Calmly, I waited as sleep overcame me. And, like a thief in the night, it crept up on me with me hardly noticing. It wasn't long before my mouth was slightly ajar and light snores escaped.

LEDGE + HALO

Boom.

Boom.

Boom.

"Shi— Shit. What's—?" I jumped from my sleep at the sound of someone banging on my window.

I cleared the blurriness of my vision by rubbing both eyes with my right hand, one after the other. My gun sat on my lap, tightly clutched in my palm. My index finger rested on the trigger, ready and willing to pull it if necessary.

My eyes darted around the darkness. It became painfully clear that I hadn't managed to get much sleep. The sun was still hiding and the moon was still glowing in the sky. Tired eyes searched for the source of my misery and the reason I was awake instead of resting. It wasn't until my eyes landed on Halo's front door did I realize where the disturbance had come from.

One side to the other, she bounced on the tips of her toes as if it would keep her warm. Inside her apartment with the front door ajar, she waved me over. Too tired to even think straight, I lowered the passenger window to communicate. Stepping out would require far too much energy.

"You good?"

She nodded, still waving her hand.

"Then, what's up?"

It wasn't until her neck stretched toward whatever space beyond the front door of her apartment that I understood what was happening. I could feel my eyes grow nearly twice their size while I attempted to process the information being received.

"Come in," she clarified, "It's really freezing cold."

It's not. I reasoned, knowing that it was more than likely her nerves that had her temperature low and her body quivering.

"You sure, pretty lady?" I sighed, unsure of what to make of everything.

On one hand, I'd be delighted to take the couch over the driver's seat, but not at the expense of her mental and emotional health. I was cool if she wouldn't be. It wasn't the first time I'd slept in a vehicle. It probably wouldn't be the last if I kept living long enough.

Up and down, she moved her head. She was convincing enough as she walked away from the door and disappeared into her apartment. I took that as my queue to get my ass out and follow. I shut off the truck and locked it up behind me.

As I approached the small set of steps in front of her spot, she finally reappeared. This time, she was wearing a long sweater over the dress that stopped near her ankles. Even with the cover-up, she couldn't conceal those curves. They were determined to hold their own space in my heart and hadn't failed in doing so.

"Good morning," I greeted her at the door.

She said nothing, stepping back as I stepped inside.

Her frame felt so much smaller in front of mine. I peered down at her curious eyes that stared up at me. She was waiting for something from me that I wasn't quite sure of. Maybe it was more words or maybe it was for me to move my ass out of the way so she could close the door. Nevertheless, I stood there, holding my ground, allowing my heart to lead since my head was in shambles.

As I leaned forward, questions surfaced that I didn't have the answer to. *What the fuck you doing, nigga? What is this? You're going to scare the damn girl. Fall back.* But, instead of taking heed to the warnings that were going off in my head, I continued on my path, finally ending with her lips on mine.

Time stood still. I felt like I'd been set ablaze. Every inch of my body burned. My heart slowed to a creep, feeling as if it would stop at any second. There was a pain within me that could only be described as one that was a result of utter bliss. Nothing in my life had ever felt so good that it hurt.

My soul stirred. For the first time in my life, it was wrapped in the warmth and fragility of another being. Without a doubt, at that moment, I knew that I'd love this woman for a lifetime. And, slowly but surely, that lifetime was beginning. *Patience.*

Like it was yesterday, I revisited a rare moment in history akin to the one before me. It was the moment our lips touched once before, almost nine months ago. The night I'd taken her home and we'd made music with our bodies like two long-lost lovers reuniting for the very first time.

My hands raised, slowly, resting on the sides of her face. When her lips parted, I tried to rearrange the teeth in her mouth and the tongue that sat between them. I familiarized myself with every inch of her mouth reachable, satisfying a craving I'd been suppressing for far too long. It wasn't until my body begged for the oxygen it was deprived of that I released her.

Wiping my lips and stepping deeper into her place, I discovered the manners my mother had given me and showed my gratitude for far much more than the moment before us. Halo was stunned in place, unable to move. She continued looking up at me, her neck still stretched and her head still leaning backward.

"Thank you," I breathed out.

"Led— Ledge, I—." She couldn't make out the words she wanted to say.

"When you give me the chance, I'm going to love you down pretty lady, until your heart can't take anymore."

Uninterested in sharing any more words with her, I pushed forward into her living room. Her home was everything that I'd expected. The neutral tones were parallel to her personality. From the moment I walked in, anything and everything on my mind took its rest. Though a bit stuffy for my liking, everything else was perfect. I quickly noted the observation, wondering if it was possible her iron was low and the need for constant warmth was more than a personal choice.

Halo darted past me and stood next to the couch where she was instructing me to lay. She lifted the oversized throw from the arm and uncoiled her arms. I stepped forward and accepted the blanket she was offering me. As I did, I noticed the open window beside us. The fresh air was cool, yet refreshing. Her eyes followed mine, landing on the slightly ajar window too.

"Mind if I raise it a little more?" I asked.

"It's fine."

For a second, she stood with a bowed head and trembling hands. So unsure of what to do with herself or what to do with someone in her home, she'd frozen.

"You sure about this?"

"Goodnight," Halo responded, "Good morning. I meant good—."

"Go get some rest, pretty lady. See you when the sun rises."

She scurried around the table, in the opposite direction of where I stood. When her knee bumped the edge of the second table which was slightly taller and slimmer than the one right beside it, I cringed. Slightly, she edged forward and applied pressure to her other leg to relieve it briefly. However, she never stopped moving. Secondhand embarrassment toyed with my existence. Though there was no reason for her to feel ashamed, somehow, I knew she did.

Shit, I'm tired. I thought as I sunk into the softest couch my ass had ever touched after raising the window a little more. *No wonder she doesn't want to leave this motherfucker.* Her crib was checking the boxes.

A cozy ass vibe. A soft couch. Cleanliness. A million candles and plug-ins to make sure it smelled nice all the time. Airy and spacious. It was a broke nigga's dream, but luckily I didn't fall on that end of the spectrum.

Even with one side of the living room occupied by baby shit, it still didn't feel crowded. A bit stuffy, but it had nothing to do with the circumference. It had everything to do with the air and its quality. It was more than likely she was running the heat.

It was far too soon to be running it inside, but it wasn't my crib and I didn't have enough details to know if I should be turning the shit off or not, yet. I saved the questions that arose for the morning when I was rested and she had gotten acclimated to my presence in her home. For now, I wanted one thing and that was some sleep.

9

LEDGE

Feeling the warmth of her presence lingering, I opened my eyes. Just as I'd imagined, there she was, sitting in front of me. I found the strength to smile as my mouth widened with a yawn. She'd thought about this for some time and finally had the courage to see it through. It was obvious by the twiddling of her fingers as she sat in the chair in front of me. It was a chair that wasn't anywhere in sight when I laid down to rest on the comfortable couch.

All I could see was flawless dark skin that stretched to accommodate our child. It was blocking almost everything else in my view. She was so close, and I could tell by the look on her face that she wanted to be closer but couldn't bring herself to invade any more of my personal space. She respected boundaries because she had so many. I wanted her to know that my space was hers and I didn't mind her in it whenever she wanted or needed to be.

"Hi."

I could hear it in her voice. She was frightened.

"Come 'er," I grunted, reaching forward and pulling her by the hand.

She stood straight up, confused as to what she should do next. She was looking for direction and I was looking for reasons to soften my morning wood. Unfortunately, she gave me none. The silk pajama number she'd changed into with the shirt that stopped above her belly and made her breasts look like melons I wanted to suck on, only making shit worse. Though it was complete with a pair of pants, the way that her hips were protruding on both sides, I knew that her ass was poking in the back.

With her hand in mine, I turned her around to confirm. Then, slowly, I guided her closer to the couch, waiting until the back of her legs touched it. She lowered her body onto the couch once she realized what I was asking of her.

"Lay down with me," I told her, patting the space in front of me.

I reached behind me and removed the large couch pillow from the back of the couch to make more room. It freed up a ton of space, allowing us both to get comfortable. I debated on removing the second pillow on the other end of the couch, but our legs didn't need as much room as our upper body.

Once she'd gotten in the perfect position, Halo laid still. I chuckled, noticing just how inexperienced she was. It made me wonder if she'd ever been with anyone before the night that we shared. My suspicions were leading me to believe that she hadn't, though she was a fully grown woman with pussy that could bring me to my knees on any given day.

"Can I?" I asked, before lowering my hand to her exposed stomach.

Her nod was slow and theatrical, giving me permission that I felt needed to be granted. I wasn't sure what Halo was dealing with, but I wanted to respect the walls she'd built and chip away at them until they came crashing down. Forcing myself over them or knocking them down wasn't my intention. I wanted to be let in, little by little, because I knew that the reward would be worth the wait.

As my fingertips grazed her skin, her body stiffened. My heart shattered a thousand times as I recalled the words she'd said to me, yesterday. I wasn't sure why or how, but they'd escaped me until this moment. I imagined the excitement and relief I felt from her agreeing to dinner and letting me inside had overshadowed all else. But, now that her words had returned, I felt sick to my heart.

My stepfather.

"How'd he hurt you?" The words surfaced without my permission.

There was a long, agonizing silence that lingered far too long before she finally spoke. My hand continued to caress her skin, assuring her that everything was okay. As long as I was by her side, there wasn't anything she had to worry about.

"He raped me... over and over and over and over again," she confessed.

In a flash, I was up on my feet and sliding back into my slippers. I patted my pockets and the hoodie I wore for my keys. Staying was no longer an option. I had shit to handle and it wouldn't get done laying on her couch.

"Ledge," she whispered.

"You seen my keys?" I questioned, patting my chest and legs.

"Ledge," she said to me, this time a little louder.

"Halo, my keys. And, what's the nigga's name? Address? Whatever information you've got on him," I barked, becoming frustrated.

But not with her, with the situation itself. The fact that a sick-ass individual had touched her brought me to the point of needing to vomit. I grew sicker as the seconds ticked away.

"Ledge."

"My keys. Where the fuck are my keys?" I asked myself, unable to think clearly.

"Ledge."

"Is that nigga still breathing?" I looked up at her and asked, feeling the crease in my brows as my expression hardened. The muscles in my face flexed as I tightened my jaw and inhaled.

"Ledge!" She yelled.

For the first time, she commanded my attention and it wasn't with her silence. Everything stopped as I watched her lift her upper body from the couch and sit in an upright position. Her palms lowered to her knees as she bowed her head and began to speak again.

"I'm sorry for yelling," she apologized.

The world doesn't deserve her. She was rare, celestial. Incredible. There was no way someone had mistreated such a pure heart. I wouldn't believe it and I knew that I wouldn't sleep too well at night until they paid for their sickness.

"I just need you to listen to me."

"I'm listening."

She had my undivided attention, always had. I was just lost at the moment. Lost in my anger. Lost in her pain. And, looking at her broken and battered, I prayed that I didn't get lost again. When she raised her head and our eyes met, I knew that through them I'd find my way. That's exactly what I needed to keep me from running to find that nigga on foot. Hunt him down like a dog and gut him like a fucking fish.

"After I tell you this, I don't want to talk about it no more today. I just need to be upfront and honest with you about my condition and how it came about. Besides Kamber and my grandmother, no one knows. My grandmother died when I was nineteen. I've been this way since. She had me since I was fourteen. I'd come to live with her after a hospital stay and emergency surgery to rid me of a pregnancy that I knew nothing about.

"My stepfather had been molesting me since the age of six when my mother first started working overnight. He was always drinking from the bottles on the counter —the grown-up juice. It made him want to do grown-up things but my mother wasn't there. That left him with me. It started with a few touches and him using objects to stick inside of me.

"Then, it graduated to him forcing himself inside of my mouth. I guess after a while, even that wasn't enough. Within a few months of the abuse starting, he penetrated me. It was the worst day of my life. Around the age of ten is when I found the courage to tell my mother. She did nothing.

"By the age of twelve, she hated me because her husband would rather have me than her. She turned to drugs. By the age of fourteen, she was always too out of it to care and my stepfather had made me his partner. He slept in my bed each night. There was no longer any use in hiding it. My mother was always self-medicating. She didn't know where she was half the time.

"One sober morning of hers, I happened to wake up with pain in my stomach that had me hollering to the top of my lungs. It just wouldn't go away. Eventually, she took me to the emergency room and that's when I discovered I was pregnant. The nurse on duty that night quickly picked up on the situation at hand.

"The second she got me alone, she asked if I was okay and if I was safe. I started talking and never stopped.

That day, I was taken away from my mother. The same day, she overdosed on her drug of choice. It wasn't until two weeks later that I was in my grandmother's custody. Prior to her rescuing me from my broken home, I had no idea she existed. She quickly became the best thing that ever happened to me.

"She didn't know the extent of my trauma or what all went on. After seeing how withdrawn I was, how I lacked social skills, and how afraid I was of just opening up and being a kid, she finally asked. The night that I told her, she went to sleep and never woke up. She died of a heart attack. I broke her heart. She died of a broken heart. When she left, I felt alone with no one in this world.

"To protect myself, I buried myself inside and haven't been out. The night I met you was the first time I'd gone outside by choice since I was nineteen. Before that, I'd only left my grandmother's home to move here after a few years alone there. The space was too big for me. I didn't need all of that room.

"Target, that was my second time being out. I can't help but wonder if this thing between you and me was just fate. Because, when I step foot out of my door, you're there it seems. And, I never, ever step foot out of my door."

"What's his name?"

"Ledge, please."

"I'm going to be back but I need to go somewhere right quick," I assured her, pacing the floor while trying to figure out where I last had my keys.

"Ledge, I don't want you to get into any trouble. I'm

getting better. Everything is going to be okay. I can't let you get in trouble on my behalf."

"When you told me that shit Halo, what did you expect me to do then? Hmmm?"

"Ledge," she breathed, again.

She'd said more to me in the last few minutes than she ever had. I didn't even know she could talk so damn much. Right now though, the only thing I wanted to hear was where that nigga lived.

"What you want me to do? Ignore everything you just said? I don't understand. What are you expecting me to do?"

"Lay down with me."

Her words stopped me in my tracks. She'd surprised herself with them.

"I mean—, I just—I," she stuttered.

The last thing I wanted was for her to regret expressing herself or asking for my presence when it was needed. I quickly removed the hoodie from my body, pulling it over my head and flinging it on the chair she'd been sitting in. I shoved my sweats to my ankles and slid them off with my shoes. In my white tee and briefs, I climbed back on the couch behind her.

"Then, that's what I'll do," I responded, finally, pulling her down with me.

Without hesitation, I wrapped my arm around her with my hand landing on her belly. My mind was still swarmed with thoughts that I'd refrain from speaking out loud, but I tried my hardest to silence them. I closed my eyes, sighing heavily.

"I'm sorry." Halo broke the silence.

"For what, pretty lady?"

"Ruining your morning."

"You haven't. I'm just... I'm tight right now, love."

"I feel it."

"Listen," I cleared my throat and grabbed her chin. Gently, I turned her around to face me. I needed her to hear my words and understand them clearly.

"At this point, I'm locked in, aight? Like, locked the fuck in. And, I'd kill anything moving about you and this little one." I pointed to her stomach while pausing.

"I want you to know that nothing will happen to either of you while you're on my watch. And, from this day forward, y'all both on it. Shit, been on it since I found out about y'all. There's nothing in this world that will stop me from keeping you two safe and unharmed. Nobody. Nobody will ever have the chance to do that shit, again. You hear me?"

She nodded. Words didn't surface, but I didn't need them to either. As long as she heard me, that was all that mattered.

"You can go outside, stand in the rain, roll around in the snow, ride with the top off, feel the wind in your fingers, feel the wind in your hair, have as much fun as you'd like and just be free. You can do that Halo, as long as I'm at your side. I won't stop trying until you've released whatever is keeping you bound in here." I tapped her chest, the area near her heart.

"Aight?"

Up and down, she nodded, again. Drawn to her, I

lowered my lips until they reached hers. She opened for me, wide and ready to receive my love. The fire inside of me had been reignited. I could feel my dick as it hardened in my briefs.

"I was your first, huh?" I pulled away to ask, still not believing how much God had favored me with this one.

"Yes, but—."

I silenced her with another kiss. Whatever she was about to say didn't matter. I wanted her to realize what our time together all those months ago meant. I could only hope it was a step in the right direction and toward her healing.

"Take these off," I told her, tugging at her pants and not giving her a chance to actually act on it.

Without her help, I managed to get them over her ass and down her legs. She wore nothing beneath them. Her thirst was evident at that moment, forcing me to pull away from her lips, again.

"When you want some dick, pretty lady, open your mouth and use your words."

Unmoving, she froze in place as her eyes shifted everywhere except in my direction. Sensing her shame and coming to terms with the fact that she wasn't ready to take such a huge step, I cupped her chin and brought her lips to mine, again.

I freed her face from my grasp and my hand began to roam her body. Just like the books I was reading daily to better understand her and my new role as a father, I wanted to study her for the rest of my days. Every day that she woke up a new version of herself, I wanted to be taught a new lesson. Get to know every single person she grew to be or regressed to meet. I wanted them all. I wanted her; *everything included*.

The warmth of her pussy radiated, leading me straight to the predestined land. From the moment I met her at the bar, I knew that I'd be there. And, after I'd finally visited, I knew that I'd be returning. What I didn't know is that it would take almost nine months and a child would be involved. However, I wasn't complaining at all about our nontraditional path. It was fitting for her lifestyle and the situation was highly adaptable for me.

Halo parted her legs, slightly, giving my fingers the space they needed to explore her warmth and wetness. My thumb landed on her clit. The swollen nub pierced the air, making its presence known. Satisfying its hunger for attention I applied light pressure and circled it.

Once.

Twice.

Three times.

"Ahhhh," Halo sighed into my mouth.

And your last. There was no way I would be letting anyone else inside of Halo. Possessiveness wasn't a trait of mine, but I didn't mind exercising it when it came down to her. I couldn't help but feel as though any other human on the planet would be undeserving of the treasure before me. It was necessary for me to protect her heart and her body from all hurt, harm, and danger. That included her pussy. *My pussy.*

My index and middle fingers joined forces to invade her deepest crevice. The snugness of her pussy wrapped them both tightly as they toured her tunnel. Combining the pressure of my thumb and the exploration of my fingers forced Halo to surrender everything she'd been holding onto since the first time we were intimate.

"Let it go," I whispered in her mouth before lowering my head to catch the one breast that had freed itself from her top.

As if I was trying to extract milk reserved for our child, I sucked her titty. She began squirming, unable to remain still as pleasure hit her body in waves, nearly consuming her. Her lower half worked against the strokes of my fingers as she rode them to oblivion.

"Oh my God. Please," she cried out, squeezing her eyelids together.

"It's best to leave other niggas out of this," I chuckled, picking up the pace.

I was ready to send her into orbit, to a world far beyond the one we lived in. One that was made especially for us that we could visit when the real world became too much for either of us to stomach.

"Leeeeeeeedddge," Halo called my name as her body curved and veins appeared near her temple.

Simultaneously, the levees broke. The sound of gushing fluids caused a constriction in my chest. I instantly felt awful for ruining her couch. *Fuck, I forgot she had a sprinkler on her.* At that moment, I knew I'd be paying for a new couch or getting the one she had cleaned because I had every intention of wringing her dry of every ounce of liquid her pussy could conjure. By the time I was done with her, she'd be severely dehydrated and shaking.

"Don't ever take so long to get at me again," I gritted, hovering over Halo as she tried her hardest to weather the storm I'd created between her legs.

I took her lips into my mouth again and continued to explore the bottom set. They were so fluffy. Her pussy was so fucking fat. Obesity at its finest and I couldn't wait to have my serving. For now, though, it was dick that I wanted to feed it.

I lifted her right leg and rested it on my shoulder. The briefs that I wore slid down easily, freeing my manhood. It sprung up the second the threads it was confined to were lowered. Her lubrication was utilized well. It made the strokes of my dick smooth and uninterrupted.

The anticipation on Halo's face sent me on a high that I'd forever chase. She was waiting and she was ready for me. The pained expression revealed everything that her words hadn't. She wanted every inch of dick that I had to give and I had a lot of them. Halo was a big girl and I had no doubt about her being able to accommodate them all. She'd done it before. There would be no problem with her doing it again.

Refusing to make her wait any longer I tapped her box. Careful, making sure to land on her clit, I prolonged the orgasm that she was still tingling from. I watched her pussy muscles as they contracted. It was a divine sight.

"Ummmmm," she moaned. Her body jerked forward as the waves continued to hit her.

When I could no longer stand it anymore, I entered her canal, head first until I hit rock bottom. *Goddamn.* As quickly as I'd entered, I removed myself, knowing that I was liable to end everything if I stayed a second longer or made any sudden movement.

My dick was covered in her slipperiness. Peering at the completely covered piece of dark, veiny meat, I groaned. There was no avoiding it. I was going to cum when I reentered her pussy and I was going to cum fairly quick. Her pussy didn't play fair. It really didn't. With the new information I'd received about me being the only nigga in this shit only made matters worse. There was no winning for me in this situation.

"Ummmmm. Yesss." Her voice was like silk against the skin. *Soft and inviting.*

Halo's foot rested in the crook of my neck. As I entered her oasis again, I tried my hardest to focus on them and their adorable features to take my attention away from the insanely tight and moist walls that I was between. White toes. Of course she was the kind to rock those. Though I was sure she did them herself one wouldn't have been able to tell. It looked like professional work. Just like her pussy, they looked edible.

Fuck. This isn't helping. My thoughts dragged on as I found myself lifting Halo's foot slightly higher and into my mouth. Every inch of her body, I wanted to taste. One by one, I rolled my tongue around and sucked on each toe.

"Yesss. Yessssssss. Ledg—."

Her pussy rewarded me with reinforced walls and

thick creaminess that spilled onto my thighs and down my nutsack.

"This shit pathetic," I admitted, squeezing my lids together to keep from looking down at the mess I knew she'd made. "Shit, Halo."

"Ledge," she cried, "It's happening again."

"Let that shit go," I instructed, finally opening my eyes and allowing her foot to fall back into the crook of my neck. "I'm bout to fucking blow."

There was always warning before destruction. Halo came undone underneath me. Her sprinkler forcefully pushed me from her pussy. I was determined to leave my legacy inside of her once again. I lodged my dick so deep inside her, I swear I felt the warmth of her soul as my rockets launched.

"Ahhhhh. Fuck," lowly, I grumbled. Ridiculousness was the only way to describe what I said and felt.

Keeping my dick to myself would be a problem. Keeping my seeds from floating in her womb would be a problem. Keeping her belly from poking out each year would be a problem. Honestly, it was hers and not mine because no pussy on the planet had any business being that fucking spectacular. How could she blame me for anything that happened after this point?

I fell beside Halo, wrapping my arms around her in the process. As I felt movement from the location of my hand on her stomach, I was reminded of the conversation I'd had with Luca's wife the previous day. However, excitement clouded my consciousness and left me with a beaming smile on my face.

"They're moving?" I whispered as if the sound of my voice would make the movement stop.

"Yes. They're moving," Halo confirmed.

Slowly, I slid down the couch until my head was near her belly. Amazed at the shape of her belly and the way it changed every few seconds, my mouth hung wide open.

"What do you think we're having?" I wanted to know what her prediction was.

"I hope we're carrying a boy," she responded.

"I thought the same thing, but a daughter would be fire. Just watching her grow. Hopefully, she looks like her mother."

"I don't want a daughter," she stated, dryly.

"Why not? What's wrong with a daughter? I thought every woman wanted a mini-me?"

I placed my hands on the places that stuck out a bit more than others.

"Not every woman has experienced what I have as a daughter," she sighed. "I'd rather not birth someone who can possibly go through the same."

"As much as I want to be offended by your remark, I get it. Never think that I'm that nigga or what happened to you will happen to our daughter. If we have a girl, she will be guarded to the best of my ability. Home will be her safe space. Nothing will happen to her while she's there. Just like not all women have experienced what you have, not all men are like the monster that you experienced. I'm far from that. I'd never do anything to our daughter other than love her unconditionally. That's all

I'll have to give her is love. Do you want more children, Halo?"

"I never thought I'd have children. Now that I'm expecting it's all I can think about. I was an only child. I hated it. I didn't have anyone. I still don't."

"You have me now. I'm here. Forevermore. You can bet your last dollar on that. Whether it's together or as friends. You can count on me, Halo. I won't hurt you, pretty lady. I won't let you down. I don't want this to be our only child, either. I want more. As many as I'm given honestly; the chances of one of them being a girl is just as much as them being a boy. I need you to understand that and to trust that they're safe with me."

She remained silent as I watched her belly move.

"I'm scared." Her words pierced my heart. "I'm scared all the time."

"Halo."

"I'm scared right now. I'm scared for when the baby comes. I'm scared of the present. I'm scared of my past. I'm scared of my future. I'm just...I'm always scared and I'm tired."

"You don't have to be scared. You shouldn't be scared. The unknown is a scary place, but it's not that bad. It's better to embrace it than to run from it and that's what you've been doing. You have to face it head on and I swear to you shit will be better. You've been here and alone for so long that fear is your comfort zone. We're going to work on getting you out of there and out of here."

"Okay."

"We can start by making sure you and the baby are straight. My brother, Luca, his wife Ever wants me to hit her up this morning. She's gotten us set up with a birthing team. You won't have to worry about the hospitals."

"A home birth. That's what I want, Ledge."

"Then that's what you're going to get. I'm going to take care of everything. Aight? I'm going to call her right now to see if we can get them out here today. I want to know what's going on with this little being in your belly. Make sure you guys are both in good health."

"I try to eat healthy and take the vitamins they suggest in the pregnancy group that I'm in."

"That's good, pretty lady. Hopefully, that's been exactly what y'all need," I said as I reached over her and grabbed my phone.

I scrolled through until I reached the newest contact on my list. I tapped Ever's name and then once more to initiate a call. When it connected, I placed the phone on speaker so that we could both hear what was being said.

"Ledge, good morning," she answered. Though there was cheer in her tone, she remained as calm and collected as the man she'd married.

"Morning, Ever. I'm here with Halo. I was telling her about what we discussed yesterday. Any progress?"

"Yes. Of course. I was waiting on your call this morning. There is availability this evening at six. How does that sound to you?"

"That's cool," I assured her, making a mental note to clear my schedule for the day. Lawe could hold it down for me. Today, my priorities revolved around Halo and our child.

"Hi, Halo. How are you momma? How are you feeling? Is there anything I can do for you before the six o'clock hour?"

"Hi," shyly, she spoke into the phone, "Do you have children?"

"Yes. I have a gang of them and I'm pregnant right now. When this one gets here, I'll have six in total. One of them is with us in spirit."

"I don't know if I have everything I need. I have a lot of things, but I don't know if it's just a lot of things I think I'll need or things that I'll really, really need."

"I can come over and go through everything with you to make sure you're all set. On your birth team, you'll have a doula, a midwife, and a natural medicine doctor. While I'm there, we can fill out your paperwork and start listing any questions you might have for them before they arrive. How about I come around four? That'll give us two hours together before they come."

"I'd love that," she answered with a smile, shocking the shit out of me.

It was becoming very obvious that she welcomed feminine energy and company. It was masculinity that scared her shitless.

"How do you feel about a plus one? I was on the other end with Lyric, my sister-in-law and best friend. She happens to be Ledge's sister, too," Ever giggled, "She wants to lend a helping hand. She has a little one, too, so she can be my second set of eyes."

"Yes," she answered right away.

My baby needs friends, I concluded rather quickly.

"Good. Good. I didn't know and wanted to make sure it was okay."

"Halo is a loner, sis. But, I think she's been waiting for the opportunity to be a part of a circle."

"Shhhh," Halo whispered, tapping me on the shoulder.

"Awwwwww," Ever responded, "Girl, you are part of a very tight circle now. Don't worry. We've got you. I'll see you at four, okay?"

"Okay."

"Ledge, please send me the address and details beforehand. Alright?"

"Yeah. I got you."

We ended the call, simultaneously. I lifted my head and stared down at a nervous Halo.

"What's the matter?"

"You think they're going to think I'm weird?"

She gnawed on her bottom lip. I felt inclined to kiss away her stressful habit. When I retracted after joining our lips together, I continued to gaze in her direction.

"No one is going to think you're weird, pretty lady. You're not. You're just a loner. Stop thinking that about yourself, aight? There's nothing weird or wrong about you. You're perfect. I see it and they will too."

"I've just never...I've never had company other than Kamber."

"And me."

"And you, now."

"You're not weird, Halo. I promise. You're just really really reserved. A little fragile and very quiet until you feel comfortable. That's a lot of people out here."

"You were right."

"About what?"

"Me waiting for the opportunity to be a part of something bigger than myself. A circle. Friends with women who can relate to me a little. I always felt like people were overwhelming and I still do, but I crave community sometimes. It would make me feel less like an alien and more like a person."

"You don't feel like a person?"

"No. Not really. I don't know. The baby helps. A lot."

"Yeah?"

"Yes. I feel like a woman for the first time. I feel useful like I have a purpose. I love that feeling."

"Good, because you might be feeling that shit pretty often after this one."

"Huh?" She didn't quite understand.

"Nothing. I'm just happy the baby makes you feel exactly how you should. But, pregnant or not, you're still useful to the world. You still have a purpose. Don't ever think that you don't have a place here. You do. From the looks of it, it's in my heart. But, that's just a start, Halo. you can be as meaningful and as impactful as you want to be."

"I only care to impact the lives of the people that matter to me. People like Kamber, you, and the baby."

"Meeee?" I yelled, loudly, making her cheeks flush a

shade of purple as she tried to cover her face.

"You want to impact little ole' me?" I joked, pulling her hands down so that she was forced to look at me.

"Stop it."

"Why me?"

"Because...I don't know."

"You know. Talk to me, pretty lady. Make a nigga feel good. Let a nigga know his efforts haven't been in vain."

"They haven't been."

"Yeah?"

"I wait for you by the window every evening. When I wake up, you're the first thing on my mind. When I lay down for bed, you're the last thing I'm thinking of. When I close my eyes, it's you that appears. At night, my dreams are filled with moments that we share, building and creating things beyond my imagination. Like a family. A home. A life together.

"Sometimes, I cry knowing that the normalcy that I dream of in my sleep is impossible for me and being the woman that you could love for a lifetime is just too big of a task for me to fulfill. Not contacting you wasn't all about the baby. It was about me, too. Knowing that I was as messed up as I am and could not be someone you deserved made my heart hurt."

"I'm not asking you to be anyone other than yourself. I like you just the way you are. Whatever you've dreamed of, it's possible to make it a reality. Even if we have to tailor it a little bit, that's our damn business. I've never been into traditional shit. Let's make this work... our way."

"Okay."

"You trying to fuck with a nigga for a lifetime?"

"I'd like that." She blushed.

"Me too. I want us to try to figure this shit out together. I'm as lost as you are when it comes to this parenting thing, but I don't want to do it separately when we have the chance to try getting it right together."

"Or wrong," she sniggered.

"Ah. She ain't got no faith in us. I don't think we're that bad. A kid can't be too hard to figure out."

"People do it every day. I just want to do it right. So much went wrong in my world."

"We have the rest of forever to right those wrongs, pretty lady. And, I damn sure plan to try."

We both fell into a welcomed silence.

"I need you to take off for the day."

"I did last night when I told you that I'd let you in for dinner."

"Good. I'll reimburse you for the hours you've lost."

"I feel sticky," she sighed.

"We need to bathe. Where are our towels and shit? I'll get them together and meet you in the bathroom. Where is it, anyway?"

"You can enter from my bedroom or the hallway. You won't miss it if you head that way," she informed me, pointing toward the hallway to the left of the door.

"The linen?"

"In the dryer. I got really nervous about dinner tonight and rewashed them all."

With a shake of my head, I stood up from the couch. I placed a hand in front of Halo to help her do the same.

"It's all good. That just means they're extra clean now."

The last thing I wanted to do was make her feel any more displaced than she already did. Whatever arose, I planned to just roll with it or figure a way around it. Halo had a different view of the world and a different way of doing things. It wasn't the end of the world. It was actually the beginning of one. The beginning of ours.

"Where's the laundry room?"

"In the kitchen next to the pantry."

"Alright."

Once she was up on her feet, I pecked her forehead with my lips. On my way into the kitchen, clothed in her dried juices and a tee shirt, I began humming. My fingers snapped to *Sunshine Lady*, one of my favorite Willie Hutch records.

"Who likes what he likes and wants what he likes. Girl you've got just what I like."

The words flowed from my lips as I opened the door of the laundry room. I lowered the glass on the dryer and grabbed the towels out one by one, folding each of them immediately after they hit the air.

"Sunshine lady, come on let your love light shine on me."

It wasn't until every towel was folded that I grabbed two big ones and two small ones for us to use. The thought of showering together crossed my mind, but I wasn't sure if it would overstimulate Halo. Discomfort in her own home was out of the question, so I figured I'd fall back and let her lead the way. Whatever she decided I was fine with.

When I reached the bathroom, she still hadn't made it inside. The second I was preparing to exit, a very peculiar scent tickled my nostrils and stopped my stride. From where I stood, I inhaled the mugginess of the bathroom. It wasn't until my nasal canal burned slightly that it registered. I knew exactly why Halo's home felt as stuffy as it did. And though the plug-ins concealed the dormant scent, I could still smell the mold when I stepped into the bathroom. The ceiling was my first guess.

"Bingo."

The large spot that hung lower than the rest of the ceiling, sagging, was evidently the location of the infectious area. I searched around me for something to stand on so that I could reach the high ceiling, but there was nothing.

"I'll shower first," Halo announced as she walked in. "I had to spray the couch down."

"How long has this been here?" I asked her, pointing at the spot on the ceiling.

"For months now. The old woman that used to live upstairs kept flooding her tub. They moved her into a first-floor unit in August," she sniffed. "Why?"

"You've been sick?"

"I wouldn't call it sick. Just a cold that comes and goes. The runny nose, however, I can't shake. Some days it's fine, other days I can hardly wipe my nose because it hurts so bad from constant tampering."

"You don't have a cold, Halo," I gritted, frustrated with the fact that she and my child had been living in such damning conditions.

"I know. Not right now. It comes and goes. Right now, it's just a runny nose."

"It's not from a cold, though, is what I'm trying to explain. I can bet you any kind of money that once I pop this bubble and expose the foundation, there is mold there. I don't want to because I don't want to expose you to any more than you've already been exposed to, but I need to see what the fuck is going on. You mentioned your nose is sore," I asked.

"Yes."

"Prolonged exposure. That happens. You see this whole circle is darker than the rest of the ceiling?"

"I thought it was water damage. For a while, I had to have a bucket beneath this part because it would keep leaking. Then, they came to fix it."

"They didn't fix shit. They patched this shit up and did a horrible job at it. Now, you're sick because they weren't on their job!"

"I didn't know."

"I don't expect you to, but they knew. They were supposed to gut this shit out and dry it out of the walls and shit. It's probably mold all in this bathroom."

"Can it be fixed?"

Worry lines creased her forehead.

"Yeah. But, you won't be able to stay while it's being fixed. Step out of here, pretty lady."

"You too. I don't want you getting sick, too."

"I'm good. I really want to open this shit up and see what's going on up there, though. Go grab me a broom."

"I can just call the office. Really, Ledge. You don't have to take a chance and get sick yourself. I'll call them. I'll call them right now."

"Nah. Pack your shit, pretty lady. Call them when you make it to my place."

She released a weighted breath. I watched as her features changed a few times before settling with the sadness in her eyes.

"Ledge, we both know I can't do that."

"Yes you can."

"You can't expect me to just pack my things and walk out of that door. I'm not like that. It's not that simple for me."

"It doesn't have to be and I understand that it's not. However, you don't have another choice. This is making you sick and probably going to have some sort of effect on the baby. Your health is the only thing that should be on your mind right now, Halo. We need you well and staying here doesn't support that."

"This is my home," she cried, tears welling up in her pretty eyes.

"And, that is my baby you're carrying. I'm not asking you to stay for a lifetime, but I'm asking you to come for a little while. You can have any room you'd like. Okay? If it makes you more comfortable, I'll crash at my brother's crib until you're ready for me to come home. Whatever it takes, aight?"

"Whatever it takes," she agreed with a nod, wiping

her tears away. "How many brothers do you have?"

I couldn't help but break into a smile at the question. I was still processing everything myself.

"I've only had a twin my entire life but my mother died a few months ago. In a letter I found at her place, I discovered who my father was. The day I ran into you at Target, I'd met him and my siblings. So, as of now, I have three brothers and one sister."

"Lyric?" Her tears never stopped flowing.

"Yeah. Lyric, the one Ever mentioned."

"And, a twin?"

"Yes. I'm a twin, Halo. Why are you still crying?"

"Because, I don't know. I just feel so happy for you. Are you happy you have more siblings?"

"Yeah. That shit cool."

"I'm happy, too," she choked out, going into full-blown, meltdown mode.

I'd heard about pregnancy emotions, but I'd never experienced them first-hand. I stood in place, shaking my head and adoring her mini meltdown as she tried to keep her eyes focused on me, even through the tears.

"I'm so sorry. I just... the thought of leaving my place, you finding out you have siblings, you finding your father, you inside my apartment, me having a baby... everything is just happening so fast."

"It's alright, pretty lady."

"And, you... you're so kind and you're so patient and I feel like a nutcase for the most part. Most women would jump at the opportunity to live with the father of their child for a lifetime. I'm really, really freaking out and it's only maybe a few weeks or so. I just don't understand me."

"It could be a lifetime," I clarified, revisiting the timeframe she'd put on her stay.

"Huh?"

"Your stay could be a lifetime if you choose. I'd love that. Having my child under the same roof as me is the goal. I'd love it if you stayed."

"Ledge, why are you like this?"

"Like what?"

"I am not like other people, other women. You have no idea what you're getting yourself into. Are you sure you want to try things with me? Me of all people? Why me?"

"I've never been more sure of anything, Halo. And, yes you. Shit. Why not you? You're unique, your pussy good, and you deserve a nigga that's going to treat you right. Why not you?"

"I don't know. I just never imagined anyone would ever want me. I'm so messed up."

"You're not. Not at all. You're perfect for the right nigga and that nigga happens to be me. Start packing your shit. We can shower at my place. I'm going to start getting all of this stuff in the car so you and Ever can go through it or whatever. You're not coming back until you're ready. Hopefully, you won't ever be."

"Can you do me a favor?"

"Whatever," I assured her.

"Can you carry me to the car? It's the only way I'll ever leave."

"Yeah. I'll carry you."

"Thanks," she breathed.

It was obvious she was trying to control the onset panic attack that was brewing. I stepped into the hallway where she stood, slowly crumbling.

"Hey." I grabbed both shoulders. "Everything is going to be fine. Don't upset yourself. I live only about twenty minutes away. You're not going far. Think about the baby. This is for the baby, okay?"

"For the baby," she repeated, "It's for the baby."

"Yes. Now, you can go pack something or I can get you some new shit. What you have is probably infested though you can't tell."

"I wash a lot. Like, everything. It's a nervous habit of mine."

"Then, everything should be fine. That's probably why you haven't seen any mold popping up. This motherfucker is spotless."

"Cleaning calms me."

"I see. Just grab a few things and we're out, alright?"

"Okay."

I watched as she made her way to her bedroom. When I turned back and took a look at the ceiling again, I cringed. Everything in me wanted to open the discolored spot to see what was inside, but Halo was right. There was no need when the complex's responsibility was to fix it. I'd make sure I paid them a visit once she was settled. She was far too nice. They needed to feel my wrath. They'd put her and my child's health at risk with their laziness. That needed to be addressed.

10

HALO

Why'd I agree to this? I shouldn't have agreed to this. I should tell him to turn around. He has to take me back. I should go back. I can't do this. Oh my God, I think I'm going to puke. Everything is spinning. What's happening here?

"Halo?" I heard Ledge's voice as he yelled my name. "HALO."

"Uh...huh?"

The darkness that once surrounded me no longer

existed. Each time I batted my eyes, light made itself known. Ledge was the darkest thing in my line of vision.

"You aight?"

"Where are we?"

"We've made it. I didn't want to wake you so I let you sleep while I got everything into the house. You ready?"

No. I'm not ready. I was sleeping? I wasn't sure what it was called, but sleep didn't describe what I had going on.

"No," I voiced.

"Baby, we talked about this."

Baby? The word made me tingle below but did nothing for the task at hand.

"I know."

"I'm going to carry you inside, aight? At least it's not all unfamiliar. You've been here before."

He's right. I've been here before. This won't be so bad.

I stretched my arms and wiggled my fingers like a child. If I didn't go now, then I'd be waiting outside in the truck all night. Ledge took me into his arms and carried me bridal-style into his home. When he lowered me to my feet the memories began flooding in.

"Consider my home yours. Nothing is off-limits. Pick a room and I'll put your things there. Don't feel pressured to choose mine. Wherever you're most comfortable, that's where I want you."

"Okay."

Without haste, I started out for the stairs. I was reminded of how stunning Ledge's home was as I marveled at the gold and black aesthetic throughout.

One by one, I climbed the stairs until I reached the second floor. I could never forget the location of his bedroom, but it wasn't my destination. I traveled to the end of the hallway, on the opposite side of the stairwell, and chose the bedroom at the deepest end.

"Here."

Ledge was close behind. I was certain he'd heard me. When his legs halted right before reaching me and his head tilted toward the right, I knew that he officially considered me insane. But, his words contradicted my thoughts.

"A girl with good taste. This one is my favorite, aside from the master suite. There's enough room in here for two. It's pretty much a mini apartment. It has everything you'll need in here except for a stove. There's a mini fridge and a little pantry for stashing your favorite snacks. This one will be perfect for you two."

"I'm sure it will be." I nodded.

"Well, I'm going to start bringing this stuff upstairs. I've already started clearing out the room down the hallway for the nursery. Do you want to see it?"

"Maybe later?" I posed the question.

"Of course. I know this is a lot for you, so I'm going to give you a second to process it all. Come downstairs whenever you're ready. In the meantime, I'm going to bring mostly everything in here. The rest I'll put in the nursery. Then, I'll be out of your hair until six," he explained.

"Okay."

"You hungry?"

"Starving. But, I need some time alone. I'm sorry. I just need to be alone for a little while."

"Don't be. I'm a big boy, Halo. I can handle my own. I'm just trying to make sure you're good. I'll whip us up something really quick and sit it by the door. Let me get this stuff up here first."

"Okay. I'm going to shower while you do that. Can you knock when the food is ready?"

"Yeah. I can do that, pretty lady. As a matter of fact, I'm going to wait to bring this shit up here and give you some time alone."

"Thank you, Ledge."

"Don't do that. I'm just doing my job."

I stepped forward into the room. As I did, the walls came crashing down around me. My throat swelled with fear and my head began spinning again. The tears I'd kept at bay in an attempt not to worry Ledge fell freely as I closed the door behind me. Unable to move any deeper into the amazing space, I lowered my body onto the floor and pressed my back against the door.

Breathe.

Breathe.

Breathe.

You're okay.

Everything is okay.

Unable to control the influx of emotions, I subsumed them all with the thick, continuous tears that rolled down my cheeks. My chest inflated and deflated with each breath that I took, yet I still felt like I couldn't breathe. As if I was suffocating. As if there was simply not enough oxygen to supply my needs and at any second, I'd collapse and life for me would end.

Loose mucus ran down my nose and into my mouth as my right hand rested against my chest. Sweat beads lined my forehead as my temperature spiked. The warmth was a direct indication that it was time to get out of the jacket that I'd covered my arms with but, at the moment, it felt impractical.

"You're okay," I whispered. "You're okay, Halo. Everything is going to be okay."

There was a small knock at the door just as the words left my mouth. I tried quieting my heart and my tears as I listened for Ledge's voice. Surely the food wasn't ready that fast; I waited for what was to come. He'd just left me alone in my misery seconds ago. He couldn't have gotten too far before turning around.

"Listen Halo," he sighed and then paused.

With baited, shallow breaths I waited for more.

"I know this shit is a little bit much. I know this wasn't ideal for you and I know you're on the other side of the door crying those pretty, big eyes out. To say that it breaks my heart is an understatement. I don't want you anywhere you don't want to be or anywhere that's just too hard to adjust. If you'd feel better if I left or you stayed with Kamber for a few weeks, then we can make that happen. I just won't be able to rest knowing you're not happy here. Happiness is part of your health. When I say that I want you healthy, it includes happiness, too. If that's not here, then I promise I won't trip. We'll make it work wherever. It doesn't have to be here if you don't want it to be."

"I do," I cried out to him, mentally, physically, and emotionally. "I do want to stay where it's safe and best for the baby. I'm just trying, you know? I'm trying to deal with it all. It's just hard, Ledge. Nothing for me or about me is simple. I wish I wasn't this way, but I am. I know I keep apologizing, but I really am sorry. I know this isn't what you signed up for."

"I don't give a fuck about that, pretty lady. I'm signing up for this shit right here and right now so you can stop apologizing. I'm not going anywhere. I've made that clear. Whatever you're dealing with, I'm dealing with too. You don't have to do this alone anymore. I'm right here, willing and able to make shit better for you.

"I'm the sorry one. I'm sorry that life has been so unkind to you. I'm sorry that you had to suffer for so long. I'm sorry that you've had to face this all by yourself. I'm sorry that your grandmother passed. I'm sorry that there was no one around to protect you. I'm sorry that you had such a shitty childhood. I'm sorry that the sickness of someone else forever altered your world and the perception of the world in its entirety."

His words crippled me, momentarily. God had taken his precious time creating Ledge.

"I'm sorry that you're afraid and always scared. I'm sorry that you haven't become the girl that you're yearning to be. I'm sorry that you spent most of your pregnancy alone. I'm sorry that I didn't come sooner. I'm sorry, Halo."

I lowered my entire body onto the floor. On my side, I rested my hand underneath my head to support its weight as I unraveled. Like a newborn baby, I bawled. All the pain that I'd been holding inside for the last decade escaped through my eyes.

"You hear me, pretty lady? I'm sorry about it all. Until I take my last breath, I plan to try right every wrong the world caused you. I just hope it's enough to help you understand how much of a treasure you are. All you see is a mess. I see a gem buried underneath the mud. I can't wait until your eyes are open and you can see it, too."

"My heart hurts," I confessed.

"Mine, too."

"When I think of you. When you're near. It's a never-ending pain that makes this feel real, makes you feel real. It's so hard to believe that you are, but this pain reminds me. It's as if my heart is actually hurting and I don't know if I ever want it to stop. It hurts so good."

Ledge said nothing for a while. I was worried I'd scared him off with my words until he finally spoke again.

"That's love happening, Halo. I feel it, too."

"Yeah?"

"Yeah, pretty lady. Soon, it won't hurt so bad or so often. But, when it does, it'll be a reminder of how deep your shit runs for me and vice versa. In those moments that you think of me, of us at our best and even at our lowest, it'll let you know that it's no fairytale and it's real."

"I like that. Nothing has ever felt like it."

"Nothing ever will."

"I feel so tired," I yawned, finally realizing my tears were settling.

They'd gone from streaming down my face rapidly to only falling down the side and to the floor when I blinked.

"Then rest," he suggested. "Right where you are."

"Can you stay?"

"Yeah."

I heard him sigh with a grunt, confirming my suspicions. He was lowering himself to the floor as well. A sharp pain shot through my heart.

"I'm not going nowhere. I'll be right here until I'm sure you're asleep."

I hadn't eaten and neither had I taken a shower, but I didn't care. The basket beside the sofa with the blankets inside was close enough for me to tilt it in my direction. Once it was on its side as well, I pulled out the blanket on top and covered my body with it.

"Ledge."

"What's up, mommas?"

"I'm so happy it's you and no one else."

That had been on my mind since I discovered the little one I was carrying.

"Me too. Me too."

I closed my eyes with tears in them and a smile on my face. My life was so far from perfect, but the moment was. For now, I was more than satisfied with that. With Ledge on the other side of the door, I fell into a deep, coma-like state.

LEDGE + HALO

IT WAS 3:24 p.m. when I emerged from the shower and 3:38 p.m. by the time I descended the stairs to find Ledge plating lunch. He'd called for me a half hour ago. I'd awakened an hour and a half ago. On the floor with no support, I'd gotten the best sleep of my life. For the first time since I felt my stepfather's hands in places they didn't belong, I felt safe.

"Feel better?" Ledge looked up and asked.

"Yes. Did you get any sleep?"

"After I convinced myself not to come in and lay you in bed so that you were more comfortable, yeah. I got about an hour in. Then, I handled a little business before putting all the baby's things in the nursery. I hope you don't mind it being there. I figured I wouldn't bother crowding out your new space with all that stuff."

"It's fine."

"I was thinking I'd run to the store after we check with Ever to see what we'll be needing. I need to get paint and shit to start off the walls in there. What do you think about a brown and cream theme? That way, it doesn't matter if we have a boy or girl, we won't have to change anything."

"I love brown. All shades. I figured you did, too. That's what most of the things you bought are."

"Just trying to keep it neutral since we don't know

269

what we're having, but I have been gravitating to that color a lot. I had an inkling it was a color you admired for some reason."

"I'm beginning to think you have superpowers," I chuckled. "You know things about me that no one knows and that I haven't told you."

"I'd lie and say it's all me but I've just been following my heart. It hasn't steered me wrong my entire life."

"Hmmm." I nodded. "What are we having?"

"I made something quick. Garlic-buttered rice, green beans, and stuffed salmon. I've done the research. It's lower in mercury and pregnancy safe."

"It is," I agreed. "And, it smells great."

"Hopefully, it tastes as great as it smells. I've had it enough times to know that I love it. I just hope you do, too."

He sat the plates down next to each other on the large dining room table. It was only the two of us. Before I joined him, he was the only one in his home. The large table made almost no sense.

"Why such a large table? There are six more chairs. Do you have a lot of family?" I wondered out loud.

"It was only my mother, my brother, and me for as long as I can remember."

"I don't have much family, either. None, really."

"I want to build something big. I've done the work and prepared the home. I'm ready to fill it."

"With babies," I tittered.

"And a wife and pets. Two dogs and maybe a goldfish. Don't kids love goldfishes?"

"I don't know. This would be my first one."

Nodding with a smile, he said, "Right. Right."

"How many children do you want?" The question was at the tip of my tongue and had to be asked.

"I'd say at least three but I hate odd numbers, so at least four. It was my brother and me, but I always felt like it just wasn't enough. At the same time, I've gained so much family in the last few weeks and I know my children won't be alone like we were. So, I'm cool if I don't make it to four. Two, for sure though. Two at least."

"Four is a nice number to settle on. Two until we're settled into our new roles and then two more when we begin to miss the baby phase and the older two have started kindergarten at least."

"You got it all figured out, huh?" He asked.

"Not really. I just learned from the group I'm in that planning is best. I've given things some thought, according to their advice. And, if I was to have more than one child, I'd like to have them in sets. If that makes sense? Two and then time to adjust. Then, two. Or, just two is fine. Whatever we decide, I'm okay with. I just don't want this baby to be the only one. My life was very lonely. I want them to grow up with someone to love and cherish forever."

"Yeah. I don't know how I would've made it without my brother."

"And you guys are twins. That's so fascinating. Who is the oldest?"

"I am."

"I imagine you guys are nothing alike."

Finally, I dug into the food in front of me. It looked so tasty and my stomach was crying for help.

"Nothing. That's the balance."

"This is really good," I exclaimed.

"I'm happy you like it."

"Where'd you learn to cook?"

"My mother had us in the kitchen right along with her. When she was working we had to figure it out ourselves. Both Lawe and I can throw down. He's more of a soul food kind of guy. I'm more of a seafood, lean kind of guy. His shit is immaculate. His dishes can take hours on top of hours. It's probably the only time he has patience except when it comes to real estate."

"That's what he's into?"

"Yes and no. But, he loves it, nonetheless. Investing and developing."

"That's good. There's a lot of money in both."

"There is."

The sound of the doorbell halted our conversation. My eyes widened in question as Ledge's lips curved upward. Obviously, he knew something I didn't.

"Relax, pretty lady. It's Ever and hopefully, Lyric. I haven't gotten the chance to officially meet her. We met one another in passing and it wasn't very pretty. This is my do over. We're both meeting her for the first time."

"Awwww," I hummed.

"I'll warn you," he vocalized as he got up, "She is strikingly beautiful. Try not to stare."

Though he chuckled, I knew that he was serious. He tossed his table napkin and headed for the front door. I was conflicted, wondering if I should continue emptying my plate or follow behind him. I settled on finishing my food and letting him and his sister have their moment. Hopefully, by the time they made it to the dining room, my plate would be cleared and I could think better. While hungry, I could hardly function.

The seconds quickly turned into minutes. Fifteen minutes passed before Ledge reappeared. My plate was almost empty and I was considering working on his. However, I knew that it would only lead to an upset stomach and my head over the toilet. I managed some self-control and refrained.

In walked two women behind him, both as dazzling as the other. I quickly picked up on who was who before he introduced them. Emotions tapped danced on my orbs as I openly admired the two women who I'd yet to officially meet. They were so well put together making me feel like a mess.

"Halo, this is Lyric, my sister."

"Hi, babe. Look at you, just so big and pretty. I love your name, by the way."

She stepped forward.

"Is it alright if I hug you? I know some folks don't like people all in their personal space, hugging them and shit."

"By folks, are you referring to yourself?" Ever asked.

"That's exactly who I'm referring to."

I wanted to tell her that I'd prefer a handshake, but the words wouldn't surface. I imagined it was because my desire to wrap my arms around her was much stronger than my habitual response to the little human interaction I received.

I looked over toward Ledge for the bit of confidence that I needed to move forward with my decision. Our eyes met as he nodded. The smile on his handsome face assured me that it was okay.

Go ahead, he mouthed.

"It's fine."

It had taken every ounce of strength I could muster to utter the words, but I managed. Immediately, I rejoiced.

Lyric wasted no time pulling me into her chest. I wasn't sure what happened or how, but something magical had taken place. I closed my eyes as our bodies synced and my heart uncurled a little more. Its expansion was new but it felt so necessary and good.

I can't wait to hug Kamber. The random thought surfaced. We had yet to reach that step, but with the new progress I'd made, we were there without her even knowing it. The next time I saw her I'd wrap my arms around her. She deserved all my love. She'd been everything to me when I had nothing and no one else.

"I'm Ever," the chic one greeted, stepping closer as I released Lyric.

"Is it me or does she have a magic touch? Like, I've never felt so... nourished and refilled after a hug from a stranger in my life. You have a warmth about you that can't be mimicked, love. I like that. Ledge, my brother, you're stuck. I can see it now."

"I am," Ledge agreed. "I already know it."

"Hi," I responded to Ever.

She opened her arms wide and waited for me to step into them. When I did, she placed them on my belly. It was very clear where her interests lied and I was okay with that. She was concerned with my child's well-being.

"How are you feeling today?"

"I'm rested now. I'd been battling what I thought was a cold, but Ledge discovered my stuffy nose and congestion were more than likely due to the mold growing in my bathroom that I had no clue about. I've only been at his place a few hours and I already feel so much better. The air quality is so much better. I feel like I can breathe better."

"It's probably because you are breathing better. Mold is unhealthy for anyone. We're going to make sure we mention that to the team this evening. They'll be here in about an hour and a half. Until then, take me to the nursery. Ledge said it's where he put all the baby things."

"Yes. He did. Unfortunately, I'm not sure where it is, either. I'm new here," I chuckled.

"Oh, don't worry. We're all in the same boat," Lyric added.

"Come on, ladies. I'll lead the way."

Ledge was absolutely right. Lyric was incredibly gorgeous. Those big brown eyes reminded me of his. And, Ever, she was truly a natural goddess. Everything about her made me want to be her friend. As silly as it sounded at my age, it was true. Besides Kamber, I didn't have a friend and never had one.

Though I wanted the same with Lyric, her presence

was overwhelmingly intimidating. She was obviously that girl and I simply wasn't. There wasn't a misplaced strand of hair on her head. Her makeup was flawless and so was the Chanel bag that dangled from her arm. I'd never seen one in person, but the double C's were dead giveaways.

She smelled like money. Not the sweaty, passed-down cash that we held in our hand, but real money. The kind that it took generations to spend and one never quite got to the end of. She was the epitome of confidence. Secretly, I despised her for having so much of it when I needed a bit. Nevertheless, she wore it well.

"You're staring," Ledge whispered as he grabbed my hand and led me toward the stairs.

"It's so hard not to. She's so pretty."

"I told you."

"And, Ever... she's a doll."

"She is."

"Y'all want to let us in on the secret or is it none of our business?" Lyric asked, following us up the stairs.

"We think you two are very pretty. Halo is finding it hard not to stare," Ledge explained, exposing us both. "I don't blame her. It was hard for me too, the first time I saw you."

"Okay, I'll have to tell my husband. This type of beauty deserves a raise in allowance. Don't you think, Ever? Apparently, I'm drop dead. Matter of fact, I should probably just come stay here where these looks are appreciated."

"Keanu understands what he has on his hands, Lyric.

Trust me. Do not call getting on that man's nerves with this. I know he's tired of your foolishness."

"Can't be. He married me. It's a lifetime of this."

"Unfortunately for him."

"He loves it here. He does. Why, I don't know, but he does."

"Without a doubt," Ever confirmed.

"Laike would love this build. He's into architecture and development." Lyric shared.

"Yeah? So is Lawe. He designed this whole thing for me. When I bought it, it looked nothing like this. I caught a deal because it was in bad shape. He made the most of the money I saved, rebuilding it almost. I have no complaints."

"Yes. Laike designed and built all of our houses."

"That's tight. It's right here."

LEDGE + HALO

MY NERVES GREW as I undressed in the bathroom and changed into the dress that I'd been given by one of the sweetest members on the staff. The birth workers had arrived twenty minutes ago and since then, we'd been going over my medical history, paperwork, and what to expect from this moment forward.

The team was composed of three women, all with different roles. There was Alec, the doula. There was

Yoshi, the midwife, and Dr. Sanders, the natural medicine physician who worked with mothers and babies.

"Halo," Ledge called out to me as he knocked on the door.

"Hmmm?"

"You okay?"

"Nervous. Like, very nervous."

"Me, too," he claimed, "But, we're going to put on our grown-up drawers and get through this, aight."

"They told me not to wear panties."

His cackling on the other side of the door made my cheeks rise and lips curve upward into a smile.

"It's all good. These are imaginary ones, anyway."

"Okay."

I emerged from the bathroom feeling slightly better. Ledge stood against the wall with his brown eyes trained on me. Though I was clothed, I felt extremely naked. It didn't matter what I had on, it was as if he could see right through me.

"Cheer up, pretty lady. This will all be over soon and you can be alone, again."

With you? The question popped into my head and hung around. I craved the silence, but only if it included him in some capacity.

"I know."

"You ready?"

"Not really, but yes. I'm ready as I'll ever be."

"Come on."

He took my hand into his and led me down the hallway where everything had been set up during my consultation. When I stepped into the room, Lyric and Ever exited. In the two hours that we'd shared alone, they learned so much about me, including my condition and how to prepare themselves for moments that triggered stress, paranoia, or anxiety. This happened to be one of those. Them giving me the space I required without me having to ask was appreciated.

"Okay, we're going to get started so that we can get out of your hair. We'll start by checking your cervix. Around this stage, according to your date of conception, you will begin to feel a bit of pressure below. It means the baby is positioning itself for delivery. You may also begin to dilate, not much but any progress is good being that you're at the full-term mark. If baby was born today, they'd be just fine. Lay on the bed for me," Yoshi explained.

Following her instructions, I reluctantly let go of Ledge's hand and climbed on the bed. The paper strip they'd laid down rattled as I climbed onto it. The protective barrier reminded me of the paper robes and table covers that were at the few doctor's offices I'd gone to from the age of fourteen until I reached eighteen.

Yoshi spread my legs, gently, exposing my vagina to the open air. A chill hit my body causing me to shiver. My trembling hands and legs didn't stand a chance once the air swiped across the hairless flesh between my thighs.

"You're going to feel me down here. I'm just checking to see where baby is and what we have going on down here."

"Okay."

I could feel fingers being inserted into the depths of me, cold ones that added to the misery I was feeling. For the life of me, I could stop shaking. Sensing my discomfort, Ledge slid out of his shoes and climbed up on the bed with me. Beside me, he stretched out and placed a hand on my stomach.

"Everything is all good, pretty lady."

His lips were like nourishment for the skin. The warmth he provided helped rebuild the nerves that had been destroyed and minimize my trembles.

"Alright. We're on our way, for sure. Especially if mommy and daddy keep having fun," Yoshi joked, pulling off the glove on her right hand.

I cringed at the thick, creamy substance on the blue piece of plastic. Both Ledge and I knew exactly what it was and how it had gotten there. He'd emptied his semen into me. Even after my shower it hadn't seeped out completely.

"If the baby is banking on that, they're in luck," Ledge boasted.

"Well, it certainly won't hurt and can sometimes help the progression."

"Say no more, doc."

There was a roaring laughter in the room that made my heart and head light.

"You're about a centimeter and a half dilated. You can be here for several weeks or continue to progress little by little. You're on the right track. We're going to get a look at the baby, run a few tests, take some measurements, and listen to the baby's heartbeat. Do you guys want to know what you're having today or are you waiting?"

"Tell us."

"Tell us, I guess," Ledge agreed with a shrug.

A white tube hovered over my stomach, dangling from Dr. Sanders' hand.

"This will be warm, so don't worry. Promise," she told me before squeezing the tube.

As she'd promised, the gel was warm and felt great on my skin. Dr. Sanders grabbed a long wand that was attached to a large machine they'd brought in and placed it on my belly. There was so much whooshing before finally, the sound of galloping horses quieted the rest of the room.

Instantly, I could feel my face stained with tears as I held my breath and placed a hand over my mouth. Everything around me blurred as the sound of my baby's beating heart was magnified. This moment was one I'd waited for since learning of my pregnancy. It was one that topped any and every other moment in my life.

The amount of love that I harbored for someone I'd never met was sickening, physically and mentally. I couldn't put into words just how profound the feeling was or how incredible it was finally getting the opportunity to love and be loved unconditionally. Unknowingly, I'd waited for this kind of love since the age of six. A love without limits, one that didn't hurt like the rest of it.

"Baby, you hear that?" Ledge's voice cracked. "You hear that?"

"Yes." Nodding, slowly, I released the only word I could muster.

"What do you think you're having, mommy?"

"Girl," I choked. Ledge's eyes left the screen that our baby appeared on in gray to look at me. I'd been honest when admitting that I wanted a son, but everything in me believed that life would play a cruel joke on me and bless me with a daughter.

"What about you daddy?"

"A girl," he gasped, eyes still trained on me.

"Well, I guess you both are getting exactly what you assumed you would anyway. You're having a girl with a head full of curls."

"Stop it!" I belted, not believing we'd guessed correctly. I was a wreck, my eyes and nose burned from the excessive crying and sniffling.

"Yup. A little girl. You see that right there?" she asked, pointing at the screen.

"Yes."

"Yeah."

"It means you'd better start practicing with some dolls or something of the sorts because this baby has more hair than me and Alec put together."

Through the tears, there was laughter, and plenty of it. Hand-in-hand, Ledge and I listened to our baby's heartbeat as Dr. Sanders snapped picture after picture and measured the baby's body to determine my official due date and the size of the baby.

For approximately thirty-five minutes, we enjoyed the company of the birth team and the sound of our baby's heartbeat as they recorded all the necessary information to confirm our health. Once the appointment concluded, I was somewhat sad to see them leave. With a due date of November 16th I needed as much time to plan and prepare as possible. As they were packing up their things, I was already going over the birth plan options they'd given me in their welcome packet.

"I left my card on file. Ever sent me the link to set up payments."

"We have your payment. It's authorized before we leave the office," Dr. Sanders stated.

"Right. Right," Ledge replied. "I'm going to help you guys get this stuff to the car."

"No. We're fine. Enjoy this moment with mom. Everything heavy has wheels on it and doesn't weigh much."

"Next time, I'll make sure we're downstairs so we don't have to bring the machine up."

"Whatever you'd like is fine with us. We've gone up and down a thousand staircases with this thing. It'll be fine and so will we. Thanks for choosing us. We'll see you in two weeks, hopefully, there's a centimeter or two added. I have a feeling baby will be on time or very close to it."

"She can stay put for an additional two days."

"Is that someone's birthday?" Alec asked.

"Mine."

"Awww. That would be the sweetest," Yoshi cooed.

"Hey." I heard Ever's voice after the room had cleared.

Ledge had gone downstairs to walk the ladies out though they'd advised him against it.

"How did everything go?"

"I wish I could stop crying long enough to tell you," I sniggered.

"I still have your list of questions. I figured today would be emotional so I'm going to send them all over through email. They'll answer them and get them back to you. Is that okay with you?"

"Yes."

"Alright. Lyric and I are going to get out of here and go grab our babies. I'm going to send you the number to my therapist when I get down to the car, okay?"

"Okay. Thank you."

"My pleasure. I'll give you guys time to process it all. Call me tomorrow."

"We're having a girl," I blurted, still conflicted but overflowing with love.

"I know. Why so sad? Girls are the best."

"I know. I just... I'm having a hard time knowing that I'm bringing one into this cruel world."

"It is cruel, but as long as she has us, we won't let anything happen to her that we can avoid or protect her from. Don't be afraid. She'll be fine."

Instead of responding, I simply nodded. Though I'd told Ever and Lyric about my condition, they didn't know the trauma that caused it. I'd left that part to myself, so she wouldn't understand the true nature of my fear of bringing a daughter into the world.

"See you later, love."

She was gone in a jiffy. I tried to gather myself before Ledge returned, but it was impossible. I was still blowing my runny nose and wiping my swollen eyes by the time he walked into the room again.

"You aight?"

"I don't know, but I'm really, really happy right now. I just want to go with that."

"Then, we will."

Ping.

Through tearful eyes, I looked down at my chiming phone to see an unknown number had sent a text message. Upon opening it, I realized it was Ever. She'd shared a contact with me.

> Kirklynn Benedict – Therapist

. The message read. I quickly saved it in my contacts and made a promise to call after the baby was born.

I exited the new thread she'd started and opened the one that Kamber and I shared. When I saw the three dots popping up before I could type a single word, I smiled. She felt me thinking of her.

> It's a girl.

I typed.

> Where are you? I just knocked at your door.

It's a lot to explain. I'm with Ledge, at his place. I'll call you soon. My feelings are a wreck right now. I heard the baby's heartbeat. I'm having a girl.

I knew it. You give girl mom vibes. Now I can buy pink shit, huh?

I think I'd like to keep buying browns and some yellows. Gender neutral.

Boring, but okay. Whatever you say. Call me later. And, get enough dick for the both of us. Your girl is dry over here.

Goodbye, Kamber.

She didn't go without putting a hundred eggplant emojis and some water emojis in the thread. Disgusted with her antics, I couldn't help but feel a little better about everything. She always did that for me.

"I know this might be asking too much, but I'm not ready to part ways, yet."

"If it involves me leaving out of the front door, then the answer is no," I replied, shutting my phone down.

"Wait, hear me out. You could stay in the truck. I'll run in and get the paint and shit. Then, we can hit up the drive-thru spot with the bomb ass ice cream. After that, we can come back to the crib and watch a movie. You in?"

"Ledge, I don't think I can manage to leave again. I've gone outside once today."

"Please. For ice cream?"

"Can it be tomorrow? I'm so worked up. I'd love to tag alone but I just can't do it today."

"What about that movie, though?"

"And, the ice cream. We left it all at my place, huh?"

"Nah. I wasn't leaving that. It's in the ice box. Let me know when you're ready for it."

"Whenever the movie starts. I kind of want some more food for now."

"Aight. Eight o'clock. We can still have our time together. We just won't be having dinner."

"Okay. But, I'm not opposed to dinner, either."

"Tomorrow at seven. We can bring fine dining to us and make it an official dinner date inside."

"Deal."

"You have to wear dinner clothes," he informed me, laying out the rules.

"I don't have any." I didn't. I never went anywhere that required clothes for real. I was the ultimate home-body with nothing but comfy clothes in my closet.

"I'll make sure you're straight by seven."

"Okay."

11

LEDGE

THERE WAS NO FEELING IN THE WORLD
comparable. Knowing I was going home to Halo at any
given moment had me on a high that was indescribable.
I'd decided against coming to work for the day, but we
were short two staff members, which called for my help.
Because it was a weekday, we'd be closing at one-thirty.
The few hours I was needed were literally just a breath of
fresh air after everything that had happened in a day's
time.

Halo hadn't gotten through the first act of John Wick before she dozed off and fell asleep on the couch. I finished off the movie right before getting the call that two of my employees had emergencies and couldn't come in. By eleven o'clock, I was walking through the back entrance.

"You'll know when it's time to go, boss. You don't have to keep checking your phone," Jade yelled across the bar.

"Mind your business, woman."

"Ummm hmmm. Got somebody waiting for you to come through, huh?"

She's already at the crib. I almost told a giggling Jade, but it was none of her damn business what I had going on. From the silly look plastered on her face, it was obvious she'd gone over the two-drink maximum for employees while on the clock. It was simply a way to loosen them up and help them relax for their shift. The restriction kept them from being sloppy drunk or allowing the alcohol consumption to interfere with their tasks.

"Don't get high off your own supply."

"You said two drinks. You didn't say what kind. You know shots are my favorite. And, because I knew you wouldn't take your two drinks, I had an extra two for you. Is that against the rules, *boss*?" She turned all the way around to face me when she asked.

"Two drinks, Jade. Now, go give this to the three ladies over at table six."

"Whatever you say."

Jade was the best waitress we had in the building. She knew the menu back to front. She also knew how to milk the pockets of the customers and keep them coming back. She was good for Jilted, but she could be a bit of a headache the few times that she consumed too much liquor. It wasn't very often, but I felt like I was in attendance every time.

Just as I was about to respond, my cell vibrated in my hand. My newest, most titillating contact popped up on my screen. I could feel the breeze from the bar hit my gums as my pearly whites were put on full display.

Okay.

She responded to the text I'd sent her on the way out of the door.

I didn't want her to wake and wonder where I'd gone so I shot her a text to let her know that I'd headed to the bar for a few hours and would be home around two.

What are you doing?

I don't know. I'm so confused from my nap. I don't know what's going on.

From side to side, I shook my head. Halo was truly special. Her innocence was still intact and I loved that aspect of her. Life had been so cruel to her in her younger years that she never quite outgrew the young woman that she was all those years ago. Watching her learn, grow, and heal would be a blessing and a pleasure.

I'd bumped into so many women whose adult life had altered their perception, turned them into beasts, or skewed their views on relationships and love. Halo was blemish-free aside from her childhood misfortunes. The only impression she'd have about men and relationships in her adult life would be the one I created. I couldn't fuck it up with her. I wouldn't.

> It's okay, pretty lady. Stay up for me? I'm leaving soon.

> I'll try my hardest.

> Bet. See you soon.

I checked the time once more, realizing we only had thirty minutes until closing time.

"Start counting the drawers down, Jade. Leave one open in case someone strolls in. Make sure everything is wiped down out there. I'll shut this down up here. We're walking out of here by 1:32."

"Yes sir. I'll get right on it."

Thirty grueling minutes passed by slowly, driving me up the wall and halfway insane. I'd never wanted to walk through my door, shower, and climb in my bed so much. Halo waiting up for me made going home hit much differently than ever before.

I couldn't wait to walk through the door, kiss her

belly, and help her to bed for the night. It was our first full night together and I was looking forward to it, although it would be spent in different spaces. As long as we were under the same roof, I was cool.

When we finally walked out of Jilted, the crisp night air welcomed us with howling winds. I started my old school and waited for everyone to make it to their vehicles. Once everyone was safe inside their whips, I climbed back into mine and burned the rubber off my wheels getting out of the parking lot.

Urgency led me, knocking four minutes off my already short drive home. I deaded the lights as I pulled into the driveway to make sure that I didn't startle Halo. If she was still hanging out in the living room, then she'd definitely see them as I turned in.

Bobbing my head to an imaginary beat, I made long strides toward my front door. The key slid into my lock with ease. I gained access to the house fairly quickly. My first stop was the living room where I knew I'd find Halo.

To my surprise, she'd changed locations. My next stop was the kitchen. I figured I'd find her there. When I rounded the corner and didn't see her standing near the dark counters or black cabinets, my brows furrowed.

I took the steps two at a time to cut my travel time in half. I reached the second floor in a jiffy. Her room was the one on the furthest end of the hallway. When I finally made it, I placed an ear against the door and tapped on it slightly. When I didn't get a response or hear any movement, I pushed the door open.

Ahhhh shit. She couldn't quite hold out. My entire body tingled as I watched her sleeping so peacefully. Quietly and carefully, I backtracked and exited the room so that she could continue resting.

Still floating from the high her presence supplied me with, I headed to my bedroom for a long, anticipated shower. It didn't matter that she couldn't wait up for me. She was here when I arrived. That brought me unshakeable happiness.

Absent-mindedly, I started the water for my shower while thinking about my plans for the day. After a few hours of sleep, I would pack Halo up, kicking and screaming if necessary, and head to the hardware store for paint and a few more things I'd need to build a few floating shelves in the nursery. I needed to swing by the outlet I'd gotten wind of and grab a rocking recliner that I'd seen online. I figured it would be perfect for Halo while nursing our daughter.

I stepped into the shower while still going over the details of my day. Dinner was still on and I wanted to make sure that I filled Halo to the brim with healthy, nutritious food. The options rolled through my head one by one before I finally settled on lobster as the meat. Alongside it, I chose garlic and lemon butter mashed potatoes, broccolini, and a bed of wild rice.

LEDGE + HALO

EVEN MY COVERS felt a bit different. When I pulled my comforter back, I tried my hardest to remember if I'd set the bed before I left. *I didn't.* I realized as I slid underneath the comforter. That only meant that Halo had managed to sneak in and take care of it for me.

Simple shit. It was exactly that, that would keep me falling fast and hard for her. Deep under the covers, I closed my eyes and sent one up to the man above. He'd shown me far too much grace in one day.

G, thank you for setting up my day to be full of blessings and surprises. There's a girl just a few rooms down the hall that I'm really into. She's having my baby. I want to do right by her. Help me. She's the most precious thing I've ever seen or held in my hands. I don't ever want to let her go. She needs a healing, a good one. It's something I can't do alone, so I need your help with that too. A nigga feels like he's begging, but it is what it is. Help me help her. Show me the ropes. Show me the way. And, I promise, I'm going to put a ring on that pretty as— that pretty finger of hers.

I'm out.

The exhaustion kept my eyelids sealed after prayer. I began drifting away and into a deep sleep that I didn't plan to wake from until I was well-rested and rejuvenated. However, the hovering presence and familiar warmth that I felt near quickly dented my schedule.

I opened my eyes to find Halo standing a few feet away. Though dark, I could feel her gaze on me. She said nothing and neither did I for a while.

"Halo, what's the matter?"

"I don't know," she sighed, heavy-hearted and seemingly still tired.

"You do," I countered. "So, tell me."

There was a brief silence before she blew out a hunk of air. I sensed her swelling anxiety and decided to coax her through whatever it was she was feeling before it overwhelmed her.

"You can tell me whatever, aight?" I sat up in bed and told her. "Don't ever feel like you can't. I've told you already, we're working through this shit together. You're not alone and will never be alone even if it feels that way sometimes. It's not the case and won't ever be the case anymore. Come 'er," I called her over, beckoning for her with my hand.

Timid, but cooperative, Halo obliged. I pulled her between my legs and rested my hand on her belly. This was the first of many late nights I wanted with her, figuring out our feelings and our future.

"Tell me what's the matter."

"I don't want to sleep alone," she finally admitted.

Chuckling at her misery, I could only shake my head.

"Baby, why was that so hard for you to tell me? I thought some shit was really happening up here." I tapped her forehead.

"No, it's happening here," she explained, reaching up to grab my hand.

She placed it over her heart and set my soul ablaze. There wasn't room for question or doubt in my mind. She was it for me. This was it for me.

"Come on, pretty lady. Climb in bed and let's get some rest."

"But wait," she pleaded, placing a hand on my shoulder to stop me from moving any more.

"What's up?"

"That's not all."

"What else, baby? Talk to me."

She said nothing.

"Halo. What is it?"

She was frozen in place, contemplating her words.

"Spill it." I encouraged her.

She placed a hand over her mouth and leaned in closer to my ear.

"I want to feel you inside of me," she whispered as if there were people in the room besides us.

Again, I found humor in her misery. It had taken a lot for her to confess the sexual urges that woke her from her sleep and dragged her into my room in search of satisfaction.

"You don't have to whisper, Halo. We're the only ones here, baby."

"Sorry."

"Climb up and let me put this motherfucker inside of you."

I could feel the shift in energy. Relief softened her frame and chipped away at her rigidness. She was so worked up with those thoughts lingering. Now that she'd let them go, she felt better. After I finished with her, she'd feel even better.

The gown that she wore made it easy to access her

pantiless pussy. Her arousal was strong, wetting my tongue and tingling my tastebuds. I didn't understand how I hadn't noticed it before with her standing so close to me. I slid her down the bed toward me and kissed her top set of lips before pushing her upward and positioning her for me to kiss her bottom set. She'd asked for dick and that's exactly what she'd get, but not before I ate. I was starved.

L, I swiped her pussy with my tongue.

E, again.

D, again.

G, again.

E, again. Etching my name on that motherfucker.

It was mine and I could do whatever I wanted with it. I knew it and so did she.

"Ledge," she cried out.

D.

O.

M.

I.

N.

O.

"Yeeeeees. Yes."

I sucked her pussy into my mouth, focusing on clitoral stimulation that made her legs tremble and her hands grip my head. She locked me in, right where I wanted to be.

"Right there. Please. Pleaseeeee."

Relentlessly, I flicked my tongue back and forward

until she numbed and slowly released me. I knew then that she'd mounted, reaching her peak with ease. And, when her well began to release its overflow, I was prepared.

"Let that shit go, baby."

My dick stood tall when I freed it. Desperate to feel her pussy contracting around my dick, I slid right into her. *Bad decision*, I taunted. I still hadn't learned my lesson. Halo's pussy was lethal and she had no idea how to use it. When she took control of her sexuality and learned how to work her pussy, it would be the deadliest weapon in the house and I wouldn't stand a chance.

"Ummmmmmm."

"This what you wanted? Hmm? To feel me inside of you?"

"Yeeeessss," she moaned. "Yes."

I could already feel the bitch entering my body as her walls caved on me. Her shit was beyond me, beyond this world. There was nothing or no one that could convince me that it didn't possess superpowers. I'd witnessed them.

LEDGE + HALO

THE SUNLIGHT WAS BRUTAL, baking my eyelids as I tried to get some sleep. It became pretty clear that the forces were against me and that I wouldn't be able to prolong my sedation. The day was waiting for me and I needed to get my ass up.

I stretched my lids as they painfully absorbed the sun that shined through the windows. However, it wasn't the only thing beaming. So was Halo and her cocoa skin. Waking up to her was like something out of a dream. I wanted to close my eyes and do that shit again, a million times over.

"Good morning," I grunted.

"Good morning."

"How long have you been up?"

"I don't know."

"How long have you been staring at me?" I asked with a smile.

"I don't know that either," she snickered.

I pushed forward and lifted my head to kiss her lips. They looked too fucking good not to.

"You're going outside today," I teased. "You ready?"

"I'm not and that's what I wanted to talk to you about."

"Naaaaah. You're coming with me. I don't want to go by myself now that I don't have to."

"But, seriously, you kind of do. I thought I'd be ready Ledge, but I'm not. I'd rather stay here and begin unpacking her things. While you're gone, I can hang up all the stuff that I started washing last night."

"You started washing?"

"Yes. I want to wash everything that we've gotten prior to it going on her skin. That's important."

"Damn, I never even thought about that. I guess you're right."

"Yes. I think you should wash clothes before putting them on the baby's skin. There's no telling where the clothes have been or what they've encountered before getting to their destination."

"True. True. But, still, you're leaving me hanging it feels like."

"I'm not. Teamwork is better, right?"

"Sometimes."

"It is Ledge. Don't be like that."

"Aight. By next week you're coming outside at least once."

"We will see. I can't make any promises."

"How'd you sleep last night?"

"I felt slimy. I still do. I was just waiting for you to wake up before I showered. I didn't want to wake you."

"Maybe we can shower together."

She paused for a second before nodding.

"You sure? You hesitated on me."

"I know. I just get in my head about everything. I'm trying to work on it little by little. I went with what my heart was feeling and not what my head was thinking and came up with that answer."

"I like that. You should tap into that more often."

"I promised myself I would."

"I'm curious. What was your head thinking?"

"You really want to know?" She shied away, falling back onto the pillow with an exaggerated sigh.

"Yeah. I really want to know."

"That I can't possibly shower with someone. It's too small and won't fit two people. Also, I was thinking about being completely naked. I've never been that way before, not around anyone."

"Neither have you busted that shit open for anyone, but you do it for me with no problem. You do it very well, might I add."

"Ledge!" She squealed.

"I'm just saying. You're capable of so many more things than you give yourself credit for. How you think that belly swelled like that? From doing things you didn't think possible. Now, here we are. Our daughter is proof of your power, Halo. Don't forget that."

"I can't. She reminds me every day with all the fuss she's always making. I don't think she ever sleeps."

"Like father, like daughter."

"You were just sleeping well, so I don't believe that for a second."

"If you felt your pussy, then you'd understand. Instant knockout. Nyquil. Sleep-aid. Medicine. Whatever you want to call it."

"You're just exaggerating."

"And, you're still slimy," I reminded her. "So, let's go get cleaned up so that I can feed you both."

"But, wait," she whined.

"What?"

"Can we just lay here a little while longer? I just... now I'm not ready to leave this moment. Can we just stay right here? Right now?"

"Under one condition."

"Yes?"

"Tell me something about yourself that no one else knows."

"No one knows much of anything about me, Ledge. I've never had friends and the person who knew the most things passed away."

"Fair enough. Then, tell me something your heart wants that no one knows."

"There is one thing."

"One thing?"

"That no one knows."

"What is it?"

"I've left home before. One time when I was twenty. I felt like I was dying inside after losing my grandmother. I went in search of her in the cemetery. I was so lost when she left me. I just needed to talk to her one more time."

"Did you?"

"Yes. I did. And, I felt so much better."

"Then, you went right back inside?"

"I know it sounds insane, but I wished I never came out. Talking to her was relieving but I had no idea what I was doing. Anything could've happened to me. All I had was an address and a few bus routes. It took me two hours to get to a cemetery that was only thirty minutes away. I missed so many stops. On the way back, it took just as long. I was out of my mind. I made a promise to stay put and I have ever since."

"Then how'd that little girl get in your tummy?" I laid my hand on her bouncing belly.

"That is a long, very long story," Halo expressed.

"We have time."

"Alright."

She laid her head on the pillow and rested her arm beneath it. Into my eyes, she stared with intent and seriousness.

"I was ready to take back control of my life, of my body. Somehow, after so long, I still felt like it didn't belong to me. Like it belonged to the man that abused it for so many years. So, as the date that marked the first time I was violated approached, I began preparing myself. I was determined to change the trajectory of my future.

"Tired of being confined to the house, confined to my past, I desperately wanted to get out. And, ultimately, have a one-night stand with someone of my choosing, that I could tell how, when, where, and to stop if I wanted to. I visited a bar and happened to run into the owner. We talked all night long and he kept my cup full of grown-up juice.

"By the time he was ready to take me home with him, I was hot and bothered. To my dismay, control is exactly what I lost the second we entered his lovely home. He made good love to me as if we'd loved each other in another lifetime and had finally rekindled our smoldered flames.

"We did things to one another and then did things to one another some more. Once the alcohol wore off and reality kicked in, I found myself on his bathroom floor, begging fear not to swallow me whole. My morning ended around four or five when he dropped me off. I wouldn't see him again for eight months when my belly was as big as it was round.

"Crazily, it was the second time I'd gone out. I don't know. That had me feeling like... maybe we were meant to run into each other. I froze up and was unable to admit that it was his child I was carrying. I let him believe I had someone else. He was the lucky guy, though. I'd never been with anyone else.

"My child's paternity was never a question, I just kept it a secret. Then, he did the math. His math added up and he realized I was indeed carrying his child. I looked up and I'm laying in his bed telling him about the time that he impregnated me."

"Oh yeah?"

"Umm hmmm."

"Slimy and all?"

"Yes. He's leading me to believe that he's trying to add another baby to the pregnancy that's at the end with the way he has been leaving his semen inside of me. I don't know if I feel good or if I feel... good about that."

"Yeah, huh?" I chuckled, finding her choice of words comical.

The frown on her face said everything she hadn't. She didn't know how to feel about everything, but she was rolling with it. She didn't quite know how to express herself either, so this was a huge step for her.

"For the record, if it was possible I would try that shit."

"He's a very dangerous man," she exaggerated.

"Na. You're the dangerous one and have no earthly idea just how dangerous you are."

"I don't think so."

"I do. Are you ready to shower now?"

"Yes. I think I'm ready. Who gets in first?"

"Come on and we'll figure it out together."

12

HALO

THE WEEKS WERE PASSING US BY LIKE SNAILS. Though I was ready to see my daughter's face, I didn't want the time her father and I were spending together to end either. It had been a blissful few weeks and I hadn't been required to leave the house to enjoy someone's company. I never imagined loving anyone else's home any more than I did my own, but his home was growing on me. I was beginning to believe I'd rather be here than anywhere else, even my apartment.

"No. She's still here. I'm only one day past my date. According to the birth team, I've dilated three centimeters, so it can be any day. Just waiting for her to come on," I told Kamber, rubbing my stomach.

It had grown so much bigger in the short amount of time I'd been at Ledge's. My feet were fatter, face was wider, body was heavier, and I was feeling so much pressure between my legs it hurt. My body was preparing itself for birth and I could feel almost every change it made.

"Awww. I can't wait to hold her little self in my arms. I'm just mad I can't kiss her. Cause honey, auntie been sucking some questionable dicks for the last two weeks. I need a clean slate before I put my lips on that chocolate skin."

"Kamber, I really really didn't need to know all that information you just gave me."

"Well, you have it now, so keep my lips off her at least the first six weeks. My system will have refreshed by then. I think. I don't know, shit."

"Sometimes, I just can't help but shake my head when it comes to you. You're hilarious."

"I give you life and you know it. You're boring and I'm ballistic. We balance one another. I think it's perfect. Don't you?"

"I do. I seriously do."

"They're here," Ledge announced when he walked into the room, shirtless and tantalizing.

I swallowed the thickness that formed in my throat and tried my hardest to rewet my mouth. I didn't want to admit to my thirst by asking for water when, truly, I only wanted to drink from his fountain. The three weeks I'd been home with him, somehow I always ended up on his pole and his face always ended up between my thighs. It was the same thing every night and every morning. We were both trying to help bring our baby girl into our world as quickly as possible.

"Hello?"

Ding. Dong. Just after the words left his mouth, the doorbell sounded.

"Hello?" Kamber screamed again.

"I— uh. I'm going to call you back later, okay."

"Alright, girl. Don't be lying either."

"I've never lied to you, Kamber." My neck snapped and eyes lowered to the phone. I could feel a tightness in my throat and that was new and uncomfortable.

"Calm down. Don't have a fucking heart attack. I was just joking."

"Oh," I sighed, releasing the breath I had been holding.

"Talk to you later babe."

"Okay, talk to you later."

As I ended the call, in walked Ever and her growing belly. Lyric was right behind her, bearing gifts again. I was convinced that spending money was her favorite thing to do. Our baby hadn't even gotten here yet, but she already had her first Christian Dior mini bag, a mini Gucci bag, and a baby bag by a brand I could hardly pronounce. She'd even upgraded the car seat and stroller combination to match the one her daughter has. According to her, they needed to be twin-cousins. I wasn't sure what that meant, but I couldn't talk her out of it, either.

"Hi," Lyric greeted, sprinting over to the couch that I sat comfortably on.

I mustered up the courage to give a small smile as I prepared the speech that I was far from ready to give. They were expecting a shopping trip and had waited two weeks for me to be ready, but now that the time was here, I was too tired to go anywhere. For once, it wasn't fear that crippled me. It was pregnancy. The thought of leaving the couch was too much.

"What's wrong?" Ever asked before I could even get a word out.

"I don't want you guys to think I'm chickening out, because I'm not. I was looking forward to today. I want to get Ledge something special for his birthday. He's been so kind and patient and loving. I just don't have an ounce of energy. It doesn't matter how much sleep I've gotten these last two weeks, I'm still very tired. I can't get up from this couch. Believe me, I've tried. I even slept here last night."

"It happens, Halo. This just means your body is doing a bunch of extra work to prepare for the baby. It just means the baby is on the way. It's doing work that you can't see but you can definitely feel. The end is near, mommy. That's the good news. It's almost over. In a few short days, you'll be seeing that little girl's face."

"I feel like it, too."

"Tomorrow is the perfect day," Ledge chimed in as he walked past.

"Of course you want her born on your birthday. Get away," Lyric fussed. "I'm making that final transaction this evening. Make sure that account is ready."

"Already did."

"Have you guys decided anything else about the official grand opening? Any acts in mind?"

"That nigga Doc is on fire right now. I'm thinking about bringing him through for sure. He has a fifty thousand per hour ticket for walkthroughs. I'm thinking two hours. I don't want the nigga to perform. I want him hanging there like it's his favorite spot or some shit."

"Yeah. That'll work. It'll make others want to stop through often to see who they run into."

"Exactly. I'm thinking run ten people through there, ten weeks straight. It doesn't have to be anyone of his caliber, just people who can get some motion in the spot. Influencers and shit with lower price tags. And, maybe two more that's hot right now. That should settle it. At least, that's been the plan since we opened the joint. Now that the cash is en route, we can make it happen."

"When?"

"Spring, once the weather switches up and the Channing winter is over. Gives us more leverage. Niggas be happy to come outside and spend bread after being in the house for months."

"That's smart. I hadn't even thought about that."

"The baby will be a few months old by then. I can focus and get my head in the game. Right now, I'm tossing around ideas and reworking the strategy I created a while back."

"Sounds like I better get my fit together because there will be money in the building that night."

"Yeah, your husband, brothers, and they might just get your father out of the house," Ever confirmed.

"I'm not talking about them. I'm talking about the other niggas."

"Lyric, you love to play with that man when he's not around. But, when he is, you don't have much to say."

"Because he's around, but when he leave, I be talking again."

Everyone around me burst into laughter. It was known that Lyric loved her husband, whom I'd yet to meet, but she also loved playing herself. The sound of loud music startled us all. Hearing Ledge suck his teeth told me everything I needed to know about its source. He only did that when it came down to one person.

"This nigga here, man," he groaned, making his way toward the door.

I heard when he swung the door open. From the swiftness of his movements, I could tell he was peeved.

"Aye, nigga," he shouted. "Turn that shit down. This Edgewood, not Dooley!"

In a haste, he was back in the front room and by my side pulling a shirt over his head. He hadn't bothered closing the front door. It wasn't until I heard ruckus near the foyer that I understood why.

"You hollering like you scaring a nigga or something. I don't have to be in Dooley, nigga I am Dooley. It's wherever the fuck I'm at."

Lawe. It couldn't be anyone but him. He was

another one I'd heard so much about but never got to actually meet.

"Nigga, you stupid, but for real. Lower your voice when you talking to grown ass men, playboy."

The person behind the second, calmer tone appeared first. From his bright skin and extra light brown eyes, I knew that he wasn't the twin of Ledge. They surely resembled, but he wasn't the identical twin I'd heard so much about. A darker version of him rounded the corner next, confirming my suspicions. *That* was Ledge's twin. He looked just like him, though there were obvious differences. He was slightly thicker and his hair stood taller on his head.

"You niggas done linked up?" Ledge shook his head from side to side. "Channing can count its days."

"What that supposed to mean?" The brighter one asked.

"Exactly what it means," Lyric added.

"I don't think I like her for real. Do she gotta be my sister even if I don't want her to be my sister?" He turned to the brighter one and asked.

"Yeah. You kind of have no other choice."

"This only my third time in the same room with her and she always on bullshit."

"Sounds like somebody I know," Ledge interrupted.

"Nigga nobody was even talking to you."

"But, you were talking about his sister," Lyric stated.

"I was his brother first."

"So, you want a cookie?" She sniggered.

"See what I'm saying, man? She really got to be my sister, too, Laike?" He asked, again, with pleading eyes.

I would definitely need stitches after watching the interaction. It was comedy at its finest. In the midst of it all, I was learning who was who and watching their true personalities unfold before me.

"Yeah. Really," Laike confirmed.

"That nigga Liam dead ass wrong for that."

"I'm the best child he has. For the record, I don't want your ass to be my brother either. The feelings are mutual, nigga."

"But, I am. Deal with it."

"You the one—," she started but was cut off.

"Ion care what I started. I'm your peoples. Get used to it."

"Ain't this about a bitch," Lyric mumbled. "Does mental illness run in this family or what?"

"Laike, Lawe, this is Halo. Halo, my brothers Laike and Lawe."

"Hopefully, we're going in alphabetical order, otherwise introduce me first, nigga. I've known you longer."

"Yeah, whatever. Alphabetical order, then," Ledge huffed, flipping him off with a middle finger.

"It's nice to meet you, Halo. Why you ain't tell this nigga 'bout this baby a long time ago?" Lawe got straight to it asking questions.

"And, why you ain't let that nigga in all that time?"

"She not answering that shit, so stop asking."

"I'm just trying to get to know her," he explained. What was hilarious was I knew he was serious and meant well. I didn't take offense to his inquiries, but I wasn't answering them.

"Not like that you're not. Matter of fact, back up some. You're too close."

"Aw. This nigga whipped!" He cackled.

"I'm not the only one. Don't act brand new."

"I ain't seen that girl in weeks. That's old news. I'm trying to see which one of y'all got a friend that needs a friend."

"If I did have a friend, I'd never leave her around you," Lyric grunted.

"You can't be my sister and my second biggest hater. Pick one."

"Who's the first?" Ledge asked.

"Hit dogs going to holler every time. Anyway, it's nice to finally meet you, Halo. Bring your ass outside sometimes."

"Nice to meet you, Lawe," I chuckled. "I'll try."

"You 'bout ready?" Laike stepped up and asked.

"Yes. I am. Hopefully soon."

"I can see it in your face. That time almost near. Baby girl will be here soon. Here," he said, digging into his pocket. "Put that in her savings account. I'm going to double that once she gets here and find her an investment property. We're going to flip it and rent it out. When she turns eighteen, that'll be her college fund if she decides to go. If not, she can use it to live out whatever dream she might have."

"Okay, uncle Laike. I know that's right. Keanu just

got her first tenant. You were on to something," Lyric cheered.

"This nigga, all he do is stunt," Lawe joked. "But that's smart as fuck. Let me put in on that."

They both emptied their pockets; leaving me with wads of money that I didn't know what to do with for the time being.

"Thanks."

"Na. Give me that back. I'll bring some more over here. A nigga need some money to hit the shops with," Lawe said as he twirled his fingers in front of me.

"Really?" Lyric sniggered.

"This is truly a match made in heaven." Ever looked on, clearly amused as me.

"I got you. Leave the pregnant lady alone. Just pay me my money back soon as you get home. I'm glad I parked at your spot."

Ledge and I locked eyes as we both wondered what was going on around us. The house was almost always silent. The amount of chatter that was happening at the moment was far more than I'd ever witnessed before. Anxiety was quickly budding in my chest. Being the mind reader that he was, Ledge caught my rising stress level before it could take me under.

"We about to get out of here and leave you ladies to do whatever y'all was about to do. Baby, I'm heading to the shops with the guys. I'll be a few hours. If you need anything, hit my line."

"Okay."

"Come on Beavis and Butt-head. We out."

Ledge rounded the couch, leaned over, and kissed my forehead. Before walking away, he rested his open palm on my belly. It was the best feeling in the world and once it was small again, I knew I'd miss these moments.

"See you in a bit, aight?"

"Okay."

I love you, I wanted to scream as I watched him follow behind his brothers. As if he'd heard me anyway, he turned around and pursed his lips together, sending me a big, fat kiss through the air. I caught it and placed it on my heart.

I love him. Wholly and heavily. I love him widely and I love him deeply. Immensely. I love him. I admitted. *So much it hurts.*

"When's the wedding?" Ever interrupted my thoughts to ask.

"Hmmm?" I turned in her direction with a puzzled face.

"The wedding, girl. You heard her."

"There won't be a wedding. Not yet, at least."

"Oh, it's coming. If he's anything like his father and brothers, there will be one very soon, too. I can't wait to be a bridesmaid. You don't have any friends other than us and the one girl you've told us about so that puts me in the wedding automatically. This is not up for debate. And, I'm planning it too," Lyric rambled.

Shrugging, I agreed to whatever she was saying. *I love him.* I repeated, realizing just how much I did.

"So about shopping," she cleared her throat, changing the subject. "I figured you'd want to stay home so I have a backup plan. I've assembled my team of experts at the stores that I love and they're going to take us on a virtual shopping spree. Whatever items we choose, they'll deliver them today. All you have to do is open the door when they ring."

"Well, there is one other problem," I admitted.

"What?"

"I forgot to get money from Ledge."

"I like how she thinks. Getting money from the man to buy his own gift. Keep that up girl and we're going to get along just fine. But, don't worry about it. Whatever you want, I'll just put it on dad's tab. It's his son, not ours."

Between her, Laike, and Lawe, I wasn't sure who was the funniest. They all had me ready to pee my pants when they spoke.

"I'm going to head out to the car and grab my wine. Yes, I'm drinking alone. I don't care what they say, we're not getting the babies drunk on my watch."

"You're not playing fair," Ever teased.

"Be right back."

Lyric left the living room and headed straight for the door.

"Have you gotten the chance to reach out to Kirklynn yet?"

"Not yet. I figured I would once the baby is here and I can actually focus on my mental health. Right now, I'm just tired and ready for her to come."

"You're being rather patient. Most first-time mothers are begging their children to pop out," she tittered, placing a hand over her mouth. She was so pretty to me.

"I'm ready when she is. I just hope she doesn't take too long."

"Trust me. She's on the way. I can tell. I've had so many, I can literally feel when it's time for me or for anyone around me to deliver. Your time is here."

"Thanks. I'm ready *and tired*."

"It'll all be worth it. Have you talked to the team?"

"Yes. They're coming tomorrow at noon to check me again and see if I've progressed any."

"Okay. Let me know how that goes if you don't mind."

"I don't. Besides Ledge, you're the only person I have to talk to about the serious baby stuff. For everyone else, it's just common questions and knowledge."

"Aww. Well, now I feel special."

"You should because you are. I was wondering if it's possible for a child to have two Godmothers."

"Is this your way of asking me? Because, if it is then yes I will be the baby's Godmother, and who cares about the rules? If you want her to have two then two she'll have."

"Kamber is the other one."

"Good. I know she'll love that."

"She will."

"Have you decided on a name yet?"

"Lailah. I knew from the start that I'd name her Lailah if she was a girl."

"Lailah. I love it."

"Me too. So does Ledge."

"A middle name?"

"Analeigh."

"That's pretty. Where'd it come from?"

"My grandmother. Her name was Anne Lee. I thought it would be cute to put a little spin on it. She was special to me and so is Lailah."

"I'm sure she'd love that."

"Me too."

"Alright, ladies. The first expert is up. Every thirty minutes, a new one will appear on the screen. Cut on the television so that I can sync it with my phone and blow the calls up on the screen."

I passed Ever the remote. I hardly ever touched it or watched television, so I didn't know how to make what Lyric was asking of us happen. As they prepared the tech, I rested my head on the back of the couch, admiring them both. I'd gone from feeling all alone to feeling as if I belonged with each member of the growing family that Ledge was now a part of. He wasn't the only one who'd found his tribe. He'd helped me find mine, too.

LEDGE + HALO

ANOTHER SHARP PAIN ripped through my body. It was one of many in the last few minutes, each one becoming stronger and more intense. The discomfort and tightness of my stomach that I suffered during each one nearly knocked me unconscious every time.

"Oh God, please," I whispered, feeling sweat beads forming on my forehead.

I held a hand to my right side and applied a bit of pressure to relieve me of the pain I was feeling. It had worked a few minutes before, but now there was no use. Everything was hurting. I pecked the screen of my phone and checked the time. It was after midnight and I knew that Ledge wouldn't be home for a few more hours. He and the guys were out celebrating his and Lawe's birthday. The last thing I wanted to do was interrupt his celebration with a false alarm. Instead of dialing his number when I picked up the phone, I dialed Ever's.

"Hello," she answered, groggily.

"Something is happening," I stated as calmly as I could.

"Something like what, Halo? Contractions?"

"Yes. Really strong ones. I tried to lay down and sleep it off, but they keep waking me up."

"I had a feeling she was on the way. How long have they been going on?"

"Since you guys left but they would just come and go. I didn't think much of it until about two hours ago. As of the last hour, they'd been coming one after the other."

"Alright. I'm going to get my nanny on the line to come over and look after the kids. Once she gets here, I'll be on the way. In the meantime, I'm calling Dr. Sanders and the rest of them. Send them a text too. They'll get it."

"Okay. Thank you."

"Have you called Ledge?"

"I wanted to make sure this was real before I interrupted his night. He deserves some fun."

"He deserves to know that his daughter is on the way, too. Call him. I can assure you this is not a drill. Get that man to the house."

"Okay."

I made the first call to Ledge but didn't receive an answer. After another sharp pain ripped through me and then subsided, I tried again. By the third call and two more contractions, I came to the conclusion that he wouldn't be answering the phone. A text message explaining my constant calls was the next option.

> She's coming. Hurry home.

I tossed the phone to the other side of the couch as another contraction hit. The sound of the doorbell was both unexpected and frightening. Doubling over in pain, I tried my hardest to put aside the fear that was creeping into my system.

Boom. Boom. Boom. There was a knock on the window. My heart nearly leaped out of my chest at the sound of it.

"Halo. It's Alec, love."

It wasn't until I heard her voice that I remembered

Yoshi, Dr. Sanders, and Alec were on their way. I'd forgotten to text them. *Ever. Thank God.*

"Ummmmmm." The pain persisted.

"Open up, Halo. I need to check you out and get everything situated."

"Co—mmmmmmmmmming," I groaned.

"I know it hurts, love, but it will all be over soon. Open up."

Energy escaped me throughout the day as I tried to ignore the pain, but I managed to stand on my feet. I took a deep breath before taking the first step. As soon as I did, I felt fluid leaving my body at an alarming rate.

"Oh my God. What's happening?" I screamed, hoping that Alec could answer the question I asked.

"What is it, Halo? What's wrong?"

"I can't stop peeing on myself. I'm peeing on myself."

"No baby, your water just broke. That's good. Baby will be here soon. Open up."

"I'm trying. I can't moooooooooooove. Oh my God."

"Breathe through it. Breathe through it. You've got this."

"It won't stop!"

"I know. Just keep walking toward the door. We'll get it cleaned up later, okay? Come open the door. I have to make sure that baby isn't coming now."

"I'm almost there."

"Good. Good, love. Keep going. I'm right on the

other side. Dr. Sanders just pulled in. Yoshi will be here shortly."

"Okaaaaaaaaaaay," I moaned, hunched over as another contraction hit me.

They were right after each other. I couldn't catch my breath.

"Another one?"

"Yes."

"Breathe. Breathe for me."

When it finally subsided, I made it to the door to open it for Alec. She rushed inside and got me back on the couch where my contractions continued. Soon, I was surrounded by Ever, Yoshi, Alec, and Dr. Sanders.

"I'm so tired. I'm so tired. I just need to sleep."

"We know, baby, it'll be over soon. You're almost fully dilated," Dr. Sanders said, stuffing her hands up my vagina. "Only a centimeter left."

"Ever, please find Ledge."

"I'm already on it. Luca just texted me back. He's leaving the club now."

13

LEDGE

"THAT'S WHAT THE FUCK I'M TALKING ABOUT my nigga!"

"This a father right here, ya'll!"

"Con-grat-u-motherfucking-lations, bro!"

"On your fucking birthday."

"Nigga, you blessed!"

"Welcome to the best hood of them all, my nigga."

Bottle after bottle of champagne was shaken,

popped, and poured on me. From the inside of the club, past the bouncers who dared to touch either of us and to the car, my brothers ran alongside of me, never missing a beat. I pulled open the door of my old school and peeled off my drenched shirt.

Like a thief in the night, I burned out of the parking lot with one destination in mind. I had to get home to my baby, both of them. I couldn't let her do this alone. She'd carried the entire pregnancy on her own. I wanted this moment for her, for us.

Traffic laws didn't exist as I pushed the pedal, causing my entire car to roar and my tires to burn. Radio silence played in the background. There was no music this time. The sound of a wailing baby could be heard in the distance. Though I knew there wasn't one around, thoughts of what Lailah would sound like once she took her first breath of fresh air had me hearing shit.

Finally. The fifteen-minute drive felt too much like forever. When I arrived, I was pleased to see that Halo was already surrounded by the team we'd hired to help bring our baby into the world. They'd been as awesome as Luca had described them. I didn't have any complaints when it came to them handling Halo's prenatal care. A team full of black women; they were knowledgeable and concise.

I jogged up the driveway, bypassing the cars parked. The door was unlocked, easing my entrance. From the moment I walked in, Halo's whimpers led me in her direction. I'd watched so many movies and heard stories of women screaming to the top of their lungs. To my surprise, Halo's low whimpering and moaning was as theatrical as it got for her.

"Halo," I called out, reaching her, finally.

"Ummmmmm," she hummed, barely paying me any mind.

"Alright. Now that dad is here, we can get ready to push," Dr. Sanders announced.

"Already?"

"We were waiting on you. She's been ready for the last five minutes."

"Shit."

"Climb in bed with her and let's get started."

The blow-up bed that they'd put in the front room felt like clouds, although it was firm to the touch. I climbed up and got right beside Halo before learning that it wasn't where I was supposed to be.

"Daddies catch the babies in our practice. Come down here," Yoshi instructed.

"Me?"

"Oh God, please. Just go. She's coming. She's commmmming."

"Listen to your body, mom. If you feel like you need to push, then push," Alec told Halo.

"I need to puuuush."

"My hands, my hands aren't clean."

"It's alright, dad. Calm down. You've got this. Hold your hands out," Dr. Sanders coaxed.

I did as I'd been told and held my hands out. She

sprayed it and my arms with a solution before wiping them down.

"Oooooooh God. She's coming."

"Keep pushing, Halo. She is coming. Hands down there dad."

I watched, nearly ready to puke, as Dr. Sanders twirled her hands around Halo's vagina, exposing the baby's head.

"She's here. Just keep pushing. Dad, get ready."

As I tried to focus on not passing the fuck out, I glared at the gaping hole that I loved sticking my dick in. It was being stretched beyond recognition and used for a much greater purpose.

"Wait mom. Wait until another contraction to push. You're almost there. We see the head. A few more pushes and—."

Dr. Sanders' words were cut short as another contraction hit Halo and she used all her might to push. Our baby girl slid out of her rapidly and landed right in my hands. Her slipperiness made it almost impossible to hold her still, but those weren't my intentions anyway. My soul was rejoicing, loudly and proudly. My heart galloped swiftly, threatening to leap from my chest. My nerves were all undone.

"Baby, baby did you see that? You see her? You— Baby. I—."

The words came as quickly as they disappeared. Complete thoughts and sentences were few and far between. I could feel my eyes stretch wider than they ever had before. Their prickliness revealed the future long before the tears fell.

"Baby, do you see her? You did it."

"I did it," Halo wailed. "I did it."

"You did it, baby."

The phantom cries I'd heard on the way over were nothing in comparison to the ones coming from the little pretty lady in my arms. To the top of her brand new set of lungs, she screamed. Hadn't I known that it was simply a trauma response after such a traumatic birth experience, I would've thought I was hurting her.

"Go ahead, dad. Now, you can lay next to mom. We're going to get her cleaned up. Congratulations to you both."

Carefully, with our daughter in my hands, I scooted next to Halo. Too exhausted to reach for the baby, she simply adored her from a very small distance. My desperation to fulfill the cravings I was sure we shared, I laid our daughter on her chest and watched the tears cascade down Halo's cheeks.

"She's everything."

"She is and she's ours."

"She's ours," Halo agreed.

LEDGE + HALO

ALEC WAS A GODSEND. It wasn't until the sun rose that she asked to be let out and for me to lock up behind her. Her postpartum duties had officially begun. For the next twelve weeks, she'd be with us four nights a week from eleven at night until seven in the morning. Her schedule would keep me from worrying too much while I worked late nights at the bar and help Halo on the nights I was unable to be with her and the baby.

"Good morning," I grunted, stretching my arms until they popped.

"Morning," Halo whispered.

I watched in pure adoration as she rubbed Lailah's hair from center to front. Her tiny body was pressed against her mother's while she nursed. There was nothing in the world comparable to watching Halo nourish and provide our daughter with everything her body needed to grow big and strong.

It was our second time waking in the last three hours since letting Alec out of the house at seven. As chill as Lailah was, she was just as demanding. Every one and a half hours, her little wailing let us know that she was expecting something from us, whether it was to be comforted or fed.

Suddenly, the distance between us was too much to bear. My heart hurt at the cognizance of it all. I scooted closer until the hair on our legs touched and sent electricity through our bodies. Simultaneously, our tired skin stretched to accommodate the smile we shared alike.

My person. A conclusion that was easily derived from the hammering of my heart as I beamed with pride, watching her adapt to our new world while caring for our little one. Still feeling like there was too much space between us, I leaned closer. The skin of our arms brushed against each other and it was only then that I felt most satisfied.

With the back of my hand, I stroked her arm as I ventured into deep thought. The tingling I felt through my body had become more and more frequent in the last few weeks. Its presence shied away from any moment that didn't include her or thoughts of her.

Closing my eyes, I pulled in an expansive breath that swept all the air from around me. A search for the words to express my gratitude was initiated. I didn't have to look far, because they were at the tip of my tongue and had been for two full weeks. Mustering the courage to spill them was lost upon me. However, clinging to them any longer felt incriminating.

"I—." Clearing my throat to rid my voice of the airiness, I started again.

"Thank you," Halo said before I was able to.

"For what?"

"Trying and trying and trying again. For not giving up on me. For not being upset about the pregnancy. For not being upset that I didn't tell you. For letting me into your home. For giving me room to grow, feel, discover, and heal."

I waited for the pain in my chest to subside before responding. But, when the time came, there weren't any other words to surface but the ones I'd been wanting to say for weeks now.

"I love you," I stressed.

"I know," she replied with a nod, ready to continue, but I wasn't ready to listen. I had so much more to say.

"Nah. I don't think you understand. Like, I really fucking love you, Halo. Deep, deep in here," I explained to the best of my ability, pointing at my chest.

"And, what's worse is I knew. I been knew. I knew the moment I saw you in Target and I had this rush of emotions seeing you pregnant. I, immediately, felt like that was supposed to be my luck. That was supposed to be our future. I was salty as fuck, trying my hardest to smile through my frustration with our status... or lack of status.

"I felt like just another nigga when I wanted to be *that* nigga. Your nigga. The one you were sharing a child with. The one who got to experience pregnancy and birth with you. And, when I finally pulled away from you, thoughts of you never left my head. Every few minutes, your voice was there, as if it was sending me signals and messages that I hadn't caught while in front of you because I was too stuck on the fact that someone else had slid into homebase while I waited for your text or call.

"That's how fucked up I was about it. About you. After a few days, when my bitterness wasn't so blinding I began calculating. The moment I stepped on your porch, I knew it was the rest of forever for me—for us. That's why I couldn't give up. I was already kicking myself in the ass for not reaching out to you sooner, finding you, hunting you down, and making you mine long before your body expanded and adapted to our growing child.

"I couldn't see myself bowing out again. I wanted this too bad. This... exactly this. And, whatever it took to get it, I was ready to face. I love you, Halo. I've never loved a woman in my entire life. My mother was the only woman I've ever truly loved and that love is nothing in comparison to this one. The thought of you not being in my world makes me sick to my stomach, physically ill. The thought of us never making this work the way it has leaves me repulsed.

"I knew I was fucked when I realized everything you considered a flaw of yours happened to be something I found beauty in. The consequences of someone else's actions made you a mad woman, but you're my mad woman. I don't take that shit for granted and I'll never take you for granted. I'm just happy that I found you when I did. I've been lost, too, Halo. It's you that's helping me find my way and I love you for it. I love you on a scale so grand that not even I have the words to express it.

"I just know that you're part of me, now. You're embedded. Your name, etched right on my heart. And, for the rest of my life, I want to keep loving on you, keep falling in love with you. Soon as you're all better and feeling like yourself again after giving me the greatest gift ever, I'm locking it down for life. I'm telling you now so don't freak out on me, pretty lady. Tell ya' nigga yes when he asks you to marry him. Alright?"

"Okay," she laughed through the tears that stained her perfect face. "This feels so new to me but it feels so right. I've never cried as an expression of happiness. I've been sad since I can remember. I thought I'd spend the rest of my life that way, but that's so untrue.

"You've come into my life and flipped it right-side up. I'd be foolish not to agree to this feeling for the rest of my days. I too, have known that I'm in love with you and how deep it runs. I just didn't know how to say it or when. Whenever I got the courage, you'd already be gone."

"It's all good, pretty lady. Just don't ever miss another opportunity. And, know that your nigga loves you back. Incredibly."

"I love you and happy birthday."

"I love you too, baby. And, how wild is that? Huh? Lailah being born on my birthday? We're in this shit together. A Scorpio princess. The world hates to see them coming."

"Oh God. I know nothing about signs or how much the world hates them but I hope it accepts this one with open arms."

"It will. It has no other choice or her father is going to act an ass."

"We're parents," she squealed, lowly so that she wouldn't disturb the sleeping princess in her arms.

"We're parents," I agreed, still not believing it myself.

Just as the words left my mouth, there was a splattering sound that made us both turn our noses up as our eyes rested on the little person it had come from.

"I got the one from this morning," Halo cackled.

"Aw shit," I groaned, tossing the covers from my body with a shake of my head.

I slid out of bed, but not before pecking those lovely lips of Halo's. As Lailah continued to make a mess of the tiny cloth diaper that Halo was obsessed with, I prepared a clean one along with wipes and a natural powder that Alec had gifted us.

.

14

HALO

My eyes popped open as I lifted from the pillow that had gifted me with the best sleep I'd gotten in the two weeks that Lailah had been born. Exhaustion had finally taken a toll on me and forced me to rest. Once my body began to shut down, I had no other choice. Otherwise, I'd still be running around the house like a chicken with its neck cut off.

"Where— where is she? Where?" The empty space

next to me on the bed told a sad, sad story that I didn't want to be part of.

Tucking my exposed boob into my nursing bra, I got out of bed. On my way out of the door and down the hallway, I closed the robe I was wearing and knotted the strings in the front. When I arrived at the nursery to find that Lailah was not in her bassinet or the crib she slept in during naptime, panic set in.

With sweaty palms, I raced down the stairs and through one common space after another until I reached the living room. There, I found a very quiet Ledge, sitting on the floor with his head and arm on the couch, admiring our daughter who was sleeping on the blanket next to a pile of pillows.

"Why'd you take her?" I sighed. "We were sleeping."

The fear of the unknown spewed from my lips as I questioned Ledge. I didn't understand the acrimony I felt or where it had stemmed from but I was peeved by his actions. It was the same action that had garnered the same feelings over the last two weeks. But unlike any other day, today was one that I was inclined to speak on them. I could no longer keep hiding my disdain for his lack of consideration when making decisions about Lailah that didn't include me.

"Please, stop taking her away from me."

"You were sleeping, Halo. She wasn't. Once she was done feeding, she became fussy and needed a diaper change. I need you to chill, aight?"

"She was fine, Ledge. You didn't have to bother her." I stood firm.

"You're not the only parent in the house. I'm good for more than a few late-night runs to the nursery or changing dirty diapers. Just like she needs time with you, she needs time with me too. What's the issue?"

I could hear the discontentment in his tone though he tried to disguise it with the love and patience that I adored so much. Unfortunately, neither of them could fulfill the hole that Lailah's absence left in my heart whenever she wasn't in my sight.

"Nothing. I'll take her. I've got it from here."

"You need some rest, pretty lady."

"I'm fine. I can take it from here. I'll take her off your hands," I assured him, stepping forward to grab my sleeping baby.

Ledge slid over, blocking her from my reach. His actions only frustrated me more.

"Ledge."

"I'm cool with you taking her back upstairs with you. She's probably about to get up looking for food, anyway. But, before you do, I need you to tell me what's really going on. Why you so uptight and visibly annoyed? What have I done?"

"Nothing," I sighed.

"Then, why are you using me as your punching bag, Halo?"

"You wouldn't understand."

"Not if you don't tell me. You're right, I wouldn't because I have nothing to go on. Sit down and tell me what's wrong and what I need to do."

Slowly, I released a long breath. "I don't want to sit down, Ledge."

Taken aback by my response his eyes grew larger. "Alright."

"I'm sorry. I'm not trying to be mean. It's just that... I don't like when you take her away from me."

"You needed rest, Halo."

"She needs to be where I can see her at all times, Ledge."

"Does she need to be? Really? Or do you need her to be?"

"She needs to be so that I can make sure she's safe at all times."

"Even when she's with her father?"

"Yes!" My voice raised a few octaves. I didn't think he was comprehending what I was saying, but I needed him to. The quicker he understood, the better off we'd both be.

"Oh wow. So, that's what this is," he sniggered, sarcastically, puzzling me in the process.

"What do you mean?"

"I thought we crossed this bridge already," he explained.

"What bridge?"

I felt as if he was talking in circles, my head, and my heart ached simultaneously. I was full of so many big feelings and so much fear and felt as though he was feeling a wrath he simply didn't deserve. However, there was no way to stop me from spiraling or hide my true feelings. Lailah scared me. Being a mother scared me. Failing to protect my daughter scared me. Having a man in the home with us scared me. There was no other way to put it.

"The one where you feel the need to protect yourself and our daughter from her father; a man that loves her with every fiber in his body."

"My stepfather loved me, Ledge," I rushed out, feeling the weight of the world lifted from my shoulders.

Just as quickly as it was lifted, I was burdened with the weight of another world. Ours. It came crashing down as silence toyed between us. It wasn't until then that I realized what I'd said and who I'd said it to.

Ledge opened his mouth to speak but closed it almost instantly. He lowered his head, suddenly unable to look me in the eyes anymore. When he dropped his head, my heart dropped to the floor, crumbling at my feet. I watched, remorsefully, as he stood to his feet.

Even at his full potential, he wasn't the tall, confident man that I'd grown to love while standing before me. He'd shrunk, not in size but in credence and pride. His ego was bruised, confidence shattered as he gathered himself to leave. And, while I watched him walk out of the door, I died a little inside knowing that I'd murdered his spirit and punctured his heart in the process.

Please. I'm sorry, I screamed, internally, but the words never left my body.

"Dammit, Halo," I bleated like a wounded sheep. "It's not his fault."

I rushed up the stairs with blurred vision and an aching chest. When I made it into the room we shared, I snatched my phone from the bed. With trembling hands, I searched through the list of contacts I'd saved. Though short, it was growing slowly. I tapped the one that my finger had hovered over many times before but I never quite had the courage to call.

"Kirklynn Benedict's office. How may I help you?"

"Uh... I.... I want to schedule a consultation please, for a new patient. Virtually, if possible. I just need it to be as soon as possible."

"Yeah, sure. Can we start with your name?"

"Halo SaraBella. I suffer from agoraphobia and a crippling fear that is a result of sexual abuse I endured for eight years of my childhood," I confessed, not stopping until I felt like I had it all out. "Can she help me?"

"Most certainly. The number you're calling from, can you be reached on this number?"

"Yes."

"Good. She has a few minutes free this evening. Would you like her to give you a call to consult over the phone?"

"Yes. Please."

"Alright. I'll need some more information for you. Hang tight."

"How much will this cost? How much are the sessions and how many do I need a week? I need to know how much I can afford right now."

"Your sessions have been prepaid for the next twelve months. Two per week. We've been waiting for you to call us."

"Paid for? By who?"

"Ever Eisenberg."

LEDGE + HALO

IT HAD BEEN hours since Ledge had walked out of the house and I was starting to wonder if he'd ever come back. Lailah was far more fussy than usual, making his time away feel even more dreadful. Being home alone with her helped me to understand his role in our lives —*especially hers.*

When she was fussing and I was unable to calm her, he did so with ease. When I wanted a little shut-eye to rest up after feedings, he was there to look after her. When I needed a shower, he kept her occupied. When I needed to grab a bite to eat from the kitchen, he rocked her until I returned or made the run for me.

To make matters worse, Alec wouldn't be joining us for the night. It was one of the three days that she was with another family. As I rocked my sleeping child in the reclining chair, every emotion possible soared through me.

10:24 p.m., the clock on the wall read. *Where is he?* I wondered. Desperately, I wanted to apologize and tell him how much he meant to us. Though I didn't think he'd ever cause our daughter harm, my head and my heart just weren't aligned on the matter. My experiences wouldn't allow me to believe that evil didn't live deep inside almost every human on earth. I just prayed that it didn't live inside the one I'd chosen.

I have to lay her down. The smell of breast milk, natural baby powder, and puke assaulted me all at once. I desperately needed a shower and it couldn't wait much longer. While she was down for a few hours I had to take advantage of the time I had. If I was lucky, I could even get in a little nap. Hers stretched for three to four hours now, giving me a bit more time to do chores and think straight.

Because the bassinet was closer and easier to maneuver around the house if necessary, it's where I laid Lailah after slowly standing to my feet. She settled well on top of the soft blanket. I placed another on top of her. It was still unbelievable for Alec, how Lailah adapted so quickly to the crib and bassinet. She admitted several times that breastfed babies were a bit clingier than bottle-fed babies and tended to prefer co-sleeping over independent sleeping.

I gazed at her brown skin and couldn't help but smile. She was the epitome of love and an accumulation of other beautiful things. Her father hadn't played much of a role in her genetic pool. The little baby was a spitting image of me when I was younger.

From her button nose to her chubby cheeks down to the perfect lips and head full of hair. Dr. Sanders hadn't lied when she shared that detail. She'd warned me and I chose not to listen. Luckily, I'd practiced on my own hair long enough to know a little something about it. Once Lailah was ready, I figured I'd do just fine with styling.

Leaving her alone was one of the hardest things ever, but I managed to sneak out of the room with ease. The baby monitor we'd chosen for the nursery was equipped with a camera so that I could check in on her at any time. If I wanted her to remain asleep while I got ready for bed, it was in my best interest to go at it alone. Otherwise, she'd be up at the sound of the shower starting. The little girl had super ears.

I began gathering my things to shower as soon as I walked into the room. Depression began to creep into my bones as the smell of motherhood swirled in my nostrils. I was repulsed by the mixture of smells, forcing me out of my clothing and underneath a towel. I peeled the slightly damp nursing bra from my breasts as my feet touched the coolness of the bathroom floor.

The shower was literally calling me. I answered by leaning over and adjusting the water to my liking. The temperature of the water perfected with each second that passed me by. When I stepped in, I hung the towel I'd been wrapped in on the hanger right beside it.

"Mmmmmmmm."

It felt like I hadn't showered in days. The thick beads of water massaged my skin and washed away the evidence of my day. My eyes grew tired as my energy level decreased. The water had quickly transformed into a sedative and I couldn't wait to be released from its spell. Once and then twice, I washed my body with the kiwi and apple body wash Ledge had picked up from the store for me.

There. I rinsed for the second time, making sure the

soap was off completely before turning the knobs to discontinue the running water. I stepped out and grabbed the towel I'd hung minutes prior. Though I was no longer under the water, I could still feel its effect. My eyes watered constantly.

"Ahhhhhhh," I yawned.

Life of a mother is exhaustion at its finest, I thought. Lailah was two days shy of being three weeks and I wasn't sure if I was coming or going.

Sleep while the baby sleeps. So many people stuck to that narrative, but it hardly worked. When the baby was asleep, I was stuck trying to get things around the house done or trying not to let myself fall apart. Sleeping wasn't always an option. The times I did decide on napping with Lailah, she decided she didn't want to anymore. Within an hour, she'd be up and ready to rumble.

My postpartum body stopped me in my tracks when I passed the mirror. I quickly backtracked, glaring at my reflection. At nearly three weeks post-baby, my body was in much better shape than I'd expected. The bleeding had subsided after the first few days and I wasn't forced to wear the large, overnight diapers that my birth team had provided.

At this stage, I was back to wearing my normal panties and only wearing a panty liner during the night and early morning when the very light yellow spotting seemed to occur. Throughout the day I was perfectly fine.

My belly had shrunk tremendously as if a baby had never stretched it far and wide. The skin was still very dark and my navel still stuck out like a sore thumb. There was also a line that ran the length of the center of my midsection that hadn't yet faded. The *Suede Serum* that I rubbed on the affected areas twice daily was proving to be a true winner. The thousands of reviews they'd garnered online weren't at all misleading.

Ledge, where are you? He crossed my mind as I entered the bedroom.

"We need to talk."

The hairs on my neck and arms stood at attention at the sound of his voice. My body found its way back into the bathroom with one hand resting on the towel I was wrapped in and the other on my chest. I leaned forward with exasperated lungs and little air to breathe, trying to process his presence.

"Halo," he called out to me.

"Sheesh. You scared me."

"We need to talk."

The silence was the only thing I had to offer as I gathered myself and headed toward the dresser that held my belongings. Ledge's hard body stopped me in my tracks. We stood face-to-face, gazing into each other's eyes and waiting for the words to magically appear. My orbs stung from the tears that welled but refused to fall.

"I'm sorry for leaving the way I did. I just... I couldn't stand the way that your words made me feel. I've been feeling that way for the last damn near three weeks since our daughter was born. I've noticed how possessive and how protective you are of her as if I'm going to harm her in some way. You won't even leave out of the room for long if I have her. You sleep with one hour open, almost, whenever you aren't too tired to keep them both open.

"Bathtime, you barely let me help and I'd be damned if I try to do it alone. Diaper changes, you're standing over me watching like a hawk. I haven't been alone with Lailah for more than ten minutes since she's been born. Your showers are shorter than they've ever been. When you're shitting, she's damn near in the bathroom with you. You're killing me here, Halo. Like, what the fuck you think I'm here for?

"I've had no issues with anything concerning your past up until this moment. Not because it exists but because it's imposing on something that I take very fucking seriously and a relationship that I cherish more than anything in this world. Fatherhood is the one thing that I'll never fold on or back down about or have too much patience with when someone is deliberately making my experience shitty. It doesn't have to be like this. It's the one thing that I can't shut up about. I won't. Because I don't deserve what's happening here."

"I know." Nodding, I agreed. "I just don't know what's wrong with me."

"You're fighting something within you that has absolutely nothing to do with the relationship between our daughter and me. I need you to understand that and keep the two separate. What that nigga did has nothing to do with me, Halo. Nothing. I'm just trying to clean up the mess he made of your heart, but I can't do that and fight for a place in my daughter's life, too. I'm here. Let me be."

"I'm trying, Ledge. It's like this voice in the back of my head that just won't let me be or let me rest or let me enjoy the relationship I know you're building with our daughter because it was never that simple with me. I didn't get that. I did, in the beginning, but then everything changed. The man that I'd loved as a father since I was three, flipped on me. He changed. He brutally raped me over and over until I didn't even recognize myself anymore. I've been numb inside for so many years because of him. You made me feel something again. You did that for me. I just can't forget what he did to me."

"I'm not him. Don't ever in your life treat me like I'm that nigga either. I'm good to you. I'm good for you. I'm good for Lailah. Don't make me pay for that nigga's mistakes any more than I already have. It ain't right. Have I not shown you that I'm nothing like the monsters that are out there? Hmmm? Have I not shown you that I'd lay some shit down before I let anyone touch a hair on your head? On Lailah's head? Have I not proved my love? My loyalty? Hmm?"

I could see the steam coming from his ears. I'd never experienced this side of Ledge and I was crumbling under the pressure against this version of him. However, I understood his vexation and it was something I'd caused. For once, I was ready to own up to the mistake I'd made. It happened to be one of the firsts of my entire life.

"Yes. Yes, Ledge. You have and I'm sorry, okay? I'm sorry I'm this way and I'm sorry I can't see past the evil I endured. I'm trying. This is all new to me. Just work with me. Just help me. Just don't quit on me. Just keep showing me and keep loving me. Just don't let me lose myself in th... in the past. I want this. I want us. I want you and I'm sorry."

I stepped forward, pleading my case. The step he took backward gutted me. Where my heart once was a hollow hole replaced it. Instantly, I felt the cold, brittleness of the world. Oxygen fled my body as I searched for the source of life. Because, at any minute, I'd fall over and die of a shattered heart.

"Ledge," I cried out to the love of my life, the author of my completion. The architect of my happiness. The origin of my freedom. The founder of my future.

"You're wrong, Halo."

"I'm sorry. I love you. So so so so much."

When he stepped forward, I felt my lungs expand with air. I could breathe again. His hands gripped the sides of my face as his lips caressed mine. Our tongues met, briefly, before I pulled away to remind him of something important.

"I'm sorry."

"I know," he breathed into my mouth.

My nipples ached as my vaginal walls began to contract. The high that Ledge supplied me with was orgasmic. It came in waves, washing my heart clean and brushing against my soul. I felt my naked body being hoisted in the air as the towel I'd wrapped it in fell to the floor.

"Ledge," I called out to him. "What are you doing?"

He laid me on the bed, gently, before climbing on top of me.

"What the fuck does it look like I'm doing, Halo?"

"But, we can't."

"Why not?"

"We have to wait six weeks."

"It's suggested we wait six weeks, not mandatory. Fuck waiting."

As the words left his mouth, I felt him enter me. I squeezed my lids together and savored our connection. It was as intense as it was appalling. I'd never get over how good he felt to me, how good we felt together.

15

LEDGE

"Merry Christmas," Halo whispered into my mouth as I hovered over her sweaty frame.

"Merry Christmas, pretty lady."

Slowly and quietly, I dislodged my tool from her box. It was coated with her sweetness; the results of a morning session that left my legs wobbly and my head spinning. Briefly, I peeped over into the bassinet beside the bed that held our five-week-old daughter. She slept peacefully, completely unaware that her parents were breaking all the *ancestor's rules* and enjoying one another's bodies at an alarming rate so soon postpartum.

After discussing things with Dr. Sanders, she assured us that everything would be fine if we continued to be careful. Our ability to be transparent with everyone involved in her prenatal and postnatal care was important to me. They understood this and gave it to us straight each time we brought a new inquiry their way.

"Merry Christmas, little baby."

Leaning down, I kissed her brown cheeks and watched as she twisted her neck in my direction. *Greedy ass.* She was always on the hunt for her mother's breast. Anything that brushed against her cheek, she assumed was filled with milk and had a nipple on the end.

"Please don't wake her. I want to shower with you. We don't have long before we're due at breakfast."

"Come on then, because she'll be up soon."

Halo slid her naked body from underneath the covers. As much as she played the concerned new mom, she loved laying in my bed without a piece of fabric on her body other than an occasional nursing bra to catch any leaks. To me, it seemed as if she wanted the dick as much as I wanted to give it to her.

"Bring that with you," I pointed to the contents of the nightstand.

I entered the bathroom before her and started our shower. She came in shortly after, bearing gifts. I opened the drawer I was standing in front of and removed the scissors.

"Hand it here." I beckoned for the plastic in her hands.

It was the second Plan B she'd taken in the last two weeks since we'd become active again. Though we both wanted more children, it felt far too soon.

"I was thinking I'd get on birth control for a few months. You know, until we're ready to try again. I've heard that it can do crazy things to your body but everyone is different. I think I'll be fine."

"I don't know, Halo. Is that something you want to do for real?" I asked, cutting into the plastic and removing the small pill.

"Not really, but neither do I want to have a Plan B for breakfast every morning."

"I'll start pulling out."

"You've never done that," she gasped, seemingly offended by the suggestion altogether.

I don't ever plan to, either.

"I can start," I said instead. "I don't want you fucking up your system with that shit if I can help. I'll start."

"Okay," she sighed.

I could see the sadness in her eyes as I uncapped the bottle of water she'd brought in as well.

"Cheer up, pretty lady. Open wide."

She tilted her head back and opened her mouth. When she stuck out her tongue, I laid the pill on top of it and placed the rim of the water on her lips. She gulped down as much as it took to finally swallow the white pill.

"Might as well kill two seeds with one pill," she joked,

dropping to her knees and taking my limp dick into her mouth.

What the fuck have I created? I asked myself as I grabbed the back of her head and assisted her in her mission to please me.

LEDGE + HALO

"SERIOUSLY, LEDGE. HOW IS MY HAIR?" Halo asked for the third time as she fixed her top again.

"I love it, baby. It reminds me of the night we met."

"It was like this, wasn't it?"

"Yeah. I like that look on you."

"You didn't like the twists I had before?"

"I liked them too, before them motherfuckers got old as hell."

"The older they get, the prettier they are."

"True, but they were like two months in, baby. It was time for them to go. I offered to help you take them down."

"I didn't feel like dealing with my hair."

"I also told you I'd pay for someone to come to you and get your shit together."

"I know. I just didn't feel like that either. I was saving all of my extrovert battery for this morning."

"I would've paid her to shut up if that's what you preferred."

"Oh God, you have a solution for everything, huh?"

"When it comes to you and Lay, yeah."

"Lay?" She sniggered. "When did you come up with that?"

"Last night. You like it?"

I'd been working on a nickname for our daughter for weeks and finally settled on Lay. It was fitting if you asked me.

"I do, actually. For you, of course. I think I'll stick with Lailah."

"Until you're jealous of everybody around her calling her Lay and then try to join in on the fun."

"That's possible," she admitted, pulling the mirror down to check her face for the hundredth time.

"Halo, you look amazing, baby. I promise."

"I'm just so nervous," she confessed, slamming the mirror up and falling back into the seat.

"You're just anxious and can't sit still right now."

"I'm meeting your father and stepmother for the first time. I'm definitely nervous."

"Mom. Momma Laura. We don't do the step thing. And, they're not the average parents. They're pretty much one of us."

I was far more drawn to Laura than I'd ever expected. She was on my line each day making sure me, Halo, and Lay were straight. She'd already reserved a spot in her center for the day we decided to bring her in. Laura was waiting and excited to meet both of the girls.

She was the epitome of a standup woman. There was no malice in her heart when it came to Lawe and me. He found his way to their home each week to be fed and treated like a baby.

His frequent trips left me slightly jealous, but I was appreciative of his adaptability and the comfort they rewarded him with. He wasn't the easiest to deal with or get through to, but they'd worked their magic. Now, he found himself on their doorstep more than a stray cat that had been given one bowl of warm milk in the winter.

"Well, excuse me then. Mom it is."

"Nah, but for real. I'm proud of you, love. You showing up for ya' nigga. I like that."

"I want so badly to be inside enjoying the gifts that he bought me and our little baby, but since he insisted."

"Thank you."

"Don't expect me to come out for the next year. I need to charge my battery again. I can already feel it."

"Well, then I guess it isn't the best time to tell you about the New Year's dinner reservations I made for us?"

"Where, in the dining room? Because I won't make it anywhere else."

"Please. Don't act like you don't feel good riding in the passenger seat right now."

"Admittedly, I do, but that's beside the point."

"Is it really?"

"Kind of. Speaking of being home, management emailed me. My apartment still isn't ready. They've offered me six months of rent to move into the unit next to Kamber. Her neighbors aren't renewing their lease and will be leaving at the end of January."

The bomb she'd just dropped on me left me speechless and hunting for words I couldn't conjure without assistance. I wasn't ready for her to leave, even if it wasn't for another month or more. Having her and Lay at home when I arrived was the highlight of my day. *Every day*.

"Baby, did you hear me?"

She was doing so well at my place, opening up more than she was almost three months ago when I pulled up to her crib. Happiness was her favorite wardrobe now. She looked and felt like the love she was receiving.

And Lailah, she didn't mind her crib or bassinet. In fact, she preferred either over us holding her while she slept. Imagining my nights without them left my mouth dry and my palms sweaty. I gripped the wheel of my truck and focused on even, steady breaths.

"Ledge?"

"Yeah?"

"Did you hear me?"

"Yeah."

"End of January and we'll be out of your hair."

We pulled up to my family's home and parked right in front of the large oak tree without a leaf in sight. I deaded the engine and laid my head against the seat. As I assembled my words, I slid my hands over my face and inhaled deeply.

"Stay," I demanded, turning to face Halo.

"Hmm?" She asked, re-glossing her lips.

"Stay. Make my house our home. Just stay."

"Ledge," she started. "I thought this was temporary."

"Those were never my intentions, honestly. Seeing

how well we work together as a team with Lay, I'm just not trying to fuck that up. I feel as if your moving back home will only take us all a few steps backward when moving forward is the goal. You're happy there... with me, with us. So stay."

"I thought you'd gotten tired of me by now," she groaned. "Are you not?"

"Baby, I'm stuck with you for the long haul, tired and all."

"I never wanted to leave," she whispered as if it was some big secret.

"You didn't?"

"No, because then I'd have to call you instead of rolling over to your rigidness pressed against my thigh or my butt or my leg."

"So, you just want to use me for some in-house dick?"

"After going my entire life without any, it's literally all I think about. I feel so ashamed, but it is so true and it is so good. I can't get enough."

"Who would've imagined Halo could talk that talk and walk that motherfucking walk. Look at you. I see you on your grown woman shit. She said she loves the dick, y'all," I screamed, rolling down the window for whoever was near to hear.

"Oh my God. Please stop. You're going to wake the baby."

"She's going to be up once we get in here, anyway. Everybody waiting for her arrival. They're ready to meet Miss Lailah."

"Then let's get inside because it's freezing out here."

Obliging, I got my girls inside as fast as I could. When her feet hit the floor, I felt Halo's body tense. There was so much going on when we walked in. Children were running around, adults were yelling, and there was laughter throughout the place. Contentment warmed my skin and pulled my lips up toward my eyes. *Family*. This was something I'd always wanted and was happy to finally have.

"She's here!" Lyric cheered, rushing toward the three of us and grabbing the car seat from my hand. "Hiiiiiiii, baby."

"She's probably still asleep," I warned her as I watched her lift the fluffy car seat cover that kept her warm.

"She's wide awake. Oh my God. Look at her. These chocolate cheeks. Lord, why didn't you give me a chocolate doll like I asked?" She joked. "My God, she looks just like you, Halo. Ledge, did you even participate?"

"I put in all the work. She just reaped the benefits, but I'm cool with that."

As the words left my mouth, Laura and Liam both came marching down the hallway in our direction. I rested my free hand on the curve of Halo's back. She softened under my touch.

"Pops, this is Halo. Halo, this is my father, Liam Eisenberg. This is Momma Laura," I introduced them.

Because they were both aware of Halo's struggles with social anxiety, they kept their distance and extended their hands. Respecting her personal space was a request

I'd made before agreeing to breakfast. I was happy to see that they'd both kept their promises.

"Nice to finally meet you. I'm going to wash my hands so that I can finally hold my newest grandbaby," Laura squealed. "It's almost time to eat. The food will be ready in about twenty minutes. Make yourselves at home."

"Finally, the woman who has my son in a chokehold. Keep sinking your claws into him, Halo. Don't let up."

Smiles and nods were all my poor baby had to offer. She was completely overwhelmed with everything and everyone but was sticking to it for me.

"And, that is Luca. I think he's the only one you haven't met so far," I yelled across the room. "What's up, bro?"

He ended the conversation with his wife and met us in the hallway.

"I'm Luca."

Halo extended her hand to match his effort, "I'm Halo."

"Ever has told me so much about you."

He was the first person she'd had any words for. I wasn't surprised. Luca had that effect on everyone. He was as welcoming as he was cold. The first time I walked in the yard, I didn't know if he wanted to kill me or embrace me more. Either way, he'd made me feel right at home from day one.

"I hope good things."

"She only takes the good from people. She leaves the rest where it's at. This my niece, huh?" He pointed to the car seat that was being passed from one hand to the other.

"Yeah. That's her," I confirmed. "Make sure that Lyric shares. I'm going to holler at Halo for a second."

"Bet. I got you."

"Right this way, baby," I redirected Halo.

Grabbing ahold of her hand, I led her down the hall and past the staircase. I knocked on the first door in sight.

"Come in!" Someone yelled out.

When I opened the door, I was surprised to find a nursing Baisleigh inside.

"Hey. Is the baby here?" Her eyes blossomed as she sat upright in the rocker.

"Yeah," I chuckled. "She's in there somewhere."

"Oh good. Let me go see her."

She tossed the cover on her shoulder over her and the baby's head and ended their session. In no time, she was up on her feet and headed in my direction.

"You mind if we borrow this room for a few minutes?"

"No. Go ahead. This is the nursing room. It's free whenever you need it unless someone is in here feeding. I assume you're Halo."

"I am," Halo replied.

"I'm Baisleigh, Laike's wife. This is our little one, Laiken."

"He's so handsome. I can't wait to have a son."

"Is that what you wanted?" She asked.

"Yes."

"Boys are awesome. I can't say that enough. Stick

around and you'll have one soon enough. It's like the fertility club or something around here. I think there's a pregnancy bug in the food they feed the women around here."

"Ever told me, but she's the only one who has more than one."

"For now, but let's keep that between you and me... and you," she said, looking over at me before leaving us alone.

"See, this why the fuck I was at Target that day. Babies everywhere."

"Yes. They're a growing family, I see."

I closed the door, shutting out the ruckus that we'd just escaped.

"Talk to me, pretty lady. How are you feeling?"

"A lot of things at once."

"I figured you could use a breather."

"Yes. Thank you. Everyone is just so... *nice*. I could've used a family like this one all those years back. Seeing everyone here, so happy, and so full of life... makes me happy but it also reminds me that I never had this. Not even once."

"I didn't either and it's been right here all along. They didn't know we existed and we didn't know they were our people. The only time I felt anything close to this was down in Berkeley with my people that way."

"Whom Lailah and I still need to meet."

"Yes. You will, soon enough."

"Everyone has spouses and children and just living the dream. Black love at its finest. This is the type of thing that the world wants us to believe isn't possible or real. Health. Wealth. Love. And Light amongst us."

"You're next. I hope you're ready."

"I'm next?" She frowned, questioning my last statement.

"To become a wife. Just like Lyric, Ever, and Baisleigh. Halo is up next. I hope you're ready to rock a stone on that left hand for the rest of your life."

She placed her left hand in front of her and wiggled the ring finger.

"Well, it does look a bit empty."

"It does."

"And, I would like to have Lailah's last name."

"Ummm hmmm."

"But, I have so much to work on before we can make that happen."

Panic rested in her eyes. I watched as her chest rose and then fell.

"Don't get all in your head about it. We'll figure it out together. Just don't tell me no when the time comes, because you're stuck with me," I explained, closing the gap between us. "For however long we're on this earth. You and that pretty little baby we made in there."

"Isn't she adorable, babe?"

"As a motherfucker," I agreed, kissing her lips once and then once more. "Come on. Let's go back in there with everyone before they swear we're contaminating the nursing room."

Breakfast amongst the family was everything Halo and I imagined it would be. By the time we returned home, the sun was setting and Lailah was out cold. Together, we enjoyed a warm shower, hot chocolate that she forced me to share with her, a movie, and a few unopened gifts I'd gotten her.

She apologized profusely for not getting me nearly as much as I'd gotten her and the baby, but that was the least of my concerns. I was more than satisfied with my new house slippers, North Face coat, clipper set, and Air Forces she'd copped. I'd tried very hard but couldn't quite remember a woman buying me anything for the holiday and vice versa.

I wasn't part of the cuffing preseason and was always left empty-handed when the day for gifting finally arrived. This year, though, I'd checked all the boxes and made sure my ducks were aligned. Ending my night with the love of my life and the child we'd made together was the highlight of my year.

LEDGE + HALO

"TO NEW BEGINNINGS," Halo repeated after me as our glasses separated.

Before consuming the contents of mine, I beamed with pride while waiting for her to sip from the flute in her hand. So much had transpired over the last two and a half months and I couldn't say that I'd change any of it if I could. I was blessed with two magnificent girls that were irreplaceable and filled me with a daily dose of bliss that wasn't comparable to any other feeling in the world.

"You're outside," I chuckled, still not quite comprehending the fact that I was sitting across from the woman I'd fallen madly in love with.

Her shoulder-length hair swayed as she shook her head and smiled back at me. She was dazzling and she was mine. I was swimming in that revelation. It blew my fucking mind every time I looked at her.

"I am and I don't know what to do with myself. I've been enjoying dinner but I'm counting down the seconds until I'm back in the house and with our sweet-faced baby."

"You look amazing, Halo. I'm feeling this look on you." I stated, referring to the simple cream gown she wore for the night. The strappy number looked like butter on her skin. It was almost as if she was naked, though she was fully clothed.

"You like it? For real?" She looked down at her body and back up at me with curious eyes.

"I love it. I love you."

"I love you."

"Immensely," I added.

"Yeah?" She groaned.

"Yes, baby."

"Any goals? Any resolutions? For the new year? I hear it's common practice to make those."

"Not really, other than getting Jilted on the map and —," I began.

"There's more?" She sniggered, "So, the not really was sort of a lie, huh?"

"Now that I think about it, I have a few."

"Spill it."

The ambiance was intoxicating and so was the woman sitting across from me. I'd made reservations on a whim, hoping that I could convince Halo by the time New Year's rolled around. Luckily, she'd agreed to our first official date after a few days of consideration and some bribing on my end.

It happened to be one of the nights that Alec was on duty, so she was much more receptive to the idea than if it was any other night. She stalked the door for a few minutes before being ready to leave, but that was expected. Christmas had been a lot for her mentally, physically, and emotionally. I was just hoping I hadn't ruined my plans by having her accompany me to break-fast with the family.

"Jilted, as I've mentioned before, it's time to get it on the map like it's supposed to be. That's the only business goal I have. The rest are personal, very personal."

"I'm listening to these personal goals," she responded, taking another sip of her drink.

She was buzzed. Relaxed shoulders and glistening orbs revealed her truth. Inebriation, I admired that look on her. Her tolerance level was immature. It didn't take much to get her there. She was only on her second glass of sweet, white wine and I could tell that we were in for a good night; one filled with sensual touches and gratifying moans.

"I don't want to leave this year an unmarried man."

"Hmmm. Good one."

"I want to travel to at least two new countries."

"Can I come along?"

"Of course. As long as you're ready."

"I have a few goals myself. I'll share them, but only when you finish."

"Teaching you to drive and helping you get out more is on the list. I want you to learn independence and enjoy the freedom of just being."

"Thank you so much."

"Closer to God. That's a big one for me. He's been too good, way too good."

"I agree."

"I think that wraps up my list."

"That was a good list, baby."

"Now, it's your turn. Spill."

"Uh... let's see," she cleared her throat. "Trust. I want to trust more and think a little less. I want to surround myself with women who understand me but also push me to be a better me."

"You like the crew? Ever and Lyric? Baisleigh?"

"Yes. They all make me jealous of how boss-ass they are and how confidence just drips from their frames. It's like they own any room they walk in, even when it's more than one of them in the same room. They command attention without even trying. I love to see that. I want that for myself. I don't need the attention, but I crave confidence. They all got their own thing going on. You know? I've just been stuck behind my computer working to build someone else's dream. I don't even have one of my own. At least, I don't think I do."

"Or, maybe you've been too afraid to dream. From the moment I walked into your crib, I got an idea of what your calling was but I could be wrong."

"What is it?" She probed.

"Interior decorating. Organization. Shit like that."

"I've always wondered how cool it would be to create home decor. I took an online class, learning to make concrete vessels, vases, side tables, and more. I think I had more fun making those than I'd ever had in my life. I've even made candles before. The art on my walls, I made with hole filler paste from the hardware store, some paint, and a knife."

"See what I'm saying? Look how exciting this shit makes you. Find somewhere to start and I'll help you from there. You're surrounded by people who will invest in your vision. I learned that rather quickly. Don't sit on your ideas. Put them to use and the rest will fall into place."

"I know, but I start work in a week. I'll need some time to get my thoughts together."

"Quit."

"Hmmm?" Her eyes bulged.

"Your job, quit," I clarified.

"I can't just do that. I can't let my team down like that. They're expecting me back next week."

"Then give yourself a timeframe. Set a date and let your team know that on that day, you'll be resigning. While contributing to their success, make sure you spend a few hours contributing to your own as well. Start researching and figuring out exactly what you want to do and how you want to do it. Set a plan in motion for the day that you're ready to make things official. That's the only way to do it. Otherwise, you'll never have your own motion and continue working for the next person."

"You're right. And, the long hours will take away far too much time from my little sweet face."

"Setting your own hours and handling your own schedule will never not feel like a win once a child is involved. I'm thankful daily that I can see Lailah whenever I'm ready, play with her, watch tv with her, change them loaded ass diapers, and put her to sleep at night. That shit won't ever get old."

"I'd love that."

"You'll never have to worry about bills as long as I'm well and able. It won't hurt to try. If it's not what you want, then go back to work. I'm just letting you know right now that I'm with whatever you're with and I support you one hundred percent."

"Thanks, baby."

"Now, back to your list. We got sidetracked for a minute."

"We did. As I was saying, confidence is a goal of mine. Therapy, too. I think it's time. I reached out to Ever's therapist and discovered she'd paid for a full year of sessions. I don't have to pay a dime for an entire year."

"Nah, for real?"

"Yes. I still need to schedule my first session. I'm just afraid that all the progress I've made in the last few months will have been for nothing. I don't want to have come this far and it all means nothing."

"It means something, Halo. I'm sure it will feel like a setback, but only so that you can restart and head in the right direction. What's the matter with that?"

"Nothing, I guess."

"Exactly. Start the sessions and we'll go from there."

"Okay. I will."

"What else?"

"I want to learn to love you better, harder, and with everything in me. I feel like I do already, but I know there are parts of me that I locked away. Hid. Burned. I'm ready to unveil them so that I can give my all to this relationship—just like you."

"In time you will, Halo. We're still fresh, still new. We have so much more loving to do. Let's just think of it as a quest and I'm on a mission to unlock doors that were shut a long time ago. Layers. Every love needs them. I'm not expecting access to them all at once. Experiences, trials, ups and downs, hardships... that'll peel back a new one each and every time. I'm willing to wait as long as I know that you're the prize in the end. Not some of you, but all of you."

"Where'd you come from?" She chuckled, taking another sip from her glass.

"Where'd you come from?"

"You're so good at this."

"At what?"

"Expressing yourself and helping me express myself."

"You're getting better. It'll take time but that's all we have and a lot of love to go with it."

"See, how do you do that?"

"Do what?"

"Make me fall in love with you a little more with every word that comes out of your mouth?"

"The same way you do it, love. Some shit we don't have to force. It's there. Plain and simple. We're facing the inevitable. Roll with it."

"I want to go outside."

"Another goal?" I sipped the brown liquor from my glass.

"Yes. A really big one. When it warms up, I want to take Lailah for long strolls through the neighborhood or shopping because we feel like it. I want to take her to parks and zoos and aquariums. Before I do, I have to get over this fear of *life... of living*."

"You will. In due time, you will."

"That's part of the reason I agreed to dinner tonight. I wanted to bring in the new year out of the house, facing my fears and feeling like a real person."

"I appreciate that."

"I appreciate you. More than you know. I really do. I'm serious."

Her smile was like rain after a drought, sunshine after a storm, and light after total darkness. *She's mine*. I couldn't get that out of my head. *All mine*.

"The feelings are mutual. I don't know how many times I've told you, but you're wondrous tonight. I love everything about your whole vibe and look. You put that shit on and I'm trying to peel it right off."

I gulped the rest of my drink and caught Halo's glossed eyes before they could leave me. The sinister grin on her face told me everything I needed to know.

"Yeah?"

"I want to take you on this table," I admitted, placing my glass in front of me.

"Then what are we waiting for, Ledge," she challenged, looking around to make sure we were the only ones in the private dining room of Velvet Road.

I'd been very specific when choosing the spot. Their private dining experience was exactly what Halo and I needed. The entire restaurant consisted of private rooms for guests who preferred time alone or needed seclusion. While everyone else charged a fortune for isolation in their establishment, Velvet Road's strategy was dedicated to solitude.

"The staff won't be returning unless we ring for them."

"Sounds perfect to me."

I scooted my chair away from the table and tilted my head to the right.

"Come 'er," I called out to her.

She stood tall, exuding that confidence she swore she didn't have. Though she shied away from mostly everything and everyone, when we were alone is when I witnessed her shine bright like the gem she was. That was the Halo that was reserved for me and I was fine with that. Not everyone deserved this version of her.

And, for as long as I could be, I would be selfish with her.

"Put your leg up here," I commanded when she reached me.

Slowly, she lifted her leg and then placed her foot on the table. I scooted up until I was close enough to smell her pussy juice seeping from her insides. I lifted the dress that I loved so much and exposed her nude panties. The lace matched her skin perfectly. I leaned in and kissed her skin through the small cracks. My mouth watered as my appetite rejoined me. I thought dinner had filled me to the brim, but I had room for dessert after all, it seemed.

With my index and middle fingers I pushed her panties aside. Her aroma tickled my nostrils and made my dick hard in my pants. I felt a hand rest on the back of my head as she led me to her pot of gold. The audacity she possessed during moments of intimacy was as sexy as it was enticing. She withheld nothing and was easily undone.

I licked the tip of her clit, bringing a low moan from her upper lips. She pushed my head deeper between her legs and her pussy in my mouth. Without words, she'd made it perfectly clear that she wanted me to ruin the pretty dress she wore. I had no issue doing so either, but not in the position we were in. I needed full, unrestricted access.

From my seat, I stood and swooped her up in the process.

"Wheeeew," she yelped.

The sound of glass hitting the floor was the least of

my worries as I spread her legs wide and lowered my lips to her neck. I kissed her brown skin, covering every inch that wasn't clothed. *Her collar bone. Shoulders. Chest. Thighs. And finally, her pussy.*

"Oh, Ledge," she wept, arching her back and digging her claws into my head.

I feasted, enjoying dessert much more than I had dinner. *This* was fine dining. My tongue became the plectrum that I used to strum her guitar. She rewarded me with satisfying moans and her personal brand of cream that tasted like nothing I'd ever had before. It was delectable.

"Ummmmm. Yes. Yeeeesssss."

I employed my fingers, inviting them to join the celebration. Curled slightly and upright, they located her textured nub which was the control center for her orgasmic experiences. I applied pressure, massaging it until I felt her limbs weaken and her body stiffen.

"Babbbbbby," she howled as a tsunami flooded the table napkin and the few dishes that surrounded us still.

After my helping of Halo, I pushed my pants to my ankles and wasted little time sinking my ship in the middle of her ocean. All that shit I'd promised her about pulling out went right out the fucking window. It was our world, whatever the consequences I was willing to deal with them.

"This feels soooooo good."

She clung to me as if I'd disappear if I let me go. I wasn't going anywhere. Not now and not ever.

"Cum on this dick, Halo. Let me see that shit."

16

LEDGE

"WE'RE COMING THAT WAY SOON. YOU'RE GOING to meet her little ass. She's a doll, man. I can't get enough of her," I explained to my cousin, Malachi, while holding the phone between my ear and shoulder.

"Don't take too long or I'm packing the old lady up and we're hitting the highway."

Though he followed his statement with laughter, I knew that he was serious. Since Lailah was born, he'd been trying to see her.

"If that's what you want to do, nigga, then come up. I'm not going to talk you out of it."

"We'll see what it's looking like over the next few weeks. My schedule has been crazy."

"Same. Same."

As the words left my mouth, Halo came strutting into the house. Her tear-stained face said everything that needed to be said about the therapy session she'd just come from. It was only her third session and she'd almost talked herself out of going. I was forced to step in and encourage her to do so anyway, reminding her of the goals she'd set three weeks prior.

"Aye, let me call you back. Baby's home."

"Aight. Handle your business. Hit my line later."

"Bet."

Without even saying a word to either of us, Halo stomped up the stairs.

"Mommy isn't feeling well," I informed our daughter as if she could understand anything I was saying. "Want to go cheer mommy up? Hmm? How about we try to get a smile on that face of hers? Huh?"

Though she didn't understand the words coming from my mouth, she sure acted like it. Her hands and feet went wild as she put her gums on full display. She liked the sound of what daddy was saying, it didn't matter what any of it meant.

"Come on, baby girl. Let's go see what's the matter with mommy."

I cradled Lailah in my arms and headed for the stairs. When we arrived, I was partly surprised that I didn't find

Halo in our bedroom. I checked the nursery and didn't find her there either. It wasn't until I got to the end of the opposite hall that I found her in bed with her face buried into the pillow. She was fully clothed and underneath the cover.

I made my way around the bed and sat next to her. Pain ripped my heart to shreds as I watched her body convulse from the affliction of it all. Knowing that my baby was struggling with something that I couldn't help with was eating me alive. Each session seemed to get heavier and heavier, reminding me of what she'd shared with me at dinner weeks ago.

I'm just afraid that all the progress I've made in the last few months will have been for nothing. I don't want to have come this far and it all means nothing.

Because there wasn't much else I could do, I placed a hand on her back and rubbed it up and down. Her trembling frame was the source of so much agony and the playground of so many scars. As much as I wanted to, I couldn't heal her. She had to manage the healing on her own. And, she was trying. The effort she was giving hadn't gone unnoticed. Though she felt like she was going backward, I knew that it wouldn't be long before she was moving forward again. Until then, we'd just tough it out.

"Somebody wants to say hi to you."

"Not right now," she cried into the pillow. "I just want to be alone. Please."

Feeling the weight of her discomfort, I stood from the bed. She needed this moment to process whatever it was she'd experienced in therapy and I'd give it to her. Lailah and I would just have to do without her for a little bit longer. There were still a few ounces of milk that Halo had pumped before leaving for her appointment, so I was optimistic about our time together.

Wanting to provide Halo with as much comfort as possible, I laid our daughter down in the spot I'd just gotten up from and rounded the bed. I flipped the covers back, leaned forward, and removed Halo's coat. Then, I removed her shoes. Her pants were next and then her shirt.

I leaned down to kiss her red, swollen lips, but she rolled over before I was able. Letting the disappointment roll off my back, I covered her body so that she wasn't cold. This time when I leaned down, I kissed the side of her forehead and pushed her hair out of her face. It was damp from the tears.

"Come on, little baby."

I swooped Lay into my arms and flipped the light switch on the way out of the door.

"Mommy needs some rest. Let's see if we can get a nap in too, before daddy goes to work. You down or you gone start tripping?"

Lailah was truly the meekest and mild infant on God's green earth. She hardly put up a fuss about anything other than milk. As long as she had an endless supply of it, she was good. She reminded me so much of her mother. *Peaceful. Modest. Quiet.* She'd taken so much from Halo. Their faces and personalities matched.

LEDGE + HALO

WITH LAILAH ON MY CHEST, I dozed off. It was my blaring phone sounding in the distance that woke me. I hurried to answer it so that it wouldn't wake her, not caring who it was that was calling.

"Yeah?" I answered.

"You trying to make time for your old man tomorrow? I was thinking we could sit down for lunch," my father replied.

"Who all coming?"

"We got to have a crowd to eat?"

"Nah, just asking if the rest of the crew coming."

"I haven't talked to anyone else. I thought I'd call you first. You've been on my mind the last few days and I just want to check in with you."

"Sounds like a plan. Halo is in therapy and doesn't feel too well the first twenty-four hours after a session. I might be bringing Lay with me."

"Well, I'd hope so. You're not the one I actually want to see."

"Then you could've just asked me to bring her by. You're using me to steal some time with Lailah. Nigga, you ain't slick."

"Hey, a man's gotta do what he gotta do. Laura is ready for her to start at the center. You two gave it any more thought?"

"We have. We just feel that she's still too young."

"What about one day out of the week? To give you two a break? You can start there. It doesn't even have to be the whole day."

"I'll talk to Halo about it."

"That's another thing I've been thinking about."

"What?"

"You making an honest woman out of her. Have you given it any thought?"

"It's all I can think about these last few weeks. I'm just holding off until she's ready. I feel like she is but she doesn't think she is. She's trying to become some perfect version of herself that I've never asked for."

"You don't have to. Women obsess over perfection like it's actually obtainable. Their version isn't anyway. They're perfect just the way they are and they have no clue about it. I've never understood that and probably never will. But, I'm saying all of that to say that if you start waiting, you'll be waiting forever."

"I can't do that."

"I didn't think so. Whatever you decide, let me know. Your mother—I mean Laura and I were talking and—."

"It's okay," I assured him. "It's cool. My mother is no longer here, Pops. She wouldn't mind having Laura step in and take her place. She wanted that. Did you forget the letters she wrote?"

"I know, son. I just don't know how you really feel about all of this. It's still so new to us all and I don't want to offend anybody."

"You're not. Have you not noticed how much Lawe

and I both needed this? You can't keep that nigga out of your house. While you're planning lunch with me, I wouldn't be surprised if him and moms not planning something of their own."

"That boy is some kind of special. Reminds me a lot of myself. He's got a good head on his shoulders, though. He and Laike are one and the same. What are the odds of them both being into the same shit? I've been making them sit their behinds down and figure out this real estate business. It's too much money in it for us not to be investing more. It could be all of our retirement plans."

"Lawe knows this. It's been his plan all along."

"So, I hear. Laike is on board now. Something good is going to come from it. I can feel it. This is what they both need to keep them from getting themselves into some trouble my wallet probably can't get them out of."

"Right."

"Well, alright. I'm going to let you go. Your sister tells me she's coming to that bar of yours to celebrate her birthday tonight. I hope you got something special set up for her or she's going to feel really basic. God knows she hates feeling basic."

"Ahhh. I knew I was forgetting something. Pops, for tomorrow just send me the time and location. I need to get the doula here early so that I can get Lyric right for the night."

"Alright."

"Love you, old man."

"Always."

The call ended as my brain went into overdrive. After

Halo had come in with sad eyes and no words for Lailah and me, everything else slipped my mind. I opened my contact list and found Alec's number. I tapped it to initiate a call.

"Hello," she answered on the second ring.

"I need a favor," I explained.

"Just say the word."

"I need you to come in early tonight. My sister is celebrating her birthday at my spot and I want to make it special for her. I need to get there a few hours early to make that happen."

"What time are we talking?"

"Now."

"I can't come now, but I can be there within the next hour and thirty minutes. I'm in the middle of something right now."

"Damn. Aight."

"Is everything okay?"

"Yeah. Halo had another session today."

"Ahh. Got it. I'll try to wrap this up quickly. Give me an hour and I'm there."

"Bet."

I didn't have an hour to spare if I wanted to make the stores before they closed. We'd celebrated a few birthdays at Jilted, but none was in comparison with what I had in mind for Lyric. I wanted to pull out all the stops for her night. Her birthday wasn't for another two days, but we were going to act like it was tonight.

A custom cake had already been delivered. There were a few decorations that we kept in the storage room for our birthday hostings, but I wanted more. I had a vision and it included large letter balloons, endless champagne, a roped-off section, hookah, long-stemmed birthday candles, a photographer for social media content, a birthday pin for monetary contributions, and custom happy birthday signs for the staff to flaunt every time a new bottle was popped.

I laid the queen of the castle on the blanket that was spread out next to us on the couch. Trying not to make a sound, I back peddled toward the stairs. I needed to make sure that Halo was alright and well enough to have Lailah the full hour it would take for Alec to come in. Two by two, I jogged up the stairs and sprinted down the hallway.

I cracked the door open to the bedroom where Halo was resting. Her back was toward the door, making it hard to confirm or deny if she was sleeping or not. For a closer look, I stepped into the room. The door closed behind me, alerting Halo of my presence.

"Ledge, please," she hissed. "I said I want to be alone."

"I'm coming up here to check on you."

"I don't need you checking up on me all the time. When I'm ready, I'll come downstairs."

The aggravation was heavy in her tone. Her annoyance was baffling, because I hadn't done anything to cause it, yet she was using me as a target again.

"Halo, I need you to talk to me like you have some sense, aight? And, waiting until you are ready ain't exactly ideal, tonight. I need to go to work early so you have to get up. Lailah will need you until Alec gets here in an hour. You think you can handle that?"

"You think you can handle that?" She barked, lifting up from the bed and sitting straight up. "Do I look like a child to you, Ledge? One who can't handle her responsibilities?"

"I never said that," regretfully, I sighed. "It's just a question that needs an answer."

Instead of responding, Halo laid back down and pulled the cover up over her head.

"Look, I've never been to therapy so I can't begin to tell you how that feels. What I can tell you is that you using me for target practice every time you're down bad, hurt, or in pain feels like shit. I have my battles as well, but am I coming home to beat up on you when they don't go my way or feel like too much?"

"Nah. I wouldn't do that because, at the end of the day, my peace lies within you. I know that you're not the enemy and I don't treat you like one. I treat you with all the love and respect that you deserve but somehow, I keep getting the short end of the stick. I told you weeks ago that we'd fight this shit together. But tell me how I'm supposed to fight your battles with you when you're fighting me? Hmm? I don't understand Halo. You're so much better than this shit."

"It pisses me off to see you lay down and let it defeat you. You have to want to win for it to happen. Trying go round for round with me when you know I'll never fight you back is pointless. I'm not that nigga. All I've got for you is words, love, encouragement, support, money, and some dick. If you're looking for a fight, I ain't got that. I'm beyond that. I refuse to let any of this fuck up my night. I've got things I need to do."

"Our daughter needs you. She's still asleep and on the couch downstairs. Alec will be here in an hour. Wipe your face, put your big girl panties on, and go downstairs. I'm heading to work."

My exit was swift. I left her alone with her thoughts as I headed to the bedroom for a change of clothes. I dug through the closet for something simple. The night wasn't about me; it was about my baby sister. Seeing her have the time of her life in my place would help resolve the shit I was feeling inside.

Dressed in all black, I made a beeline for the stairs. I wanted to get out of the house before Lailah woke up because once she did I knew it would be harder. It always was on work nights. Leaving her, I didn't think I'd ever get used to it.

When I made it downstairs, Halo had taken my place on the couch. My aspirations of being out of the house before the baby woke were crushed as I watched her drink milk from her mother's right breast. It was her favorite and the one she drained first every time.

Halo's eyes locked with mine briefly before I tore away. I entered the kitchen and went straight for the minibar area. With everything that I was thinking and feeling, I needed a stiff one. I didn't have a preference for the night. The first bottle my hand landed on, I removed the cap and lifted it until the liquid poured down my throat, eventually burning my chest.

"Ahhhh," I coughed.

Realizing I wasn't quite pleased, I turned the bottle up again.

"Aight. I'm out." As the bottle hit the counter, I whispered.

Straight out of the door and past Halo, I escaped her grasp. If I mumbled a single word to her I knew that I wouldn't be leaving the house any time soon. We needed to talk but now wasn't the time.

She'd cool off eventually and I'd be right there waiting to pick up where we'd left off. Therapy paused everything in Halo's world. Motherhood, relationships, and work. That's why she preferred Friday sessions over the one Wednesday session she'd attended. Her entire world shut down when a session was over. Nothing moved. There was a twenty-four-hour hold on every-thing. But, once the pain subsided, she was back to being my Halo, the woman that could do no wrong in my eyes. I couldn't wait for morning so that I could meet her again.

LEDGE + HALO

"JADE, finish setting up the table. She'll be here by twelve," I yelled out as I passed the bar area and approached the empty section that was reserved for Lyric and guests.

"I'm on it," she slurred, plainly intoxicated.

"Jade, how many drinks have you had tonight?"

"Uh... probably about the same amount as you."

Her point was made, forcing me to seal my lips and head back to the office where Lyric's decorations were waiting on my desk. I collected as many of them as I could with two hands and brought them back to the table.

"Is this all of them?" Jade questioned.

"Nah. I'm bringing the rest out."

My phone vibrated in my pocket. I patted them all until I found the one. On the screen Lyric's name danced. I swiped the screen to answer, knowing exactly what she wanted.

"Yeah, I'm getting your section ready, Lyric."

"Alright. Just making sure."

"What time will you be here?"

"I don't know. I'm waiting on Keanu to come back. I'm not sure where he's off to, but he's staying with the baby tonight."

"He ain't coming?"

"No. No boys allowed. It's girl's night. We'll celebrate with the guys on my actual birthday. For now, they're all home with the kids. Well, everyone except you."

"That's because I'm here making sure y'all have a good time. Besides, Halo ain't coming out. We all know that. Not tonight and not on your birthday either."

"One day, my girl is going to surprise us all and come hang."

"Yeah, well, I'll be glad when she does."

"Me too. With a body like that, you wouldn't be able to keep me in the house."

"You aren't ever in the house, anyway."

"Mind your business. You get what I'm saying."

"I do."

"Alright, well I'll see you in like an hour, I guess. Whenever this man pulls up, I'm on my way. I have to stop and get Ever then we're dropping by to get Baisleigh."

"Bet. I'm here."

As I ended the call, I felt a tap on my shoulder, prompting me to turn around. I was evidently surprised to see the man Lyric was looking for standing in my face.

"Your wife is looking for you, dog."

"I know. She can wait a little longer. She has the whole night to herself."

"We're getting her set up right now."

"That's why I'm here. I got some gifts I want to leave in her section and I want to pay her tab upfront. I know she's about to run up a bag in this bitch. You'll discontinue the family discount completely by the time she's done. She invited the staff from Baisleigh's House too. They drink like fish."

"I got her covered."

"Nah. Trust me. Take this," he offered, forcing the banded hundreds in my hand. The white band that held the bills together displayed the count in red.

"She spending ten g's tonight?" I whistled.

"Minimum. That's just to start the tab. If she goes over it, then let me know."

"I'll handle it if she does."

"Where's the section? I need to unload."

Keanu lifted his hands to show me the bags he was trying to get rid of.

"Right there. Jade is getting it together now."

"Aight. I need to run to the car and get a few more things. I'll be right back."

I admired the love he had for Lyric. It ran much deeper than the typical husband and wife titles. He was her friend. Her best friend. I witnessed their friendship in the way that he cared for her. It reminded me of the love of a brother or a father.

Lyric was getting the best of both worlds and that made my chest swell with pride. She'd chosen wisely. That was one less ass I had to kick and one less chance I had to take for going to jail because I would behind her and Halo. There would be no questions asked.

Leaving Keanu to handle his business, I made my way back to the office to handle mine. I needed to get the rest of Lyric's things to Jade and then finalize the inventory count so that I could put in orders to our vendors before calling it a night. If it wasn't too late when I finished up, I planned to pop a bottle with the birthday girl and then head home to climb in bed.

My phone went off again. I looked at the screen to discover a text message from Halo. As simple as it was, I knew that there was so much more to the words.

I'm sorry.

She'd sent.

Progress. She understood her actions were hurtful and decided to acknowledge that instead of waiting until things blew over. With a smile on my face, I pushed the door to my office open. Her message only made me want to end my night sooner than I'd anticipated.

There wasn't a response that could accurately express the message I wanted to convey. When I got home, I'd show her much better than I could tell her. I grabbed the rest of Lyric's things with one hand and turned up the shot glass that still had brown liquor in it with the other.

17

HALO

"HE READ IT, BUT DIDN'T RESPOND," I SIGHED into the phone, waiting for Kamber to give me some helpful advice. "I feel awful, Kamber."

"You should. Girl, I don't know what the hell is wrong with you. If you're expecting me to pacify you right now, then call somebody else."

"I'm not. I know I shouldn't have been so mean. I feel awful and I miss him."

"When that man walks through the door, you need

to be right there with your mouth stretched wide the fuck open. Suck that nigga dick until he forgives you. Then, don't do that to him again."

"I'm not. It's always so much, though. I feel like I'm drowning after these sessions. They're killing me and putting a damper on my relationship. I feel cripple when I walk out of that office."

"It's all for the better, Halo. Think of it that way. And, give yourself some grace. You've been through so much."

"I know."

"And, look at the bright side honey. You've been going out of the house. It doesn't matter that it's only two days a week."

"I still can't wrap my head around it. Ledge has a service that picks me up and drops me off when I'm done."

"I'm so happy for you, friend. You got out of that apartment, got you a nigga, and are getting your life. Damn, does this mean I need to move?"

"This move wasn't on my list of plans."

"That's what makes it so much better."

My other line buzzed. Remembering the text I'd sent a few minutes ago, my frame firmed.

"He's calling," I reported with wondering eyes and a hammering heart.

"Answer then and call me back."

"No wait. I'll just click over."

"Okay, hurry before he hangs up."

I pulled the phone away from my face to see that it wasn't Ledge calling. It was Ever.

"Oh."

"Oh?"

"It's Ever. One second."

I clicked over before Kamber could begin to complain. "Hello?"

"Get dressed."

"Hmm?" Confused by her request, I asked, "What?"

"Get dressed. We voted and we all agreed that you should come out with us to celebrate Lyric's birthday."

"Yup."

"Sure did, so get dressed."

I heard a variety of voices on the line.

"Who is we and why do I have to go?"

"Lyric, Baisleigh, and I. And, we're on the way. That's why you have to go. If me and my pregnant belly are in attendance, then why can't you be?"

"I have Lailah."

"Nice try," Lyric sang.

"Alec is there with Lailah. I already asked."

"Wow. Are you guys serious right now?"

"We're on the way. You have about fifteen minutes," Lyric warned.

"That's not enough time, guys. I need more."

"Twenty minutes. We'll wait for five. Make sure you get really fine. Your man is at work tonight." Listening to Lyric probably wasn't the smartest thing to do, but she was making sense.

"I know and he's upset with me."

"See, the perfect reason to get fine and make him forget whatever he's tripping about."

"He's not. I'm the one that was tripping."

"Okay, well, hey. Apologize in person. You're wasting time. Come out in twenty minutes or we're coming in."

"Bye."

I hung up the phone completely, forgetting that Kamber was on the other line. By the time the phone buzzed in my hand again, I was already upstairs going through the bags of clothing Ledge had gotten me for Christmas. I was sure there was something inside that I could wear for the night.

"Hello?"

"Just hang up on me then."

"Sorry. That was Ever and the rest of them, requesting my presence tonight."

"Oh my God, I'm jealous. I'm on my way to work. Y'all about to have all the fun."

Kamber still hadn't met any of the girls but swore she was their best friend in her head.

"Hopefully. Black or white?"

"Shirt or bottom?"

"Shirt."

"Black. I'm sure it'll look sickening against your skin."

"Alright, black it is. And, the bottom?"

"What do you have?"

"Black, cream, uh, red, and... denim."

"Red. Go with red."

"Okay. The pants flare slightly at the bottom."

"Oh, that's perfect. What kind of shirt is it?"

"A silk button down."

"Button half and then tie the rest in the front. Show a little boob and some stomach."

"Kamber, I think it's fine the way it is."

"Maybe so, but put a little spin on it. Have you forgotten you made your man mad before he left the house? Unbutton the top buttons and tie up the bottom."

"Okay."

"Now, shoes?"

"Lyric got me some black shoes. Tom Forward or something like that."

There was silence on the line before Kamber burst into laughter. I didn't understand what was so hilarious.

"Tom Forward? Who the fuck is that, Halo?"

"I don't know. Whoever made the shoes, I guess."

"Tom Ford?"

"Tom Ford?" I repeated.

"How do you know about shit like Chanel and Gucci but don't know Tom Ford?"

"Everybody knows about Chanel and Gucci. If they had been Chanel or Gucci, then I would've gotten the name right."

"Well, don't tell nobody it's Tom Forward. It's Ford. F-O-R-D."

"I get it. I get it. Anyway, I think they'd go well with this outfit."

"Shit, any outfit if I had them in my closet. You

wouldn't be able to keep me out of them. But, yeah, put them on."

"Accessories?"

"What do you have?"

"Ledge bought me a diamond necklace for Christmas that I haven't unboxed. He got me a watch too. I could wear those."

"You'd better wear those. Let that nigga see you dripped in his coins. They love that."

"Love what?"

"Nevermind, Halo. Focus. Make sure you wear perfume and fix your hair. I'm sure you cried all in it."

"How'd you know?"

"Because you're that fucking dramatic."

"Whatever, Kamber. I need to call you tomorrow. They'll be here in twenty minutes and I need to get dressed."

"Bye. Suck enough di—."

I ended the call before she could finish. Her foolishness had no place in my life tonight. I'd deal with that another day. For now, I needed to focus on getting myself together before the girls showed up. Luckily, the swelling of my face was going down and I didn't look like a blowfish. Otherwise, I'd be staying inside and everyone would just have to go on about their night without me.

LEDGE + HALO

I smoothed my shirt down with my damp palms. *Maybe I should untie it. It's probably wrinkled now. How is my hair?*

"Slow down, y'all. Princess Halo ain't used to walking in heels," Baisleigh chortled, reminding everyone.

I was struggling to keep up but after deciding that my feet just couldn't go fast as everybody else's, I put all my energy into not falling face-first on the pavement. Luckily, the distance from the reserved parking to the door wasn't that far.

Collectively, everyone slowed down to match my speed. Little by little, we progressed until we were finally at the entrance. Memories flooded me as I tried to hand over my identification to the security guard who simply waved me off.

"She's going to show you to your section. Enjoy your night ladies, and happy birthday, Lyric."

"Who told you it was my birthday?" Lyric paused.

"Your brother let us know to be expecting you. He hasn't shut up about this shit all night."

"Since you know so much then, go ahead and dig in your pocket and put something on this pin. Be the first. Do the honors."

"What this is, a shakedown?" He sucked his teeth, but still managed to reach in his pocket. He pulled off a twenty from the roll and handed it to her.

"Oh, I know you can do better than that," she encouraged him.

"This definitely Lawe's fucking sister," he told the other guard.

"Since you know that, gone peel off one of those hundreds I saw."

"Man, I'm getting robbed at my own job," he complained, putting the one hundred dollar bill in her hand.

"It was nice doing business with you."

The waitress led the group into the bar and down the long hallway. I remembered it like it was yesterday, the first time I walked the length of it. It was the night that Lailah was created and the beginning of the rest of my life.

"I'm Passion. I'll be your server tonight. Your section is straight ahead and to the left when we walk in. You won't be able to hear me much in there. Is there anything you all need before we step on the other side of this wall?"

"Juice for the liquor," Lyric responded.

"Alright. I'm going to go tell the boss man that you've arrived."

"Nah. She'll do it," Lyric told her, pointing back at me. "I need you to grab the juice."

"Alright. I'll meet you ladies at the table in a bit. Enjoy your night and welcome to Jilted."

"Why me?" I cringed.

"Because, he's mad at you, not us. Besides, I'm sure he'll be pleasantly surprised that you're outside tonight," Lyric expounded.

"Might even give you your punishment right now

instead of waiting until you get home," Baisleigh added.

"Don't do it, Halo, not unless you want to end up like me." She rubbed her pregnant belly.

"Don't listen to her. Do you know where he is?"

"Yes. I've been here before. The night that Lailah was made."

"Run that shit back, then. Make another Lailah," Lyric cheered.

"Has she been drinking?" I asked Ever.

"Please don't remind me. I'm the designated driver for the night. She's the first person I'm dropping off if I don't call her husband to come to get her first."

"Hopefully you won't have to. I'm going to go get Ledge," I breathed. "Wish me luck."

"Have you seen your ass in them pants? You don't need luck, baby. You've got it."

I shook my head, unsure of how much Lyric had said was true. Nevertheless, I proceeded through the bar and toward the area I recalled visiting before we headed out of the door last February. I entered another hall after crossing the entire bar in search of the sign that I vaguely remember being on his door.

Ledge, CEO, it read. I could see the letters in my head as my memory was jogged.

Conference.

Staff Only.

LEDGE. Here it is! I shouted inside, happy to have stumbled across the door without feeling crazy for remembering a little sign that probably didn't exist. I raised my hand to knock, but the door inched open before I could.

Urrrrrrrrrn. The sound of the door widening triggered every emotion I'd ever experienced, but what was revealed behind it only summoned one. *Hurt.*

Rapidly, sharp pains shot through my chest, paralyzing me. I was immobile, unable to move, and unable to speak. Like a statue, I stood, trying to figure out what I'd done in my past life to deserve everything I was witnessing in this one.

"Jade," Ledge called out to the woman that sat in front of him with her butt on his desk and her skirt hiked in the air.

"Yes, *boss*?"

"What did I tell you?"

"If you can break the rules, then why can't I?"

"Jade, we'll discuss this later. Right now, there are people out there that need your service."

"And you don't?"

The wallet in my hand fell to the ground, startling us all. Instantly, Ledge and I shared perplexed gazes. In a flash, he was up from his seat and putting distance between himself and the girl on his desk. Now that he was in full view, I could see the smeared lipstick on his cheeks and right where his lips creased. Just like me, he was frozen in place. Stuck. Unsure of what to say and unsure of what to do.

"Can I help you?" The mysterious girl asked.

Without a word, I bent over and picked up the wallet that held my valuables.

"Halo. Baby, hold up a minute."

I could hear Ledge's footsteps as he followed me down the hallway.

"Halo. Wait.

He caught up to me in no time. Too ashamed to go back into the lounge area, I slammed my palms against the nearest door with an exit sign attached. The night breeze hit my face, helping supply my lungs with the oxygen I needed to breathe.

"Halo!"

I kept walking, unsure of where I was going or where I'd end up. All I knew was that I didn't want to be in the same space as Ledge. I'd never felt this way before, especially not about him, and the feeling was crushing me.

I committed to walking as far as my legs would take me. However, that wouldn't be very far with Ledge on my heels. He left no room to spare. Still, I kept trekking down the street that led to wherever. I was lost, mentally and physically.

"Slow down and talk to me."

"Go back inside and leave me alone."

"Nah, we both know I'm not doing that."

"Don't let me be the reason you put your activities on pause. Continue."

"You're being foolish right now. Stop for a second and listen."

"Go away, Ledge."

"You give me such a hard time, Halo."

"I gave you my fucking heart!" I spat, not recognizing the monster I'd quickly become.

"That wasn't what you think it was," he explained, trying to grab ahold of me.

"Don't touch me. Don't touch me."

I unlocked my phone and searched for the number I'd last dialed, hoping that Kamber picked up.

"Who you calling?" Ledge inquired.

I didn't answer. My focus was elsewhere. When the phone rang out and rolled over to voicemail, I wanted to toss it across the street. The one time I really needed her, she couldn't pick up.

"Who are you calling, Halo? And why you keep walking? You're going to fall in them fucking shoes."

"Worry about yourself, Ledge. I'm perfectly fine." The wind whipped my wet face, making it feel much colder than it actually was.

"Let me take you home!"

"No."

"Let me take you home, Halo. We can talk about it there. It's cold as fuck out here. You're going to be sick. Stop walking and let me take you home."

I stopped in my tracks, unable to go on any further. My knees were weak. My head was spinning. My heart was hurting. The pain I felt in my chest was so broad and so big that I didn't even feel the pain from walking in the shoes I could barely stand in. And, as I looked back at the man that I loved with everything I had to love with, my heart shattered like glass.

"You know what, Ledge. Fine. Take me to your place. When I get there, I'm packing my things and Lailah's things. We're going to Kamber's until my new apartment is ready. I am so happy that I didn't give it up when you asked me to. I knew something like this would happen."

Stunned and silent, Ledge shook his head from one side to the other.

"You signed for the apartment, anyway?" He cocked his head, staring into my teary eyes.

"What do you care, Ledge? I'm just some fucking project to you. I'm really messed up and I've been telling you this from the start. You came into my life and tried to make me someone I'll never be. I am damaged. I am nothing. I am scraps. I am bits and pieces and no matter how hard you try, you'll never be able to put me back together."

"I was cool with you the way you were, Halo. You wanted to change. I supported that just like I support anything and everything else when it comes to you. That's how love works. You put your eggs in the basket and you sort them motherfuckers out. A cracked egg isn't any less valuable than a whole one. They can both feed the soul. Your life was fucked up. I get that."

"But why you trying to fuck ours up? Why you keep running away from us? Why you keep dipping your hand in our basket and taking your eggs out when shit ain't going so good? Why you keep fucking with my head? Fucking with my heart? Why you keep doing that shit, Halo? What I ever do to you?"

"Take me to get my things."

"I'm not taking you no motherfucking where until I get some answers. And, Lailah ain't leaving. That's her crib. I'll find somewhere else to go. Just answer me and

I'll let you gone about your business. My feet are tired. I've been chasing somebody that doesn't want to be caught. I'm willing to cut my losses but tell me why? Why let me fall for you the way that I did knowing you wouldn't catch me? Why take me through all this shit if you knew you weren't ready for a nigga to love you down like I do? Why? Why you do that, Halo?"

"Because you left me no other choice. I tried to keep my distance. I tried to stay away from you, but you wouldn't let me. You did this, Ledge. Not me. You tried to love me back to life and it just ain't working."

"You're right." He threw his hands in the air. "And, I'm sorry to have upset you. Let me take you home and I'll grab my shit."

Without an ounce of fight left in me, I turned around and headed back toward the bar. As I passed Ledge, he lifted me into his arms and tossed me over his shoulder. The pain of the shoes I wore was finally starting to kick in. He knew that it would, so he solved the problem before it even arose.

I hated that he was so good to me. I hated that I couldn't reciprocate it. I hated that he remained calm in any given situation while I unraveled. I hated the way his love still outshined all else even when we were fighting. I hated fighting.

I hated that I'd come out tonight. I hated that I'd shown up at his office door. I hated that I'd witnessed him with someone besides me. I hated how normal she was. I hated how confident she looked. I hated how she could probably make him a happier man than me. I hated that I couldn't make him happier.

We reached the truck in no time. He opened the door and placed me on the passenger seat. I avoided his eyes as he stopped to wipe my face with his shirt. There was no use in him clearing the tears because more came.

"Stop crying," he begged me.

"I want to go home."

"Aight. I'm going to take you, but stop crying." The strain in his voice only made it hurt worse.

I loved this man. All of him. Every bit of him. Why things between us couldn't work, I just didn't understand.

"Listen, I don't want you painting an image of me in your head that is untrue. That is an employee of mine. I've never been anything but professional with her since day one. Tonight, she had way too much to drink. I'll admit that I had too much as well. She came into my office on some other shit. Trying to keep it chill, I ignored her for the most part. That was until she sat on top of my desk and began putting her fucking lips on me."

"Nothing more than what you saw was going to happen. I was too focused on getting my work done so that I could come home to you and Lailah. After I got your text, I was ready to fuck and make up. Another woman never crossed my mind. Jade was just on bullshit tonight. She was forcing herself on me," he claimed.

"Did you stop her?" I posed.

His silence said enough.

"Take me home, Ledge. Now."

"Wait. Wait. Baby, you're right. Aight? I can admit that. I thought ignoring her would get the fucking point across. When the morning came, I intended to discuss this with her and let her off with a warning. If she ever tried it again, she'd be let go. When you showed up, I was about to leave the office with her in it, giving her time to sober up enough to drive home. Nothing was going to happen, Halo."

What he was telling me and what I'd seen were two completely different things.

"I'm ready to go home," I whispered, bowing my head and picking imaginary lint from my pants.

The slamming door startled me. The moment it connected, my body jerked forward. I inhaled deeply before exhaling a long, exasperated breath. Ledge climbed into the truck shortly after, starting it and turning the heat all the way up. No words were exchanged during the entire ride. Not even music played in the background.

When we pulled into the driveway, the truck had barely stopped rolling before I opened the door to exit. Ledge caught my wrist and stopped me from the escape I'd played over and over in my head on the way. I tried freeing myself from his hold but he wouldn't let go. He had a grip on my hand, my heart, and my head.

"Please."

"Not until you calm down. Lailah picks up on energy, Halo. She did nothing to deserve whatever version of you that you plan on giving her right now. Whether that's a sad, angry, or upset mother. It doesn't matter. Before you go inside and transfer that energy, I need you to calm down. That's all I'm asking."

"You don't make the rules for me, Ledge."

"All I'm asking is for you to chill."

"Chill? After walking in on my boyfriend sitting front row while an employee who he's been working with for some time now shows him her lady parts like it's a normal day in the office. You want me to calm down?" I scoffed, "Are you serious right now?"

"That wasn't just another day in the office, Halo."

"Could've fooled me. While she was in your face, exposing her pussy, maybe you shouldn't have been so calm and we wouldn't be having this conversation right now. No, as a matter of fact, I'm glad we're having this conversation."

"Gives you another reason to run from this huh? Right up your alley?"

"If that's what you think, then fine."

"She didn't show me her pussy, for the record. And, I'm always calm. What other way is there to be?"

"Nothing. Don't worry about it. Can you please let my wrist go?"

"I really want to talk about this, Halo. I don't want you to go in that house and we not get the chance to talk about this. I know you. You'll run and hide and I won't be able to get to you, again."

"Should you have that privilege?" I wanted to know, honestly.

"Halo."

"Seriously, Ledge, if we had an argument and I left

the house upset, went to work, and you walk in to find another man's dick in my face. His pants are at his knees, but he has on boxers. Still, right there in my face, however. And, then, his cologne is all over my body. How'd you feel?"

He said nothing.

"How would you feel?" I slowed down, asking once more.

"I would've killed the nigga on the spot," he admitted, finally seeing my point and freeing me from his grasp.

I rushed out of the truck and up the driveway. Disrupting Lailah and Alec was the last thing on my mind. I ran to the furthest corner of the house, closed the door behind me, and released everything that had built up inside of me over the last hour. I knew at that moment that I'd never stop crying.

Letting go of Ledge was worse than anything that had ever happened to me. Letting go of Ledge was like cutting off the very machine that gave me life, helped me breathe, and kept me alive. Frankly, I didn't think I could survive without him.

18

LEDGE

"CALL HER BACK, THEN. IF SHE'S NOBODY, THEN call her back."

"I'm not calling her back. Lay the fuck down and shut up before I give you something to shout about."

"Call her back! You said she's nobody."

"Is she nobody? Yes. Am I fucking her? Yes! How long have I been fucking her? About a year. Will I fuck her again now that you know about her? Yes. Do I give a fuck that you know about her? No. Come on, don't play like you don't know what it is. I don't question you and be all up in your shit. Show me the same respect. I'm single and you're single until we're together. Long as I'm in your presence, you've got me to yourself. That's what we agreed on so that's what it is. Tripping ain't going to change shit. If you don't like it you can leave. But, if you want to stick around, then bend over and shut the fuck up."

"Urrrrrrgggggh!" I pulled the pillow up until it covered my ears.

Two weeks of the same back and forth was driving me up the wall. Choosing to crash at Lawe's place seemed like a good idea at first. At least it was for the first week. But, with Bianca back in the picture for the last two weeks, I was starting to regret my decision a little more every day.

Morning, noon, or night, it didn't matter. There was always fussing followed by the headboard banging and loud, obnoxious screaming. The type of toxicity I was witnessing with the two of them was enough to have a nigga analyzing every decision I'd made the night that Halo broke things off.

The more I went over it in my head, the more I understood her point of view. There was nothing that she could tell me that would make me feel better or keep me from catching a case if I walked in on the same thing. The only difference was, I wouldn't have called shit off. I didn't have the heart to, not when I knew Halo like the back of my hand.

If a nigga was pressing up on her, then that's just

what it was. She wasn't indulging. I figured she knew me just as well, but I never factored in her past. Faith in men was a lost art for her. She didn't have any faith in us. It had been destroyed long before my time and I'd aided that decision with the bullshit that I let go on.

Jade felt every bit of my pain the next morning. As soon as the sun rose, she was fired. If there was any chance that Halo and I could work our shit out, then she couldn't be in the picture.

I rolled over and grabbed my phone. Before the madness started, I wanted to be prepared. I made sure the Bluetooth was connected to the speaker before tapping the music app. I scrolled through the playlists I'd created and settled on the one that had been hitting the hardest lately. The shuffle feature was handy, switching up the order of the songs I'd selected.

I Can't Make you Love Me was up first. It sounded a lot different than it ever had with Halo in mind. I exited the app and pulled up our text thread. As I had each morning since everything transpired, I greeted her in hopes of a response.

Good morning.

I shot over.

I waited for the gray dots to appear. The screen darkened after a while, but I tapped it to keep the light bright. There was no use in waiting, but I did anyway.

Time seemed to be the only thing on my side this morning. I glanced at the top of the phone to see that it was almost time to scoop up Lailah while her mother got some work done. Though she let go of the apartment, she hung onto her job. Every day, she worked from eight until twelve. She'd cut her hours tremendously to accommodate our new co-parenting schedule.

> Be there in a few.

This time, I didn't wait for a response. I knew that I wouldn't get one. The thread was full of blue bubbles. Anything Halo needed to say to me, she said while I was in her presence. She never communicated with me by phone anymore.

I stretched my limbs and climbed out of bed. Changing the black sweats I'd slept in didn't even cross my mind when I tossed on a white shirt to match them. I pulled on the same hoodie I'd worn the night before and topped it off with a Nike cap. My Nike slides would have to do the trick. The only person I wanted to impress wasn't thinking about my ass right now, so I didn't give a fuck.

I hadn't driven my El Camino much since Lailah was born. I'd been riding the truck like it was my official dad-mobile. The loud pipes and engine on the old school were not ideal for Lailah's ears or the long naps she liked to get in during car rides.

Because Lawe's three-car garage was already full, I was forced to park in the driveway. That left my interior as cold as the exterior some mornings. This one was no exception. I hiked the heat up so that it would be nice and toasty by the time I got Lailah in. To keep my body temperature up, I rubbed my hands together and waited for the chill to subside.

Lawe didn't live very far from me, which was one of the reasons I'd chosen his home. It was merely an eight-minute drive from his house to mine. When I pulled into the driveway, I noticed the open blinds. It had become a habit of Halo's since I'd started picking up Lay for her morning shift. Going inside wasn't an option. She passed off the baby at the door without as much as a look in my direction if there wasn't something wrong or something she needed.

I kept the engine running as I stepped out. By the time I made it to the door, so had Halo. With Lailah buckled into her car seat and ready to go, she pushed it open and handed her over. I grabbed the handle of the car seat but didn't allow the door to close. Sensing my desire to communicate, she stood with her arms folded against her chest.

Even when she was mad, she was still the prettiest girl in the world. Her eyes darted in every direction but mine. Yet, the pain was evident. She couldn't hide it and neither could I.

"Your birthday is coming up."

"Ledge, it's cold outside. Lailah needs to get into the truck."

"Can I step inside?"

"I don't think that's a good idea."

"Why not?"

"Can we not do this? I have work in a few," She groaned with a shake of the head.

"We're not doing nothing, Halo. We're just talking. You can stay mad at a nigga. I'll give you that but you don't have to hate me. That's not you so don't let it become you."

"I don't hate you," she cleared up. "I'm just not ready to talk to you."

"Can I take you out for your birthday?"

"No." Her response was as short as it was stern.

"Why not?"

"Because Ledge. Is that all? My baby needs to be inside."

"Here. Put her seat back in the house so she can stay warm."

"You can just put her in the truck and she'll be warm."

"You'll shut the door on me."

"I'm supposed to."

"Not when I'm trying to talk to you," I explained.

Aggravated, she grabbed Lailah's car seat and put it back inside the house where it was warm.

"Now, what is it? I have to clock in at eight."

"You have a few minutes."

"It doesn't mean I want to spend them talking to you."

"I miss you."

Although she remained silent, I didn't miss the gleam in her eyes. It didn't last long but it didn't go unnoticed.

"Ledge, I don't want to do this with you."

"Then tell me you miss me too and you can go in the house."

"I'm not going to do that," she fussed, rubbing her hands together.

"Why not? It's true."

"Because it doesn't matter. They're just feelings. They'll go away."

"Just feelings," I tittered, sarcastically. She hit me in the center of my chest with that one.

"Yeah. They're just feelings."

"Stop playing with me, Halo. We're wasting valuable time to prove what?"

"I'm not trying to prove anything, Ledge. What did you expect? Me to just ignore what happened and move on in hopes that it won't ever happen again?"

"It won't."

"I know because I won't let it. And, it shouldn't have ever happened in the first place."

"I agree."

"So leave it alone. Move on."

"Move on?" I tilted my head to better understand what she was asking of me.

"Where the fuck is all of this coming from? Who are you right now? Do you not understand what you're asking me?"

"The same thing I asked you the night it happened. I gave you something valuable to me, Ledge. Things. Things I'd never given to anyone else. And, you did nothing to protect it. I'd never let that happen to you. You promised me that you would never hurt me and all you did was lie. You keep telling me you're not him and not to ever compare you to him but why not? Hmmm? He fucked me and so did you, Ledge. The only difference is, yours actually hurt a lot worst."

Blow after blow, she knocked the wind from my chest.

"So, please spare me the antics, okay? I have work to do. Please get Lailah and bring her back at twelve. She'll be ready for another feeding by then."

Unable to stand the pain on her face as she spoke to me, I found my hands on her jaws. She froze, refusing to look at me, refusing to let me see into that soul of hers, refusing to show me how much I'd hurt her, refusing to give me the chance I needed to set things right between us.

"Look at me," I ordered.

"No. Please, just leave."

"Look at me."

"No." She shook her head from side to side.

"Halo, look at me. This is me. Look at me," I begged.

"I can't," she disclosed, placing a hand to her mouth to muffle the scream that she let out. The tears from her eyes hit the white sweater she wore. Shaking and trembling, she still hadn't found the strength to look at me.

I'd done that to her. I'd caused this. I'd managed to break my promise. I'd resulted to breaking her heart when all I ever wanted was to heal it. Now, I was put in the same category as the man before me and I just couldn't rest there. That wasn't where I needed to be.

"Halo, look at me right now and tell me I'm a

monster. Tell me that you hate me and that you want nothing more to do with me. Tell me you don't want this to work and you want me to stop trying. Tell me to give up. Tell me that you don't want to love me anymore. Tell me to my face, because it's the only way I'll receive it. Look at me and tell me this is the end and I'll do as you ask of me."

"Please," she wept. "Please just leave."

I lowered my hands until they were at my side. Stepping back, I waited until she retrieved the car seat. When she handed Lailah over, her eyes finally met mine.

"Give up on me," she demanded.

"Can't do it, pretty lady."

LEDGE + HALO

I CLOSED my eyes and for a brief moment to gather my thoughts. No matter how hard I tried, I couldn't get Halo out of my head. It had been two hours since I'd picked up Lailah and our conversation was still the only thing I could think of.

"You look stressed, nigga," Luca acknowledged as if I didn't already know.

"You think? My old lady deep in her feelings, thinking she's ready to end the whole shit. I've gone from living with my family to staying with a lunatic who can't decide if he wants his ex or not. I done got demoted from full-time father to a fucking co-parent. What the fuck is that, anyway?"

"You, shit," he chuckled.

"You can laugh, you're here with ya' kids every day. It's been damn near three weeks without mine and I'm sick. I know a nigga done lost ten pounds at least."

"You did look a little slim when you walked through the door. That's why I offered you something to eat."

"Can you quit with the jokes? You haven't been this funny since I met you."

"I'm not joking, though. I'm for real."

"Whatever man. I been eating. Just not what the fuck I want to eat."

"Not what you need to be eating because if you were then you wouldn't be on my couch moping and shit. Take your ass home and eat her fucking insides out. I bet she forgives you, then."

"She won't even let me in the house."

"Ahh. It's bad, then."

"It is, for real. I'm just trying to figure out how to get back on track. I can't keep staying with this boy. They're going to drive me crazy. Hearing them almost every day makes me cherish what I have with Halo even more. We were good. Besides some hiccups, we were straight. Like, legit, never felt so confident about anything else in my life. I was sure 'bout her. Still sure 'bout her."

"Then what's the issue?"

"She ain't sure 'bout me."

"You said you guys talked this morning, right?"

"Yeah."

"Instead of her slamming the door on you like she usually does?"

"Yeah."

"Then, she sure 'bout you, too. She just needed time to place her feelings. Is she still hurt? Damn right. But, is it over? Nah. She's ready. You just have to apply the pressure. Once you do, she'll burst at the seams for you. She understands what you guys have and she's afraid to lose that or give that up to someone else. She's literally scared."

"That's why she's in her feelings like this. She thinks someone else has a chance with you and it's not sitting well with her. Watch, when this all pans over, she's going to be switching up her hair, the way she dresses, the way she does things... but, don't let her. Now that you've given her reason to believe that someone else has a chance to have what you promised her, it's your job to unpack that and prove to her that you want her for exactly who she is."

"Women are very complex creatures, bro. It's like, they don't blame men for fucking up. They automatically blame themselves. Most of them, at least. I wasn't nice enough. I wasn't cute enough. I wasn't spontaneous enough. I wasn't this and that and the truth is that shit has nothing to do with them."

"I didn't fuck up, though."

"You did. You think one of the women at our factories would make her way into my office, sit her bare ass on my desk, and kiss over my face? Hmm? Like, right now. Do you think that would happen? Drunk, high, whatever. You think one of them gone try me like that?"

I shrugged, unsure of the answer he was looking for.

"They can't and they won't. Why? Because they know I don't get down like that. I don't play that shit. I have a wife and at all times she will be respected. Whether she's beside me or not. Any motherfucker that can't respect her doesn't belong in my presence. It's as simple as that. Whoever that bitch was that was all on your desk knowing you have a woman at home doesn't respect Halo."

"Jade. You met her when you came through the first time."

"Yeah. Figured it was her. That's why I haven't even asked. I knew she was trouble from the moment I saw her. That's why I asked about her. She was thirsty then, trying to hook the biggest fish available."

"I know. Just never thought she'd try me, but she did."

"And, I hope you let her go. Women like that are dangerous with nothing to lose. They'll get you caught up in a jam every time if you let them."

"She's fired."

"Good. Now, there's no need for you to be pulling your hair out over there at Lawe's house. I got a spot you can crash at until you get your shit together. Now that I know what I know, you got a week to do that. Take your ass home. Don't let this little mishap crumble what you're trying to build."

"Appreciate it. I need some fucking peace and quiet so I can think."

"You do. How much time have you got? You trying to hit the jewelry store? Your girl needs a ring and Ever needs a new one. It's time to upgrade her."

"I got to get Lailah back to Halo in less than two hours."

"I've got all day. We can go once you drop her off."

"Bet. For now, I'm going to get some shut-eye while she's napping."

"Aight. I'm going to head up to Ever's bakery and drop off a few things. The door will lock on its own when you leave. The key to the condo will be on the console by the door. Get your rest and then go get your woman."

"I definitely plan to. For real."

LEDGE + HALO

THE SOUND of my phone vibrating in the distance woke me from my sleep. I grabbed it from the blanket that Lailah was resting on. Not sure how long I was asleep, I realized her little ass was wide awake as I answered the call.

"Yeah?"

"Where are you? It's one o'clock. I said twelve, Ledge."

"I know. We fell asleep and your call woke me just now."

"Where is she?"

"Right here, looking at me."

"Okay. I'll be waiting."

"Aye?" I tried to catch her before she ended the call.

"Yeah?"

"You ate?"

The line died, forcing a smile on my face. She hadn't eaten. I could tell from the attitude she called me with.

"Come on, little baby. It's time to go home. We're going to stop and get mommy some food on the way. Are you good with that? Got to make sure she's good and full so that she can be a little nicer the next time she sees daddy. Yeah? Daddy is ready to come home and see you all the time. You miss daddy?"

Lailah showed no signs of sleep as she bobbed her big head and watched me through wide eyes. I began putting on her coat so that we could get out of the door.

"Daddy misses you all the time and mommy and our bed."

She was such a good baby. Hadn't her mother called, then I'd still be asleep and she'd still be watching me sleep.

She called. Her name hadn't crossed my screen since the night of our split. The call was about Lailah, but that didn't matter. *She called.*

LEDGE + HALO

3:26 A.M. My phone screen displayed as I scrolled through my never-ending catalog of pictures I'd captured of a sleeping Halo. *An angel on earth.* That's what she was to me and I'd give whatever to be laying next to her instead of the lonely bed I lay in.

In less than twenty-four hours she'd be celebrating another year of life and the plans that I'd made for her special day were pointless. She was willing to spend the day without me. When I dropped Lailah off earlier, she asked if I could get her tomorrow evening because she had made new plans. As much as I wanted to ask what the plans were, I refrained. Whatever she had in mind, I hoped it made her feel as special as she was.

"Fuck!" I squeezed the sides of my phone, frustrated with my life at the moment.

One night. That's all it took for everything to come crashing down on me. I had no one to blame but myself. Instead of putting Jade in her place, I had to stroke my own fucking ego and allow her in my personal space where she didn't belong. Lots of liquor and a bad judgment call had ripped through my home and torn Halo and me apart. It didn't matter that nothing happened or was going to happen, I shouldn't have let her get so close to me.

"I got to make this right," I voiced, rolling over onto my side.

The velvet box that sat on the nightstand held a ring almost as breathtaking as the woman I wanted wearing it. To see her in it would bring me so much peace. When the time was right, she'd have it and she'd agree to be mine.

Our time apart left me with so much to think about. There was work to be done between the two of us, but it wasn't nothing we couldn't handle. As long as we both wanted what we had to last, then we'd stand the test of time. The bumps and bruises along the way would only strengthen us, not tear us apart. I saw this as one of those bumps and a few of those bruises. Once we got through it, we'd experience another level of closeness.

"She's been through enough already."

My phone put me out of my misery by ringing. Lyric's name popping up on the screen made me sit up and divert my attention.

"What's up?" Worry lines creased my forehead.

"Why does it sound like you just ran a marathon?" She questioned.

"Why are you calling so late as if something is wrong?"

"Because, I told her to, nigga," Laike chimed in.

"It's too early in the morning for prank calls and shit. What's up?"

"I told y'all. We could've waited until sun up to call him."

"Lawe?" Perplexed, I laid back down on the pillow and massaged my temple.

"Yeah. I heard you don't like being at my crib no more. That's good, cause you were never welcomed in the first place. You just showed up."

"Cause I can."

"That's not what I gave you a key for."

"Well, that's what I used it for. What's up? Why is y'all calling me at this time of night?"

"That info you wanted, I got it."

"Stop playing." I was back up at the sound of Laike's confession.

"Nah. I'm not playing. That's why Lyric hit your line. I'm on a burner and didn't have your number saved. My phone is at the house. That's the only place it needs to ping if the people ever come looking, so leave yours, too. Me and your foolish ass twin on the way."

"Say no more."

One second. Before you move on to the epilogue, be sure to **scan the code** to get the **deleted scenes** for this book and many others.

or sign up for deleted scenes at **https://theliteraryheroine. ck.page/e2956a645b**

EPILOGUE

HALO

I THOUGHT THINGS WOULD BE SO MUCH different this year. What started out as a dream swiftly ended as a nightmare. There was no more Ledge and there was no more us. That ship had sailed and I was still seasick from the turbulence.

Opening my eyes on the morning of my birthday hadn't felt good in such a long time. With each passing year, they got a little heavier and a little harder to open. This year, even the thought of getting out of bed was too much for me. So, together, Lailah and I stayed tucked under the covers, ignoring the calls and text messages until I couldn't anymore.

"Hello."

"I know you canceled our plans because you don't feel like doing much of anything but at least let me take you to dinner," Ever cheerfully stated.

"I have Lailah."

"You're telling me that like it matters," she chastised.

"Have you ever broken up with Luca?"

Seeing them gave me so much hope at once but after the last few weeks I had, there was no hope left.

"No. And, I never will. Aside from the vows we made to each other, I made a vow to myself to never experience life without him. He's my person. The life I lived before him was so minuscule compared to the life that I'm living now. He makes this whole thing worth living. My heart would stop beating if I had to live without him. I don't fear much with him by my side, but I fear that. I'm scared to even think of doing life without him."

"Me too."

"Then, don't. You're not doing yourself any favors by suffering."

"I feel like I can't breathe without him," I moaned, the pain residing in my bones and all over my body. "I don't want to feel like this. I hate this feeling so bad."

"When you love a man the way that I love Luca, the way that you love Ledge, you won't ever stop. You can spend the rest of your life gasping for air that's right there or you can spend the rest of it with an endless supply at your disposal. Your feelings are hurt, baby, and that's okay. But, I am very confident when I say that nothing was going to happen there, whether you walked in or not."

"Still. I just keep seeing her in his face like that. So comfortably."

"Halo, I have to cut it to you straight and tell you that this has little to do with Ledge's actions and everything to do with whatever is holding you back from your true self. There are some underlying issues that you and Kirklynn will sort out eventually, but don't punish yourself anymore in the process. Her comfort, her confidence, the access she had... none of that was under his control. Employees have access to their boss' room. At Jilted, it's where they leave their belongings when they are working."

"How'd you know?"

"I asked. I wanted to know what she was doing back there, too. It wasn't my business but it didn't hurt to ask when he brought it up."

"Ledge?"

"Yes."

"You've seen him?"

"Several times. He's over here for the most part when he has Lailah. Otherwise, he's at the center in Laura's room with her. He doesn't like taking her to Lawe's. He says it's too much going on over there."

"What did he say?"

"He knows he messed up and he's just trying to fix it."

"I still feel like he could've stopped her much earlier on and made her close her freaking legs."

"I agree."

"That's all I'm saying."

"I know exactly what you're saying and you're right. He didn't do what he should've done. Now, he's paying for it."

"Me too."

"I just don't think this is worth walking away from him for. It's a lesson for you both, but the deciding factor for your relationship... it's not worth it."

"He and I talked the other day."

"Good. What came of that conversation?"

"Nothing."

"Halo."

"I just can't help but see her face and her lipstick smeared on him when he's standing in front of me."

"She's fired. He told me that," she revealed. This was news to me, but I felt good about it.

"Good."

"He bought me food when he dropped Lailah off the same day."

"I hope you didn't send it back with him."

"I was starving. I couldn't. I wanted to, though," I laughed to keep from crying.

"Poor Ledge."

"I miss him so much. I wanted to spend the entire day wrapped in his arms. Instead, it's just Lailah and me, trying not to drown in our sorrows."

"Has he called you?"

"I don't know. I haven't checked my missed calls. You're the first person to get through to me."

"Halo," she fussed.

"I just haven't felt like being bothered."

"Well, I'll let you go. I'll be over to get you and Lailah at six-thirty. How does that sound?"

"Fine, Ever. We'll be ready."

"Good. See you then."

"See you then."

I tried very hard not to begin scrolling through the long list of notifications on my screen. Because I knew they'd etch away at my sanity, I searched for a distraction. Socializing was not on my list of things to do for my birthday; I didn't care who it was. Everyone could wait.

"Let's see what you and daddy be watching, mommas."

I reached across a wide-eyed Lailah and grabbed the remote from Ledge's side of the bed. Upon pushing the power button, the twelve o'clock news broadcast appeared. I moved to turn the channel, completely uninterested in what was happening in Channing but halted at the name that was plastered across the screen. I'd never forget it.

"That's right. Behind me is where they found the remains of Charles O'Brien. Investigators say that it was the most gruesome murder scene they've witnessed in over a decade. The victim's testicles and male organs were found hanging out of his mouth. Apparently, he died from a single gunshot wound to the head. However, it's being reported that he would've succumbed to his injuries hadn't the killer shot him. There are no suspects at this time. If you have any information, authorities are asking that you contact them at the number listed on the screen. This is Jane Hornet reporting for Channel 24 News."

I couldn't believe my eyes. Every inch of my body numbed while continuously staring at the television screen. *Charles O'Brien*. The monster that lived under the same roof as me, the one who'd altered my brain chemistry and turned me into a woman I didn't recognize, was him.

He's... he's gone? I ached inside out. Everywhere, it hurt. *He's gone?*

My phone vibrated beside me. Absent-mindedly, I picked up, mouth still hanging open and head still swimming.

"Happy birthday, pretty lady," Ledge sang into the phone. "Happy birthday to youuuuuu."

"Ledge," I gasped.

"I told you, as long as I'm breathing you ain't got shit to worry about. Open the door."

"You're here?" I asked, feeling the weight of a thousand anchors being lifted at once.

"Nah. I'm not trying to fuck up your day, but your gift is there. Tell Lailah I love her."

The call ended before I was able to respond. I rose from the bed only to fall on the floor beside it. My knees gave out and my legs gave in. Like a wounded animal, I wailed. Right there, on the floor, I howled.

He's gone.

LE DGE + HALO

"Here, you can look at the dash screen right here to keep an eye on here," Ever explained, adjusting the camera angle remotely so that it was aimed at Lailah.

"That's nice. I'll have to get one of these."

"Laike installed it. I don't know where he finds these gadgets all the time but I'm never complaining. Everything is helpful."

I stared at the live feed of a sleeping Lailah. It felt like the only time she wasn't sleeping was when she was eating. Even then, she was half asleep.

"I almost hated to bring her out. Just keeps reminding me that Ledge is no longer home with us."

"Don't go getting sad on me, Halo. It's your day. Let's make the best of it."

"I'm trying."

"Alright. I'm going to hold you to that."

"He called to wish me a happy birthday when I hung up from you this morning. He told me to come to the door. Ever, I'm almost ashamed at how happy I was thinking it was him there."

"It wasn't?"

"No. It was a delivery. Several, actually. Lyric sent me the same Chanel bag I was obsessing over the first day we met. Do you know it costs almost ten thousand dollars? I looked it up online."

"I know. She got me the same one. I haven't worn it yet. I'm saving it for a semester of college for one of my fifty children," she snickered.

"It can cover one, maybe two."

"Right. Depending on where they are. What did he get you?"

"The dress I have on now, roses, a card, an envelope full of money that I've yet to count, and a new pair of shoes."

"Well, he has great taste, at least. I love this. The color is giving Valentine's Day."

"With my birthday being so close to the holiday, I figured I'd wear it tonight."

"I don't blame you."

A loud, blaring sound disrupted my train of thought. I wasn't sure what I was about to say after it ripped throughout the entire SUV. It wasn't until I looked at the dash that I realized it was Ever's ringing phone.

Luca Bear appeared on the widescreen. A pang of jealousy stung me like an upset bee. They were as cute as it got.

"One second," she told me before answering. "Hey, baby."

"Aye. You left your purse. You far? Do I need to bring it to you?"

"No. I'm still around. I'm going to swing by and get it. I have to use the bathroom, too. I'll be there in a few minutes."

"Aight."

"I hope you don't mind." She turned to me and said.

"Not at all."

I didn't. The stop would give me time to collect myself and truly tap into the fact that it was my birthday and not just another day without Ledge.

"If you want, we could leave Lailah at my place. Our nanny is there with Luca and the children."

"You don't think it'll be an issue?"

"No. It's already four children running around. What's one more?"

"One more breastfeeding infant?"

"Lucas is still a breastfeeding toddler, what's the difference?"

"Do you think we will be long? I didn't bring any milk but I fed her before we left so that she won't be hungry at the restaurant."

"An hour and a half, two tops. If she gets too upset, we can just leave, but I doubt that happens. I have an emergency stash of frozen milk as well. It won't hurt her."

"Okay. I guess she can stay with her cousins, huh?"

"The girls will love that."

I wasn't exactly sure how I felt about leaving Lailah or how I felt about anything, honestly. The day had presented so much in such a short amount of time that I was still trying to process it all. By the time we made it to the enormous pad that Ever parked directly in front of, I still didn't feel much better about anything.

"Come on. Do you need me to grab anything?"

"Her bag. The rest, I can handle."

In the red dress that resembled the one I'd worn for

New Year's, I slid out of the front of the massive SUV and into the back. I unhooked the straps to set Lailah's car seat free. With her dangling at my side, I followed Ever into the house.

"I'm going to go find Luca and the children. They're more than likely in the other wing. You can go right through there and into the sitting room. I'll be right back. This little girl is sitting on my bladder."

Flabbergasted. It was the only word to describe my state. The large family required lots of room, but their home was insane. I couldn't quite put my finger on it, but there was something vaguely familiar about it all. *Daddy and momma Eisenberg*, I concluded. There were a few resemblances in the homes, but this one was on a much grander scale.

As I followed the instructions that Ever had given, I took my precious time to get a good look at the dream of a home that she shared with her husband. I didn't think I'd ever feel comfortable in anything as big, but I'd enjoy my time there whenever I was invited over.

Right through here? I wondered. *And, into the sitting room.* Her words registered as I made the turn and found the room she was referring to. *Who has an actual sitting rooooooom?*

Red balloons covered the ceiling, casting dark hues over the entire room. Long strings hung low, nearly touching the floor. There was a small table complete with a cloth, napkins, and set for two. *What is—what is going on?* My eyes danced around the room until that familiar thing resonated with me. *Him. He's—he's here.*

I whipped my head around, searching the entire room for the man who'd stolen my heart and refused to give it back. Though I couldn't see him, I could feel him. My heart sensed him. His nearness made my nipples ache and my lungs tighten. *Where... whe... where is h—*.

"I'll take her," his voice serenaded my soul, forcing my eyes closed as his fingers grazed mine to remove the car seat from my hand.

So many seconds passed before his return. I felt incompetent as I waited. Incomplete, far from whole. Gutted, once again.

"You ever loved someone to the point of pain?" He reappeared behind me.

I couldn't see his face, but I could smell his skin and feel his breath on the back of my neck. The hairs on every inch of my body stood. The ones I'd recently shaved grew half a centimeter, stinging as they broke my skin and sprouted, again.

"So much that you'd rather die than live without them?"

He moved slightly to the right of me.

"Feels like you're drowning when they're not around, anymore."

He sighed long and hard, stepping back a bit to center himself again.

"Feels like your heart will slow to a creep and put you out of your misery at any moment. And, you almost want it to, but then you realize how much it would hurt them if you ever left for good?"

He stepped closer, again, this time on my left side.

"You tell yourself that if you ever got the chance to be in their space one more time... just one more time... you'd make sure that neither of you ever had to feel that way again? Like your chest is caving in. Your lungs are at capacity. Your brain is imploding. And, your soul, your soul just won't stop crying."

He rounded me, finally revealing his handsome face and saddened eyes.

"What I'm asking you is, have you ever been in love, pretty lady? The real kind. The deep kind."

"Our kind," I finished for him. "Yes."

My heart pounded against my chest.

"Then, you'd understand when I tell you how sorry I am for ever jeopardizing that love."

Nodding, I answered him.

"I meant your heart no harm."

I tried blinking away the tears, but they fell anyway. The pain in his eyes was as evident as the pain in my heart. There was no way of hiding it.

"I meant you no harm."

I placed a hand over my mouth to silence the sobs that erupted.

"Don't make me live my life without you. I won't make it."

With his final words, he lowered until he was on one knee with a velvet box in front of him.

"Don't make me try. Just tell me that we can move forward and relish in that love we just talked about."

"Our love?" I choked through the tears.

"Our love. Halo, in any lifetime, I'd choose you. I'm just asking you to choose me for this one. Be my wife."

"Baby." I broke down until I was kneeling with him.

"Hmmm? Tell me you feel this, too. Tell me I'm not alone."

"I love you," I cried.

"Immensely," he shared the same sentiment. The tears in his eyes told me. The drumming of his heart told me. The sincerity of his voice told me.

"Be my wife," he repeated himself, still on bended knee.

"Okay," I agreed.

"Yes?"

"Yes." I nodded.

"Yes!" He huffed, visibly relieved.

"Shit, I thought you were going to turn me down, pretty lady."

"It was the easiest *yes* I've ever given."

"Then why the fuck you take so long? Got a nigga sweating bullets."

Ledge blew out, swiping his dewy forehead.

"I'm sorry. I'm just... overwhelmed."

"I love you, Halo." He slid the prettiest diamond onto my finger.

"Immensely," I replied, unable to hold myself together anymore.

I wrapped my arms around him and shoved my face into the crook of his neck. The heaviness I'd been feeling in his absence was shed little by little with each tear that landed on his shirt. *This* was my person and I was his. Whatever I faced, I never wanted to do it without him.

"Hey. Hey. Hey," he whispered. "What's the matter?"

Because I couldn't find the words, I grabbed his hand and placed it on my rapidly growing bulge. The hardening revealed what was beneath long before the positive pregnancy test I'd taken two days ago. The morning he'd shown up at the door, I wanted to share the news but I couldn't pull myself together long enough to say much of anything.

"Baby, we're pregnant?"

From the height of his pitch, his feelings toward the news were apparent. He sounded like a kid who'd just entered a candy store. With a nod, I confirmed.

"My young niggas don't miss," he boasted.

"You're okay with all of this?"

I worried myself sick thinking of the many possible ways he'd react to the news. So much was happening between us and I wasn't sure if bringing a baby into the equation would make things better or worse. Nonetheless, another was on the way. There was nothing either of us could do at this point but accommodate the new addition and whatever came with them.

"All of what? Making you my wife and sharing a second child with you? Damn right. Are you not?"

"I'm just hungry," I admitted.

"Of course you are," he chortled.

His hand never left my stomach as his lips rested against mine.

"Don't give up on me," I begged, recanting my statement.

"Can't do it, pretty lady."

THE END.

Prepare for **Lawe**, set for **Spring 2023**. Available for pre-order now.

Want more of these two? Be sure to **scan the code** to get the **deleted scenes** for this book and many others.

or sign up for deleted scenes at **https://theliteraryheroine. ck.page/e2956a645b**

MORE FROM GREY HUFFINGTON

SYX + THE CITY
SYX + THE CITY 2
SYX THIRTY SEVYN
SXYTH GIVING
SYX WHOLE WEEKS

WILDE + RECKLESS
WILDE + RELENTLESS
WILDE + RESTLESS

MR. INTENTIONAL
UNEARTH ME

THE SWEETEST REVENGE
THE SWEETEST REDEMPTION

HALF + HALF
THE EMANCIPATION OF EMOREE

WEB EXCLUSIVES:
ghuffington.com

450

PAPERBACKS
HARDCOVERS
SHORT STORIES
AUDIOBOOKS
MERCH
AND MORE...

Printed in the USA
CPSIA information can be obtained
at www.ICGtesting.com
LVHW021517281023
762400LV00014B/128